The

"Not since *Practical Magic* have two literary sisters felt as distinct and animate as Dot and Dash Wilson. I was so attached to both these richly, lovingly developed characters, and stayed up far too late hungrily devouring their stories. This is the most unputdownable book I've read in a long time. Impeccably researched, educational, emotional, and immersive, *The Secret Keeper* is Genevieve Graham at her finest."

Heather Marshall, #1 bestselling author of *Looking for Jane*

"Genevieve Graham unveils the strength of Canada's women in their efforts during World War II with her incredible research. Dash and Dot are intrepid heroines you'll want to root for, and *The Secret Keeper* is a story you won't want to put down."

Madeline Martin, bestselling author of *The Keeper of Hidden Books*

"Genevieve Graham never fails to fascinate with incredible stories of Canada's past, and *The Secret Keeper* is no exception. A sweeping novel about the bonds between sisters and the burden of secrets in a time of war, it will thrill and charm readers in equal measure."

Julia Kelly, international bestselling author of *The Lost English Girl*

"Reading a Genevieve Graham novel is like reading a love letter to Canada. In *The Secret Keeper*, impressive research, tender family dynamics, and an absorbing plot intertwine to pay homage to the quiet heroes of the second World War."

Ellen Keith, bestselling author of *The Dutch Orphan*

"Through impeccable research, harrowing flight scenes, and equally tense code-breaking ones, Graham deftly captures the emotional and physical toll of war on the home front, while beautifully illustrating the capacity for human resilience, camaraderie, and connection inside us all."

Natalie Jenner, bestselling author of *Every Time We Say Goodbye*

"I fell in love with Dot and Dash from the get-go. These two sisters were brilliant and full of heart, and I was rooting for them equally during their harrowing and sometimes heartbreaking journeys. A fabulous read!"

Sara Ackerman, bestselling author of *The Unchartered Flight of Olivia West*

"A riveting tale of the steadfast bond between sisters in the midst of wartime adventure. In Dot and Dash's extraordinary journey, Genevieve Graham vividly captures the courageous heroics of women in World War II."

Paullina Simons, internationally bestselling author of *The Bronze Horseman*

"Graham is the reigning queen of historical fiction about Canada, and *The Secret Keeper* is her most sweeping, searing story yet, an intricate tale of the Canadian women of World War II, many of whom were sworn to keep their wartime heroics secret."

Kristin Harmel, *New York Times* bestselling author of *The Paris Daughter*

"Genevieve Graham once again takes a deep dive into the world of women at war with Dot and Dash, twin sisters from Oshawa who overcome male prejudice to make a massive contribution to the defeat of evil. Vivid characterizations and pinpoint research bring that dangerous—yet exciting—world alive."

C. C. Humphreys, bestselling author of *Someday I'll Find You*

"My favorite historical fiction author has done it again, bringing to light the untold story of women in wartime whose oath of silence protected the fate of the free world."

Elinor Florence, bestselling author of *Bird's Eye View*

"Thrilling and heartfelt, *The Secret Keeper* showcases the oft-forgotten contributions of Canadian women to the war effort through twin sisters Dot and Dash, whose commitments to serve puts them at odds with their commitments to each other. With a particularly heart-pounding third act, *The Secret Keeper* is Genevieve Graham at her masterful best."

Bryn Turnbull, internationally bestselling author of *The Paris Deception*

"*The Secret Keeper* is at once touching and harrowing. Graham masterfully and lovingly recreates the lives of two women engaged in wartime service, capturing their youthful idealism, sense of duty, and sheer energy. You will follow the adventures of sisters Dot and Dash with your heart in your mouth. Not to be missed!"

Iona Whishaw, *Globe and Mail* bestselling author of *To Track a Traitor*

ALSO BY GENEVIEVE GRAHAM

Bluebird

Letters Across the Sea

The Forgotten Home Child

At the Mountain's Edge

Come from Away

Promises to Keep

Tides of Honour

Somewhere to Dream

Sound of the Heart

Under the Same Sky

The
Secret Keeper

GENEVIEVE GRAHAM

Published by Simon & Schuster
New York London Toronto Sydney New Delhi

A Division of Simon & Schuster, LLC
166 King Street East, Suite 300
Toronto, Ontario M5A 1J3

This Simon & Schuster Canada edition April 2024

SIMON & SCHUSTER CANADA and colophon are trademarks of Simon & Schuster, LLC

Simon & Schuster: Celebrating 100 Years of Publishing in 2024

For information about special discounts for bulk purchases, please contact Simon & Schuster Special Sales at 1-800-268-3216 or CustomerService@simonandschuster.ca.

Interior design by Erika R. Genova

Manufactured in the United States of America

1   3   5   7   9   10   8   6   4   2

Library and Archives Canada Cataloguing in Publication
Title: The secret keeper / Genevieve Graham.
Names: Graham, Genevieve, author.
Description: Simon & Schuster Canada edition.
Identifiers: Canadiana (print) 20220394563 | Canadiana (ebook) 20220394660 | ISBN 9781982196981(softcover) | ISBN 9781982196998 (EPUB)
Classification: LCC PS8613.R3434 S43 2024 | DDC C813/.6—dc23

ISBN 978-1-9821-9698-1
ISBN 978-1-9821-9699-8 (ebook)

Dedicated to the memory of
Lynn-Philip Hodgson
(1946–2023)

And to Dwayne, always

"There are millions of women in the country who could do useful jobs in war. But the trouble is that so many of them insist on wanting to do jobs which they are quite incapable of doing. The menace is the woman who thinks that she ought to be flying a high-speed bomber when she really has not the intelligence to scrub the floor of a hospital properly, or who wants to nose round as an Air Raid Warden and yet can't cook her husband's dinner."

C. G. Grey, Editor of *Aeroplane* magazine (1942)

The role of women has always been undervalued in the spy world, always undermined in terms of recognition. Unfairly so. It's a world that needs women.

Helen Mirren

prologue

— 1928 —

Margaret Wilson clambered onto the kitchen chair, her four-year-old brow knitted with concern. She had a very important question to ask her mother. Her twin, Dorothy, climbed up beside her, fascinated by how neatly her mother could fold the laundry. All the seams matched up perfectly every time.

Their mother smiled. "What are you two up to?" Her gaze dropped. "Oh, Margaret. You skinned your knee again."

"I put a bandage on it for her," Dorothy said.

Margaret didn't care about her knee. It was fine. Dorothy had washed all the blood off it, and Margaret had hardly cried at all. "Why's the back room empty, Mommy? Where did all the stuff go?"

"I'm glad you asked. Sit down, please. We don't climb on furniture." She set the laundry aside then sat at the table with her daughters. "Do you remember Gus Becker? The little boy from up the street? His father is going away tomorrow, so Gus is coming to live here with us. That will be his bedroom."

The twins exchanged a glance.

"But this is our house," Margaret declared, arms crossed. "We don't want boys in it."

Dorothy sat beside her, saying nothing but mimicking her sister's pose. The idea of having a boy living in the house didn't frighten her as much as the idea of *anyone* new moving in. How would it feel, having five of them at the table, not just four? Who would he sit beside? Would she have to talk with him?

"Of course, Margaret. This will always be your house. Yours and Dorothy's. But I want Gus to feel like it is his as well. You two have each other. He doesn't have anyone when his father is away, and he knows very little English. I am counting on you girls to make him feel welcome."

"But what if he's a *bad* boy?" Margaret asked.

"He is not a bad boy. I expect you to be nice to him," their mother replied. Margaret doubled down on her pout, so Dorothy did, too. In response, their mother's left eyebrow shot up. The one that always meant the discussion was over. "Come and help me get his room ready, please."

Grudgingly, the girls followed her to the room at the back of the house, and Margaret swept the floor while Dorothy helped make up Gus's little cot. Afterward, Margaret decided she and her sister should play in there, since the room was so tidy, but their mother took their hands and led them back to the kitchen, where she made it very clear that they were never to go into that room again unless Gus invited them.

"It's like you have a brother now." She crouched in front of them. "He's probably going to be shy at first, but we must make him feel like part of the family, and that means giving him privacy."

Dorothy twisted a lock of her blond hair between her fingers, feeling badly for the boy when she thought about it that way. She couldn't imagine not having a sister—or a brother in Gus's case. Dorothy's sister was everything to her. Maybe it would be all right to have a big brother. Maybe she wouldn't have to talk to him if she didn't want to.

Margaret had no such illusions. Their house was just fine without a boy in it. Boys were big and bossy and sometimes smelled bad. "He should live in his own house, Mommy. We don't want him here. What if he's mean to Dorothy?"

"Gus is not a mean boy," their mother replied. "If he was, I would not have agreed to take care of him in our house. Now, I want you to imagine being in his place. What if Daddy and I were not here to take care of you, and a family offered to take you in? Wouldn't you hope that they would love you as if you were already a part of their family?" Her expression cleared as if she remembered something. "You know, I think he might be very good at baseball, Margaret. Maybe you could play catch together."

Gus arrived with his father the next morning, his blond hair disheveled under a black cap, his wary gaze darting around the front entry. Margaret stood in silent judgement of the boy while Dorothy concealed herself behind the grandfather clock. Her stomach hurt.

The two grown-ups spoke for a bit while Margaret and Gus remained in the entry, eyeing each other like a pair of dogs—without the wagging tails.

"Come in, Gus," their mother said after his father left. "You can call me Mrs. Wilson. I think you already know my daughters, Margaret and Dorothy." She peered around the grandfather clock, then scowled. "Come here, Dorothy. Say hello."

Dorothy tiptoed over and whispered, "Hello."

"Hello," he replied, observing her closely.

"Margaret?" their mother prompted.

"Hello," she said tightly.

Concern flickered across Gus's pale brow then was gone. "Hello."

Their mother took the boy's little suitcase and told him where to hang his coat and cap, then he followed her to his room. Margaret and Dorothy trailed behind, then they loitered in the doorway after their mother got him settled and returned to the kitchen. He sat on the edge of his bed, feet dangling halfway to the floor, and regarded them through big blue eyes.

Dorothy wondered if he was as nervous as she was. When she was scared, she could hide behind Margaret. Gus didn't have anyone to hide behind. She tilted her head, feeling a little sorry for him.

"How old are you?" Margaret asked.

"Six," he said.

Margaret was impressed. Six was practically grown up. Maybe he wouldn't be so bad after all. Especially if her mother was right and he knew how to throw a ball. She decided to give him a chance.

"Mommy is making beef stew," she informed him.

His eyes widened, but he didn't say anything.

"You have to help with the dishes after," Dorothy put in, feeling brave.

"*Ja.*" He hesitated. "Does your mother cook potatoes in the stew?"

"Lots," Margaret informed him. "I like potatoes."

He nodded slowly. "I also like potatoes."

Both girls were pleased, having established this important common ground. He couldn't be all bad if he liked potatoes in his stew.

"Anyway," Margaret continued, "we're going outside to play if you want to come."

Margaret led the parade into the yard, indicating points of interest. "That is Daddy's shed. Don't go in there. That's the swing he built for us." She narrowed her eyes at him. "Think you could push us high in that?"

"*Ja*, I could."

His accent sounded odd to Margaret's ears. Dorothy thought it was nice.

"All right." Margaret stopped by the tall maple tree beside the house. "This is my tree. I'm the only one who climbs it."

"Why?"

"Because Dorothy doesn't like to climb trees. She sits on the stump."

Dorothy nodded. She preferred to watch her sister climb. Just to show him what Margaret meant, she hopped onto the old stump and swung her feet a little. Gus seemed to take that in, then he stepped closer to the tree, looking up.

"Can I go up?" he asked. There was a pause.

"I don't know about that." In an instant, Margaret had scrambled up to her favourite spot, a sort of "V" in the branches where she'd built a nest of leaves. Nobody had ever sat there before, except for her. "Can you climb this high? Because this is pretty high."

"I can."

Dorothy studied him. He stood right beside her, observing Margaret, and she thought he probably could climb it easily. He *was* six, after all, and a *boy*.

"It's very high," she warned him quietly. "I don't want you to get hurt."

He faced her, and Dorothy could tell he was thinking carefully about what she'd said. His expression was serious, but he had pretty blue eyes, and so far he wasn't bossy at all. He hadn't even argued with Margaret. Then he smiled, and it was such a nice smile that she returned it.

"Can you climb *this* high?" Margaret asked again, now higher in the tree.

Dorothy's stomach flipped. Her sister was showing off. "Margaret! That's too high!"

"No, it isn't," she called back.

"Come down! Mommy will be angry!"

"I don't care. Can you climb this high, Gus?"

He took another step closer to the tree, frowning a little. "I can."

Margaret shifted in place, a little off balance without her nest on this higher branch, but that was all right. She wasn't scared. She wanted to show Gus how grown up she was. She folded her arms and leaned as far out as she dared, watching his face. "Prove it!" she yelled.

Then her foot slipped, and she screamed as the other one went as well. Suddenly she was flying—and then she was on top of Gus, gasping and trying not to cry. Dorothy rushed to her side and pulled her off the boy, who lay quite still on the ground.

The front door slammed, and their mother rushed out, apron flapping. "Gus! Margaret! Oh, what did you do?"

"Don't tell Mommy!" Margaret begged. "Promise!"

Gus blinked up at Dorothy, who shook her head and whispered, "Don't tell!"

Their mother knelt beside Gus before he could answer. All they could do was hope he wouldn't say anything.

"Don't worry, Mommy! I'm okay," Margaret told her, though her chin wobbled. She pointed up at the tree and started explaining, but her mother didn't appear to be listening.

That's when Dorothy saw Gus's eyes were shining. She crouched beside him, concerned.

"Oh, Gus," their mother said. "You poor thing. I'm afraid you might have broken your wrist. I'll call the doctor at once." She glared at the girls. "How did this happen?"

"I fell," Margaret said. "He's okay, though."

Dorothy didn't know what to say. It was Margaret's fault. She shouldn't have been showing off. But she would never tell on Margaret.

"You and that tree," their mother muttered, helping Gus sit up. "Are you all right, dear?"

The girls held their breath, waiting to hear what he would say.

"He's okay," Margaret assured everyone again, though she was a little worried since Gus hadn't said a thing.

Gus sniffed. His attention shifted to Margaret then came to rest on Dorothy. He had a small cut on his forehead, and Dorothy felt an urge to run and get him a bandage, but she had to make sure he was all right first.

"I am okay," he told their mother. "It was my fault. I got in the way."

one

DOT

-.. .. --- -

—June 1942—
Oshawa, Ontario

Dorothy Wilson tucked a strand of blond hair behind her ear and scowled at the mystery novel in her hand. The author's latest reveal didn't seem plausible, and it made the character seem so much more dim-witted than Dot imagined he was. On the other hand—

"Dot!"

She glanced up. Her twin sister was leaning over Mr. Meier's black Chevy truck's engine, groaning as she stretched for something. Dot could type a mile a minute, add six-digit figures in her head in no time flat, and speak three languages like a native (not including Morse code), but she'd never been interested enough in engines to bother learning what was inside them. She didn't mind coming out here, though. The garage was poorly lit by one hanging bulb, and the rain outside the closed door chilled the air, but she always liked to be near Margaret.

In contrast to Dot's navy-blue dress with its spotless Peter Pan collar, her sister was clad in a grease-stained, exceedingly unladylike pair of overalls, and her thick black hair was tied into a haphazard ponytail. Most people shook their head in wonder, seeing how different the Wilson twins were. Different, yes, but also inseparable.

"Yes, Dash?" Dot asked.

Everyone, except their mother, called Margaret by her nickname. Considering the way Dot's sister always rushed around, it suited her to a T.

Dash twisted around, her cheek smeared by a thick swipe of oil. "You didn't hear me? I've been saying your name for five minutes at least."

Dot was aware that she missed out on a lot of what people said if she was engaged in a book, but often she felt—somewhat selfishly, she allowed—that whatever they might be saying couldn't be as interesting as what she was reading. This time, however, she was contrite. Dash was annoyed. Not with her, but with the truck.

"*Désolé. Que veux-tu?*" she asked. The novel in her hands was a French translation, and sometimes the words overlapped in her head. Her mother had gotten her started on mystery novels a few years back, but this was the first one she'd read that wasn't written in English. Her father had found the book hidden away in a bookstore and given it to her, knowing she'd enjoy the challenge. She was already wondering where she could find more translations.

"Hand me the half inch, please?"

Setting one finger on the page to hold her place, Dot scanned the scattered assortment of tools on the table beside her. She picked up a wrench, eyed it for size, then placed it in her sister's hand before returning her attention to the book.

"That should do it," Dash said to herself, sticking her fingers into the engine and checking the tension of whatever it was before climbing into the driver's seat. The engine gave a noisy series of clicks, but that was all. "Damn," she whispered under her breath as she marched back to the hood.

Dot's mouth twitched. She loved when her sister swore.

She understood Dash's determination. There was nothing Dot liked better than solving puzzles, and engines were her sister's idea of puzzles. Her mother often said that Dash's fascination with mechanics and Dot's puzzle-solving skills came from their father's side of the family, then she rolled her eyes and finished with, "Thank heavens you inherited my practicality." Usually, their father popped in at that point and added "and your beauty," making their mother glow. Dot figured her mother was right. Her father was a whiz at math, and he almost always had a crossword puzzle going. His brother, her uncle Bob, was a solid man with a devilish grin who always had engine grease under his fingernails.

Uncle Bob, Aunt Louise—Lou for short—and Dot's cousin Fred came over for dinner often, since they lived close by. Dot still fondly remembered the night more than ten years ago when the whole family had been celebrating the girls' very first day of school. Her mother had made the grand concession of allowing them to sit at the grown-up table for the evening. At age seven, Fred and Gus were practically adults, so they got to sit there as well. Dorothy was always happy when Fred came over, because he and Gus were friends. It was good, she thought, that Gus had a friend who was a boy, not just Margaret and her.

After supper that night, her mother and aunt had gone to the kitchen, leaving the children with her father and Uncle Bob.

Fred beamed at his father. "Tell Gus about the war and your airplane."

Uncle Bob obliged, and Gus listened carefully, his eyes wide. Uncle Bob's voice rose louder and louder as he lost himself in the memory, and Dorothy watched his fist move forward, left, forward, right, shifting in front of him as if he were holding the control stick of his "Canuck." When at last the doomed enemy plane crashed dramatically into the sea, everyone yelled hooray, and Uncle Bob puffed his chest, pleased with their reactions.

He was a flight instructor now, but back then, he had served with distinction as a pilot in the Royal Flying Corps. Fred loved to remind the girls that Captain Robert James Wilson was on the short list of Canadian flying aces, having shot down sixteen enemy planes.

Dash, who they still called Margaret back then, adored her uncle and hung on his every word. She had wanted to fly her whole life, so when Uncle Bob started to tell his pilot stories, she got stars in her eyes.

Dot loved Uncle Bob, too. Her favourite thing about her uncle, and the only part of him that didn't intimidate her, was his dashing moustache, its ends waxed to a curly perfection. She was impressed by his exploits, of course, but she was confused. She was almost certain he had told them that he'd shot down fourteen planes, not sixteen. But surely he knew best. She must have simply forgotten. She was only five, after all.

In Dorothy's view, though, Uncle Bob lived in her father's quieter shadow. Her father was a gentle man with a thin, out-of-fashion pencil moustache and a postwar habit of constantly checking a door or window. His smiles were quick and self-conscious, and he had very few visitors outside of family. But beneath his understated exterior, he radiated intelligence, and when he did get into a conversational mood, Dot listened to every word. He was, as her mother fondly said, very good at working with his hands, and he kept a small woodworking table in the backyard shed. Two years before, he'd built the sisters a dollhouse for Christmas, complete with tiny furniture, and her mother had sewn two perfect little dolls to fit inside. One had blond hair and wore a grey dress to match Dorothy's favourite. The other had dark hair and a bright emerald dress, since green was Margaret's favourite colour. A year after that, her father constructed a bookcase for Dot's burgeoning collection of books.

Uncle Bob might be a flying ace, but her father didn't have to fly a plane to be a hero in her eyes.

"Tell us *your* flying stories, Daddy," Margaret prodded, and Dot felt a twinge of betrayal. He had flown? Had he kept his history secret from her?

But her father only chuckled, his pale cheeks flushing. "I wasn't a pilot, Margaret, dear. You mustn't think I was one of those brave lads. No, no."

"But you were in the war," she insisted. "Did you go in airplanes?"

Sometimes Dot thought Margaret was altogether too bossy.

"Yes, I did, but I was not a dashing pilot like your uncle. My job was to sit in the airplane and transmit locations through my Marconi."

"Macaroni!" Margaret cried, delighted. Beside her, cousin Fred guffawed.

"No, dear," her father said patiently. "Marconi."

"What's that?" Gus asked.

"Marconi was the name of my radio. Operating it was not nearly as exciting as what Fred's father did."

Dot leaned forward. Her father rarely spoke about himself, so this was a rare treat.

"Your dad is being too humble," said Uncle Bob. "You should be proud of him. He held a very important position as a telegraph operator for the Royal Flying Corps. He saved many, many lives by sending locations from the airplane to the military. With that information, they were able to direct artillery fire to that position. He also . . ." Uncle Bob consulted his brother, and Dot noticed her father scowling slightly. "Well, he wrote regularly to your mother, keeping her happy."

Dot was intrigued. "How did you do that with the fire, Daddy? If you were in an airplane, how did you tell them?"

"I tapped the coordinates in Morse code, and they reached the receivers on the ground. For example, if we saw a munitions cache, I would do this."

He tapped his middle finger rapidly on the table in an unpredictable rhythm. To Dot, it sounded like there was a purpose to the uneven taps, as if they were trying to say something.

"Do that again, Daddy!" So he did.

She gaped at him in wonder. "What's the tap tap tap? What's it saying?"

"You heard that, did you, my little genius? That is Morse code. It is a different kind of language made up of a series of dits and dahs. Each letter of the alphabet has its own pattern. Listen. I'll show you your name." He tapped once slowly, then twice fast. "We call that a dah, then two dits. That is the first letter of your name, Dorothy, which is . . . ?"

She sat up straight, staring at his finger. "D! Do more, Daddy! What's an 'O'?"

He tapped three times again, but evenly, and a little slower. "Dah-dah-dah is 'O.' When you write it down, it is in dots and dashes."

"What's an 'M'?" she wanted to know. "For Margaret."

"'M' is dah-dah."

She beamed at her sister, catching on right away. "Your name starts with dah-dah!" Margaret looked interested, but she was not caught up in her sister's excitement. "Will you learn with me?"

Margaret's mouth reluctantly twisted to the side. "Okay."

Her mother returned from the kitchen, carrying a jiggling dish. "Who would like some Jell-O pudding?"

Margaret squealed with delight. "You made green! I love the green one best, Mommy!"

Aunt Lou followed with the dishes. "Special dessert for a special day. How exciting that you girls get to go to school now!"

Dot sat back, watching her mother serve, but her mind was spinning. "What's J, Daddy? What's 'J' for, Jell-O?"

He tapped dit-dah-dah-dah.

So began Dorothy's quest to learn and memorize the Morse code alphabet. She already knew the regular alphabet, of course. Her mother had taught them that two years earlier. Now Dot's father had given her a key to a whole new puzzle that promised worlds of fun. Day by day she took on more of the patterns, and once they were stuck in her head she went to her father for more.

"First you must learn to spell," he had told her, pulling out paper and a pencil. "What word would you like to spell?"

She didn't hesitate. "Sister."

"All right. Here's how to spell it in regular letters." As he wrote out the six letters, they both said them out loud. Then he handed the pencil to her. "How would you tap each letter? Draw it underneath in dashes and dots."

Pencil grasped tight in her curled fist, Dot drew three little points under each S.

"That's right. Now the other letters."

She bit her lip, her mind ticking through everything she had learned and memorized over the past few days. Her pencil pressed against the paper again. "Two dots for 'I.' One dash for 'T.' Just one little dot for 'E.'" She hesitated. "What's 'R'? I forget!"

"Think, Dorothy." He patted her head affectionately. "The answer is right in here." As if he had brought it to the surface, "R" appeared. "Dit-dah-dit."

"Excellent! How do you write that?"

"Dot-dash-dot."

"That's my girl. Now we put them together to make a word. Show me."

It was as if a window opened in her mind, and her heart whirred like hummingbird wings. She read the code out loud, tapping with one finger as her father had done. "Margaret is my dot-dot-dot dot-dot dot-dot-dot dash-dot . . ." She grinned at him. "Dot-dash-dot."

Morse code bored Margaret within a day or two. She learned it only so she could communicate with Dot, but her heart wasn't in it. Their father noticed, and instead, he presented her with a small brass cylinder. The metal was tarnished and dented, but the vibrating needle in the centre caught her attention.

"What's that?"

"This is a compass. It tells you which direction you're going in."

Margaret frowned. "Like forward?"

"A little more than that. You see this little needle? It will always point north."

"North?"

He turned to Dot. "Dorothy, please bring me the map on my desk. The big paper rolled up, with the funny lines on it."

"I know where that is," Gus replied from down the hall. A moment later, he and Dot appeared in the dining room with the map. They helped her father spread it out on the table.

"Ah, yes. Thank you," he said. "This, my dears, is a map of the whole world."

"The whole world?" both girls exclaimed, their noses almost touching the paper. How fascinating to see it drawn like this, when all they'd ever imagined of the world was grass and trees and sky.

"Gus, have you seen this before?" her father asked.

"In school. A little."

"What can you show me?"

Gus squinted at the small print, then brightened. "This big part is Canada."

"Good! And what are these up and down lines?"

"Provinces," he declared. He jabbed a finger on one. "This is Ontario, where we live."

"Excellent, Gus. Can you tell me exactly where we live?"

Dot and Margaret stared at Gus, flabbergasted, as he leaned over the map. He noticed their wonder and assured them they would learn it too, in two years.

"We're learning it right now," Dot replied, matter-of-fact, "from you."

"Go ahead, Gus," her father urged. "Where are we?"

"We are . . ." He grinned. "Right here!"

"That's right. That is Oshawa." Her father slid one finger up the page from the spot Gus had marked, and he faced Margaret. "North is anything in this direction."

She held the compass up. "Why do I need to know where north is?"

"If you have a compass, you'll never be lost. I'll show you." He pulled a piece of paper from his pocket and presented it to all three children. "I've made you an adventure. Dorothy, you will read these Morse code letters to Gus. Gus, you will spell out what she's saying and pass those directions to Margaret. And Margaret, you will follow the compass. Do you understand? Look again at the compass. What is it pointing at? Remember, 'N' means north."

She frowned at the compass then looked up. "It's pointing at the picture of Grandfather."

"Yes! Correct! Grandfather's picture is north of where you are standing right now. Now out you go, the three of you. Have fun!"

It was a beautiful summer day, with the kind of warm breeze that felt like a kiss. Their mother was hanging laundry on the line, clothespins in her mouth, and she waved at them as they passed.

Dot clutched the paper in her hands, delighted by the puzzle. "Dash Dot-dot-dot-dot Dot-dash-dot . . ." she read to herself, then out loud she told Gus "T-H-R. . ."

That led to Gus telling Margaret to take "Three big steps north," then "four baby steps east." Margaret's eyes were glued to the compass, and Dot's were on the paper. Neither of them saw the big rock that tripped Dot and would have sent her sprawling if Gus hadn't rushed in and caught her on the way down.

"Good catch!" Margaret said, laughing.

"Thank you, Gus," Dot said quietly as he set her back on her feet.

His cheeks were bright red. "You're welcome."

"Come on, everybody! No dillydallying!" Margaret called, marching on.

At the end of the quest, their father had stashed a little bag of sweets. All three rushed back for another adventure, which he happily produced.

A month or so after that, when it was just the five of them at supper, Dot's mother set her warm hand on her fingers.

"Please, Dorothy. The tapping is driving me mad."

"But I'm spelling."

"I know what you're doing," her mother said, smiling with infinite patience. "Let's leave the spelling until after supper, please."

From the corner of her eye, Dot saw Gus smiling. At first, she thought he was laughing at her, but then his finger silently tapped the table.

.. / .-.. .. -.- . / .. —
I like it

"My grandmother was named Dorothy," her father said then, brightening with a thought. "A very intelligent woman. We named you after her, actually. But no one ever called her Dorothy. Do you know what they called her?"

Everyone shook their heads.

"They called her Dot. And it seems to me that if you are so interested in Morse code, we could call you Dot from now on. What do you think?"

Her mother pressed the corner of her napkin to her lips. "Oh, I don't know."

"If it was good enough for my grandmother," he said, "it's good enough for our daughter."

"Well," she said after a moment, "if Dorothy is Dot, then Margaret, with all her exhausting energy and running around, must be Dash."

All of them howled with laughter at that.

"What about Gus?" Dot asked.

"I just want to be Gus," he told them.

Her mother held up her hands. "Now, now. I am only being silly. Dorothy and Margaret are perfectly beautiful names. We won't have any of that nonsense in this house."

To her disappointment and the girls' delight, the nicknames had stuck. Everyone but their mother and schoolteachers used them after that day. As far as Dot could remember, the only time their mother ever called them by their nicknames was the night she proposed the idea.

Even now, most people knew them as Dot and Dash, though they were seventeen.

The sound of Mr. Meier's engine starting up brought Dot back to the present.

"What was the problem?" she asked when Dash turned off the car.

"I must have bumped the battery post," she replied, wiping her hands on the cloth hanging from her waist. "All's good now. Fan belt's perfect. Not too tight to break the bearings, just enough to fix that squeal. Mr. Meier will be happy."

Dot closed her book and rose, glad to go. "I hope he pays you this time."

"He doesn't need to pay me," Dash said, hauling open the garage door. The rain had eased off, and the last rays of sunshine burst through, resulting in a glorious rainbow. "If Sam was here instead of marching through England, he would have fixed it. It's the least I can do."

War was constantly in the news, more sobering by the day, and the mention of Sam Meier brought it all back. The Germans had captured

Europe and set their sights on Britain. Then, in December, the conflict had come to America on the wings of Japanese dive bombers—the *Aichi D3A*, Dash had informed her, since she had recently developed an interest in identifying airplanes—and the Allies breathed a sigh of relief when the horrific bombing of Pearl Harbour forced the Americans into the fight as well. Sam Meier, Gus, and Fred had left to join the fight a year before that happened. In fact, most of the boys from school had signed up and shipped out, making it more and more difficult for Dot to picture the war as something very far away.

"Still. You should be compensated for your work. A man would be paid," she insisted as they walked. "How many hours have you spent on that truck so far?"

Dot felt confident about this topic. She was paid for her work, after all. Once a week, six students plodded a mile and a half from the Centre Street School to her house for French lessons, for which each child's mother paid Dot thirty cents an hour. She could have taught them German as well, but she had decided that was probably a bad idea nowadays. Dot was proud of having her very own savings account, and she visited the bank often to keep a close eye on the figures. So far, the only withdrawals she made were her monthly donations of two dollars to the Red Cross.

"You know, there are other ways to earn money." Dash kicked a rock down the gravel road. "In the city, I mean. I could do that."

Dot's step faltered. "What are you talking about? You'd go to Toronto?"

"Lots of girls are working in the city now that the men are gone. Loads are joining the Wrens or the Women's Army Corps. I could be a driver with them, or maybe a mechanic." She bit her lower lip, considering. "Of course, there's the Air Force, too, but the Wrens have such beautiful uniforms."

Horrified, Dot grabbed her sister's arm so she stopped in place. "You're going to the *city*? To join the *army*?"

At least Dash had the good grace to look abashed. "Thinking about it. You could come with me."

Dot couldn't honestly say she was surprised, but the thought of Dash leaving filled her with anxiety. She knew her sister was restless. What else was there for a beautiful, lively young woman to do in Oshawa, other than hang out at the Four Corners or dance to a band at the Jubilee? Sure, the head office for General Motors Canada was here, but so far they hadn't replied to any of Dash's enquiries about work other than to say she was too young. Which was a ridiculous requisite, Dot felt, since her sister could out-mechanic anyone else, no matter their age. Even more ridiculous was that while GM was ignoring Dash, they had offered Dot a sewing job, and she was exactly the same age. Of course, Dot had declined. Dash pretended GM's rejection didn't matter. She said they were only making parts there, not fixing engines, which was what she liked to do. Still, Dot knew it hurt.

Without something like GM to hold Dash's interest, Dot had secretly feared that her sister might be happier in Toronto. She'd never said anything about that out loud, because if Dash left, what choice would Dot have but to follow? Nothing frightened Dot more than the thought of a busy, noisy city full of strangers—except for a busy, noisy city without Dash.

"You're not really going to go, are you?"

"Why not? We're almost adults, Dot. It's time to do something. Aren't you bored?"

"No."

Dash narrowed her eyes. "Don't do that. Don't make me feel bad for wanting more."

"I don't want you to leave."

"Then come with me!"

"How long have you been thinking about this and not telling me?"

"There's so much you could do in the city," Dash pressed. "The military would be lucky to have you. You'd have them shipshape in no time."

Dot dropped her eyes to the wet road. She was happy at home, living a quiet life. The last thing she wanted was change. Especially if that change separated her from her sister.

"What would I do there?"

"Anything," Dash said, walking on. "Secretary, clerk, telephone operator . . . Think about it. Working isn't just interesting, it's our duty."

The passion in Dash's voice made Dot's heart pound. She caught up to her sister. "I don't understand," she said quickly. "What's so exciting about working in the city? And why is it our duty?"

"Calm down, Dot. You're talking a mile a minute."

Her family was always reminding her to speak more slowly. Dot tended to forget that in the heat of the moment. "Why. Is. It. Our. Duty."

"Because women are a big part of this war now. We have to work so men can fight."

Dot reluctantly let the idea percolate as they walked. Frankly, she'd prefer to sit out the war at home, but without Dash the house would be so bleak. It might be diverting to be a secretary, she supposed; she liked to type, her shorthand was excellent, and maybe she could help with Morse code. If they let her, she could reorganize files and folders until she was blue in the face. She did love to organize things. Her mother was always thrilled when Dot suggested she could set the kitchen to rights. Maybe whoever she worked for would have a Marconi, like the one her father had told them about. Now *that* would be interesting.

But no, she couldn't go. Not only did the thought paralyze her with fear, how could she possibly leave her parents behind? Especially her father. Her mother went out with friends on occasion, but he rarely did. Dot welcomed those nights when she could have him all to herself. When he didn't have one of his headaches, they would sit contentedly at the kitchen table in near silence, seeing who could solve the crossword first, or they'd set out a new jigsaw, or they'd share whatever other amusement caught their interest. No. Dot couldn't possibly go to the city and leave him.

Beside her, Dash was skimming a screwdriver under the tip of her nail, cleaning out the dirt. Sensing Dot's attention, she put her arm around her. "Calm down, silly."

"When?" Dot demanded.

"Oh, I don't know. I'll go see what it's all about in a few weeks, I guess. Why wait?"

Dot could think of a hundred reasons.

"It's going to be fun," Dash said with confidence. "A big adventure."

Adventure. Well, that was just about the last thing Dot wanted to think about.

two

DASH

—July 1942 —
Oshawa, Ontario

With bobby pins between her lips, Dash ran a hairbrush through her thick, dark waves until they crackled with electricity. She gathered it all together in a practiced move, tied it with a red ribbon, and pinned the flyaways. Leaning close to the mirror, she applied lipstick, pressed her lips together, then turned her head to the side, making sure all was well. She frowned at a blemish on her cheek, but it was too late to do anything about that now.

It was also too late to change how she'd told Dot she was considering going to the city to work. The idea had been burning in her mind for months, and she felt so much better now that it was out in the open, but surely there'd been a kinder way to do it. One that wouldn't have caused such a stricken expression to flash across her sister's face.

Poor Dot. After their walk home that night, she'd acted like the crab Dash had chased around on their one and only beach vacation to California and disappeared into her shell. She had barely spoken a word to anyone since then. She wondered if Dot's silence came from anger or if she was actually considering the idea of getting a job in the city, but it was impossible to know. Either way, Dash wasn't backing down.

"I've waited long enough," she told her reflection.

It felt like forever since cousin Fred, Gus, and almost all the other boys from school had shipped out to war. Their departure had left Dash as the only young mechanic left around here, which she had appreciated at first, but the shine had faded. She wanted something else now, and whatever that was, she wanted to do it anywhere but in this small town.

She thought about the boys often. Especially Fred and Gus. Fred was a pilot like his father, so he had joined the RCAF. Shortly after he'd gone, Gus had quit his job at Pedlar People sheet metal and enlisted in the army. If only Dash could have gone with them, though she knew that was impossible. Growing up, she had always preferred playing games with the boys over sitting politely with girls and discussing the weather. Her mother might cluck her tongue, but Fred and Gus never looked twice if Dash went outside on a bone-chilling day, hockey stick in her hand, skates tied over her shoulder. If she didn't come out to play ball with them in the summer, they figured she was sick.

It ate her up that they were over there being useful, and she was doing nothing. Knitting socks didn't count, in her opinion.

She paused, sucking in her cheeks as she regarded her image in the mirror. None of the other girls could throw a softball like she could, and they couldn't tell a fan belt from a throttle, but Dash still knew the value of a good lipstick and a formfitting dress.

Gosh, she missed Gus. He'd been gone over a year, and even after all this time, she felt like there was an empty seat at the table when she sat down for supper. She knew Dot felt the same way, but they hadn't spoken about him much. Dot preferred not to talk about anything to do with the war. Gus was the absolute worst at writing letters. Couldn't he just send a little note saying he was out there somewhere, either miserable or happy? Honestly, she didn't care which. She just wanted to know he was alive.

The door to the girls' shared bedroom swung open, and Dot walked in. Without a word, she dropped onto her bed and pulled out a crossword book and a pencil. As she always had, Dash felt a weight lift from her shoulders with Dot around. Her sister had a gift for turning the volume down on drama, so Dash automatically calmed a bit when she was near. When she was stuck inside on rainy days, Dash could sit quietly with Dot for hours. She could even manage to get through an entire book under her sister's influence. But not often.

The tip of Dot's tongue peeked out between her lips as she read. A sure indicator that she was deep in thought.

"Aren't you going to get dressed?" Dash asked. Dot bent down to scribble in an answer, oblivious. "Hello?"

Dot looked up, her eyes slightly out of focus. "Hmm?"

"Birthday dinner, remember? Are you going to get dressed?"

Dot glanced down at the grey dress with black flowers and matching belt that she almost always wore. The dress did nothing for Dot's fair complexion, Dash thought for the hundredth time.

"What do you call this?"

"Come here," Dash replied. Her sister never paid much attention to her appearance, but occasionally Dash liked to remind her how pretty she was. "Let's doll you up."

"*Un minuto, per favore.* I want to finish this."

Dash peered down at the page. "Umbrella," she said, unable to resist. "Thirteen down."

"That's an easy one," Dot grumbled.

"Do the rest later. Please?" She sniffed, inhaling the scent of cloves and cinnamon from downstairs. "Smell the cake? Come on. Let's get ready."

"All right, all right," Dot relented. "Do with me what you will."

Dash loved that invitation. She flung open the wardrobe doors and went straight to her favourite emerald-green dress. The one with the most darling sweetheart neckline.

"First of all, your dress."

Her sister gave her a look. "Are we trying to impress someone? It's just Aunt Lou and Uncle Bob, isn't it?"

"Come on. We're eighteen! Let's dress nice. Try it on."

Dot slipped the dress over her head then let her sister paint colours on her cheeks and lips. Ten minutes later, Dash declared Dot was just as gorgeous as she was.

"You're biased," Dot said, but Dash could see how pleased her sister was by the discreet smile she gave the mirror. She pretended not to notice Dot straightening up the vanity behind them, making sure the lipsticks were on one side, the mascara on the other, and the two little dolls their mother had sewn for them years ago stood at the back, leaning against the mirror.

Both sisters had things they wanted to fix.

"Here they are!" Uncle Bob announced as the girls came downstairs. "I thought we were going to have to celebrate without you."

"You can't have a party without us!" Dash declared, making everyone laugh.

"You both look beautiful," their mother said. "Happy birthday, girls. I made your favourites."

Dash glanced at her father. He and Dot had a lot more in common, but Dash had her own way of communicating with him. He smiled at her and nodded in his quiet way, filling her heart.

"Mmm," Dash said, privately winking at Dot as they went to the kitchen to retrieve the food. "Corned beef fritters. We *love* those."

"Now, now." Her father was awfully good at reading sarcasm. "There's cake for after."

Really, Dash didn't mind fritters. At least there was no parsnip or carrot pudding tonight. They brought the food to the table, then Dash sat beside her uncle.

"What's the news from Fred?" she asked him. "Where's he flying? He's with the RAF now, right?"

Dot frowned. "RAF? You mean RCAF."

"Quite a few of our boys are flying for the Brits now," her uncle explained. "Fred wrote a while back that most of their pilots are from here. Last I heard, he was in Malta, but he can't really say much. Everything has to be kept quiet, for obvious reasons."

"Where's Malta?" Dash whispered to her sister.

"Little island south of Sicily," Dot replied quietly. "East of Tunisia."

"Why would they go there?" she asked, vaguely recalling the map.

"They'll be blocking convoys trying to head to Tunisia or Italy," her father put in.

"The Mediterranean must be beautiful," Dash mused, already moving away from the geography lesson. "Did you fly over water, Uncle Bob?"

"I did. It's beautiful as long as you make it back to the runway in one piece."

"Bob," Aunt Lou chided.

"And Fred is a master at that," he said with confidence. "He'll be just fine."

After they finished the main course, their mother carried the spice cake to the table and set it in front of the sisters. Dash smiled dutifully around the table while her family sang "Happy Birthday" off-key. Then she cut the cake, and Dot passed the plates around.

"I am not giving you any gifts this year," her mother declared, sitting back down and winking at their father.

The plate in Dot's hand hovered uncertainly on its way to Aunt Lou. "That's all right, Mom. We're eighteen. We don't need presents."

Dash heartily disagreed. After all, she still gave her mother flowers for *her* birthday. "Why not?"

"Because, darling girl, someone else is," her mother replied, smiling.

"Here you go," her father said, handing Dot a box. Her face lit up when she peeked within.

"Dad! *Das Geheimnis von Sittaford?* Agatha Christie in *German?* This must have been so difficult to find! Where did you get it?" Speaking far too quickly in her excitement, Dot flipped open the front cover. "When was this published? I can't imagine recently."

"There were a few to choose from, but yes, they are fairly rare." Her father radiated pleasure. "Most were translated in the thirties. I was told the Germans are still translating her work today."

"That's astounding," Dot replied, digging deeper. "Oh! And what's this? *Le Meurtre de Roger Ackroyd. En Français aussi!* Dad! What a treasure chest!"

Dash winced. Foreign versions of mystery novels? She and Dot might be fraternal twins, but Dot and their father were identical.

"I am so pleased you like it. Five of each language."

"He's been collecting them all year," her mother said.

Dash sat expectantly, hoping her father hadn't gathered any books for her. If he had, she'd do her very best to say how grateful she was, but books really weren't her thing. Instead, he turned to his brother. With a flourish, Uncle Bob produced a folded piece of paper, which he handed to Dash.

To Margaret (Dash) Wilson.
FLYING LESSONS *for the summer — or as long as it*
takes. Love, Uncle Bob

Dash stared at the page, stunned. "You mean it?"

Her uncle's laugh rolled straight from his heart. "I never say something—or write it down—if I don't mean it. You ought to know that. My dear niece, you will become a pilot, if that's what you want to be. I'll teach you just like I taught Fred, and he's the best flyboy in the RAF."

Dash had wanted to fly for as long as she could remember. Her mother claimed her obsession had started the moment she could walk. She wanted to be a bird, a bee, a witch on a broomstick, anything as long as she could soar in the clouds. Nearly every day of her childhood, she had climbed the big maple tree beside the house, wanting to be high above the ground. She still remembered when Gus had first arrived and she'd gone too high. Poor Gus. He'd ended up flat on his back with a broken wrist when she landed on top of him. He never did snitch on her, though. He was a true friend even then.

To this day, Dot had never climbed that tree—she seemed inexplicably content to stay on the ground—but she always came out to keep an eye on. One day, Dot and Gus had been sitting on the grass together, watching Dash in her nest. They had been about eight, so Gus was ten. Dash was working on her aim by dropping rocks into a bucket far below. Most of them were going in with noisy clunks, but quite a few littered the base of the tree.

"Gus?" Dash called. "Please?"

"Okay," he groaned, getting to his feet, "but this is the last time."

"Thank you," she sang sweetly as he collected the leftover rocks. He put them into the bucket with the others then scaled the tree to exchange it with the empty one Dash held.

"Ready?" Dash asked, holding a rock in one hand.

"Aim better this time," Gus muttered, climbing down and placing the empty bucket on the ground.

The first one landed only inches from the bucket. "Stupid rocks."

"It's not the rocks' fault," Gus said. "Lean over so you're right over the bucket then drop it. Don't twist your wrist."

The next one landed perfectly in the bucket with a plop, and they all cheered.

After a few more, Dot jumped up. Something about the sound had caught her attention. "Do it again! A big one and a little one together."

Taking careful aim, Dash dropped two at the same time.

Dot's brow creased with concentration. "Again."

Dash complied, and Dot grinned at Gus. "It doesn't matter how big the rock is. They all go the same speed. Count fast, like this." She'd tapped her finger on the back of her other hand, saying, "One-one-one-one."

"I see," Gus said, nodding with apparent interest.

Dash laughed, thinking how silly it was that her sister could find patterns in everything, including falling rocks. But she and Gus had gamely counted along with Dot and found, not surprisingly, that she was right. Then Dot took a furtive look around and whispered for Dash to climb even higher so she could hear if it made any difference. As Dash dropped more rocks from a precarious tree limb, Dot counted *One-one-one-one Two-two*—and stopped at the sound of them hitting the bucket.

When their father came out, Dot told him about her discovery while Dash descended to a safer height. He nodded, explaining that that was to do with physics and something called gravity, which did not interest Dash in the least. If she ever got a chance to fly in real life, she'd just keep on flying. Gravity wouldn't catch her. She'd never come down.

She had flown for the very first time on their tenth birthday, when Uncle Bob took her up in his crop duster biplane, which he called Jenny. While her parents, Dot, and Gus watched nervously from the ground, Dash buzzed happily over farmers' fields as Uncle Bob sprinkled long clouds of tiny white crystals—lead arsenate, he told her—over the plants to rid them of pests.

"Go, Jenny, go!" she cried rapturously, extending her arms like wings, swooping and tilting with the plane. It was only years later that she learned the name of the plane wasn't an affectionate label; the aircraft was the Curtiss JN-4, nicknamed "Jenny" by the manufacturers.

After they landed on solid ground, Dash was still walking on air.

"There you are, Margaret," her mother said, leading her off the field. "Now you've flown and gotten it out of your system."

As if Dash was done with it. "I've flown for the *first* time, Mommy," she laughed.

Uncle Bob took her up regularly after that. He even took both sisters and Gus to an Air Tour where Dash had fallen in love the rest of the way. Gus hugged Dot when she got scared of the planes and the noise, but Dash could see from his face that he was enjoying the show almost as much as she was. That beautiful summer day had been *it* for her. Some girls loved horses, Dot loved mysteries and puzzles; all Dash wanted was to fly.

Now Dash was eighteen, and her dream had just been handed to her on a piece of paper.

"I can't believe it," she said breathlessly, reading the letter again. "When can I start?"

Uncle Bob shrugged, as if he hadn't really considered that. "Oh, I don't know." He turned to his wife. "What do you say, Lou? I think I'm available tomorrow morning."

Dash sprang from her chair with a shriek and ran around the table to give him a hug. Then she hugged everyone else one by one, just because.

"You don't need lessons," Dot said, grinning over her sister's shoulder. "You're already soaring, and you haven't even climbed into the cockpit!"

three

DOT

▬ •• ▬▬▬ ▬

— August 1942 —
Oshawa, Ontario

Dot leaned against the wall, scowling at all six of her students as they
slumped over the dining room table. It was this stinking summer
heat, she assumed, as a drop of sweat trickled down the back of her neck.
She could see from the trees through the window that there was a slight
breeze outside, but she wasn't about to move them all to the yard just for
that. These lessons were not about comfort, they were about learning. She
was being paid to teach, not to babysit, and she did not believe in coddling
children. She made a point of working hard and was quite proud of her
lesson plan: verb conjugation to start, conversational French after that,
then a repeat of the earlier verb but with a different conjugation to finish.

This week's verb was *pouvoir*, which ten-year-old Michael—Dot
called him *Michel* during class, of course—had a bit of a snit over.

"Why is it *que j'eusse pu*?" He pronounced it "poo" just to annoy Dot.
"The verb isn't about poo. And why is it *je peux*?" he continued, dropping
a rebellious "x" at the end. "It's not fair that they make it up like that. It
makes it too hard."

It was a waste of time trying to reason with the boy when he got like
this.

"That's the way it is," Dot answered cheerfully.

She glanced at the clock. The past hour had moved so slowly it felt as if the class was twice as long. Pressing on, she pulled out a piece of paper on which she had written the next lesson.

"Now let's move on to conditional verb conjugations. Sit up tall, children. Eyes up here, please. Let's use *parler, c'est ça?* Do you remember what this means? Conditional means I *would* talk, rather than I *am* talking. First, the present tense: *je parlerais*. Everyone together, *tous ensemble maintenant. Je parlerais, tu parlerais, il parlerait . . .*"

Anna, the eldest and brightest of her students, propped her cheek on her hand as she recited, her eyelids heavy. Michael's feet were bouncing under the table, and though he eventually delivered the words correctly, Dot wanted to scream at the three mechanical syllables he recited, "Je par. Le. Ray. To par. Le. Ray." Finally, the clock struck five o'clock, and she sighed with relief along with the class. She held the door for the children, and they bolted into the sweltering heat outside.

Before the lesson had started, she'd placed a glass of water in the refrigerator to chill, as she always did. Now she pulled open the wide white Maytag door, and though she knew she should always conserve electricity, she paused, savouring the delicious breath of cold air that rushed out. After a moment, she grabbed the glass and shut the door. As she gulped the water down, she spotted a couple of letters on the kitchen table. Neither was from Gus, she noted miserably.

Ten years ago, a letter had arrived that had changed all their lives. It was a hot afternoon like this, and Dash, Gus, and she had just arrived home from school. As her mother picked up the envelope from the table, she'd asked them about their days, wanting to hear what they had learned and who they played with. There was so much more to talk about once they were eight years old, and Gus was already in grade five, which was even more interesting. While she listened, she opened the envelope. Dot still recalled the sound of her mother's little gasp, the way her palm had rushed to her mouth. Without a word, she turned from the children and retreated upstairs to her bedroom.

A little later, she came back down and called the three of them to the living room.

"I have some very sad news, children."

Her eyes were red. She'd been crying. That was alarming, since she was almost always calm and happy. Dot leaned against Dash's side for reassurance, and her mother reached for Gus's hands. He looked uncertain, as if he should run away.

"Gus, I'm so sorry, but your father had a terrible accident today."

"I will help take care of him," Dot offered immediately.

That made her mother blink quickly. "I wish you could, Dorothy. But the sad news is that your father died, Gus. He will not be coming home."

Gus stared at her, not moving. Dot and Dash stood on either side of him, unsure what to do. Dot had never felt so miserable.

"I'm sorry, dear," her mother said.

Gus's chin quivered, but Dot knew he would not cry in front of them.

"Thank you," he said.

Then he turned and walked quickly to his bedroom, quietly shutting the door behind him. Dot knocked on his door a little later. He made a sound she couldn't interpret, so she assumed he'd invited her in. He was lying in his bed, a pillow hugged over his face. Dot's heart was in pieces for him. If she had been crying, she wouldn't want anyone to speak to her, but she wouldn't want to be alone, either. Maybe he needed her to listen. She was very good at listening. So she sat at the foot of his bed, not saying a word. Eventually, he lifted the pillow and looked at her. His expression was so despondent she started to cry. He sat up and pulled her into a hug.

"Will you go away now, Gus? Are you going to leave us?"

"I hope not," he sniffed.

"I don't want you to go."

Meanwhile, Dash had been hounding her parents about the very same thing. When it was time for supper, her father put his hand on Gus's shoulder. "I'm very sorry about your father, Gus." Then he met their mother's gaze. She nodded, and he continued. "We would like you to live here with us as you have been. What do you think of that?"

"Yes, please," Gus whispered.

And so he did. He stayed with them until he turned eighteen, and then he went to war. Ever since then, Dot had been waiting to hear from him. They all had. His silence concerned her greatly, though she hadn't mentioned that to Dash. Her sister was so deliriously happy, distracted by her flying lessons, she hadn't talked about much else lately. In turn, Dot was deliriously happy that Dash hadn't set off to work in the city, so she kept quiet about anything that had to do with the war.

But she did miss him. Terribly. She missed the reassuring smiles he'd give her when he knew she was scared or sad, and she missed the warmth of his hugs. Without them, she found it a little harder to cheer up.

And then there was the one other thing she wasn't talking about. Not to anyone.

A few months before he'd gone away, Dash had come home all excited about a big dance coming up. It was for anyone over sixteen, so the girls were eligible to attend. Though it sounded exciting, Dot vanished into her shell at the mere mention of it. Dash never pressed her to come, but on the day of the dance, Gus had.

"You're not coming?"

She was in the tire swing, and he was gently pushing her.

"I don't know how to dance."

"I could teach you. It's not hard."

She'd blushed, imagining that. To teach her, he'd have to put one hand on her waist and hold on to her other one. An odd curl of heat traveled through her belly, thinking of that.

"That's all right. I'm happy to stay home and read. You go. Dash loves to dance with you. She says you're very good."

Gus grabbed the rope connecting the tire to the tree, stilling the swing. "I want you to come, Dot. I want to dance with you. I won't let anything bad happen."

It was impossible to say no to him when he looked at her that way. So Dash had dressed her up, and Gus had driven them in their father's car, and the only time he'd left Dot's side was to get her a refreshment. When the piano player started crooning "The Way You Look Tonight," Gus had come up behind her.

"Ready to try dancing?" he asked, his breath tickling her ear.

"You promise you won't laugh at me?"

"I have never laughed at you, Dot. I never will. Unless you say something funny, that is."

He was hard to resist. She gave him her hand, and he led her to the side of the crowd, where it wasn't too busy. Then he was holding her, and butterflies danced in her chest while her feet tripped all over themselves. She felt strange, and she didn't understand. She'd hugged him so many times. They'd spent loads of time talking in private. Why did this feel so different?

"It's not hard," he had said. "Look up here. In my eyes."

Now, Dot's finger circled the rim of her water glass, and she stared at its contents, lost in reflection. Gosh, she missed him. Sometimes it hurt when she thought about him. If only he would write.

At least they heard from Fred occasionally. He was very proud to be part of the Canadian squadrons that formed the RAF's No. 6 Group, Bomber Command. He wasn't allowed to say much more in his letters, so they were a little boring to read, but at least they heard from him.

When Dot entered the living room, her father was there already, squinting at a newspaper.

"Well," she said, sinking into the sofa. "Class is over."

"That sounded painful."

"I could never teach a whole classroom. Just six of them is exhausting." He set down his paper, and she studied him. "Are you all right? You look pale. Can I get you something?"

"No, no. I'm fine. Just a headache," he assured her. "You know me. When the weather changes . . ."

The front door swung open. "What a wonderful day!" Dash cried happily.

"Shh! Dad has a headache."

"Oh, sorry. What a wonderful day!" Dash whispered, joining them. "I was at Uncle Bob's."

Their father brightened at the mention of his younger brother. The two were very close, like Dot and Dash. A couple of years before the Great War had begun, cancer had taken the boys' mother, then their father had reportedly died of a broken heart shortly after. The brothers had grown up in their grandparents' house, but they were mostly on their own. Dash's father had practically raised Uncle Bob, and their affection for each other had never waned.

After the war ended, Uncle Bob had married Aunt Lou, and she inherited her father's wheat farm. Faced with a life he knew nothing about, Uncle Bob declared that he was more of a landlord than a farmer and rented about half the land to actual farmers. He sold most of the rest to the county, which had quickly planted houses rather than wheat. Before that, he'd given Dot's father a choice of one of the lots, on which he had built his own home. As a result, the families lived about a mile and half from each other. The only substantial part of the farm Uncle Bob had kept for himself was the portion he reserved for Jenny and her own little airfield.

Dash plopped onto the sofa beside Dot, looking wildly beautiful. Her long black hair was in mad disarray beneath a beret, and her cheeks burned bright red from the wind.

"Uncle Bob showed me the instrument panel today, and I understood it pretty easily because there are a lot of similarities with automobiles. But there were new ones too, and it was so interesting. Then we went for a flight, and that was the icing on the cake." She spread her arms out over the back of the sofa and raised her face to the ceiling. "He said I'd done well with the practical lesson, so I should sit back and enjoy myself, so I did. Honestly, I couldn't be happier."

"I couldn't tell," her father said, giving Dash one of his sweet smiles.

"You're paying attention to Uncle Bob, right?" Dot asked, concerned. "Not just soaring around with that big grin on your face?"

"Of course! I want to learn everything so I can fly everywhere. Maybe someday I'll fly for a living."

Dot doubted that, but she would never say so. As much as she questioned her sister's outrageous dreams, Dash almost always proved her wrong.

"I could teach like Uncle Bob, or I could fly people around, or . . ." Dash petered off, seeing Dot's lifted eyebrow. "Don't worry. I know those are pie-in-the-sky thoughts."

"You can do whatever you work at," her father assured Dash. "I've never seen you quit."

"Thanks, Dad." She leaned toward her sister, elbows on her knees. "Oh, you'd love it, Dot. The way the engine purrs, then Uncle Bob pushes the throttle in, not all at once, just kind of urging Jenny along, and she roars!"

"So it purrs, then it roars," Dot teased. "Is it a plane or a lion?"

"Jenny the lion," Dash mused, toying with the idea. "Will you come watch me?"

Dot wasn't certain she could. What if something happened? Her stomach did a little flip just thinking about it.

"Please?"

There was nothing she wouldn't do for Dash. "Of course."

"You, too, Dad. But only when I'm ready. When I get to fly by myself, maybe you can even come up with me."

Her father chuckled, sounding a little nervous. "Oh, I don't know about that. I've done my share of flying, thank you. I will stay on the ground with your sister."

"I can't wait to show you!" Dash bounced.

Much as it shamed her, Dot was envious of her sister's joy. Would she ever find anything that captivated her so entirely?

"The only thing I didn't like today," Dash continued, "was that Uncle Bob says we are only going to fly once a week. He doesn't want to do it all at once. He says he has other things to do beside teaching me. Imagine!"

As she chattered away, Dot relaxed slightly. The idea of Uncle Bob limiting the lessons to once a week pleased her very much. The longer the instructions took, the longer it would be before Dash could head to Toronto for a job.

four

DASH

— Oshawa, Ontario —

Early one Saturday morning in mid-August, Dash gave her mother a kiss on the cheek then grabbed her green sweater on her way out the door.

"I'm off to uncle's," she said.

"Of course you are. Is today the big day?"

"I sure hope so." She plucked at her sleeve. "Green's my lucky colour."

She didn't have to ask what her mother meant. After weeks of lessons, they all knew Dash was more than eager to head out on her very first solo flight. She had done all the land training she could, and she'd mastered peering over Uncle Bob's shoulder at the controls. For the last two weeks, she had taken over the controls and flown the plane with him sitting in the aft cockpit, and the sense of being in charge of her own flight had been blissful. She'd never wanted to land. When she had left his yard last time, he had suggested today *might* be the day when she did the whole thing by herself. She had barely caught a wink of sleep in anticipation.

It would be a warm day, she could tell, but it would be cold in the sky, with her head sticking out of Jenny's open cockpit. Her coat hung over her arm as she headed out, her gloves in her pockets, and a scarf was jammed in one sleeve. She practically skipped the mile and a half down the sun-speckled road to Uncle Bob's farm, figuring she could get there blindfolded, since she'd gone so many times. When she finally turned the corner at the end, Jenny came into sight, her parallel, tan wings shining in the early dawn light, her gleaming wood propeller at rest. Technically, her uncle could have moved the plane to the Oshawa airport when it had opened in '41, especially since he was an instructor there for the Elementary Flying Training School. The RCAF had a whole fleet of seventy-five Tiger Moths there, all being used as trainers, so Jenny would have had company. But Uncle Bob had wanted to keep her nearby.

Today's airplanes looked so different from the old biplanes, she thought, approaching the field. With their single wings and aerodynamic shapes, they couldn't help but impress. But Jenny was a classic. Dash skimmed her palm over the smooth fuselage, admiring her simplicity. Instead of painting the plane's entire cockpit and fuselage that bright lemon yellow many others had, Uncle Bob kept his plane an understated olive green with a pale blue fuselage. She was already such a fine-looking airplane, he said. A natural beauty. There was no need to dress her up.

"Shall we fly, you and I?" she asked the plane, tapping a wing, then she turned, hearing her uncle approach. His shoulders were uncharacteristically hunched.

"Good morning!" she called cheerily, hoping she was misreading him.

"Bad news, Dash."

Her heart sank. "Oh no. What's wrong?"

"I'm a little under the weather. Don't plan to fly today."

So much for her lucky sweater. "I hope you feel better soon."

He stopped beside the plane and leaned against the fuselage. "You can't lean on me forever, you know. So I thought today I'd leave the flying to you, start to finish. I'll watch from here."

Dash caught her breath, then anticipation rushed in. "My first solo flight? Really?"

"You think you're ready?"

Her whole body tingled with excitement. "Don't you worry about me, Uncle Bob. I was born ready."

"Oh, I do know that about you. All right. Up you get," he said, helping her onto the lower wing. "I'll do the walk-around checks, you do yours, then you can go."

Her palms were sweating as she lowered herself into the cockpit and eyed the seven familiar glass dials on the instrument panel. Automatically, her mind traced the routine of starting the plane: slide the green fuel lever forward to let fuel into the cylinders, press this valve on the carburetor... While she went over her checklist for inside the plane, Uncle Bob strode around the outside inspecting flaps, rudder, wheels, propeller, tires, and everything else. She knew it would all be fine, but he'd made it very clear to her that doing the checks every single time was the most important thing she could do.

Once she was done, Dash snapped her helmet on, then she pressed the little lever to prime the fuel line.

Satisfied, Uncle Bob stood alongside and looked up. "You ready?"

She fastened her seat belt, fingers vibrating with adrenaline. "Roger."

"How on earth do you know to say Roger?"

"Dot told me. I can't believe you even need to ask. She knows everything."

"What did she tell you about that?"

"Well, she said that when a telegraph is sent in Morse code, the receiver always sends back confirmation that they received the telegraph, so they tap in the letter 'R' for Received. Then, when they started using two-way radios, they used the phonetic alphabet, like Able, Baker, Charlie, Dog for ABCD."

He was grinning. "Go on. This is fascinating."

"The rest is common sense."

"Oh? Give an old man a clue."

"Well, Roger is phonetic for 'R.' If you're already using 'R' for Received in a telegraph, that means you use Roger for two-way conversation."

"Dot told you all that?"

"She could put an encyclopedia to shame."

That made him laugh. "She might know everything in the books, but she doesn't know how to fly, does she?"

He stepped to the front and pulled the propeller down in a few revolutions, pushing fuel into the plane's workings. When he nodded, she reached outside of the cockpit to flip the ignition switch on, then she lowered her goggles.

In his smile she saw a rare flash of her father, full of pride. "Ready?"

"Contact," she called, and he gave the propeller a final revolution.

It caught, spinning so quickly it gave the illusion of stalling. The engine roared to life, vibrating under and around her, surrounding her in noise and filling her with a sort of breathless euphoria. From her perch, she watched her uncle pull out the chocks, the little triangles that held the wheels in position while the plane was parked, then he gave her a stiff salute and Dash was on her own. At first, a cold uncertainty flipped in her belly, but it was replaced immediately by fire. The plane bumped along the tarmac, taxiing to the start of the runway, then she faced Jenny's nose into the wind, lining her up for takeoff. Ahead stretched a long, open road, then the vast sky she longed to be a part of. If only her family was here to watch. She increased the RPMs to 1000, and the plane growled with impatience. Her pulse raced with it.

"Let's go, Jenny," she said out loud. "It's you and me now."

She punched the throttle, and they roared down the pavement. Dash muttered *nose up, nose up, nose up* as she jostled over the uneven runway, ignoring the tangles of hair now pasted to her face. When the plane reached sixty-five miles per hour, she helped it lift into the air, then her stomach swooped as she left the earth behind. Relishing the sensation, she headed up, up, up to what her uncle called a comfortable cruising height, at two thousand feet. Then it was just her and the plane and the clouds and the sky.

Right where she'd always dreamed of being.

From the corner of her eye, she saw the world spread beneath her, the snaking rivers and roads, the tiny houses. But when the plane wobbled, her focus went to the dials. Her awe would have to wait. She calmly manipulated the stick, lining up to the level of the horizon so she could soar across the sky, then she flew the pattern she'd followed so many times with Uncle Bob. Everything felt different now that she wasn't shielded by someone else's wing.

"Woohoo!" she yelled, her heart full. "I'm flying!"

More confident by the second, Dash leaned her head over the edge of the cockpit and took in the unspeakably beautiful view: the greens and browns, the places she had known all her life but had rarely really seen. The colours seemed deeper now that she was on her own, the land below more intriguing. She banked slightly, turning toward home, and was a little disappointed not to see anyone in the yard. She'd have loved to wave at them. There was the old school, tiny beneath her, the redbrick building empty for the day. And in the distance, the long, blue coastline of Lake Ontario. Eventually, she pulled her head back, glad she was bundled up. Between the double wings, the motor, and the constant wind whipping past, it was freezing up here.

It was patently unfair, Dash thought as she leaned the plane to the right, that women pilots weren't permitted to fly in the war. Who could say that Fred was a better flyer than she was? She'd always had better aim when they played ball. If the people in charge could only change their rules and allow girls like her to fly, who knew what might happen? She could easily picture herself as part of a squadron, coming in low over a German target . . .

She shook her head, clearing her thoughts. She couldn't bear to think of it, because it would never happen. The best thing she could do would be to sign up for the Wrens as soon as she could. At least then she'd feel like she was helping in some way.

Dot wouldn't be happy about that at all.

Far, far below, her uncle stood outside the hangar, observing Dash's flight. She noticed Aunt Lou walking out to him, so Dash tilted her wings side to side to wave hello. She waited for them to wave back, but instead, her aunt and uncle fell together in an uncharacteristic embrace. Dash felt a jolt of concern and decided to cut her flight short. She lined up the runway, then *nose up nose up nose up*, she touched down with a disconcerting bump and taxied the plane home.

Uncle Bob was not smiling when Dash rolled up. He was pale, and he was still holding Aunt Lou tightly against him. Dash couldn't see her aunt's face.

"Uncle Bob?" Dash asked, killing the engine. When he didn't answer, she dropped onto the tarmac and ran to them. "What's wrong?"

That's when she noticed the piece of paper he held in one hand, pressed against Aunt Lou's back. A telegram. Her stomach rolled.

Dash raised her eyes to his, terrified. With all her might she hoped she was wrong. "Fred?" she whispered.

That's when her uncle lowered his head onto his wife's shoulder and began to cry.

five

DOT

-•• --- -

— September 1942 —
Oshawa, Ontario

Kneeling on a burlap bag, Dot dug her trowel into the black earth of their front yard, harvesting vegetables and clearing weeds. It was only the end of summer, but beets, carrots, onions, and almost everything else already needed to be picked and canned for the approaching winter. The squash and pumpkin had put out healthy vines for their fruit, and the potatoes, always the easiest thing to grow, edged two sides of the garden with bushy green leaves. She'd come back for those in a couple of weeks. Her first basket was full of perfectly ripe green beans, which she'd can this afternoon. Then she'd patch her father's coat. And she'd knit. She'd probably make supper, too. Anything to keep her mind off what was happening around her.

Dot hadn't asked for Dash's help today, even though she thought a bit of digging might do her sister some good. Ever since Fred had been shot down at Dieppe—could it have been only two weeks ago?—Dash had been miserable. They all had, but Dash had never learned how to control her emotions. *Dieppe*. What a horrible disaster. She'd read that nearly nine hundred Canadians had died that day, and thousands more had been wounded or taken prisoner. This was exactly the reason why Dot tried not to think about the war or those boys' eager entry into it.

Fred had been impatient to fight in the Canadian Army's first actual battle. He had written home just a few days before, saying he was tired of waiting. And now he was gone.

Everyone counted on Dot to be level-headed, but the fact of the matter was that Fred's death was tearing her apart, too. She just didn't want to talk about it. All talking did was haul her grief back to the surface, where she couldn't manage it. Dot's instinct had always been to keep her feelings inside. She didn't like to tell anyone but Dash what she was feeling, and even then she kept some things to herself.

"Hello there, farmer."

She lifted her gaze. "Oh, hello, Dad. You're home early."

"I needed to get some paperwork done, and the office was too noisy."

He adjusted his glasses on his nose, and she noted the black rings beneath his eyes. He suffered from such awful headaches. She wished there was something she could do.

"I wasn't in a mood for talking," he added.

Neither was she. But so much emotion was building inside her, she feared she might burst.

"Are you all right, Dorothy?"

She hesitated. "I still can't believe Fred is gone."

"No. I don't suppose any of us can. It will take a long time to get used to."

They both lowered their eyes to the dirt, and she wondered if he could possibly be thinking what she was. She didn't know if it was out of place to have this one pressing thought that was *not* about Fred, but if anyone would understand, she thought it might be her father.

"I can't stop thinking about Gus. We haven't heard from him in months. We have no idea where he is. What if he . . ." She stopped, unable to continue. Fred's death made everything so real. She couldn't imagine living without Gus.

"I promise I'll come home," he had said to her and Dash at the train station on their last day together. "And I've never broken a promise to either of you."

That was true, and Dot had clung to that promise despite his lack of letters. But the days kept marching on with no word.

Once upon a time, Gus had been a neighbour boy who barely spoke a word of English. A new curiosity. Then he had a chair at the dinner table and a bedroom of his own tucked in the back of their house. They taught him their language, and he taught them his. They'd understood each other perfectly. He was a part of them. A crucial part, it turned out.

In his first week at school, Dash had introduced Gus around. Dot had walked with them but only observed. The thought of voluntarily speaking with people, even the kids at school, had always terrified her. She avoided doing that at all costs. She knew that by not joining in, she was making her isolation worse, but it felt like an impossible barrier to cross. Besides, Dash was always more than happy to step in for her.

But when Dash wasn't around, Dot's timidity occasionally made her a target. One day, when the children were coming out of the school for lunch, one of the bigger boys had given her a shove. She'd landed hard on her knees and palms, skinning them. Stunned, she looked up at him, unsure what she'd done to deserve it, but she was too afraid to ask. Then Gus was there. He was younger and smaller than the other boy, but that hadn't mattered to him. He pushed the boy down and stood over him.

"Only a bully pushes girls," he said. Then he'd helped Dot stand, careful of her scratched hands. "Are you all right?"

"Thank you," she whispered.

"I don't like bullies," he told her.

When it had come time for Gus to leave to fight the Nazis, Dot had known it was the only thing he could have done. He'd never liked bullies, and the ones in Europe were much worse than the boys had been in school.

Dot's father gave a weak shrug, and she knew he had been thinking about Gus, too. After all, he was practically his son. "He promised he would return. That is what we must hold on to." He eyed the garden's empty rows then her two full buckets. "I think you have enough there to can for a week. I'll carry one in for you."

As usual, Dot had prepared everything in advance. The clean jars stood upside down on a towel, and the kitchen sink and pots were filled with water. She lit a burner then moved to the sink to wash the vegetables while she waited for the water to boil. Beans first, beets last, since they were the dirtiest. Canning was long, dreary work, but also rewarding, and much appreciated through the winter months. After the last jar had been filled, she reached up and stretched her aching back. That's when she noticed Dash walking purposefully through the front door.

"Where have you been?" Dot asked. "I thought you were upstairs all this time."

Dash hesitated, then she held out a blue and white pamphlet.

"What's this?" Dot asked, taking it from her. The illustration on the front was of a smiling woman in a navy-blue uniform, and the banner on top said, W.R.N.C.S. *Women's Royal Canadian Naval Service*. "'Join the Wrens'? Why should I—" Her jaw dropped. "No. You didn't just sign up, did you?"

Dash didn't answer, but she raised her chin a bit, prepared for battle.

"Without me?" Dot cried. "You didn't even tell me?"

"I did tell you. I just, well, I sped up my plan."

Dot's vision blurred. "I can't believe it. You're really leaving?"

"They said I will hear from them within two weeks, and then yes." Dash's gaze softened. "I gotta go, Dot. I know half a dozen girls at least who are already signed up and working. Remember Jean? She's a sailmaker. Cindy is a delivery driver. I even heard that in England some of the British Wrens load torpedoes onto submarines! Can you imagine? I applied to be a mechanic. Wouldn't that be perfect? You should really think about joining, too."

But all Dot could picture was the twin bed beside hers, empty.

She watched Dash head upstairs, unable to move. This couldn't be happening. She dropped her gaze to the piece of paper in her hand.

"Join the Wrens, and free a man for the fleet," she read.

She tossed the pamphlet onto the table as if it burned her skin. Oh, how she hated this awful, selfish war. It was taking everyone from her. Soon Dash would be gone, and Dot would miss her like mad. It wasn't only that, though. Without her, Dot would have no one to hide behind. She understood she should be ashamed of her weakness, and she supposed she was, but she was also dreadfully afraid to do anything about it. Taking risks meant facing the unknown. It meant unpredictability. Everything Dot had ever done—from the inflexible rules of numbers and Morse code to the routine of conjugating verbs in any language she learned, and solving mysteries before anyone else—relied on knowing with certainty what would happen next.

You should think about joining.

But she couldn't do that. What would be the point? She already knew she wouldn't be able to handle such a drastic change. Besides, she would never be courageous enough to follow in her sister's footsteps.

That was the one certainty she still had.

six

DASH

— *Oshawa, Ontario* —

Dash sat cross-legged on her bed, feeling glum. The bedroom window was slightly open, and she could hear the swish of autumn rain against the leaves of the old maple tree. Normally she loved that sound. Not today. Ever since Fred had died, death had felt like something tangible. A threat she could feel coming closer, and the rain made her feel trapped. To escape that feeling, she had gone to the recruitment centre and done something about it. She refused to sit here like a bump on a log and wait out the entire war. She was glad she had done it, but by doing that, she had changed everything between herself and her sister.

"*J'espère qu'il cessera bientôt de pleuvoir*," she heard Dot say downstairs, followed by a lazy chorus of her students' voices. "That's right. Does anyone know what we just said? Yes?"

"I hope it'll stop raining soon," a little voice replied.

A storm cloud hung over Dot's head these days, and it was hard for Dash not to take at least partial responsibility for that. Still, just because Dot was afraid of being alone, that didn't mean Dash shouldn't do what she thought was right.

Then again, Dash had her own problems with leaving. The reality of not having Dot around was daunting, but she wasn't about to admit that.

She'd told her parents, Uncle Bob, and Aunt Lou about the Wrens. They'd been excited for her, and proud, but every one of them had quietly asked how Dot was taking her decision. She was a little annoyed that they had taken the shine off her news with that question.

"Dot's stronger than you think," she told them. "She won't need me."

Which was true, though it would take some time. But knowing that Dot would eventually manage just fine on her own was a difficult thing for Dash to face as well. That would take time, too.

She heard the front door open, and through the window, she watched Dot's half dozen students leave the house, clutching school bags to their chests in a futile effort to keep them dry. At the sound of her sister's feet on the stairs, Dash turned to face her. When Dot entered the room and saw her like that, her step faltered.

"We should talk," Dash said. "We haven't said more than two words to each other since I told you about the Wrens."

Dot didn't reply. She placed her lesson plans on the table between their beds, then she sat on her own and mirrored Dash's pose.

"Where do you want to start?" Dash asked.

Dot set her jaw. "You called this meeting, not me."

"Let's talk about Gus," Dash suggested, and Dot's face softened.

"I miss him so much it hurts," she admitted quietly.

Dash nodded. "Sometimes I sit down for supper and expect him to pull up his chair and join us."

Dot was staring over Dash's shoulder, toward the window. "I miss his voice. I miss turning around and seeing him there. I miss the smell of his clothes when I am doing the washing." She squeezed her eyes shut, and her words rushed out. "But I am so, so angry at him. I would never abandon the people I loved without at least sending an occasional note to let them know I was all right. It's like he doesn't care about us at all. Like he's forgotten us. And then I start wondering—" Dot stopped.

There was a beat as Dash wondered what to say.

"He's alive, Dot. We'd know if something had happened, wouldn't we? We're his only family. They would have to notify Dad if something happened. I agree with you on his letter writing though, and when he eventually comes home, I plan to give him a piece of my mind."

"I wish he'd come home right now," Dot said with a sigh. "This house is going to feel so empty without either of you in it."

"Fred," Dash said, changing the topic.

"Fred," Dot echoed. "You go. I don't know where to start."

Neither did Dash. She thought about Fred a lot, imagining what his last moments might have been like. Flying was Dash's passion, but there was obviously a terrifying aspect to being airborne. Fred would have been streaking through the sky, then something had struck his plane—the fuselage? a wing?—and he would have scrambled for some way to level it. To make everything right again. Then he'd grasp the fact that he couldn't, that he was *going to die*, and what then?

"People say things like 'He knew what he was getting into when he signed up,'" Dash said, dabbing a tear from the corner of her eye. "But how could he have truly known? I mean, he got shot out of the sky. One minute he's flying, and the next . . . We don't even know how he died. Was he alive when he crashed?"

Dot looked away. "I changed my mind. I don't want to talk about that. It's awful."

"If we don't talk about these things, they'll just stew," Dash warned.

"Let's talk about the Wrens, then," Dot snipped.

Dash blinked. "I'm not going to apologize for my decision, Dot. It's what I need to do."

Dot's expression was tight, a mixture of anger and grief. *Betrayal.* Dash had never seen that before. This was the first time she'd ever come close to betraying her sister. And boy, had she done it.

"You should join," Dash said, filling the silence between them. "You really should. You could join the typing pool or work the telegraph machines, I don't know. They'd love to have someone as smart as you. If you tell them about your French and German, they'd leap at the chance to bring you on."

She knew Dot didn't want to go. She wouldn't want to leave the quiet haven of their house. She wouldn't want to work someplace where she didn't know anyone and didn't know what was expected. Dot would have already convinced herself that she wouldn't fit in. That she would fail.

"Couldn't you wait a little longer?" Dot tried. "With everything that's happened with Fred—"

"Fred is precisely why I have to go now. Men are dying over there, and I'm doing nothing. My own cousin was killed while I was flying around without a care in the world. I don't want to sit around feeling this way when maybe I could somehow prevent it. Fred died doing something important for the rest of the world. I want to do what I can as well."

"So your mind is made up."

"I love you, Dot, but if I stay here I will go nuts. You know that. You'll be fine without me. The best thing you can do is keep busy. Think about joining." But it was more than that, and they both knew it. Dash's hands tightened to fists on her lap. "I want you to step out of this house without me and not be afraid."

Dot's voice was cold. "I am not you, Dash."

"No one is asking you to be me. There's so much you could do for the Wrens that would be of use. Things that are nothing like what I can do. Imagine a brain like yours working for them. You could really make a difference."

A barrage of rain hit the window, but neither of them flinched.

"I don't want to fight with you, Dot."

"Then don't leave me."

"I'm not leaving *you*, I'm—"

"Yes, you are!" Dot exclaimed, sitting straight up. Dash was alarmed by the rush of hurt that filled her sister's eyes. "I don't know what will happen around here without you. I don't know what will happen to *me*. I don't know how I will live without seeing you every day. I don't know how to . . . I don't know anything except I don't want you to go. Please, Dash. Stay with me. Don't leave me."

Every part of Dash longed to rush to her sister and hold her tight, assure her that she'd always be with her no matter where she was. But she did not move. It was the hardest thing she'd ever done, and it needed doing.

"I'm not leaving you," she repeated calmly. "It's not about you or the rest of the family. I'm going for my own sake. It's impossible for me to sit here, knowing that Gus and all those other men, all those boys we grew up with, are going through hell and I'm not doing anything about it. I believe joining the Wrens is how I can do something."

"How can you say you're not helping?" Dash demanded. "We've been doing a lot of good. We volunteer for the Red Cross, we built the victory garden in front, we collect and donate metal, and we've knit hundreds of things for the men over there."

"You're right," Dash allowed. "All of those things are helping. But I need to do more."

The flush faded from Dot's cheeks as defeat set in. She reached into her pocket and handed Dash an envelope. "I guess you need this, then," she said.

It was from the recruitment office. "You hid this from me?"

"Not really. It only came this afternoon, and I was going to give it to you anyway, but then we started talking and I forgot." She sniffed. "What does it say?"

Dash's hands shook a little. "I have to go to HMCS York the day after tomorrow for a medical examination."

———

On the morning of her appointment, Dash left the house early and walked to the bus station. She knew the schedule, so after she'd settled into a seat, she sat back to enjoy the hour-long ride to Toronto. She'd done this about a year ago, to go to a dance with Gus and some of her friends from school, then again last July when they'd gone to the Miss War Worker Beauty Contest. What a riot that had been. More than a hundred women, all of whom worked in the local military manufacturing plants, had competed for the title of Miss War Worker. Dot had stuck close to her all that day, gesturing at the women. She'd insisted that none of them would have stood a chance against Dash, if Dash had a job.

This was the first time Dash was taking this trip by herself, and the freedom gave her a little thrill. At the end of the line, she got off to wait for a streetcar. When it arrived, she paid her dime then paused to speak with the driver.

"I'm sorry to bother you, sir, but I'm not exactly sure where I'm going. I have to get to the HMCS York. Is it at the docks?"

"The docks? Well, it's near there," he said.

Dash was still confused. "How do I get to it?"

"I'll just drop you off," was his response. Then a light went on in his eyes. "You're thinking the York is a ship. You'd think that from the initials, but it's the Automotive Building of the CNE. The military muster there before training."

She thanked him, slightly embarrassed, then she spotted a free seat at the back of the car and made her way toward it, squeezing between the standing passengers. At least she knew how to get to the CNE, since that's where the Miss War Worker contest had been held. Once she was settled, she peered out the window at the wet road. As the streetcar rolled past a park, she spotted army men doing exercises on the hill. *Is Gus wearing one of those uniforms?*

Signs of war were everywhere, even in this city thousands of miles away from the conflict. After three years, a lot of people looked haggard and stooped, tired of it all. Despite the mild fall day, Dash shivered, remembering last winter. There'd been a coal shortage, so the government had imposed a restriction on how warm people were allowed to keep their homes. Sixty-five degrees meant Dash, Dot, their mother, Aunt Lou, and other volunteer knitters had made good use of wool and needles, though sometimes it was almost too cold for their fingers to work. With the war still dragging on, Dash imagined this winter would be worse.

Yet even with so much unhappiness, people were carrying on. They stopped to chat with one another, standing in front of lawns that had been dug into victory gardens. Instead of hauling bags of groceries home to their families, they carried ration tickets in their pockets, doing the best with what they had. And yet, there were signs of optimism. Just the other day, her father had read something to her and Dot from *The Star* about the Toronto Transit Company's plans to build a second streetcar line either parallel to this one or *beneath* it to help out with the rising demand. A train underground. Just imagine. People came up with the most unexpected solutions. So far nothing had come of the idea, but even if the plan worked, she figured it must be practically impossible to find enough construction workers. They were all fighting overseas. Just like Fred had been. Just like Gus.

When the streetcar eventually dropped her off at Exhibition Park, Dash didn't see any signs at all indicating the Women's Royal Canadian Naval Service members belonged here, but the letter in her hand was clear. She wandered into the massive agricultural complex then stopped the first man in a uniform and asked for directions.

"This area's for the air force," he said. "I don't know where the Wrens go."

She thanked him and continued on, pausing by one of the renovated stalls where the men lived during training, the stink of cows and horses, pigs and chickens thick in her nose. Overhead she spotted a sign bearing the word SWINE and a smaller one below indicating this area was reserved for officers. According to another, all other ranks belonged under CATTLE AND SHEEP. She'd laughed out loud, and despite her excitement she felt a twinge of regret that she wasn't sharing the joke with her sister. Dot would have loved the irony.

When a woman in a navy-blue uniform strode past, Dash called out, asking where she should go.

"You're in the Agriculture Building. You want the Automotive Building," she said, pointing. "Medical exams for the Wrens are in the upper gallery."

Dash found her way to the tiny room, marked by a doorway with no door. It was divided in three by a set of short, flimsy shower curtains, and the largest section held a desk, a filing cabinet, and two chairs. She took a seat, filled in the required forms, then was told to go behind the first curtain, remove her clothes, and don the required open-backed gown for her medical exam.

"All my clothes?" she clarified, peering at the indicated curtain. Beneath it, she spied two pairs of legs: one male in navy trousers, and one female evidently in nothing at all. The curtain was so light it swayed with the hint of a breeze, and when it suddenly parted and gave her an unexpected glimpse, she looked away, cheeks blazing.

"Every thread."

The doctor was professional, thorough, and quick, but she still felt humiliated by the indignity of it all. Afterward, he checked her paperwork, flipping over a couple pages to be sure of something, then he dismissed her. Slightly flustered but energized with anticipation, Dash left the tiny office carrying a different letter. This one said she must be ready to report for duty when called.

It wouldn't be long.

seven

DOT

—●● ━ ━ ━ ━

— *Oshawa, Ontario* —

Dot was like a bat when it came to her hearing. Bright and early this morning she had heard the rustle of Dash pulling on her clothes, then the groan of each step as her sister snuck downstairs and out the front door. Once she was gone, Dot remained in bed with an upset stomach. She felt a deep sadness that Dash was really leaving, but she also acknowledged a twinge of envy. If only she could find the courage to be like her sister just this once.

But Dot had never been that way. Just after they had started school, she'd realized she was different. The other children used Dash's new nickname in a way that suggested she was fun and popular. Dot, on the other hand, was only Dot the Dormouse: meek, small, and hidden away.

When Dot was fourteen, she had asked her father why she was this way, and he'd turned it around on her: What way? He saw nothing wrong. Dot was the smartest girl on earth, and there was nothing wrong with that.

She asked her mother the same question, and at least she'd been sympathetic. She tucked a strand of Dot's hair behind her ear and assured her that she would find her confidence in time.

She asked Dash, who had squeezed her tight. "Because you're my perfect sister. You're Dot, and this is how you're meant to be."

She even asked Gus. She'd been sitting on the stump with a book, the summer breeze ruffling the pages, but her concentration was broken. It bothered her that her father said everything was fine when Dot didn't feel it was, and that her mother seemed so certain that Dot would eventually find courage, because Dot had no idea how to do that. She wanted instructions. Something factual, though she knew that was unrealistic. Gus was walking up the drive, and when he saw her, he came over. He sat at the base of the maple tree and studied her, his expression soft.

"Why so gloomy?" he asked.

She'd always thought he had the most beautiful blue eyes. They only seemed to get nicer with age. "I'm not gloomy."

"Yes, you are."

"I'm just . . . ruminating."

"I see. What about?"

They often sat like this, when Dash was off with friends or something. Gus could be energetic, laughing with Dash, or he could be quiet and introspective, which was soothing to Dot. Sometimes, when Dot stayed in her room rather than attempting to play catch with the two of them, she secretly watched him through the window, fascinated by the lines of his body as he threw the ball. In tranquil times like this, she felt warmed by his presence. He never teased her, and he seemed genuinely impressed when she shared something she found interesting. He made her feel important, not self-conscious. So she asked him her question.

"Why am I the way I am? So meek. So scared. Nobody else is like this."

He held her gaze. "You are whoever you choose to be. You could change if you want, or you could be satisfied. Either way, I'll always love you."

Dot would never forget his answer or the way he'd said it. His words had eased her mind in so many ways. Maybe everyone's response had been right after all.

A red-winged blackbird called from outside, his buzzing song breaking Dot's morning reverie. It had been a while since she'd last sat on the old stump beside her sister's tree, and it felt like where she needed to be just then. She made her bed then headed downstairs and grabbed a coat from the cupboard. Only after she'd finished doing up the buttons did she notice it was Dash's favourite.

Outside, the grass was still wet from last night's rain, but the sky was clear. Dot brushed the damp surface of the stump clean, then she took up her childhood seat. For years she had swung her feet from here, unable to touch the ground. These days the stump seemed so small.

One summer, her mother had led Dot, Dash, and Gus on a hunt for monarch caterpillars. At her direction, they filled jars with leaves and grass then popped one bright yellow and black worm in each. They twisted on the lids, into which her mother had poked breathing holes, and set them on their windowsills. Within a few days, each caterpillar had climbed the glass walls to the lid and begun to form a chrysalis. Gus announced his worm's progress at breakfast, Dash was mesmerized, and Dot took notes. For the next two weeks or so, they watched in wonder as the chrysalis underwent changes in colour and shape. Then the shell began to peel away, and tiny black legs curled around the edges. With no apparent effort, the creature pulled loose of it, revealing to the world a new, beautiful form.

Dot had spent eighteen years in her own chrysalis. She liked it in there. Until the war had come along, she'd never really thought about leaving it. But with all the changes going on around her, she wondered again what was wrong with her. She felt certain she should have outgrown this anxiety by now. The bravest thing she had ever done was to become a teacher, though only of a small group. She enjoyed doing something worthwhile with her brain, and it gave her confidence when she heard the children improve. But she'd been scared stiff to try anything beyond that.

The autumn wind stirred the leaves overhead, knocking some off, and a couple landed on Dot's coat. The monarchs were all gone, having flown south for the winter. Dot had never understood how they did that, flying through the wind and storms on their tissue paper wings. She'd love to see the migration in motion, all those tiny beings brave enough to cross the continent like that.

Maybe that's what Dash felt like, heading off to join the Wrens.

She shivered, imagining her sister on the streetcar in the middle of Toronto, surrounded by strangers. She'd be excited, perhaps a little nervous about doing something new, but mostly she'd be eager. Had Dot ever felt like that? Impatient to face the unknown? No, never. Did she want to?

She took a deep breath, trying to clear her mind. Even just thinking this way filled her with anxiety.

Dash would soon be leaving, joining other butterflies on an enigmatic journey. Dot would still be here, all alone, curled up in her warm, safe chrysalis. What would it take for her to peel back the shell and climb out, she wondered, then spread her nervous little wings and see if she could fly like her sister?

eight
DASH

—————————

— *Oshawa, Ontario* —

Dash didn't head straight home after her medical. There was one place she wanted to go first. The sky was blue, the autumn air still. A perfect day to soar. The last time she and her uncle had been on the field, they'd received the news about Fred. She hadn't flown in the weeks since then, and she suspected it was the same for Uncle Bob. She wasn't sure how he would take her arrival and request, but she hoped it might help them both.

Aunt Lou was sitting on their front porch swing, knitting something in grey.

"Margaret." She smiled softly. "It's good to see you. I suppose you'll be leaving soon."

Dash nodded. "I'm just waiting for the letter now. I'll miss you both."

Aunt Lou set her knitting on her lap. "We'll miss you, too."

"How's Uncle Bob?"

"He'll be all right one day. We all will." She placed a hand on Dash's forearm. "He'll be glad to see you, sweetheart. Go on in. I think you're just what he needs right now."

Dash arranged a smile on her face and breezed into the living room, where her uncle sat in his old yellow armchair, reading a book. He'd stopped waxing his moustache and had trimmed it to something more mature. Dash thought it made him look hollowed out. Old.

"I passed my medical exam for the Wrens today. Turns out I'm perfect," she told him. "I'm just about ready to go."

"Of course you are. Perfect, I mean," he said. "Best mechanic around. Soon to be the best pilot, too. The navy is lucky to have you."

"I won't be flying, but I hope you're right about the mechanical stuff. I figure I'll be working in Toronto, since a mechanic isn't about to be shipped overseas. Especially a girl mechanic. That's all right. I just want to be busy." She gestured toward the airfield. "Think we could fly today? I'd really like to go up one more time before I leave."

She saw the indecision in his eyes as he gazed out at the field, where the windsock hung limply against its pole.

"Yeah. Let's go," he said at last, his voice a little husky. Halfway to the field, he patted her shoulder. "You take me up, kiddo. Start to finish."

"I was hoping you'd say that."

"We'll have a better landing this time," he managed.

Dash stuck her arm through his, and they strolled toward Jenny. The plane stood quietly in the sun, her double wings shining, ready to go. The closer they got, the faster her uncle walked.

"Let's go," he said, giving her a leg up onto the wing.

It was a perfect takeoff. Dash's face nearly froze at two thousand feet, but she didn't care. Her uncle hollered over the wind for her to enjoy herself, so she flew farther than before. Beneath the racket of the engine, the airplane's shadow slid silently over the ground, glittering with the vestiges of last night's rain, and the beauty took her breath away. Gosh, she'd miss this, she thought, a lump in her throat. She'd miss a lot.

Dot's words rang in her head. *I don't want you to go. Please, Dash. Stay with me.*

Well, Dash thought, choosing not to dwell on the hurt, *I don't want you to stay here, Dot. I want you to fly.*

Squinting into the wind, she soaked in the glorious view below and the heavenly blue above. Beyond the horizon there was so much more, she knew, and her heart ached to explore every part of it. After a while, Uncle Bob tapped her shoulder, and Dash reluctantly turned back toward the airfield. It would be her last flight for who knew how long, and the reality threatened to pull her down, but there was too much to look forward to. Right now, she idled on the runway of her life. By joining the Wrens, she would take flight.

She touched down without a bump then rolled to the spot where Uncle Bob liked to park. After she turned off the engine, she faced him, wanting to thank him for this gift. He had already taken off his helmet, and his flyaway hairs danced in the breeze. His cheeks were bright red from the flight. Like hers, they were wet with tears.

"Thank you, Dash," he said. "Being up there . . . It helps, you know?"

"We'll get through this," she promised as they climbed out.

He skimmed his fingers along the plane's fuselage then curled them around one of the struts between the wings. "I know you aren't going far," he said, eyes on the plane, "but please take care of yourself wherever you are. I couldn't bear to lose you, too."

"Oh, Uncle Bob." She gave him a hug, and she felt his strength tighten around her. "You never need to worry about me. I'm always careful with everything I do."

The irony of that made him laugh, which was exactly what she'd been aiming for.

———

Days passed, but not fast enough for Dash. When the date finally came, she crowded into the car with her parents and Dot, and her father drove them all to Union Station. Dash's letter from the Wrens had said she was being sent for training at a place called HMCS Conestoga, in Galt, Ontario. Having never heard of the place, Dot had looked it up for her on a provincial map. Not too far, but far enough for a little adventure.

The four of them stood together on the platform, waiting for the train to arrive. Her father, looking dapper in his Sunday coat with a tartan scarf wrapped around his neck, situated himself behind their mother. Where he was quiet, she was busy, and now she fussed, folding and unfolding Dash's coat collar while running through a checklist of things she might have forgotten to pack.

"I have everything," Dash assured her. "Dot packed for me."

"Sweetheart." Her mother's eyes shone. "We're so proud of you. It's just so hard to believe our little bird is leaving the nest."

Dash grinned. "I wish I was a bird. Then I'd really be flying."

"You know what I mean. Now, don't forget to write to us about everything, and—" She bit her lip and pressed a handkerchief to her nose.

Her father stepped in. "Write when you can, but don't worry about us. Your priority must be your work. I imagine you're in for a very interesting time."

"I hope so."

He hugged her, but when she squeezed him back, she was startled by a jolt of panic and held on a little longer. What was she doing, boarding a train on her own? She had no idea about any of this. Had she lost her mind?

He smiled with understanding when he let her go, as if he'd felt it, too. "Don't worry about yourself, either. You've never failed at anything you've done."

"Oh, Margaret," her mother cried, pulling her into an embrace. "Be smart out there. Please, please be safe."

Then both parents backed away to let the sisters say goodbye.

"It's going to be okay." Dot's sweet attempt at a reassuring smile practically broke Dash's heart. "We'll be fine."

"I'm sorry."

Dot pressed her lips together, embarrassed. "It's me who should be sorry. I've been a baby. I see how this lights you up. You're reaching for something you want, and you're going to get it. I will miss you every day, but you'll be where you belong. I understand that now."

Dash took her twin's mittened hands in her own. "You'll be in my heart every step of the way."

Dot's brave expression collapsed, and Dash held her tight. "I won't be far," she promised through the lump in her throat.

"We'll be fine," Dot said again.

The train arrived on a rush of air, lifting coats and hats, and Dash reached for her suitcase. The porter opened the nearest door and set out stairs, then all at once she was on board, her face pressed to the window. Her family, huddled together for support, smiled and waved, and Dash did the same. The train whistled, a railway man yelled something she couldn't hear, then someone blocked her view as the engine lurched into motion. When she could see outside again, the train had left the station—and her family—far behind.

nine

DOT

‑ . . ‑ ‑ ‑ ‑

— October 1942 —
Oshawa, Ontario

M*erci!*" Dot called, but the young newspaper boy was already moving on to the next house. She crouched to retrieve their copy of *The Oshawa Daily Times*, then she returned to her father in the living room.

"*Tu dors?*" she whispered, noticing his eyes were closed.

He blinked slowly. "Just resting."

"This just arrived," she said, handing him the paper. "Would you like a cup of hot water?"

"That would be lovely, thank you. Cream and sugar as always," he joked.

Before the war, Dot and her father had enjoyed a little coffee on Saturday mornings while they worked on their weekly crossword puzzle together. Rationing had put an end to that. Their calendar reminded them every week that they had to wait until the fourth Friday of the month to pick up tea and coffee rations. Rather than do without completely, they'd decided between them that it was simple enough to boil water and convince their imaginations that it was coffee. It didn't work, of course, but it was better than nothing at all.

When she brought in his steaming cup, she could see he was distracted by something in the paper. Curious, she set the cup on the table beside him and peered over his shoulder.

The article was about a U-boat attack. That was a little odd, because distant war events didn't usually show up on the front page of *The Oshawa Daily Times.*

"Port aux Basques," she read out loud, alarm quickening her words. "That's at the southwest coast of Newfoundland, am I right?"

"It is. A small community." He passed her the paper then took off his glasses and rubbed the bridge of his nose with his thumb and forefinger.

Practically in Canada, she thought, shocked. How had the war come so close? She read on and caught her breath on the next sentence.

"The SS *Caribou* . . . They torpedoed a passenger ferry in the middle of the night? Oh, Dad," she whispered.

One hundred and thirty-six men, women, and children on their way home had perished. Their families, who had probably done much the same as Dot had, holding the war at bay for as long as possible, had lost everyone they loved.

"Aren't passenger ferries supposed to be safe from attack?"

He put his glasses back on, his face pale. "No one is safe in war."

"But how? How could this have happened?"

"I cannot imagine the U-boat was aware this was a civilian ferry," he said. "Not even the Germans would do that on purpose. They would have been hunting something more valuable to their cause. It's simply a terrible tragedy."

"What would have happened to the U-boat after?"

"Who knows? It would have dived immediately after firing, and the escort ship would have dropped depth charges, but the article does not say if the U-boat was caught."

Dot's mind brought her the screaming victims, the churning black water, and the Atlantic's icy teeth. All the little children, lost and confused and freezing to death in the depths. All those mothers . . . Bile rose up her throat at the thought of so much violence. So much death. She had almost accepted that bloodshed was practically an everyday occurrence in Europe, but that was far away and easier to bear. Not here. Not in Canada, where she felt so secure. Her father must be right; this attack had to have been a mistake.

She sank onto the couch, mulling over the story. Shouldn't there have been a way for the ferry to communicate with the enemy? To let them know they were not a warship? Could the tragedy have been prevented?

"I have a question, Dad. I know what you did in the Great War with your Marconi radio. If you'd been doing that now instead of then, using new technology, could you have flown over the U-boat and transmitted its locations? Could you have warned the ferry or notified the submarine?"

"That would have been a very different situation," he replied. "I would not have been flying over the open ocean or in the pitch black of night. Even if I had been there in the daytime, it would not have been easy to detect a U-boat underwater. Of course, things have changed over the years. It is possible now to send messages great distances through radio transmissions."

"You were able to prevent some attacks back then, I imagine," Dot said softly. "It must have felt good, knowing you were saving lives. Did the military tell you if your efforts were successful, or was it all kept secret?"

"Most things in war are top secret, but occasionally someone in a high-up place would let something slip, or I'd receive a little 'Well done!' message." He paused. "Once in a while, I learned about a small victory that had come about because of my transmissions. Yes, it was a fulfilling sensation, knowing I had helped in some way."

Dot leaned back in the cushions, wondering. What if a message could have been delivered ahead of time through radio transmissions, like her father said? How did that work? Might it have saved lives?

Was there something she could do?

"I see you received another letter from your sister," her father said, interrupting her train of thought.

"Yesterday. The third in three weeks. I can't accuse her of being a lazy correspondent. Not like Gus," she added uncertainly.

"We would know if something happened to him, Dorothy."

"I suppose you're right. I just have to think positively."

She touched the latest letter from Dash, folded in her pocket. It was brimming with news, high spirits, and even a couple of photographs. Dash wrote so well, Dot could almost hear her sister saying the words out loud. She pulled the note out again and read to herself while her father returned to the newspaper.

I met some lovely girls on the train, then even more when we arrived at the training station in Galt. The place itself is not much "to write home about," as they say, but there's so much to keep us busy. We do everything from physical exercises (I've never run so much in my life!) to Morse code (easy for me!) to semaphore, and we scrub floors like nobody's business. Oh, and you'll be happy to hear, Dot, that I am now being compensated for my work! Ninety-five cents a day. See? Mr. Meier never needed to pay me after all.

By now you've seen the best news of all. What do you think? Isn't it the snappiest uniform you've ever seen? In case you can't tell with the black-and-white-photograph, it's navy-blue wool. It would look great with your hair. I know, I know, but it really would. I'll tell you, I was smiling an awful lot more in this picture than I did when I first put it on. As soon as I was issued the uniform, Chief Wren Merrivale, the woman in charge, sat me down and stuck a smallpox needle in one arm and typhoid in the other. They told us that we'd feel it the next day, and boy, did we ever! I could barely move!

By the way, that's Virginia on my right (I call her Ginny). Ginny's from Parry Sound and has a couple of brothers (fighting overseas). She and I are bunkmates, and she's the funniest thing. Honestly, she should be an actress. The most fun thing is that she likes doing mechanics! We're hoping to get posted together somewhere.

Dot drew the photograph in close, inspecting her sister's porkpie hat, which she'd set at a jaunty angle. The white band around it said H.M.C.S. in bold black letters, just like it would with any able seaman, indicating that Dash was part of the navy. Part of the war.

For the longest time, Dot had purposefully avoided reading or talking about the conflict. War was the very picture of uncertainty, and there was little that Dot liked less than the unknown. She wanted facts. Logic. Then Fred had been killed, and Gus had vanished into thin air. Nothing about them being gone made any sense at all to her. Then Dash had left. In the moment when she had joined the navy, Dash had brought the war right into their bedroom.

As much as that terrified Dot, the idea had begun to intrigue her. Her sister looked so happy. She made it sound like such fun.

Her gaze went to Ginny, a tall girl whose blond curls were mostly hidden under her hat, and she felt a pang of jealousy. What of? Was she envious of the time Dash's new friends got to spend with her? Or was it the fresh and excited expressions on their faces? Maybe it was the courage that had put them all out there in Galt. The courage Dot couldn't seem to summon.

With both Dash and Gus gone, Dot forced herself to ask the obvious question, though she'd tried very hard to avoid it. The answer was that yes, she still felt she was helping with the war effort. She had even gone with her mother to donate blood, just to prove she could. But were her small, safe contributions enough? Could she do more?

"I'm thinking of joining the Wrens," she blurted out.

Her father peered over the newspaper, startled. "Why, that would be commendable, Dorothy, but I am somewhat surprised. Are you certain that sort of life is for you?"

"I am absolutely *not* certain. But I want to help. Like Dash. I want to do more."

The paper slowly lowered, and he regarded her closely. "I know how frightening it can be for some of us to step beyond our established limits."

She swallowed. Suddenly it seemed like an awfully rash decision. "Would you and Mom be all right without me?"

"We would survive."

"Dash says there is a lot I could do."

He smiled at that. "You, my dear, could most likely do whatever you wanted. Like your sister, I've never seen anything that can stop you."

"Except engines."

"Yes, yes. Except engines. We'll leave those to Margaret, shall we?"

An unexpected prickle of anticipation crept through her body. Was this what it felt like to be Dash? To make a choice to do something, then head right out and do it?

"I think I should look into it right away, before I back out. I'm not used to feeling this courageous, and I'm afraid the sensation might fade."

"That is wise, my dear girl, though I suggest you go to the recruitment office Monday, not today. I imagine it's closed on weekends."

"I should tell Mom first, of course."

"Tell me what?"

Dot paled as her mother came into the living room. There would be no going back if she declared her intentions to her mother. She debated dismissing the idea altogether, but her father calmed her with a simple nod.

"I am going to join the Wrens," she said. "I'm going to sign up on Monday."

Her mother's eyebrows shot up. "Are you sure? Do you think it's the right thing for you, dear? From your sister's letters, it's a lot of work."

"Like I said to Dad, no. I don't think it's the right thing for me, but I do think it's a good thing. I want to prove to you and Dash that I can do it, and to myself as well. I want to make you proud."

"Sweetheart! You make us proud every day."

Dot closed her eyes when her mother came to hug her, and she inhaled the flowery powder she always used. She would miss this smell. That and a thousand other things. But then she thought of Dash and her porkpie hat, and she dared to believe that she would discover so much more.

ten
DASH

— *Toronto, Ontario* —

You sure this is the right place?" Dash asked Ginny.

Tall and a little awkward, but with fingers long enough to reach the most impossible engine parts, Ginny was an observer and a thinker. And a heck of a mechanic. She studied the paper in her hand then squinted at the building across the street.

"Yep. This is it. Eisen's Garage."

Both girls could hardly wait to get into the garage and return to doing what they really enjoyed. They were counting on this job being very different from the one they'd had at GECO, the top secret munitions building where they'd been employed for the past couple of weeks. That job had been unexpected in itself, since it was a civilian company, but evidently they'd been given special dispensation since they had a military contract. The General Engineering Company of Ontario was massive, with miles of hidden tunnels underground that the girls hadn't even begun to explore by the time they left. GECO operated twenty-four hours a day, six days a week. It was almost entirely run by thousands of women who filled fuses and shells with explosives for $19.60 a week. Since a munitions plant obviously posed a risk of explosions, the factory was in Scarborough, away from most of Toronto's population.

"You ready?" Dash asked, wiggling her fingers in the air. The chemicals in the explosives had stained them yellow, and she was looking forward to replacing the yellow with black engine grease.

"Am I ever. I don't suppose they're going to make us sign another oath of secrecy here."

"Ha! I doubt it."

The Canadian government had mandated the oath at GECO. They said everyone had to be wary of a Nazi invasion, and the company had to be sure no employees ever gave any hints as to where the munitions factory was located. Security was tight. At the beginning of every shift, the women had to show their identification, and their names and employee numbers were embroidered on their uniforms. The company was also careful when it came to safety measures. To prevent dangerous materials, even dust, from entering the factory, Dash and the others had to wash when they arrived, then put on their spotless white coveralls and wrap turbans around their hair.

Dash's supervisor—thank goodness!—had given Dash and Ginny the ticket out of there. She knew the two of them were mechanics, and when her brother and a friend left their jobs at a garage to serve in the war, she let Dash know about the openings. Fixing engines suited both Ginny and her just fine, and working together was even better.

Dash straightened her friend's collar. "Let's make a good impression."

They crossed the street, and Dash knocked on the door beneath the sign. No one answered. She tried again, a little louder, but there was still no response.

"I hear them in there," Ginny said. "Maybe they just can't hear us over all the noise."

They exchanged a nervous glance, then Dash opened the door. After the bright sunshine, it was difficult to see at first, but shapes soon began to appear in the gloom. The clanging of tools and the sudden revving of an engine echoed around the place, and Dash took it all in. It was a big garage; there looked to be ten bays, and all were occupied by vehicles under repair. She spotted three men bent over inside the car hoods, their hands busy within.

"Well, well, well," a man said, approaching from the side, his hands sunk in his trouser pockets. "Look what we have here."

Dash and Ginny turned toward the voice, smiling politely. He was about Ginny's height, about a half foot taller than Dash, with dark hair and dark eyes. As he came closer, Dash thought he wasn't particularly handsome, but he wasn't awful to look at. An older man trailed behind him, and he did not look the least bit pleased to see the girls.

"We're from the Wrens," Dash told them, aware of the sudden silence in the garage. She wasn't overly surprised that they were the only two women in the place, but having spent most of her time surrounded by women lately, she felt more conspicuous than ever.

The younger man gave them the once-over. "I never coulda guessed, considering those fancy uniforms you got on."

The older man's gaze traveled up from under heavy lids. "You're the two so-called mechanics?"

Dash bristled, but Ginny responded, her voice even. "Yes, we're them. Petty Officer Wren Margaret Wilson and Petty Officer Wren Ginny Thomas."

"Petty officer," the older man scoffed. "Is that right? Girl officers *and* mechanics. The world's a crazy place these days. You got anything else to wear?"

Ginny held out her bag. "We have everything we need."

The younger man's attention was on Dash. "Feel free to change in my office," he said, indicating the glass-enclosed space at the far end of the room. Dash saw a desk, a couple of chairs, and no privacy.

"*Your* office?" the older man asked.

"Sorry. My dad's office. Ladies, meet Mr. Eisen, your new boss. I'm his son, Jim. I'll be looking after you two."

"Is there somewhere else we can change?" Dash asked, tamping down her annoyance.

Jim slipped a chummy arm around her waist. "Maybe the head, but it's pretty small."

Dash sent a silent thank-you to the Wrens for teaching them navy terms. The "head," they'd been taught, was the washroom.

"That'll do," she replied, circling free of his grasp.

"Would you mind giving us a tour?" Ginny asked.

"A tour. Okay. Those are the bays." Jim pointed around the garage while his father stood in place, arms crossed. "They got all the tools you need stacked behind them, but you can borrow the other fellas' if you need. Just be sure to put them back. They get touchy if their things are missing. Monday to Friday, you show up at eight, half-hour lunch break, then you can leave at five. If you're late, you get docked, or else you stay late. Payday is every two weeks on the Friday." He indicated two bays halfway back, directly across from one another. "Those are your stations, and you'll have a vehicle in there every day. The trouble with them is written on the clipboard on your workbench. You finish one, you get another."

A grumble came from Mr. Eisen. "I told the navy I didn't want girls working here, but they said you knew what you were doing. I say prove it."

Fine, Dash thought. "Where's the head?"

Dash stood guard outside the tiny washroom as Ginny changed into her coveralls. She emerged a few seconds later, her face a mild shade of green.

"What is it?"

"If it smells like that in there every day, we're changing at home."

Dash stepped into the washroom, careful to breathe only through her mouth. Just before she closed the door, she scanned the garage, conscious that every man in the place was watching. "We are definitely changing at home after this."

They'd checked into their assigned "home" the night before and met their roommate, a bubbly Wren named Mary who had already worked the hospital switchboard for a year. The three of them got along right away. Their prim landlady, Mrs. Pidgett, was another story. The woman was probably in her fifties, and she constantly paced, wringing her bony hands and muttering under her breath. Dash caught a few words, like *brazen!* and *scandalous!*, and she understood that Mrs. Pidgett was uncomfortable with women doing men's work. It wasn't the first time she had heard those kinds of adjectives, and while it was annoying, she ignored it as best she could.

At one point, Mary pointed out that Mrs. Pidgett never wore anything but grey and black, and it hadn't taken much after that for the girls to make the leap to calling her The Pigeon when she wasn't around. And they started referring to their tiny, shared bedroom as the Pigeon Coop.

At least in the Pigeon Coop, there were fewer eyes on them. When they were dressed, Jim led them through the garage. Between the bays, Dash felt his hand touch the small of her back. She sped up to keep out of his reach.

"I think we can find our places on our own," she told him.

Heads held high, the girls walked on, painfully aware that everything they did was being observed and judged. At their allotted bays, Ginny turned left and Dash turned right, where she came face-to-face with an ancient Dodge, riddled with rust. All the other bays contained cars and trucks from 1935 and newer. This one was about twenty years older than those. So this was a test. Dash went to the workbench for her orders. The clipboard read, "Bring her back to life."

It had to be a joke. This old car probably wouldn't ever make it out of this garage again. She glanced up from the note and saw all the men leaning on their cars, smirking.

"There a problem?" Jim asked innocently, and she knew he was laughing at her.

Nothing made Dash angrier than being laughed at. "No problem at all," she assured him. She gathered her hair and tucked it under her cap. "Just hoping there'd be more of a challenge, I guess."

"Oho!" he said, grinning. "I'll tell you what. You get this car going, and I'll treat you to dinner."

So that's how it was gonna be. "Thanks, but no. I'll tell *you* what. I'll get this car going, then you'll bring me something else to work on. And you'll pay me after two weeks. I'm here to do my job, sir."

His brow twitched. "I see. Well, get to it then."

Dash worked through lunch. She changed the old filters and checked the spark plugs and battery, but from the start she had a feeling she knew what the trouble was. This ancient car had been left to sit for so long, it had to be the carburetor. She removed that—a Kingston 5 Ball, which most of these old cars used—then she clamped the bowl to the counter with a vice so she could put all her weight into loosening it. Once it released, she used a half-inch wrench and a screwdriver to disassemble the whole part. She was right. The thing was filthy. She started by cleaning the float, which controlled the needle, because with it all gummed up like this, gas couldn't get in. Then she turned to the main jet, which was caked with fuel residue inside and out. After she removed the gunk, she soaked each piece in Varsol and put her muscles into scrubbing with a hard brush for the rest of the day.

An hour before closing time, she reassembled the carburetor and put everything back where it belonged, then she climbed into the driver's seat and started the old car up with no trouble at all. She was aware of the men gawking, but she showed no indication that she noticed except to wink at Ginny. Her friend kept a straight face, swallowing a laugh that they could share later. Without a word, Dash shut off the Dodge's engine and headed down to the office. Jim came out as she arrived, reluctantly impressed.

"Where do you want me to park her?" she asked.

"Sure you don't want a fancy dinner to celebrate?"

"Celebrate cleaning a carburetor? I don't think so, Jim. Just tell me where to park her, and I'll be back tomorrow for something new. Try to find me something a little tougher, would you?"

eleven

DOT

-- .. --- -

— *Toronto, Ontario* —

She'd done it. Dot had taken the hour-long bus ride to the main transit station in Toronto all by herself. Now she sat in a streetcar, pressed solidly against the window, questioning everything about what she was doing. Fortunately, no one sat with her, so she didn't have to worry about that at least.

She'd made sure to wear Dash's lucky green coat today, figuring she needed all the help she could get, but the closer she got to her destination, the more doubts popped into her head. What if they didn't want her? How could she ever face anyone ever again if that happened? Or worse, what if she walked into the recruiting office and they offered her a position right then and there? Panic fluttered briefly in her chest, but she dismissed the thought. She hadn't packed a suitcase, so she reasoned they couldn't send her away today. But what should she say to them? What would Dash do?

As the streetcar approached the recruiting office, Dot pulled the string for the bell then climbed off. Swallowing a knot of nerves, she tiptoed into a quiet room decorated with recruitment posters and staffed by a couple of men in uniform. Three women, also in uniform, sat behind them at desks, typing.

Dot grabbed a pamphlet off a nearby table then presented it to the man at the counter as if it were her ticket in.

"May I help you?" he asked cordially.

"I hope so. I hope I am at the correct place. I have never been here before. Never been to any recruitment office, actually." Her cheeks blazed. She was aware that she was speaking quickly, but she also knew from experience that she couldn't slow the waterfall of nerves until she'd finished her thought. "I suppose that makes sense, doesn't it? If one needs a recruitment office, they certainly don't need two, do they? I wonder how many of these offices there are in the city. Has this one been here long? My sister was here before, though that was a while ago. Her name was Margaret, but everyone calls her Dash. Dash Wilson. Did you meet her? She's a Wren now. We're all so proud of her. And so I was thinking it might be a good idea for me to see if I could join as well."

"I beg your pardon?"

Slow down, you idiot. She tapped the pamphlet with her finger. "I would like to join the Wrens."

"Excellent. You are in the right place."

He thanked her for coming, then he reached behind the counter and handed her a form to fill in. She carried it to an empty table, planning to treat the task as seriously as if it were an examination, but it asked for little more than her name, birth date, and address.

"Thank you," he said, taking the completed form from her. "Now, if you don't mind, I will bring over a couple of items for your attention. The Women's Royal Canadian Naval Service believes in helping each woman reach her fullest potential, and we begin with a simple test to establish the best fit. One is mechanical, and one is administrative. If there is something with which you are uncomfortable, simply go on to what you feel are your strengths."

She watched him disappear into a back room, her nerves jumping. A test? Dash hadn't mentioned a test. Dot was unprepared. She hadn't studied. She watched with trepidation as the man returned with a box, which he placed before her.

"The first is a mechanical challenge. We ask you to assemble Meccano parts to resemble this finished example." He extracted various steel bits from the box and set them on the table. Beside them, he placed a completed model of a building. "I will be right back with the other item."

Dot's stomach dropped. She stared at the little box, completely at a loss. Dash would have put this together in no time flat, but there was no hope for Dot. Coming here had been a big mistake, she realized. She'd gone and done exactly what she'd most hoped to avoid: she'd made a fool of herself. Heat radiated off her face, and she was sure everyone in the office could see the sweat on her brow. She glanced at the door, wondering if she could somehow escape the rest of this appointment without anyone noticing, but the man was already returning.

Right beside the Meccano pieces, he set down a typewriter and a handwritten letter. "This one has to do with administrative work," he said. "We ask you to transcribe this handwritten letter, and I will time you. Any questions?"

Dot almost burst into tears with relief. She pushed the first box aside. "I'm afraid I am completely useless at mechanics, but I am ready to type anytime."

"All right. Turn the page over." He pulled out a watch. "Begin now."

She didn't bother to read through the messy print, just got right to the typing.

> *Dear Mrs. Sandring,*
>
> *It is with great sadness that I send my personal condolences regarding your terrible loss. Harold was a leader in our battalion, both in the heat of battle and after. If someone was in need of advice, it was to Harold that we turned . . .*

In the back of her mind, she was vaguely aware of the content of the letter, which went on for three more paragraphs, but she said nothing. She was not being tested on comprehension. When she was done, she pulled the letter swiftly from the roller and handed it over.

He wrote her typing speed on the bottom then checked the page for accuracy. "Very impressive," he said. "Now that's out of the way, do you have any other skills you'd like me to include? Do you drive? Cook?"

Her face warmed. "I'm not particularly good at either."

"Do you speak any languages other than English?"

"*Mais oui.* I write, read, and speak *le Français, und auch Deutsch*. I am also fluent in Morse code."

"Even more impressive than your typing speed, Miss Wilson." He made a note on her form and drew a star beside it. "Anything else?"

She leaned forward, curious about the star. That seemed to be a positive sign. Perhaps it hadn't been a mistake to come here after all.

"Miss Wilson? Anything else?"

"I don't believe so, I'm afraid." On impulse, she gifted him her approximation of Dash's winning smile. She felt a sudden need to convince this man that she belonged with the Wrens, and she was aware that her own thin smile didn't turn heads like her sister's could. She even gave her eyelashes a little flutter, though it felt silly. "Not unless you count crossword puzzles and mystery novels as a skill."

His eyebrows lifted. "I see."

She was interested to see him print the words "crossword puzzles" beside her name and the star. What odd observations to record.

He set his pen aside. "Thank you for coming today, Miss Wilson. You will be hearing from our office soon."

"I will?" Now that she had taken this first step, she required a definitive answer as to whether or not she should make plans.

"Oh yes, Miss Wilson. Most definitely. You have many desirable skills."

Dot clamped her lips together. She didn't want to let on that her success made her happier than she'd been in a long time. "Thank you."

She gathered up Dash's coat and stepped out once more into the jarring noises of the city, but this time she barely noticed.

So that was it. All done within fifteen minutes. So much dread and second-guessing herself, and she'd breezed through it. He had even been impressed by her. All that fuss had been rather embarrassing, if she thought about it now. This was what confidence felt like, she realized, warmed all the way through. Now if only she could remember this feeling when it came to her next challenge, whatever that might be.

twelve
DASH

———

Dash rolled out from under the truck, glad to be done with the last oil change of the day. It wasn't that she minded the job, it's just that she'd changed the oil in at least a dozen vehicles today, and another dozen yesterday. She wondered how many a man could have done in that same time frame. Probably not as many. A man would be bigger, so he'd have to squeeze under the car, whereas Dash was small enough to simply slide in and out.

It had taken a few days before she could get a read on the men working at the garage, and after that she'd decided not to try too hard. She was here to work, not socialize. The only issue so far was Jim, the boss's son. She'd learned he was married, but that didn't seem to matter to him. He couldn't get it through his thick head that she did not want to go out with him. Nor could he understand that leering at women and touching them without invitation was not acceptable. She'd slapped his hand off her waist the other day. Everyone in the garage had seen him put it there, but not one of the other men had stepped in to help her. If anything, they'd seemed amused by her reaction. She tried not to think about that too much, but she couldn't help tensing up any time one of them came over to talk.

With a groan, she got to her feet. Friday night was here. Time to get her thoughts out from under the hood so she could enjoy the city.

"Did you remember we're going to see *Holiday Inn* tonight?" Ginny called from across the garage, wiping grease off her hands.

"I did," she replied. "How could I forget, with Mary going on and on about Bing Crosby's 'dreamy' voice?"

Their roommate, Mary, was a lot of fun. She found humour in almost everything, and her laughter cut through the noisiest crowd like a cannon shot in the middle of a church service.

"You brought clothes? Or do we have to go back to the Coop?"

Thank goodness Dash had remembered. "I brought clothes."

"Mary got off work a half hour ago. She said she'd meet us near the theatre."

"Where's the theatre? Can we walk to it?"

"She said it's playing at the Midtown. Bloor and Bathurst, across from the Dominion Bank. We can take a streetcar if it's too cold."

"It's warm enough," Dash said, "and I need fresh air."

That's when she realized she'd forgotten to pack any money. When her hands were as clean as she could get them, she got changed then dug into the pocket of her navy-blue Wrens' coat, hoping she wouldn't have to beg one of her friends for a dime for her ticket. She drew out a speck of lint and a couple of coins, producing twenty-five cents. Perfect. She might even get some popcorn. She lifted her winter coat off its hook and headed into the chill with Ginny.

"How's your sister?" Ginny asked. "Have you heard from her?"

"Oh! I forgot to tell you! She signed up for the Wrens!" Dash patted her pocket. "I got a letter from her yesterday."

"Good for her! That must have been tough for her, from what you've described. My sister's the same. Worries about everything. I don't think she'll ever sign up. That's all right, though. My mother is always sick, so she's a big help."

"I'm sorry to hear that. Thank goodness your mother can lean on her," Dash said, picturing her own parents. They'd miss Dot, but they'd do fine without her. "I really am glad Dot took that step. She'll do well. She'll see."

A couple of blocks from the theatre, Dash spotted a young woman in a bright red beret, hopping on her toes on the sidewalk.

"Mary hardly looks excited at all," she laughed.

"Hey, hey, hey!" Mary called as she ran up to greet them. "Friday night at last! So?"

"The Midtown?" Dash asked.

"Yes, please! I was counting on that all day. I even brought along three extra nickels so I could buy each of us our own bucket of popcorn. My treat."

Dash was touched. "That's swell of you, Mary."

"I love going to the movies," she gushed, her eyes squeezing into crescent moons.

Ginny chuckled. "My grandmother calls movie theatres 'dens of iniquity.'"

"Then let's do something wicked just for her," Mary suggested. "Come on. We're almost there."

The tall black marquee spelling MIDTOWN vertically from top to bottom was all lit up. The girls paid for their tickets, lined up for popcorn, then claimed the three best seats they could find together.

"Lots of people here tonight," Ginny whispered, scanning the theatre.

All at once the lights went down, and Dash felt a flurry of anticipation in her stomach. "Ladies and gentlemen," boomed through the speakers as the curtains pulled back from the screen. "Welcome to Midtown. We hope you enjoy the movie. All together, everyone, let's follow the bouncing ball!"

The cartoon that lit up the theatre featured a girl walking around an apple tree, accompanied by a popular new song by the Andrews Sisters. Dash, Mary, and Ginny happily sang along.

Don't sit under the apple tree with anyone else but me
Anyone else but me, anyone else but me

No! No! No!
Don't sit under the apple tree with anyone else but me
Till I come marchin' home!

The news reel came on after that, and Dash tossed popcorn into her mouth. Her favourite films were the ones when the cameramen wandered through camps where Canadians were. She always scoured the background, spying for Gus or one of the other boys from school. Tonight's reel was entitled "Rommel's Defeat in Africa" and showed British and American troops intercepting the German marshal's supply ships, leaving him with nothing. The scene ended with cannons blasting dramatically into the night, then a long row of Allied planes—Hawker Hurricanes, she thought—speeding down the runway toward the camera. The directors loved happy endings.

At last the feature began, and Dash lost herself in the song and dance. She didn't find Bing Crosby attractive at all, but the way he sang . . . she understood why some women said he made them melt away. When the movie ended, the lights came on, and the girls headed out with the rest of the crowd.

"I feel like dancing," Dash said, sweeping into the lobby with her friends.

She fastened her coat around her and tucked a white scarf around her neck, feeling the cold as soon as they stepped out of the theatre. Either the temperature had really dropped over the last two hours, or the theatre was extra warm. Behind her, Mary squealed then spun around to catch her hat just as the wind tried to steal it.

"You look like you could have been in the movie!" Dash laughed, spinning herself.

"Oh, you're a hoot, Dash."

"I'm a cement mixer when it comes to dancing. I bet you can dance," Ginny said.

Dash grinned. "Sure can, given the right partner."

"My Arnold can dance," Mary mused, pulling on her leather gloves. "I remember when he and I—" The smile slipped from her face.

"Now, now, don't be blue," Ginny scolded. "That's not allowed. We came out to forget about the war and everything in it, including the boys. Plus, he's fine. He just wrote to you last week. He hasn't even shipped out yet."

"I suppose. It's just that the movie was so romantic."

As fun as all the singing and dancing was, Dash's idea of romance was a little different. For her, it came down to that scene on the airfield in *Casablanca*. The way Humphrey Bogart told Ingrid Bergman that she had to leave without him, despite everything he felt. The longing in her eyes, and in his, though he was trying so hard to be tough. Oh, that, *that* was the romance Dash craved.

"I'll be humming that song all night," Mary was saying. "I was right, wasn't I? About Bing Crosby, I mean. He has the dreamiest voice."

"Yeah. 'White Christmas.' That's a beautiful song," Dash said, thinking of home.

It was already November. Her parents would be bundled up in the house, keeping the furnace turned down as low as they could stand it. Suddenly that's where Dash wanted to be, snug by the fireplace in the living room with her mother and sister and Aunt Lou, her fingers around knitting needles. And she didn't even like knitting.

"I heard there's going to be a Christmas party in December at the Palais Royale," Ginny said.

"I wonder who's going to be there," Mary said. "I mean, the girls at the switchboard, we'll all go. Maybe the girls at the garage will come."

"There's only two of us. The rest are men," Ginny said. "Jim Eisen and his greasy buddies."

Dash stiffened at the mention of Jim. He had cornered her a few days ago, asking her to dinner again. She'd refused politely, but he had smiled in that ugly way of his and said something about wearing her down over time. Then he'd patted her bottom when she turned back to her bay. Shocked, she'd spun back to face him, but he only grinned over his shoulder as he walked away. She wished he'd been closer so she could have slapped him.

"If he's going, I'm not," she told her friends. "He chases a lot of skirts that don't belong to his wife. I don't want to be in the same room with him if I don't have to."

"He watches Dash like a lion watches a lamb," Ginny told Mary.

Mary shuddered. "He sounds like a pig. My Arnold has an uncle I try to avoid. I don't like the way he looks at me."

Dash wasn't naive, she just hadn't ever had to face any of this before. Growing up, she'd always been one of the boys, albeit one who could dress to impress. She'd thrived in a world of baseball and hockey, car engines and dirt. Fred and Gus and all the other boys cheered when she was on their team. She'd gone to dances and she'd flirted, but no one had ever taken advantage. If they had, she knew she could count on Gus and the others to defend her. The boys she'd grown up with had shown respect. This aggressive behaviour was new to her, and unsettling. She'd told Jim no, then she'd told him no again, but it hadn't changed anything. She tried changing tactics by coming to work with messy hair and no makeup at all. She was curt with him, but he always followed. Either he thought her rejections weren't important enough to acknowledge, or he was just plain stupid. Dash was at a loss for what to do.

She needed this job, and the last thing she wanted was to annoy the boss's son. The Wrens had placed her here because she was a good mechanic, and she was determined to earn their respect. Every day she did her job to the best of her abilities, and she knew the men in the shop were impressed, though none of them would say anything out loud. But along the way she'd discovered that her skills wouldn't be enough. When she'd felt the slap of Jim's palm against her backside, she'd understood this wasn't something she could simply hope would go away.

She felt Ginny's sympathy constantly, but her friend was trapped as well. Jim wasn't coming after her in the same way, but if Ginny said anything about his conduct, she could jeopardize her job as well. They'd talked about the problem on their walks home, and Dash had told her not to worry about it, since there was nothing she could do. It was an awful feeling. The more they spoke about it, the more humiliated Dash felt. She didn't want anyone else to know, so she left it out of her letters to her family.

But Jim was getting more brazen by the day. She'd have to be more forceful, though that could spell the end of her job. What choice did she have?

thirteen

DOT

■ ·· --- ·

— *Oshawa, Ontario* —

I t was after a particularly encouraging French lesson that Dot received the same letter Dash had gotten a month or so before, only this time it was addressed to her. She broke into a cold sweat just holding it. Soon she would board her first train, ride the rails toward HMCS Conestoga like Dash had, and she would become a probationary Wren. A member of the navy. The very idea would have been inconceivable to her a few weeks ago.

The night before she was to leave, Dot pulled out her suitcase and stared at it, wondering what on earth she should bring. When she had packed for Dash, she had filled the suitcase with a lot of sweaters, but they took up far too much space and they'd had to repack. Shoes? She hesitated, then tucked two pairs into the sides. Would she need that many? After all, she would be getting a uniform identical to Dash's—

"Don't you dare close that suitcase yet," her father said, appearing in the doorway.

"Oh, Dad. I have to." She felt homesick already. How on earth would she survive this ordeal without her father's sage council and company? Who else would understand her like he did? "I'm sorry."

"Not without this."

He pulled a bag from behind his back and presented Dot with a new crossword puzzle book. She hugged him and tried valiantly not to cry. She shouldn't leave. Who would he do crosswords with? Who would bring him a cup of pretend coffee? Who would look after him when he had one of his headaches?

"I'll miss you so much, Dad. Are you positive you and Mom will be all right?"

"My darling Dorothy. You must stop worrying about us. Your mother and I have each other, and we've been around a long time. Still, I will miss my crossword buddy."

Dot held in a sob and gave him another squeeze.

The next morning she stood on the crowded train platform, her parents on either side of her, feeling unbalanced. Gosh, she was scared. If only Dash was there. When Dot had written to her about joining the Wrens, she hadn't mentioned her reticence. She'd never told Dash about the hours she'd sat alone, paralyzed by anxiety. She hadn't needed to, because Dash knew her inside out. She would have known this was the most difficult decision Dot had ever made.

"*All aboard!*"

"Oh no," Dot whispered. "Is it too late to change my mind?"

"You're going to be fine," her mother said, dabbing a handkerchief to her eyes. "Have fun, learn lots, and don't take any garbage from anyone. Make lots of friends."

"We're so proud." Her father's voice wavered, and she nearly broke. "I know you will do so much good out there. You will be saving lives. There is no greater honour."

When it was time, Dot climbed onto the train, found a seat, and smiled gamely out the window at her family, trying to mask her fear. Dot was eighteen, a grown woman, like Dash had said before. It was time to grow up and take responsibility for herself. This was exactly what she needed to do.

A tall, slender girl with a tweed coat and a head full of bouncing orange curls paused by her seat. "May I sit here?"

Dot froze, then said, "Of course." Goodness. If she was this nervous meeting a friendly stranger on the train, how on earth would she manage the Wrens? She cleared her throat as the girl settled next to her. "My name's Dot Wilson."

"What a fun name," she said. "I'm Alice Renwick. I don't suppose you're with the Wrens, are you?"

"I am."

Alice grinned, revealing a mouthful of slightly crooked teeth. "I am, too. Maybe we'll be roommates. I'm excited, aren't you?"

Dot reminded herself to speak slowly. "I suppose I am. I've never been away from home before."

"Me neither, except I've come all this way from Manitoba, so I guess that counts."

"Manitoba!"

"Little place called Flin Flon. Way up north, near the Saskatchewan border. You've probably never heard of it. Anyway, I think we're going to have a jolly time. Know what I heard about this place where they're taking us? HMCS Conestoga? It used to be the Grandview School for Girls, a detention centre for 'wayward' girls. So you'd better behave!"

They talked of this and that, and Dot was amazed by how easy it was to chat with Alice. Almost immediately, she showed Dot a photo of her boyfriend, who was in the navy. He was slender with a sharp chin and a smile that looked carefree.

"Does he have red hair, too?"

"He does!" Alice said with delight. "Just the right red."

Their conversation made the next two hours fly by, and when they pulled into the station in Galt, Dot was optimistic that she might already have made a friend. She could hardly wait to write to Dash and tell her about Alice, the train, and whatever else was about to happen.

"This looks like our crew," Alice said, approaching a group of young women on the platform. Dot trailed behind and smiled shyly at the other girls as they introduced each other.

"Ladies!"

A woman in a crisp, navy-blue uniform had emerged from the cab of a truck and was striding toward them. Dot glanced at Alice, who had gone silent along with the others.

"I am Chief Wren Merrivale," the woman announced, and Dot bit her lip against a grin.

Lt. Merrivale, Dash had written, *is like a Tootsie Pop. Hard on the outside, soft on the inside—though she's not nearly that sweet. I tried to butter her up on my first day, and I quickly learned that was a mistake. She rather neatly put me in my place, saying she was not there to be my friend.*

"Welcome to Galt, where you will begin your training with the Women's Royal Canadian Naval Services. You know our slogan, that by signing up, we 'free a man to serve.' Here, you will learn discipline and trades. By taking their places, you enable our brave men to win this war and come home sooner. The Women's Royal Canadian Naval Services is a professional, well-trained, and highly dedicated branch of the military. We expect your utmost dedication and disciplined attention to everything you are taught. Is that understood?"

Dot's head bobbed like a doll's. Chief Wren Merrivale was not like any Tootsie Pop she had ever had.

"Excellent. Well, ladies, we have a hill to climb before we officially arrive at HMCS Conestoga." She extended a hand toward the truck. "So please get aboard. There will be a tour when we arrive, and you will receive your uniforms. This will be a long day. The hard work starts tomorrow."

Lt. Merrivale wasn't wrong—the day went on and on. At the end of the tour, which gave Dot and the others a complete picture of where they would eat, exercise, learn, and socialize, they were led to the barracks. Dot stopped just inside the door, taking in the rows of bunks, and felt a familiar panic sweep into her chest. If Dash had been there, she would have reached for her hand, giving reassurance. But Dot was on her own.

In her absence, Dot reached for logic to calm her. *Why am I here?* To help in the war effort, of course. To fight the Nazis however she could and help Gus get home soon. Certainly it was all that, but deep down she knew it was much more. Her mind returned to the kitchen table, to the security and love of her small circle at suppertime, to the crosswords at breakfast. She wanted her family to be proud that she could do this by herself. She wanted Dash to see she could be alone and not afraid.

She studied the other girls moving into the room, some with confidence, some unsure, and she thought maybe she understood a little better. Here, in this place where she knew no one and nothing, where the very idea of sleeping among strangers chilled her straight through, she might discover another part of herself. Here she wouldn't just be a sister to one, she might just become a friend to many.

fourteen
DASH

On their way home from the movie, Dash lifted her face to the sky. The first tiny flakes of snow kissed her nose, bringing back memories of snowball fights and skating on the rink that her father and Uncle Bob made every year. Of Dot's red cheeks above her scarf, and the way they laughed, holding each other upright on the ice. Ginny and Mary were talking about something, but Dash let herself drift out of her friends' conversation, distracted by the beauty of the night. The war might have stolen many things, but she could still find moments like this to soothe her.

A man was walking toward them, tall and confident in the falling snow. His hands were in his pockets, and his long coat fell open over a tan-coloured army uniform. She watched him approach, struck by the familiarity of his stride and posture. Then he reached up to brush the snow off his hair, and her heart stopped.

"Gus?"

Their eyes met, and he froze in place. "Dash?"

"Gus?" she cried. "Is that really you?"

Then they were both laughing, and she ran into his open arms. She couldn't help that she was crying, and she didn't bother wiping her tears away.

"I can't believe it," he said, hugging her hard. "It's so good to see you."

"We haven't heard from you in so long!" she admonished him, drawing back. "We were afraid—"

"I'm sorry. Things have been . . . busy. I guess I—"

"Hello," Mary said, fluttering her lashes and holding out a hand. She and Ginny had sidled up next to Dash and were eyeing Gus with curiosity.

He shook it. "I'm Gus. I'm an old friend of Dash's."

"Oh! Dash talks about you. She's been so concerned," Ginny said.

His smile flashed in the streetlight. "I'm a terrible letter writer."

"That is very true," Dash replied. "The family is going to be so relieved when I tell them I saw you! Can we go somewhere to talk?"

"Lovely to meet you," Ginny said tactfully, tugging Mary away. "I imagine you two have a lot of catching up to do. We'll see you back at the Coop, Dash."

"Don't stay out all night!" Mary sang, dancing down the sidewalk.

Gus was still smiling at Dash. "Where shall we go? There's a diner nearby that stays open late."

"That sounds perfect."

They found a little table by the window, took off their coats, and settled in.

"I can't believe you're here," she said, bubbling over with questions. "Tell me everything. Where are you stationed? Did you have to go overseas? I want to know it all."

He leaned back in his chair, looking as happy as she felt. "Ladies first, Dash. Where are your manners?"

They talked for hours, and as they did, Dash grasped the extent of the hole Gus had left when he'd gone away. Sitting with him now, she felt like an empty mug being filled with warm cocoa. They chatted about home and friends and memories, and she told him all about the Wrens. She contemplated telling him about Jim, but she decided against it. Knowing she was having trouble might upset him, and there was nothing he could do about it anyway. She could hardly sit still when she told him she had flown Jenny on her own. When he asked about her parents, she'd ended up telling him about Fred, and they'd grown silent.

"And Dot?" he finally asked, his voice softer after Fred's sad news.

"Oh! I can't believe I didn't tell you straightaway." She banged the heel of her hand against her forehead. "Dot's with the Wrens! She's training right now."

"I knew she would join."

"You did? I didn't."

He chuckled. "You joined. There was no way she was going to let you do something without her. She just had to work up the nerve. Have you heard how she's doing?"

"She writes to me all the time, like clockwork. She's a little overwhelmed, I think, but she's making friends and enjoying herself."

"I'm proud of her. That must have been quite a hurdle."

"I wonder where she'll be assigned."

"I imagine there are so many departments that would value her skills. Communications for sure. The way she thinks is so unique. I think it's safe to say she won't be joining you." He flipped one of her hands over. "I see you're still working with engines."

She laughed. "Occupational hazard." She told him more about her job, still avoiding any mention of Jim, and eventually she wound it back to Gus.

"You still haven't told me what you are up to."

His shoulders lifted and dropped. "I wish I had something exciting to tell you, but you'd be disappointed. I'm not fighting, obviously, so they keep me busy with other stuff. Your life sounds much more interesting than mine, which is composed mostly of push-ups and marching and fascinating things like that."

"I bet it's more interesting that what you're letting on," she pressed.

"It's not."

Dash studied him, unsure how to feel about his statement. "The army's missing out on someone really great, but then again, I'm happy to know you're not over there fighting."

"Thanks, Dash."

Eventually, she glanced out the window and admitted she needed to get some sleep.

"Are you coming home for Christmas?" she asked. "Everyone would love to see you."

He winced. "I don't know. I'm not stationed here. I was just sent to the city as an errand boy. I have no idea when they'll need me again or where."

"Can you at least try to stay in touch? Even if it's a few lines of your messy handwriting, I'll take it."

"I'll do my best," he replied.

"And if they ever ask for an errand boy again, raise your hand."

He stuck it up. "I promise."

"I gotta go," she said reluctantly. "This night has flown by."

He stood and held out his arm. "I'll walk you."

The snow had stopped before it really got started, but it was still chilly. The streets were dark, with barely a car to cast a passing light along the shiny street. They were the only two on the streetcar, and they sat quietly, lost in their thoughts. Dash felt like there had to be a million things to say, but she couldn't find them. They'd run through everything, it seemed.

After a few minutes, she reached up and rang the bell. "This is my stop."

He walked with her toward the darkened windows of the Pigeon Coop. The remains of Mrs. Pidgett's fallow vegetable garden poked through the dark like ghosts, looking sad. Just above the front door Dash could picture her roommates, sound asleep.

"I'm so glad we had tonight," Gus said. "I miss you." He pulled her into a hug, and Dash squeezed him tight, fighting tears. "Please tell Dot I said hello, and that I miss her, too."

"I will."

For a split second she saw the little boy she'd grown up with, his mouth puckered with disappointment. "I wish we had longer."

"Me, too."

"Good night, Dash."

"Good night, Gus."

She closed the front door quietly behind her and hung up her coat, leaving her wet boots on the mat. On the stairs, she paused at the window and watched him walk away. He'd been so vague about what he was doing, and she was sad about that. Even if it was dull, she still wanted to know. Maybe he was ashamed about not physically helping the war effort. In a way, she felt sorry for him.

Mostly, though, she was relieved. Seeing him tonight, with his familiar blue eyes and that smile that warmed her all the way through, had been everything. Exactly what she'd needed, though their time together had been far too short.

Down the block, he turned the corner and was briefly lit by someone's headlights. Funny how grown up he looked, and yet how young she suddenly felt, being with him again. He might not be happy about what he was doing, but she was. It was such a comfort knowing he wasn't in danger. She couldn't imagine living without him.

fifteen
DOT

─ ·· ─── ─

─ Galt, Ontario ─

Dot bolted upright at the sound of the wake-up call: a blasting, dis-
torted recording of a bugle reveille played through a loudspeaker.
She had been at HMCS Conestoga for three days, and she still couldn't
get used to that noise.

"Let's go, ladies! Ten minutes!"

She groaned without meaning to, trying to move stiff and sore limbs.
All around her, similar sounds came from other bunks.

"Oh boy," Alice muttered.

"Do you suppose we'll have to run again even though we hurt this
much?"

"I think, dear Dot, that they'll make us run every day, no matter
what."

"I don't think I can."

"Nonsense. There's nothing we can't do, my friend." Alice swung her
long legs over the side of the bunk. "Let's get something to eat."

Dot and her two dozen classmates had fifteen minutes in the mess hall
for breakfast, where they downed a quick serving of oatmeal, bacon, and
coffee. On her first morning, she'd barely eaten anything she was so nervous.
Now that she knew what was coming, she gobbled down the entire plate.

That first day, Chief Wren Merrivale had gathered all the girls together and told them what would be expected of them over the next three
weeks, in addition to their lessons and training. She made it clear that no
matter how hard they worked during the day, there would be no getting
away from scrubbing floors, pots, and toilets, and peeling vegetables for
soup. It hadn't surprised Dot to hear that they were not only there to
learn, but to work. After all, the Wrens were a branch of the military.

It was the next part of the lecture that had taken Dot by surprise.

"Among the many classes in which you will participate is one con-
cerning specific health risks associated with fraternizing. You will have
seen, no doubt, that there are a number of men in this facility. You may be
asked to work with some. On occasion, you may meet socially."

A few of the girls around Dot shifted, and she heard a muffled ripple
of giggles. During their tour, Dot hadn't noticed a lot of men around
Conestoga, but she hadn't been looking. The ones she had seemed to be
working far from wherever the women were.

"Wrens," Chief Wren Merrivale continued, "are under strict orders
to limit these interactions and avoid socializing whenever possible. The
Royal Canadian Navy and the Women's Royal Canadian Naval Services
will not accept any sort of ill or untoward behaviour. Still, we are aware
mistakes do happen. So during your time here, we will be including
lectures on illnesses that could result from fraternization, such as vene-
real diseases. On that note, you should know, pregnancy is a dismissible
offence."

"*Oh, mon Dieu*," she breathed. Of all the things Dot had expected to
learn, it wasn't the by-products of the birds and the bees.

"I have never heard of *that* being called 'fraternization,'" Alice whispered.

To Dot's relief, they'd moved on from there. Lessons began with
the history of the Royal Canadian Navy, introductory Morse code, and
semaphore. Despite her knowledge of languages, Dot had never learned
semaphore, and it interested her. She copied out all the little figures on
the display Chief Wren Merrivale posted then memorized the semaphore

alphabet while the other students were still working on the few first letters of Morse code. When each girl was handed a pair of flags made of two large red and yellow triangles then was told to stand, Dot jumped to her feet, ready to go.

"The movement of the flags is crisp and clear," the Chief Wren explained. "Your message must be visible from a distance. Semaphore is habitually used to deliver messages from ship to shore or ship to ship, and often via telescope. Move with me now." She held both flags straight down so the red triangle pointed at the ground. The one on her right was just outside her leg, and her left flag pointed directly at her knee. There was a flurry of material as every girl imitated her. "That is the letter 'A.' Now this." Her left flag remained where it was, but the one in her right hand rose sharply so it was extended at the level of her shoulder. "That is the letter 'B.'"

Over and over they practiced, until the sharp snap of moving flags occurred at almost the exact same moment around the room.

As they exited the classroom on that first day, Dot hugged her notebook to her chest and smiled at Alice. "That was fun."

"If you say so. My mind is spinning."

"What's next?"

"The gymnasium."

Dot's happiness vanished. From the moment she'd decided to join the Wrens, she had been anxious about the physical exercises she knew would be a part of the military. When they had begun to run, she puffed along behind Alice, daring to hope it wouldn't be so bad. Unfortunately, it was worse. Dot struggled through sit-ups, push-ups, burpees, and a half-hour lesson on how to salute to the Chief Wren's satisfaction. As the lesson ended, Dot stood straight then gasped, feeling a powerful cramp in her stomach. To her mortification, she was forced to sprint to the head and throw up. No wonder Dash hadn't warned her. Dot never would have signed up if she'd known about this.

The second day had been no easier, but when the other girls ran, Dot did as well. About halfway through, she became convinced that she was going to die before the end of the hour. Afterward, she sank onto the floor at the side of the gym, her chest heaving, specks floating through her vision. She felt utterly humiliated. Joining the Wrens had been a mistake. She never should have listened to her family when they'd said she could accomplish anything she put her mind to. She was going to fail.

Except she couldn't get enough of the morning classes. Those made it all worthwhile.

Labouring for breath, Dot scanned the room, asking herself how she could ever earn a place with the Wrens. A few feet away, a couple of rosy-cheeked, sweaty girls laughed together, leaning on each other while they recovered from the run. The way they seemed to revel in the perspiration all this effort had produced reminded her of Dash, and she felt a familiar twinge of envy. Ashamed, she turned away and her gaze landed on a few quiet girls who remained on the fringe of the activity as she did. Taking in their stricken expressions, it dawned on Dot that she might not be the only one having trouble, which meant she wasn't alone in her self-doubt.

You can change if you want, Gus had said once, and she realized he had been exactly right. Especially here. No one really knew her yet. She could be Dot the Dormouse or she could be someone else entirely. It was up to her.

And so today, the third day, Dot decided to try harder. She had been sabotaging her own efforts by doubting herself, and she was determined not to dwell on self-pity. She staggered stiff-limbed into the mess hall and ate all she could, then she hobbled to the classroom to translate Morse code to semaphore and back again. When it was time to head to the gymnasium, she stretched out her body as she was told to do, then she began to run. Yes, it was harder than anything she'd ever done before, but clearly, no one would let her die from her efforts. Now she surprised herself by not only surviving, but improving. She no longer saw stars when she ran. Eventually, she even smiled while she did it.

What helped Dot adjust the most was the navy's strict adherence to rule and order. Structure kept Dot calm. Each morning, then again after supper, she smoothed out every wrinkle and crease on both uniform and bed, then she turned to the little table she shared with Alice. Her friend tended to place her things willy-nilly, and Dot felt more comfortable when everything was organized. For Dot to properly display her framed photographs of Dash, her parents, and one of both girls with Gus, she needed to shift Alice's to a higher shelf. At first she'd worried about what Alice might say, but fortunately, her friend hadn't seemed to notice, and Dot got comfortable moving things around.

That first week, Alice and Dot became close, which was a relief. She had assumed making friends would be much more of a challenge. Alice had a social personality, like Dash's, and she was also very smart. She quickly caught up to Dot on semaphore, and they shared an interest in the more technical aspects of what they were doing. Other than Gus and herself, Alice was the only person Dot had ever known who thought Morse code could be fun.

At the end of the week, Alice came into the room where Dot was tidying the shelves and sank onto Dot's bunk. Dot flinched internally as Alice laid waste to her perfectly straightened bed, but she reminded herself that it was all right. She would tidy it again later. How many times had Dash rushed in and dropped her things all over the freshly organized vanity, consumed with the need to tell Dot something?

"What's happening here?" Alice asked, seeming to notice what Dot was doing for the first time.

Dot glanced nervously at her, hoping she hadn't upset her friend by touching her things. "I was thinking that if you display your photographs up here by your bunk, you'd have a better view of them. Your other items can be stored underneath, on that shelf. Since I am on the bottom bunk, I'll put mine on the lower shelf, beneath yours." She braced herself for rejection. "What do you think?"

"I see." Alice steepled her fingers and regarded Dot. "You're one of those girls who likes things just so."

"I'm afraid so. Will that bother you?"

"Not at all. My sister is the same way. You are now officially responsible for these shelves." Alice paused, thoughtful. "But I want you to know that if you make mistakes, it's okay with me. No human being is perfect. Not even you."

Dot opened her mouth, prepared to argue that point as she had so often with her family. She'd always viewed the implication as condescending, and it had felt like an insult. This time she stopped herself and smiled instead. Everything here was new, and bit by bit, that included her attitude. Maybe she could accept the fact that what she'd heard was the opposite of what Alice had said. Maybe now she could let herself believe it.

———

Every day over those three weeks at Conestoga, Dot learned more, got stronger, and made more friends. She made sure to include the fact that sometimes she couldn't help smiling, and her sister's responses were filled with happiness for her. Near the end of their stay, the trainees were sorted according to their strengths—some were bound for the laundry, some for driving, some would be cooks—and Dot was thrilled that both she and Alice were selected for the administrative side of things. They joined a speedy typing pool and continued working with Morse code as well.

"I wonder what happens after this," she said to Alice one evening over supper. "Our three weeks are almost up."

"We'll know soon enough, I'm sure. In the meantime, we'll be home for Christmas!"

But the next morning, Dot was summoned to Chief Wren Merrivale's office. Her stomach clenched with nerves.

"Why me?" she whispered to Alice. "What did I do?"

"It will be fine," Alice assured her. "Merrivale loves you."

That didn't calm Dot nearly enough. She knocked then waited outside the office door until the Chief Wren invited her in. Dot pasted on a calm expression in an effort to disguise her terror.

"Please take a seat," the Chief Wren said. "I have been going over your file. In particular, I read the note left by the recruiter at your initial interview to join. I'm sure you are already aware that your typing speed is very impressive, as is your Morse code."

Dot sat on her hands, waiting for the *however*.

"We are seeking young women who are particularly suited as wireless operators. Wireless telegraphists, actually. Could you see yourself in that role?"

For a split second, Dot wasn't sure she'd heard her correctly. She'd been so focused on expecting bad news, this came out of nowhere. Then she understood the question, and her heart soared. Wireless telegraphist! She'd known all those laps around the gym would pay off some day! Her hands moved to her lap, where they linked together.

"I would like that very much, Chief Wren," she said, keeping her words as slow as possible. "I feel I would excel in radio communication. My father operated a Marconi in the last war."

"That's very interesting. I imagine you've spoken with him about it, and you understand the point of radiotelegraphy."

"Communication between two points," Dot recited from her father's lessons, "made through pulses of radio waves sent out in Morse code patterns, spelling out messages."

"Precisely. We use it to receive messages from various points around the world to track our own positions and those of the enemy."

"You can receive messages from all around the world?"

"Yes, and send them. Through radio waves. You will learn more about that later. For now, you will be trained to translate the sounds you hear so you can track the enemy or provide navigational support to our men. Think of how important that is. Your work with Morse code might one day prevent a tragedy a world away."

Her throat tightened with emotion. The conversation with her father about the SS *Caribou* seemed like so long ago, but she remembered it clear as day. She'd asked if that tragedy could have been prevented, and if he could have done anything to stop it in his day. He had shaken his head, but he had also told her that technology had changed. This was exactly what he had been talking about. She couldn't wait to tell him.

"Thank you for this opportunity, Chief Wren." She hesitated, unsure if it might be too personal a story to share. "My love of Morse code is what resulted in my nickname. My sister Margaret is called Dash."

Chief Wren Merrivale graced Dot with one of the first genuine smiles she'd seen so far, and Dot was reminded of Dash's Tootsie Roll comment. The chief Wren was quite pretty when she smiled. Dash was always suggesting to Dot that she relax for exactly that same reason.

"I recall your sister, but I didn't know the origin of that nickname of hers. I don't remember her being as talented as you with Morse code, though."

"No, ma'am. I mean, she's good, but she is called Dash because she's always moving. My sister is a mechanic."

"I remember that." She stood again. "Come with me, please."

Dot followed her past the typing room, where she spotted Alice at work. Her friend glanced up from her work, her raised eyebrows questioning, but Dot could only shrug. At the end of the hall, the chief Wren opened the door to another room, and Dot's pulse picked up. A dozen or so radio receivers were lined up against the walls, and she couldn't help thinking of her father.

"I'd like to see how you might do as a receiver. Take a seat, if you would, and slip on those headphones. They are, as you can see, connected to this radio. I want you to listen and tell me what you hear."

Dot put them on eagerly and closed her eyes to concentrate, but the sounds were faint and indistinguishable from each other. A whirling universe of peeps and beeps flying by at lightning speed. She glanced up, confused.

"Don't give up yet."

Chief Wren Merrivale adjusted one of the dials, and the cacophony of noise suddenly concentrated, as if she'd turned the knob on a pair of binoculars and focused the view.

"Listen for one line of Morse code. You are not expected to understand what it says, since most is done using ciphers. I just want to know if you hear what they are sending. Can you hear it?"

Dot's mind opened wide with wonder. Oh yes, she heard it. Now that she understood what to listen for, the dots and dashes formed letters in her head as clearly as if she were writing the alphabet. Was she hearing a directive from the German Navy? Was it a location beacon? A world of messages floated out there, and in Dot's mind, each one was a puzzle to be solved. When the chief Wren slipped a paper and pencil into her hand, Dot dove in, printing out the letters as they sped by.

"Excellent. That's what I thought," Chief Wren Merrivale said after Dot reluctantly removed her headphones.

"You should be very, very pleased with the work you have done here, Wren Wilson. Don't think I haven't noticed the effort you put in over the past three weeks. You have excelled in every department throughout your term. Your enthusiastic participation in all classes has been exemplary, including the basic training in the gymnasium. And for someone who arrived here so terribly shy, you have made great strides in expanding your social circle. Your fellow trainees seem quite fond of you. As am I." She touched the radio. "I believe working with wireless telegraphy is where you belong, and I can tell you're pleased with that." She handed Dot an envelope with an official stamp from the WRCNS. "You have earned this. Congratulations."

Dot read through the letter once then again, astounded by what was printed there, then she raced breathlessly back to her bed to grab her stationery.

Dear Dash, she wrote.

I am afraid I have some bad news and some rather wonderful news.

First the bad news: I will not be coming home for Christmas. I am brokenhearted over that. I miss you and Mom and Dad terribly, and I have so many things to tell you all!

But now for the good news: I am being transferred to a new base. It's a little speck on the map in Quebec called HMCS Saint-Hyacinthe. I am leaving first thing tomorrow morning, up before the sun. Why am I so excited? I am going to copy the exact words that they put in the letter I received just now so you'll understand:

At HMCS Saint-Hyacinthe we focus our efforts on signalling, wireless telegraphy, radar operations, and coding. . .

You were right, Dash. This is where I belong. I will write more when I can, but for now I must get packed and ready to go. Since you will be speaking with our parents before I will, and because I am too short on time to write another letter, I am trusting you will share this news with them. Please tell Dad I cannot wait to tell him about the radios!

I hope you all have a wonderful Christmas. I miss you and I wish I could be there, but my heart is singing, just thinking about what I'll soon be doing!

All my love, Dot

sixteen
DASH

—— December 1942 ——
Toronto, Ontario

The dark sky held barely a suggestion of a sunrise when Dash and Ginny neared the garage. It was the first day of December, and winter had come in fast and hard. An inch of fresh snow already squeaked under their boots. The temperature in the garage wasn't much warmer than it was outside, but at least they'd be out of the wind. Maybe Mr. Eisen would be forced to turn on the heater he swore so much about.

"Are you heading home for Christmas?" Dash asked. "I can't wait to get home and wrap myself around the stove."

"Sure," Ginny replied noncommittally. "But my brothers won't be there, so it's gonna be subdued to say the least."

"They're in the navy, right? Pilots?" Dash made a little sound of frustration. "They're so lucky."

"I don't know, Dash. I think you should be relieved they don't let women fly."

"American women get to fly, why shouldn't we?"

"They're not fighting."

"No, but at least they're flying." Dash had pictured it so many times:

roaring through the sky, chasing German planes. The best part would be when the *Luftwaffe* pilots discovered they were getting shot down by a woman. "I would love to be over there, ending the war."

Ginny chuckled. "Okay. Well, you can shoot down as many of them as you want, but in my opinion, knowledge is what will win this war." She tapped her temple. "Intelligence and determination. Smart people like your sister."

She pulled open the door to the garage, and Dash stomped snow off her boots before heading inside. As usual, they were the first two in.

"Here we go again," Ginny said, taking her spot in the bay across from Dash. "Have a good one, Flying Ace."

It was another long day. Vehicles came in without brakes, without working radiators, needing new spark plugs, any number of things. While some of the men paused for cigarettes or coffee, Dash didn't take breaks. She could sense Jim watching her, making sure she was busy, and she didn't want to get any adverse attention. She understood she was being punished for not going out with him, but that was all right. If working hard was her penance, Dash was happy to pay it.

At closing time, everyone rushed out, having heard there was another snowstorm coming. Dash stayed behind, adjusting the linkage on a Ford truck since Jim had specifically requested she finish it today, even if she went into overtime. She wished she'd left with Ginny, though. If she had, she'd be back at the house already, sipping on something hot instead of freezing her fingers off.

The garage was quiet now, except for the clunk of the pipes freezing in the raw chill and Dash's own chattering teeth. When the Ford's steering was finally done, she stuck her frozen hands into the armpits of her stained coveralls, trying to restore some kind of sensation.

"I'll warm 'em for you."

She tensed. "Jim. I thought you'd left already."

He stepped out of the shadows, his boots scuffing the floor. "Just you and me, sweetheart."

"Leave me alone, Jim."

"Give a fella a chance, why don't you?"

She stood her ground. "I have told you many times, I am not interested. Please believe me when I say that. I. Am. Not. Interested. Go away, Jim. Truck's done. I'm tired. I'm going home."

His eyes narrowed, and he took another step closer. Much too close. "Not quite yet."

"What's your wife think about your activities outside of the house?" Dash asked hotly, though there was a quiver in her voice.

All at once he closed the distance between them, backing her against the wall, his thick forearm pressed against her windpipe. She clawed at it, but he was locked on tight, his face inches from hers.

"Get off me," she growled.

"Don't talk about my wife," he hissed through bared teeth.

Dash wheezed. "I can't breathe."

"Lemme help with that." His arm was like an iron bar, holding her in place. She couldn't move when he started kissing her, scraping his teeth against hers. She twisted her face sideways and gasped for air, but he kept his hold on her.

"See?" Despite the freezing room, the sweat on his cheeks shone in the dim light. "I'm not such a bad guy. Just relax. You might enjoy yourself."

"Get off!" she screamed. Her knee swung up toward his groin, but she missed. The pressure on her throat increased until stars floated in her vision.

"Come on, baby."

Bang! Jim's eyes popped wide open for an instant, then he crumpled to the floor. Behind him stood Ginny, a shocked expression on her face and a shovel in her hands. It dropped with a clang, and she rushed to Dash's side.

"We have to report this," she insisted, holding Dash upright. "Right now. Let's get out of here. He'll wake up soon. I didn't hit him too hard."

"Hard enough. Thank you, Ginny."

seventeen

DOT

—•• --- -

— HMCS Saint-Hyacinthe, Québec —

The only thing better than going to HMCS Saint-Hyacinthe for five weeks of training was doing it with Alice. She, Dot, and four others from Conestoga hit the ground running as soon as they arrived. This time it was Alice who started off a little nervous, but Dot reassured her.

"There's nothing we can't do, isn't that what you told me when we first started?"

Their days at Saint-Hyacinthe were much like they had been at Conestoga: practical lessons, history classes, and the gym, but everything was more focused. They were drilled on signalling and Morse code, taught radio theory and repair, and they learned the locations and call signs of the German Navy's coastal stations. Endless letters and numbers were placed in front of the girls, and they translated what they saw both into and out of Morse code as quickly as possible. Sometimes they used semaphore flags or lights to change things up. When it came time, Dot didn't hesitate to climb a ten-foot-tall signals mast to keep up her training for semaphore. A few of Dot's classmates drooped under the concentrated hours, but she could not have been more in her element. At the end of the month every girl would be expected to achieve a minimum of twenty words per minute in Morse code. Dot was determined to leave that number far behind, and Alice took that as a challenge.

They still hadn't been introduced to the headphones with those magical sounds pattering through them, but Dot took heart, knowing that was coming.

And there was even more good news. Yesterday, she had received a letter from Dash, and it had felt like an early Christmas present.

I saw Gus! Dash had written. *He was walking down the street and I kidnapped him. We spent hours talking in the diner. Oh, Dot! It felt so good to see him and be able to scold him in person. He said he misses you so much, and he said he would try to write to us, but I have learned not to hold my breath . . .*

Gus was alive. He was well. Dot had cried tears of relief into her pillow at the news.

At Saint-Hyacinthe, they had a new commanding officer, Chief Wren Stevens. She was shorter than Dot, and heavyset, with a sharp, direct gaze that could mean she was either paying close attention, or she was furious. Dot didn't quite understand her yet, but she wasn't intimidated. Chief Wren Merrivale had been scary in the beginning, too, and by the end Dot had quite liked her. This morning, Chief Wren Stevens stood at the front of the classroom and announced that it was time for the girls to learn about radio signals and wireless telegraphy. Dot sat up straight, pencil in hand, ready to go.

When the Chief Wren turned to the blackboard and began to outline the physics of both the atmosphere and the ionospheres, Dot wilted, disappointed. She didn't understand a thing. She snuck a peek at the girls around her and was slightly relieved to see her own confusion reflected in their strained expressions. Chief Wren Stevens did not appear to notice.

"Physics," she was saying, "helps us understand how wireless telegraphy works, and how it is possible to obtain line bearings for use in direction finding. Though it is complicated in theory, it is vital for those interested in the field to understand, since pinpointing specific locations based on a single radio signal is our job."

The Chief Wren drew a square on one side of the blackboard, which she tapped with the chalk. Dot quickly copied it in her notebook.

"This is us. I shall mark it 'Station.' Out here," she said, drawing a circle some distance away, "is the ship whose messages we are monitoring. Let's imagine this is the Mediterranean Sea. You might think that communicating between here and there would be too far, but I will demonstrate that it is accessible from any distance."

Still facing the board, Chief Wren Stevens drew a line connecting the two shapes, calling it their "line of sight," then she added two arcing lines around it. Determined not to fail, Dot blocked out every sound in the room but the chief Wren's voice and copied the diagram exactly.

"The area inside these arcs is what is called a Fresnel zone. It accounts for anything that might interfere with the line of sight, like an underwater mountain, another ship, or something like that." She turned back to the girls. "Does anyone understand what I just said?"

So far, Dot was following along, but she wasn't sure where it was leading, so she kept quiet. No one else said a word.

The chief Wren smiled. "You will. Have you drawn this in your books?"

There was a quick shuffling while the other girls grabbed their pencils, and the chief Wren gave them a few moments to copy it for themselves.

"Now I am going to draw two straight lines from the ends of the zones, and they will converge. This, as you might guess, is called the convergence. Pick up your rulers and draw yours, please."

Dot put up a hand. "How do we know which angle to use or how large to draw the ellipse?"

"Excellent question. The zone varies depending on the length of the signal path and the frequency of the signal. Since this is a hypothetical signal at the moment, there is no wrong answer."

Dot chose an angle then compared her drawing to Alice's. They were different, but both illustrated the convergence that Chief Wren Stevens spoke of.

The chief Wren scanned the room, waiting for everyone to finish. "What we just did was give you an idea of what we will be working with. Now we will get to the real thing. Here at Saint-Hyacinthe, we will teach you how to find the coordinates for convergence through specific radio units known as high frequency direction finders, also called HF/DF, or Huff Duff. We will now head out to the hut, and I will introduce you to the radio, your new best friend. Please follow me, and bring your coats."

Dot placed her hand over her mouth as if she were yawning, but in truth, she was covering her grin. The joy of hearing those sounds for the first time back at Conestoga still felt fresh. It had been like passing into a different universe, sparkling with puzzles to solve. Dot could hardly wait to hear it again. Beside her, Alice gave a little hop of excitement.

In the hut, a dozen desks were set up in a U-shape. Each held a radio receiver and a set of headphones. The receivers were about a foot and a half tall, and their black metal faces were covered in dials and knobs. In the centre was a large circle, and above that at both sides were three-inch rectangular glass windows with numbers behind. Dot's fingers itched to grab the headphones and slip them over her ears, but she needed to understand everything first.

"This is your Huff Duff," Chief Wren Stevens said, touching one of the radios. "Your high frequency direction finder. In older systems, if you were trying to determine a bearing, you would have had to mechanically rotate an antenna, then listen. It was complicated and took time that operators sometimes could not spare. Fortunately, the radio before you will only require slight tweaking of the dial." She indicated a glass pane crossed by a moving sound wave. "A high frequency radio band is what we use to locate or communicate over long distances. You will be able to see the signal on this oscilloscope display." She looked pointedly at each girl in the room. "Ladies, this is how we hunt U-boats."

Alice nudged Dot in the ribs, making her squeak. "Here we go!" she whispered.

"Please choose one desk for yourself," Chief Wren Stevens said, then she waited for all the girls to sit. "When we begin, you will be overwhelmed at first, but I will help you find what you need to hear. After you listen for a while, your brain will pick out the sounds and sharpen them into Morse code. Your job is to translate and write the letters you hear."

She walked slowly behind the girls' chairs, leaning in and placing paper and pencils in front of them as she went. "Write what you hear as it comes in. I only want letters from you. Do not, I repeat, do not try to decipher the message. Deciphering is for others who have been specifically trained to break them down, and doing that would demand time we do not have. Only use printed capital letters, please, since handwriting can raise confusion between letters. When you sense the message has come to an end or is repeating itself, put the paper aside to be picked up, then start again with the next message." She surveyed the room. "All right. Put your headphones on and begin."

Dot wasn't overwhelmed. She was euphoric. When the deluge of sounds hit her, she did what Chief Wren Merrivale had done at HMCS Conestoga and fiddled with the radio dial until it all became clear. Listening hard to the air waves, she closed off any other thoughts so her consciousness could drift uninterrupted among the sounds. From her only other experience, she'd learned that cool, unemotional concentration, not thought, fueled the communication. Now, when one sound in particular reached for her, she grabbed onto it and began to print. She heard what sounded like a series of five letters before they repeated. Five, then five more. She printed every one of them in neat, capital letters, then she moved onto the next. And the next. It was exhilarating.

Dot jumped, startled by someone tapping her shoulder. Looking up, she saw Chief Wren Stevens signalling for her to remove the headphones.

"That's it for the day. You have excellent focus, Wren Wilson."

There was no one else left in the room.

The Chief Wren held up some of Dot's little papers. "Clearly, you have grasped what this is all about. You are a natural, and I am excited to see how you do after this initial experience. But this is only your first day of listening, and you may not realize it, but you've been working for two hours straight, not even pausing for a sip of water. It's time to stop for the night."

You are a natural. The words of acknowledgement made it easier for Dot to set the headphones aside, though she wished she could just keep going. A natural? Yes, I am! she thought, energy buzzing through her. When she reached the barracks, she barely remembered walking there, but she knew she was wearing a ridiculous grin the whole way.

Day after day, she plugged herself into the sounds, feeling like a race car starting its engine, impatient for the finish line. Sometimes the letters came in groups of three, sometimes in pairs, sometimes five in a row, and Dot wrote every one of them down. They rarely spelled anything or made any sense, but she knew to expect that. The hours were never long enough for her. This wasn't work; it was energizing. In contrast, the other girls threw themselves onto their beds at the end of every day, worn out. Even Alice complained that all she could see and hear these days were dots and dashes.

"I am dit-dit-dit-dit done!" she groaned, climbing into her bed at the end of the second week. Her bright curls tumbled over the edge of the upper bunk when she leaned over to look at Dot. "That's all I hear now!" she cried, a wild sort of light in her red-rimmed eyes. "The pipes clank, and I hear a message. The springs of this"—she bounced slightly, jarring the bunk—"mattress are talking. Do you know, I was waiting for the kettle to boil today for tea, and I found myself listening to the sound of the steam and trying to hear dits and dahs. I don't know how much more of this I can take!"

Dot felt no such strain, but she didn't want anyone to think she was strange—like when she had recited double-digit multiplication tables in grade four and all the other children had stared—so she didn't let on that this was her idea of fun.

"We've made it this far, Alice. There's nothing we can't do, remember? Don't give up yet. There's a lot more coming."

Alice made an agonized noise of frustration as she flopped back onto her pillow, disappearing from view. "Da-da-dit Da-da-da Dit-dit Da-dit Da-da-dit Da-dit-da-dit Dit-da-dit Dit-da Da-Da-dit-dit Da-dit-da-da!"

Dot smiled, translating her friend's noises. "Going crazy."

Dot loved what she was doing, but as time passed, she realized it wasn't enough. She could hear the Morse code beeping through her headset, but what was it *really* saying? After a while, despite the warnings, Dot gave in to the siren call of the letters. It was obvious the various combinations were puzzles. Other people had been trained to decipher them, but Dot could see no reason why she couldn't try as well. While she was hunting for a new message, why couldn't she spend a little time sorting through the last one, to see if she could figure it out.

Three hours into her next shift, she decided to try. She wasn't doing anything sneaky or against the rules, just playing with letters a bit on the side while she listened for more. She slouched in her chair, rubbing the back of her stiff neck, and stared at the letters she'd just written.

These had arrived in a series of four at a time. Like most of the thousands of letters she'd written, they appeared to be arbitrary. But through all her listening, she'd picked up patterns, and she was certain she had heard these ones before. Between incoming messages, she bent over her desk and wrote different combinations of the same letters, trying to make something come together.

B-O-E-J

F-H-S-V

Q-Q-F-X

The double Q seemed suspicious. A possible clue, if she could parse it correctly. Especially since there was no letter U in the message. Maybe each line was separate but backward. JEOBVSHFXFQQ. Or maybe *that* was backward XFQQVSHFJEOB. JOB SHE, she wrote, mixing up the letters then crossing them out. Obviously it was a code, but what was the key to unlocking the meaning? She assumed the Germans would constantly change the keys around; the people doing the deciphering had them and would know which to use, but she'd get no hints.

What if she looked at it like a simple alphabet code, with one letter off? B-O-E-J would be A-N-D-I, then F-H-S-V would be E-G-R-U, and Q-Q-F-X would be P-P-E-W. ANDIEGRUPPEW.

She dropped her head into her hand, frustrated, then all at once, something shifted in her brain, as if she'd flicked on a lamp. Just as the letters emerged from sounds, now they floated before her eyes, switching positions and spelling out a message she saw clear as day. That's when she understood why she hadn't spotted the answer before: the message was in German.

It was so simple. How had she missed that?

A-N D-I-E G-R-U-P-P-E. The W had to have been added to throw her off. A-N D-I-E G-R-U-P-P-E: *To the Group*. A salutation. To whom?

Now that she saw it, she could see there was so much more. Her pulse sped up as she turned to solving the lines and lines of letters that followed. The next group of letters was much longer, and at first they meant nothing to her, so she slowed her thinking.

J-D-H-M D-A-D-R . . .

Sticking to that simple code, the six rows of four letters spelled out *Keine besondere Ereignisse*. No special events.

"Ha!"

"Shh!" came the response from all around the room.

Flushed, Dot set her headphones on the table and put up her hand. Chief Wren Stevens approached, speaking quietly as to not disturb the others. "Yes?"

Dot tapped her finger on the long string of letters she'd just written. "This is a German transmission," she whispered. "And it's a common one. I've seen it before."

One corner of Chief Wren Stevens's mouth curled up, but her tone was serious. "I thought you understood we *listen* here, we do not decipher."

"Yes, ma'am, but I had time, and I've been very curious."

"Let's take a look." She gestured for Dot to follow her back to her desk. "We purposefully did not mention that the transmissions were in a different language. Tell me the steps you took to find this."

"Well, it's obviously a cipher, and I love ciphers. I've loved puzzles all my life. Crosswords, mysteries, I love it all. My father was my greatest influence. Every Saturday morning he and I— Oh, that's for another time." She knew she was speaking quickly, but the Chief Wren did not slow her down. It was as if she understood that Dot saw things better at that pace. "I feel a little foolish for not recognizing this one until now because it's a rudimentary cipher, but I overlooked the fact that it might be in German. Such a silly mistake, considering the war and all."

Dot wrote out the first series then rewrote them one letter earlier. "B is A, C is B, D is C, and so on." She drew lines from the first group of letters she had printed, putting them in the order she now understood. "You see? Once I figured that out, I translated in German. This short series says *An die Gruppe*, which translates simply as 'To the group,' a common opening to a message."

She sensed the chief Wren leaning over her, but she couldn't break her trance to check if the woman approved or not.

"I tried to see the rest of the message the same way as I had the beginning, but it didn't work. The letters obviously had to mean something universal, otherwise why connect them to a group message? That stumped me briefly, but I'm not one to quit mid-puzzle. Just ask my family. I tried the one-off code again first, and it still worked. It had to, considering there were eight Ds in there. An obvious key. To me, those *had* to be Es. After that, all I had to do was rearrange. I moved this to there, and this . . ."

When she was done explaining, she sat back, triumphant. "You see? It's not a very interesting message, but it does work. *Keine besondere Ereignisse.* That translates to 'no special events,' or 'nothing to report.' Now that I recognize it for what it is, I know I have seen it used before."

Chief Wren Stevens nodded noncommittally, a beat of judgement that, in the past, would have sent Dot down terrifying spirals of anxiety, but not this time. She knew she was right.

"Excellent work," the Chief Wren said softly. "Very, very well done. From a listener to a codebreaker with no training. I'm interested to learn how the initial idea for using German came to you. How did you figure that out?"

Seeing a message appear amidst a scramble of letters, well, it wasn't that different from some of the puzzles Dot had played with growing up. Just another anagram that basically showed itself to her. She'd never thought about *how* she did it.

"I don't really know. I just saw it."

Alice must have been listening, because later that evening she sat beside Dot at supper with a pencil and paper. "Show me how to see what you see. I want to do more than listen."

"I'm not sure I can," Dot replied.

"I will try to keep up. Say it like you're explaining it to yourself, only do it out loud."

Dot stared at the blank page, wondering where to start. Then she wrote down the message she had told her instructor about, seeing it again in memory.

"A code is essentially a form of substitution," she told Alice. "If you can figure out the key, you can work backward from there. The key is the trick. Sometimes we know what it is, but often not. Also, I discovered today, and I really should have realized it all along—"

Alice held up her hand, her brow twisted. "Slow down, Dot. No one talks as fast as you once you get going, you know that?"

"I'm sorry. My family tells me that all the time." She inhaled, slowing herself. "I discovered today that I needed to think in German, not just English."

"That was your 'aha' in class today?"

"Yes. I couldn't believe I hadn't seen it earlier. It was so straightforward. They weren't trying to hide anything, and that made it easier for me to see. Look for repeated patterns and repeated letters." She explained about the Ds and the Es.

Alice nodded slowly.

"Another way to recognize what is being used is by looking for certain words used a lot. Once you identify them, you can use that word as a key. For example, the British often use the word 'STOP' when a message is over. They might even say 'MESSAGE OVER.' The Germans say all different things, depending on the sender. One that I have heard a lot is 'ENDE,' which just means 'End.' Once you see that, it's not difficult to use those letters as part of the key, and go from there."

A light began to come on in Alice's eyes. Sensing her friend's eagerness, Dot made up a few short test sentences to see if Alice could solve them. After a little head scratching, she did.

"What do you think?" Dot asked.

"I think you are amazing, but I need a lot more practice."

———

The next morning, the class was sent out to the semaphore area. From her spot ten feet up the mast, Dot could see the girl at the other end of the parade square, her yellow and red flags whipping in the cold wind. Dot's job was to read the letters, then Alice would write them down.

The girl at the end held one flag straight down and one straight up.

"D," Dot said. Then "I," when the girl whipped her left flag down to the lower left, then switched her right flag to the left and held it in the high position.

She yawned. "So that's M-V-O-D-I."

"Keep going, Dot," Alice said. "Remember? Chief Wren Stevens said we're not supposed to translate, just read the flags. They're timing us. I don't want to clean toilets again."

"U-P-E-B-Z. It's a puzzle, Alice. An easy one. Like if I look at letters just one past . . . If I go back from there . . ."

The flags kept signalling, over and over. Dot did what she'd been assigned, repeating what she saw so Alice could write it all down, but she couldn't stop translating in her mind. Whether it was supposed to or not, the message was beginning to reveal itself.

"Just the letters, Dot," Alice said. "It's cold out here."

"Q-F-B-O-V," Dot read dutifully, "S-C-V-S-S." She was pretty sure they were coming in series of five. The triple SS was telling. What if . . . "Repeat those last five again?"

"S-C-V-S-S." Alice sighed. "Come on. We both know you can solve it. Just finish so we can go in."

"F-S-B-O-E, K-B-N." She turned to Alice, smug. "Got it."

Alice couldn't suppress a smile. "What is it?"

"Peanut butter and jam for lunch today." Dot's expression tightened. "What is that? I know I've heard of it, but from where? The Americans?"

"Yes!" Alice hooked her arm through Dot's. "With their rations, the American soldiers get bread and peanut butter, then they got bread and jam, so somebody decided to put them together." She wiggled her pale eyebrows. "I can't wait to try it."

═══════

After five weeks, Dot and Alice were tested on everything they'd learned for their final examinations. Both breezed through every category, including the physical challenges, although when it came to speed, no one could come close to Dot at Morse code. The minimum speed required for graduation was twenty words per minute. Dot was at forty-five, and Alice was at thirty-four.

On the day of their graduation from Saint-Hyacinthe, Dot stood beside Alice on a small stage. Their uniforms were spotless, their shoes scrubbed so hard they reflected the ceiling lights as they earned the rank of Petty Officer Wren, a rank equal to sergeant in other military branches. Chief Wren Stevens presented each of them with a blue embroidered badge of a crown above two crossed anchors, which Dot would sew on her sleeve the minute she had time. There was also a certificate of graduation and a sealed envelope. Slightly less important, but still exciting to Dot, was the fact that she and Alice would receive a pay raise to $1.15 per week.

After the presentations, Chief Wren Stevens came to the podium to congratulate each of them for their exemplary work over the past five weeks.

"I would also like to read a statement to you, written by the minister of National Defence for Naval Services." She cleared her throat. "'The expectations of the navy in the Wrens have been justified by your hard work and dedication to duty. You who are members of the sister branch of the senior service have won the respect of all Canadians by your acceptance of requirements, readiness for responsibility, and your invaluable contribution to the work of winning the war. You will share in no small measure the gratitude of the Canadian people when victory is ours.'" She set the paper down and smiled at the graduates. "In addition, I would like to share my own personal gratitude for the commitment and diligence you have shown. You have earned this honour, and I know you are eager to see what happens next. All of that information is in the envelope you now hold."

As soon as the ceremony was over, Dot and Alice sliced open their envelopes and read the letters within. Dot's heart leapt, discovering where she was going next, then she looked up slowly, meeting Alice's eyes.

"HMCS Coverdale," they both said. Grinning, they quickly read the letter.

HMCS Coverdale, Dot read, was a special wireless station in New Brunswick. It was not a training centre at all. It was an actual listening station.

"No more classes," Dot said, stunned. "We're done!"

Alice grinned. "What do you say to that, Petty Officer Wren Wilson?"

Hearing her name attached to the military rank filled Dot with an exhilarating sense of pride. She'd done it. She'd made it all the way through, and she was no longer afraid.

"Well, Petty Officer Wren Renwick," she replied. "I say we'd better get packing. No more school for us."

This time, it was the real thing.

eighteen
DASH

— Toronto, Ontario —

D ash and Ginny rushed out of the garage, and Dash nearly slipped on an unexpected patch of ice. The forecasted snowstorm had arrived.

"Where's the police station?" Ginny asked.

Dash had no idea. She still felt shaky and sick after Jim's attack. All she wanted was to curl up in her bed and try to forget it had ever happened. "Let's just go home. They won't do anything. Nothing happened in the end."

"Nonsense," Ginny replied. "Something happened, and I saw it. We can't just let this go, Dash. What if he tries it again on you or someone else?"

Wordless, Dash lowered her chin to her chest, shielding her face from the storm, and followed Ginny up the street. It was the oddest feeling, being cold on the outside and numb on the inside. She couldn't think straight, just kept feeling that pressure on her throat and seeing Jim's wild eyes. Ginny was her lifeline, and she relied on her judgement. She trudged through the rapidly darkening evening, using the weak streetlights and her friend's boot prints to get through the snow.

"Ah!" Ginny cried out after a while. "Look!"

A squad car rolled gingerly down the street toward them, navigating the slippery surface, and the girls waved at him to stop. The driver rolled down his window and smiled at them expectantly. He was middle-aged, with saggy pouches under his eyes that reminded Dash of a basset hound. He looked like somebody's sweet old grandpa.

"What are you two ladies doing out here?"

"We need to report an attack," Ginny said breathlessly, leaning toward his window.

"What kind of attack?" he asked.

She pointed at Dash. "A man tried to . . . uh—"

"Where is he now?"

"Probably just waking up," Ginny admitted. "A shovel fell on his head."

The policeman studied the two of them. "I'll drive you to the station. You can make a report there."

They piled in gratefully, scattering snow onto his black upholstery. It felt good to be out of the wind, but anxiety welled in Dash's stomach. She knew Ginny was right, but she didn't want to talk about Jim. Didn't want to think about what had happened.

"Why are you out here, sir?" Ginny asked. "You're the only car on the road."

"That's what we're hoping," he replied. "I have to watch out for any other fools driving in this, make sure everyone is all right. And I get to play the knight in shining armour for pretty young girls like yourselves."

He dropped them off at the station and told them to check in at the front desk. There, a constable listened as Ginny told him what had happened. This man, Dash noted, did not look like anybody's sweet old anything. Just a cocky young policeman appearing impressed with himself.

"Was anyone hurt?"

"Look at her neck," Ginny said. "That's going to be a bruise."

"That's it? What do you want me to do about a bruise?" he asked.

"I should think that's obvious." Ginny stretched to her full, impressive height. "He should be thrown in jail."

"For making a pass at a girl?"

Dash and Ginny exchanged a glance.

"It wasn't a pass. It was an attack," Dash said, her voice coming out hoarse.

He lifted an eyebrow, considering her, then he let out a huff and reached for a paper and pen. "Right. Right. Well, I'll tell you what. I'll write it all down, and someone will look into it tomorrow."

Nothing in his tone of voice suggested he took them seriously.

"Let's go home," Dash said, and they stepped back into the storm.

———

Early the next morning, the girls went to their Wren supervisor.

She listened, then said, "I'm sorry this happened to you, Petty Officer Wren Wilson; however, I'm afraid you will have to get used to that sort of behaviour. We may be helping in the war effort, but we're not running it. Men haven't changed throughout this time. I advise never being alone in the same room as a man without proper supervision. You're fortunate your sister Wren came back to check on you."

She dismissed them, and the girls stood silently in the hallway.

"So that's it?" Ginny asked at last.

It twisted Dash up, knowing Jim would get away with this and there was nothing they could do about it.

"We still have to go to work on Monday," Dash replied, resigned.

"Are you going to tell Mr. Eisen?"

"What would be the point?"

"I'm not letting you out of my sight. And I will be carrying that shovel everywhere I go."

"Maybe that will be enough. I'm sure it won't happen again. I will never be stupid enough to be alone in the garage again. Besides," she pushed herself to smile. "You and that shovel were pretty intimidating."

Mary was writing in her journal when they returned to their room that afternoon, and she rushed to meet them at the door. "Where in heaven's name have you been? I went to bed last night and you weren't here, and you weren't here when I woke up this morning." She gasped when Dash took off her coat and revealed a line of angry bruises around her neck. "Dear Lord, Dash! What happened?"

It was a little easier to talk by then, so Dash told her everything and Ginny filled in the blanks.

Mary's eyes were big as saucers. "Don't go to work on Monday."

"We have no choice."

Jim Eisen was the first person Dash saw when they walked into the garage Monday morning. She turned away as fast as she could.

"If looks could kill," Ginny muttered, "we'd be goners. Okay. He's gone back into the office now."

Shaking, Dash headed toward the truck requiring her attention. The only time she lifted her head all day was to make sure Jim was nowhere in sight. Part of her wanted to yell and scream, to let everyone know what a louse he was. The other part wanted to avoid breathing the same air as him.

When they left at the end of the day, she still felt as if every move she made was being watched.

"Was Jim even at work?" she asked Ginny. "I saw him in the morning, but nothing after that."

"That's because you were doing a very good job of keeping your eyes on your work. He was there, all right. He looked a little frightening, to be honest."

When Dash arrived at the garage the following morning, she was told to go to the boss's office. She tucked a few stray hairs back into the bright red kerchief she always wore then went in, heart racing. She was relieved to see it was Jim's grumpy old father who sat at the desk, not Jim.

"Sir?"

"Inspector went around the vehicles last night, and your Dodge was knocking like a son of a gun."

In a flash, Dash remembered everything she had done on that truck. "It was all right when I left, sir."

"Yeah. Sure it was." He slammed a fist on his desk, making her jump. "What I wanna know is why a so-called mechanic would leave an air filter loose like it was. What's a loose air filter do, Wilson?"

"Uh, well, it would suck in dust, sir. The engine would smoke, because it's burning oil. The cylinders would need to be rehoned, and it would need new rings." She stood her ground. "But I didn't leave it loose. I would never do that."

"You letting somebody else do your work, then? That wasn't your Dodge?"

"N-no, that was mine, but I would never make a mistake like that."

"You're sloppy, Wilson, and you'll be paying for those repairs out of your paycheque."

Dash went to protest, but she knew there was no point. "At least let me fix it myself. Please, sir."

"Just make sure you do it right this time." He shook his head as if he had the weight of the world on his shoulders. "The navy sends me girls to fix engines and distract the fellas. What's next? Gonna give them guns and send them in to fight? Honestly. The world has lost its mind." He waved a stubby finger in Dash's face. "I'm watching you, Wilson. One more and you're out. Now get lost."

Biting her lower lip against tears, Dash quick-walked to her station, passing a wide-eyed Ginny on her way. She kept to herself for the rest of the day, working hard on the Dodge. She was so shaken she didn't tell Ginny what had happened until they were almost home.

"But you'd never do that!" Ginny exclaimed. "Everyone knows you're the best mechanic in the place." She narrowed her eyes. "Do you think Jim . . . ?"

"I wouldn't put it past him," Dash grumbled, opening the door to the house. Mary paced just inside, waiting for them.

"Is everyone okay?" she demanded. "Want some tea? Let me help."

"We're fine," Dash assured her, "though tea would be great. All we have to do is get through the next couple of weeks until Christmas. Things will have to be different after that, don't you think?"

Dash kept her head down the next day and the next. When she scouted for Jim, she was relieved that he wasn't looking her way. She dared to believe he'd forget about her and go away for good.

"Look. There's the boss's new secretary, Sally," Ginny said at lunch break later that week. "Jim's been sniffing after her all day."

She gestured with her chin toward a tiny thing with shiny blond hair, a tight skirt, and high heels. From the way she was nodding quickly at Jim, her hands fidgeting behind her back, Dash automatically thought of Dot. Without meaning to, she touched the place on her neck where Jim's forearm had held her captive.

"That poor girl doesn't have a hope against him," she said.

Just before their break was over, Sally headed outside for a cigarette, and Dash took the opportunity to offer a little sisterly advice.

"You'll want to keep your distance from Jim," she suggested softly. "He's the boss's son, and he thinks he can do whatever he wants."

But Dash was wrong. Sally was not like Dot at all. She scoffed. "Don't tell me who I can or cannot talk with. If you can't keep your boyfriend under control, that's not my problem."

"My boyfriend? You've got me wrong, Sally. I'm just telling you because that fella's a whole heap of trouble wrapped up in shiny packaging. I'm trying to help."

Sally's reply was cool. "Duly noted." Her eyes fell to Dash's coverall, stained with grease. "Shouldn't you be working?"

At the end of the day, Sally sashayed past Dash's bay and right into Mr. Eisen's windowed office, giving Dash a complacent smile that confused her entirely. Trying to be discreet, Dash dropped to a squat behind the car she was working on.

"Why are they pointing at me?" she whispered.

Ginny's face was tight with alarm. "I don't know, but Mr. Eisen is standing up."

"What should I do?"

"I think we should make tracks. It's closing time anyway. Maybe he'll cool down by tomorrow morning. You ready?"

Dash put all her tools away in record time, pulled on her coat and boots, then she and Ginny almost ran toward the exit.

"Wilson! Thomas! Get over here!"

They froze. With no other options, they turned and walked back to Mr. Eisen's office, trying to ignore the other men's stares.

Mr. Eisen sat waiting behind his desk, a storm on his face. Sally stood pertly in the corner, arms crossed.

"You're done," he told them. "Pack up and go."

Ginny gasped, and all Dash's blood drained to her toes. "Sir?"

"Since day one, you girls have been a pain in the neck and a distraction to the rest of the garage. I was charitable. I gave you a warning, but it seems you can't help yourselves. Well, you've been nabbed. Time to go. I'll tell your major or chief Wren or whatever it is she calls herself."

Dash stood at attention as she'd been trained, scrambling for some sort of dignity in her confusion.

Ginny vibrated beside her. "I'm sorry, sir. I don't understand."

As slow as cold molasses, Mr. Eisen lifted his bulk off his chair and set his hands flat on his desk. "Anyone stupid enough to steal from me ain't getting another chance."

"Steal?" they cried as one.

"Don't flash those eyes at me, missy. Sally here heard you talking about the missing petty cash, which is something you shouldn't have even known about."

Dash and Ginny exchanged a glance, horrified. "No, Mr. Eisen. We would never—"

He looked directly at Dash. "Then she found it, hidden rather poorly at your bay."

Stunned, she stared at Sally, who was inspecting her nails, hiding a smile.

"Why, you little sneak!" Ginny took a step toward Sally.

"That's enough." Mr. Eisen blocked her way. "Both of you get out. Don't come back."

"Mr. Eisen, we would never—"

"Get out!" he roared, not blinking.

The Wrens had taught Dash not to flinch in the face of such fury, but it was difficult. Back then, it had been *Yes, Chief Wren! No, Chief Wren!* Standing before a man who was accusing Dot of being a thief was much more complicated, and her face burned with the effort of holding in her outrage. The rest of the garage had gone silent, and she knew they were all observing the girls' humiliation with interest.

"Mr. Eisen, we did not steal," Dash insisted.

"We would never steal," Ginny said.

"Oh yeah? More than one of my guys saw you. And I trust my guys. Always have. What I don't trust is some gussied-up grifters wasting my time and lying to me."

"We never lied to you," Dash said. "We never lied to anyone. Your spoiled, horrible son set us up, didn't he?"

"Or it's all the other fellas, leering at us, making us feel like dirt every time we walked in," Ginny added. "We're the best mechanics in here, but you'd never know it, how we're treated."

At least Mr. Eisen had the courtesy to hesitate at that. But it didn't change his mind. With no other option, the girls turned toward the door and strode across the garage, heads held high. It was only when they were outside that they burst into tears.

nineteen

DOT

-•• --- -

— Moncton, New Brunswick —

Dot and Alice stood at attention with four other Wrens in the wood-panelled office of Chief Wren Alder. Their new boss was tall and slim as the tree in her name, with a no-nonsense look about her narrow face. Dot's old anxieties began to surface, then she reminded herself that she was no longer a student. She and Alice were now employees of special wireless station HMCS Coverdale. They were now the experts.

"After having seen the impressive results of your training," Chief Wren Alder said, "we are pleased to have you join us at HMCS Coverdale. Here we will be utilizing your skills to end this war."

Dot's confidence swept back in, along with a healthy dose of anticipation.

"Before we begin, there is something of great importance that you must understand, and with which you must comply if you are to remain here."

In her periphery, Dot saw Alice turn her head slightly, no doubt checking her reaction, but Dot refused to look over. This place could offer many opportunities to prove herself, and Dot didn't want to jeopardize any of them. She wanted to make a good impression right away.

Chief Wren Alder walked around her desk, and her long fingers closed around a piece of paper covered in type. "At HMCS Coverdale, we are engaged in very important, top secret work." She held up the paper then spoke deliberately to each of the girls, every syllable crystal clear. "This document is the 'Official Secrets Act.' To work here, each of you must swear an oath of secrecy that will remain in place for a minimum of forty years. You will be an important cog in the war machine and a potential keeper of extremely dangerous secrets. By signing this document, you swear never to speak with anyone about any part of your work. Not your family, not your boyfriend, not the girl sitting beside you. Not even me. You will play a vital role here; however, no one but you will ever know what you are doing."

From the silence, Dot could tell the other girls were just as stunned as she.

"In case you are wondering if this is serious or not, I assure you, it is crucial. Sharing secrets, whether purposefully or accidentally, would be regarded as treason."

Dot's blood ran cold. *Treason.*

Chief Wren Alder showed no change in her expression as she hammered in the last nail. "And as I am certain you already know, treason is punishable by death."

Now Dot glanced at Alice. She could practically hear her friend's thoughts. They were the same as hers, she imagined. Keep secrets from her family? Never in her life had Dot considered lying to Dash or Gus or her parents or anyone else. Could she do that?

"Excuse me, Chief Wren," Alice said, her voice unusually meek. "Our families and friends will wonder where we are and what we're doing. How are we to answer them?"

"You must help them believe that your position is a very dull one. You take dictation, you type reports, you get coffee for your boss, and you pass on unimportant memorandums. You will convince them that there is nothing exciting in your life."

The room was still as Chief Wren Alder gave the women a moment to decide what to do with the rest of their lives, and to sort through a lifetime of emotions from before this moment and after. Signing this oath would alter their lives forever. It would change the core of who they were. Dot would be forced to lie to everyone she loved until she was almost sixty years old.

It was back: the crippling anxiety that had gripped her for so many years. The impulse to escape the room shot through her veins, and the remedy was simple. All she had to do was tell these people she'd changed her mind, then she could race home to safety.

Or, she could keep her mouth shut and help save the world from a crazed dictator.

Practically every poster said it: LOOSE LIPS SINK SHIPS. The world was already knee-deep in secrecy. Why should Dot be excused from that? When she thought of the war, she pictured Fred and Gus. There was nothing she could do for Fred, but maybe by doing her job and keeping quiet about it, she could help keep Gus safe. That's what this oath was all about.

Gus's open expression returned to her, from that day long before when he'd said that she could change if she wanted to, but she didn't have to. He loved her either way, he'd said.

It was up to her.

From somewhere within her claustrophobic dome of panic, an unexpected strength rose. Her heart slowed, beating with purpose now. She would not run. She had come this far, and she had earned the privilege to do something important. She was being trusted in a position of such confidentiality that the word *treason* had been uttered. Yes, it would be difficult to hide the truth from her family, but by working in a special wireless station, she could make a real contribution.

Chief Wren Alder's black heels clicked on the wood floor. "Does anyone have a problem with signing this? You can tell me now, and there will be no penalties. You will simply be reassigned."

No one spoke, and Dot felt a weight lift from her shoulders. She was not alone.

"Excellent. Please raise your right hand and repeat after me," Chief Wren Alder said. "I, state your name, solemnly and sincerely swear . . ."

"I, Dorothy Lillian Wilson, solemnly and sincerely swear . . ."

Her mouth was as dry as the paper the Chief Wren held, and her pulse pounded like a drum in her throat. The moment Dot signed that paper, no one would know where she was or what she was doing. It was for all the right reasons, but it was the hardest thing she'd ever done.

". . . so help me God."

I'm sorry, Dash.

She pressed the tip of her pen to the paper, and the ink curled and crossed as she signed, *Dorothy Lillian Wilson.*

Looking at her signature, Dot felt a shift within. Months earlier, she had trembled in fear when her sister even hinted that she might leave home without her. She had never imagined she might one day do that herself. Then she'd worked her way up through sheer determination and a refusal to fail. Now this.

Nothing in Dot's world would ever be the same.

But she was no longer afraid. Never again would she wait for someone else to take care of things, because she understood now that she could do it herself.

She set down her pen and stood straight again, ready to fight.

twenty
DASH

—————————————

— Oshawa, Ontario —

"Merry Christmas, Mom!"

Dash gave her mother a big smile, but she knew she looked a sight, standing in the doorway of their house. She'd lost her hat on the streetcar, and the blizzard had turned her hair into a melting drift. Her scarf hung loose around her neck, and though her cheeks were cheerfully red from the cold, she knew her eyes looked dog-tired. She'd been up all night, unsure what to tell her parents.

Her mother blinked. "Well, Merry Christmas to you, too! What are you doing here? We didn't expect you for two more weeks. Come in, come in, before you catch your death out there. Oh, let me have a look at you."

Dash stepped inside and took off her boots, not wanting to track in snow. As she set down her suitcase, she took in the familiar kitchen and was surprised by a hot push of tears behind her eyes. How could it feel so good to be home, and yet make her want to disappear out of humiliation?

Her mother took her coat. "I'm so happy to see you. But was I wrong? Weren't you coming in about two weeks?"

I failed, Mom. I was fired. "Yes, that was the plan, but things changed, so I thought I'd come home early. I hope that's all right." She'd have to explain, but not yet. Her fingers went reflexively to the high neckline of her new turtleneck. She'd bought it especially, wanting to hide any bruises. "Where's my hug?"

She escaped further conversation by agreeing with her mother that she looked tired, then she hauled her suitcase to her bedroom. When she pushed open the door, she felt even worse, because the room looked so empty without her sister in it. Dropping her bag, she went to her bed and sat, her back to the wall, knees hugged to her chest.

Dot would know everything soon. Dash had written to her the night she was fired. She'd told her about Jim and the awful helplessness she'd felt, then about Mr. Eisen's accusation, and the way he'd roared *Get out!* so furiously that the hair on her neck had stood on end. She had told her everything. She had to. She never kept secrets from her sister.

Oh, what she would give to have Dot here. Writing a letter was one thing, but feeling Dot's hug and hearing her sister's cautious encouragement was completely different.

There was a tap on the door. "I'll wake you in an hour, all right? Aunt Lou and Uncle Bob are coming for dinner, and I know they'll be happy to see you."

"Thank you, Mom," Dash called back, then she lay down, just as she'd said she would.

She and Ginny had gone to speak with their supervising Wren and explained everything. After some thought, she told the girls they could take some time off for Christmas, but they were expected to return to her office in January for a new posting. From there, they reluctantly said goodbye to Mary, then they'd gone their separate ways. Everything would be solved in the new year. For now, Dash needed her family. How strange that the very house she'd wanted to leave behind had been the one destination she'd run to when it all went wrong.

She awoke to her mother's gentle knock, feeling woozy, as if she'd slept for days. Pulling her turtleneck back over her head, she caught a glimpse of her reflection in the mirror and flinched. Melted snow, her pillow, and a deep sleep had left one side of her head flat and the other side wild. Her only option was to tie it all back or wear a hat. Hats weren't permitted inside, so she reached for a hairbrush.

"They'll still love you," she assured her reflection, tying a ribbon. She gave her cheeks a pinch for colour. "They'll be disappointed, but they'll still love you."

She couldn't remember too many times in the past when she'd been reluctant to leave her room to face the music. Maybe once, when she was twelve and had broken her mother's vase by throwing a ball indoors with Gus. Oh, and once when she was seventeen. She and Gus had wanted to go to a dance without permission, and she'd gotten caught sneaking out the window with his help. Tonight felt even worse somehow, even though none of it was her fault.

"Well, well, well!" Uncle Bob was the first to spot Dash coming down the stairs, and his happiness boomed through the house. "Isn't this a treat!"

"Margaret!" Aunt Lou said, holding out her arms for a hug. "A delightful surprise!"

Dash looked to her father for his gentle smile and it calmed her a little.

"Your mother said you were home. I'm glad." He held her tight enough that she felt the outline of bones in his shoulders. "We missed you."

Sharing supper with them felt wonderful. She was happy to tell them all about Ginny and Mary, and they laughed, hearing about Mrs. Pidgett and the Pigeon Coop. She described Eisen's Garage but kept the description brief, not yet brave enough to say anything further.

"And what about Dorothy?" Aunt Lou asked. "What is her latest news?"

"Last I heard, she's training at Saint-Hyacinthe. They specialize in wireless telegraphy, radar, and coding."

A special sort of pride lit up Dash's father's expression, and she saw a little more colour in his cheeks. He knew better than any of them how much a placement in this field would mean to Dot.

Her mother beamed. "All the things she loves."

The awkward quiet that followed told Dash she hadn't fooled anyone. After she finished eating, she folded her napkin and set it on the table.

"You've all been very patient," she said. "Now that we've celebrated Dot's well-earned success, I think it's time I tell you that I'm in the opposite position. I was fired."

There was a momentary silence, then their shock melted to disbelief. *No, not you, Margaret*, they all insisted. *They must have made a mistake.*

"It wasn't a good place for me," she hedged. "The boss's son, he, uh . . ." She dropped her gaze to her lap, trying to get past the swelling in her throat, then she raised her chin. Burning with shame, she rolled down her turtleneck to reveal the marks Jim had left behind. "He wanted . . . He tried to take something from me that I wasn't willing to give."

She'd thought that she was strong enough to handle what had happened, that she could just get past what he'd done as if someone had tossed an insult, but saying it out loud, she felt the force of his arm on her neck again, the push of his mouth against hers, and her desperate need to escape.

Everyone at the table exclaimed in horror, then her mother was at her side, holding her.

"N-nothing happened," she whispered as her embrace tightened. "I'm all right."

Over her shoulder she saw her father staring at her, shocked.

"I'm all right, Dad." She let go of her mother so she could see them all. "When I wouldn't . . . play along, he told his father lies about me. They called me a thief and a 'gussied-up grifter,' and told me to go. So I left."

"'Gussied-up grifter,'" Uncle Bob said with disgust. "Best mechanic he ever had is more like it."

"I am so sorry, sweetheart," her aunt said, her hands clenched under her chin.

Her father's eyes shone. "Margaret."

"You can't always protect me, Dad," she replied, reading his helplessness. "I'm all grown up. I have to take care of myself now."

"What will you do next?" her uncle asked.

"Not yet, Bob," Aunt Lou scolded.

"No, no. It's all right," Dash said. "I have to report back in January, and the Wrens will tell me. I don't know if I'll ever get to do mechanic work again, but I'm sure there will be something."

"I saw something that I think might interest you. It was in the paper." Uncle Bob turned to her father. "Do you have last Saturday's edition?"

Nodding, he left the room then returned with *The Oshawa Daily Times.* Uncle Bob muttered to himself as he flipped through the pages.

"Aha! Here we go."

He folded the paper so one article was easy to see, then he handed it to Dash.

"Elsie MacGill, Queen of the Hurricanes" was the headline.

Dash frowned at the article. "Who's Elsie MacGill?"

"Oh! I've heard of her!" her mother exclaimed. "She's Canadian, from Vancouver. She was a Woman of the Year in 1940. Brilliant woman. Designed her own airplane, I think. Why? What's this all about?"

Dash began to read, and every sentence gave her a little boost of adrenaline. "This says she helped design the Hawker Hurricane, that slick new fighter plane I saw in a shorty before a movie the other night."

"Good for her," her mother said.

Uncle Bob pointed at the article. "Keep reading."

Dash knew the moment she had reached the part he wanted her to see. "She's . . . she's at a factory up at Fort William called the Canadian Car and Foundry Company. She's *in charge* of building hundreds of Hawker Hurricanes." She blinked at her mother. "She's the *boss*. And . . . and it says most of the factory workers are women."

"That'd be something. Work for a woman?"

"Work for a woman *and* build planes?" Dash closed her eyes, dreamy. "Just imagine."

"Why just imagine?" Uncle Bob asked. "Write to her tonight."

Somehow the dishes got washed, though Dash barely remembered doing them. Her mind was on Elsie MacGill, the fascinating woman in the paper. She read the article twice more, increasingly awed with every read. Miss MacGill had been the first woman admitted to the engineering program at the University of Toronto, then she'd taken a job in Michigan as a mechanical engineer with an automobile company. When she got interested in aircraft, she'd returned to school and become the first woman aeronautical engineer in the world. From there, she'd been hired as the chief aeronautical engineer at the Canadian Car and Foundry Company in Fort William, where she designed aircraft and eventually ran the Hurricane project. Dash could not imagine how a woman could have gotten so far in a man's world, but she wanted to know more.

When the others went into the living room to play bridge, Dash headed upstairs to the little table she also used as a vanity. She pulled out paper and a fountain pen then hesitated, an uneasy swirl of doubt building in her chest. What if she wasn't up to this? She felt so uncertain—so *unDash-like*—these days. If only Dot was here to talk her through it.

"You're not thinking logically, Dash," she would say. "What are you afraid of?"

Dash knew exactly what she was afraid of. Before last week, she hadn't known what it was, but then she'd faced Mr. Eisen's rage, and now she did. She'd failed. She'd never failed at anything in her life, and she never wanted it to happen again. What if she wrote to Miss MacGill, and she didn't want her? Dash had always been good at what she did, but what if she wasn't ready for the next level?

"*I* did it," the Dot in her head reminded her.

What an amazing girl her sister was. Despite every fibre of her shy little being fighting against the challenge, Dot the Dormouse had graduated from HMCS Conestoga and had been transferred to a specialized camp all about radios and coding and stuff she loved. She'd done all that by herself. Without Dash's help.

Working for Miss MacGill wasn't just what Dash wanted, she thought, curling her hands into fists. It was what she needed. And if Dot could beat her own paralyzing fear, why then, so could Dash. She picked up her pen, searching her memory for everything her high school English teacher had told them about writing formal letters, then she placed the tip of her pen onto the paper.

Dear Miss MacGill . . .

twenty-one
DOT
‐ •• ‐‐‐ ‐

— February 1943 —
Moncton, New Brunswick

D ot stared longingly across the white expanse of Coverdale's snow-covered field then returned her gaze to the hulking black shapes lurking by the fence. She shifted her boots in place, realizing her toes had hardened into frozen pebbles from standing in place for so long.

Was it her imagination, or had the creatures moved closer?

"Come on, Dot!" Alice was twenty feet ahead, her voice muffled behind a thick yellow scarf. The day-old snow reached the tops of her boots. "They're just cows!"

Technically, yes. Just cows. The sensible thing would have been for Dot to march alongside Alice as they crossed the vast field to get to the Huff Duff hut, keeping her gaze averted from the big animals. That would be the smart thing. But people were smart in different ways. Dot figured she was being pretty smart in her own way right now, staying cagey around the herd. They seemed more curious about her every time she passed this way.

"Dot!"

Alice was right, too, though. They couldn't afford to be late for their shift. This wasn't school any longer; they couldn't just run extra laps if they were tardy. A hundred and forty Wrens worked at Coverdale, trading off in three eight-hour shifts so there was never a moment when the radios were left unmonitored.

Most of the girls disliked the graveyard shift, but Dot preferred it. At night, the cows were tucked safely away in the barn. Now she slid a tentative boot into the indent Alice had already made in the snow, her eyes on the bovines. As if on cue, all eight of them swung their thick black heads in her direction, blinking at Dot against the snowflakes on their lashes. She took one step, then another, heart pounding, then she broke into an awkward run, sprinting and stumbling through the deep snow, flailing her arms for balance.

When at last she reached Alice, her friend was doubled over with laughter. "Well done. You made it, matador. Let's go to work now."

When they reached it, Alice tugged the door to the hut open with a grunt, freeing the ice from its hinges, and they stepped inside. The large room was mostly an open space, with a long table on either side. At each table, a dozen or so women hunched over their Marconi CSR5 receivers, searching frequencies for enemy signals.

Dot stomped her snowy boots at the entrance and stuffed her mitts in her pockets, but she kept her coat on. The girls on the midnight shift, who they were replacing, still wore theirs. Dot tiptoed to her assigned chair, eyes on the curly-haired girl she would soon relieve. She was leaning in, absorbed in a transmission she had caught, and her right hand was printing madly. The fingertips of her left hand barely touched the radio's dial, but Dot could tell she was ready to adjust it the slightest bit if the sound or voice in her headphones faded into static.

There could be no break between the girl leaving her post and Dot arriving. So when Dot arrived behind the seat, the girl turned up the volume and kept taking notes until Dot swooped in for the headphones. Assuming her warm chair, Dot picked up the message where the other girl had left off, and her workday began.

For eight hours straight, every day until she lost track, Dot and the other girls listened and wrote, shivering from the cold. No one was permitted to leave their radio during their shift unless she raised a hand to visit the lavatory. When they finished for the day—or night, depending on the shift—there was time for a quick meal in the mess hall, then they collapsed onto their beds and were snoring before Dot could count to ten. Sixteen hours later, it all began again.

And yet, Dot's enthusiasm for the job never waned. Whenever she stepped into the HF/DF hut, her body buzzed with anticipation.

Every ship in the world was able to broadcast messages, and each message could be caught and intercepted by a focused hunter like Dot. The trickiest part was singling out a lone dit dit dah among a literal sea of dits and dahs. Ironically, the regimented systems of the Germans had made that task a little less difficult. Their U-boats were positioned within a grid system, a large rendering of which was posted on the wall of the hut. Twice a day, Grand Admiral Dönitz ordered the submarines to surface and report their location, weather reports, and other nonemergency information, all in under thirty seconds. Every time a U-boat checked in, Dot and the other listeners swiftly located it in the grid. From there, they could search for the frequency on which it was broadcasting. The submarine's bearings were teletyped to Ottawa, then to England, where the people in charge could take whatever evasive or aggressive action the situation warranted.

Dot was made for this: listening, translating, thinking like the wind. The work fueled her mind like nothing ever had. It gave her great pleasure to know that the enemy underestimated the power, speed, skill, and determination of the young women at Coverdale. The young women nobody talked about.

And yet, despite Dot's confidence in her abilities, some moments still caught her off guard. She got satisfaction from recognizing specific transmitter operators by their idiosyncrasies, such as their word choices or keying rhythms, but she never got comfortable with the occasional blast of a human voice, joining or overlaying the monotone dits and dahs. The mechanical sounds were no more than a puzzle to her, but the voices— whether German, American, British, or any other nationality—reminded her that every signal came from an actual person. Somewhere out there, someone's son or brother was in danger.

The Wrens never shared the actual messages they'd intercepted, but sometimes they chatted over supper about familiar voices. Dot usually stayed out of those conversations, but Alice tried to bring her in. She'd told Dot that she had a wonderful sense of humour, and that she needn't be so shy. At first, Dot had scoffed, a little hurt by Alice's teasing, but Alice assured her that she wasn't joking.

"You have to talk more, Dot," she'd said. "You are hilarious, but nobody knows it except me."

One night at supper Alice decided to prove her point. She asked Dot in front of everyone if she had heard from the Menace lately.

Dot was taken off guard. "The Menace?"

"He's German, but he speaks in English," Alice said, giving her a wink of encouragement. They'd talked about him before, but just between them. "You know him. He talks directly to us, trying to scare us."

Dot cast a glance at their coworkers, uncertain. "The Menace? Oh yes, I heard him the other day." Normally, hearing voices bothered her, but the Menace didn't. In her mind, he was more of a caricature than a man.

"Oh?" Alice asked coyly. "What did he say?"

Sucking back her natural reserve, Dot dropped her voice and sharpened her words into a German accent. "Hello, listeners! Ve are here in U-boat and ve are coming to kill you!'"

Surprised to hear Dot playing like that, the girls laughed so loud the room rang with it, and Dot warmed through. Alice lifted a sassy eyebrow. *Told you so!*

Later that night, as Alice settled into the bunk over her head, Dot's mind returned to the discussion in the mess hall.

"It must really annoy the Menace and his fellow Germans, not knowing if we hear what they're saying," she said.

Her friend shifted above her, rocking the bunk as she got comfortable. "What would you say to them if you could transmit? Do you ever think about that? I mean, they're the enemy and all, but really, they're just men from another country, doing what our men are doing. Sometimes I hear shouting, but it's not clear enough to translate. I wonder what they're saying."

Dot had asked herself the same question many times. Every so often, she longed to reach out to those under fire and answer the most terrible broadcasts. To offer some sort of comfort. Like the American pilot who screamed as his plane plunged earthbound in a helpless spiral. Or the strangled voice of a German sailor in a doomed U-boat, screaming for mercy that would never come. The boundaries between countries and nationalities blurred at times like that. So many times she'd listened with tears in her eyes and questioned the horror of it all.

"I think," she said quietly, "we already know. Fear sounds the same in any language."

twenty-two
DASH

—————————————————

— *Fort William, Ontario* —

Thank goodness Dash had listened to her mother when she'd told
her to dress warmly for Fort William's northern climate, and not
to forget her winter boots. The drive from Dash's hotel to the massive
Canadian Car and Foundry Company buildings was dicey at best. Her
driver, a serious young man named Charlie, blasted through snowdrifts
and fishtailed over icy roads. A couple of times she wondered if she might
have to get out and push the car out of the snow, but somehow they survived. As Charlie bumped against the sidewalk and parked, Dash told
herself that if she got the job, one of the first things she would do was
offer him driving lessons.

The snow had stopped for now, thank goodness, and the sky was a
blinding blue over a soft white world. Sunshine beamed straight down
from heaven and twinkled on the frozen surface. The day was far too
beautiful for anything to go wrong, she told herself, so as she waited in
the back seat of the car for Charlie to open the door, Dash smiled with
optimism. He'd told her that part of his job was to open the door for her,
so *please, miss, stay put.* It was charming, really. Through her window,
Dash watched him labour around the car through knee-deep snow, yank
the door open through a drift, then he saw her safely to the sidewalk.

As he lurched back to the driver's seat, she heard him mutter something about the stupidity of living in northern Canada in the winter, then he shut himself within and turned on the engine.

Dash turned and gawked at the huge building before her, struggling to believe that another one of the same size loomed behind it. The two of them had originally been constructed to house a half-dozen wooden-hulled, steel-framed trawlers, since CanCar, as Charlie called it, had built ships for the French Navy to use as minesweepers in the last war. Prior to that, the company's first factory, located in Montreal, had produced railway cars. Now they built and contained an entire fleet of Hawker Hurricanes. These people knew what they were doing, and Dash wanted to be a part of that.

Everything about being here was a thrill. On the train ride to Fort William, Dash had read up on the planes until she knew all she could. In addition to impressing the interviewer with her knowledge, she planned to keep her eyes peeled—maybe she'd see a Hurricane today. If she was lucky, she might even meet the legendary Miss Elsie MacGill herself.

Charlie must have misunderstood her hesitation on the sidewalk, because he stuck his head out the window and pointed. "That's the entrance over there."

She waved her thanks then headed in that direction. Once inside, she was swallowed up by an echoing cavern with high ceilings and cement walls. Twenty feet away she spotted a desk, behind which sat one of the prettiest women Dash had ever seen. On her desk was a small sign that read MISS ROSE.

"Good morning," Dash said quietly, then she cleared her throat and tried again. *This is no time to be shy*, she reminded herself. "My name is Margaret Wilson. I'm here for a job interview."

The woman consulted a page before her, her lips pursed. "I have no such appointment listed here."

"Oh, but you must," Dash insisted, her face burning. "I received a letter, and, well, the company even sent Charlie in the car for me. He drove me from the train to the hotel last night. He just dropped me here . . ."

The woman was unimpressed. She glared at Dash with perfectly made-up eyes. "I do not have any appointments for Margaret Wilson."

Dash couldn't help thinking of what Dot would have said at this point. *Of course her name is Rose. A beautiful face with a thorny disposition.*

"Obviously there's been some sort of misunderstanding," Dash said, slightly panicked. "I'm—Oh, wait." She almost laughed, realizing her mistake. "How about Dash Wilson?"

Miss Rose checked the paper. "Yes. Please take a seat."

She bustled past Dash and knocked on a door while Dash clenched her hands in her lap. She had spoken with her Wren supervisor before coming, and the woman had been very understanding. If Dash passed the interview, the Wrens would simply transfer her to CanCar. If not, they would find something suitable for her in January. This interview meant everything to Dash.

A moment later, another woman appeared in the open doorway. Her short black hair was rolled neatly back, and all her weight was braced on two metal canes. Dash shot to attention as she'd been taught back at HMCS Conestoga, stunned that she now stood before Miss Elsie MacGill. Fifteen years ago, just before Miss MacGill had graduated from the University of Toronto, she'd been struck by polio, and the disease had ruined one of her legs. She could have quit working right then, but from what Dash had read, that idea had not fit into Elsie's plan. Despite doctors' warnings, she hadn't let her disability slow her down.

She observed Dash through intelligent eyes. "At ease, Miss Wilson. Thank you for coming. Won't you please come in?"

Speechless, Dash trailed her into a large office. Her knees wouldn't stop knocking with nerves, so she was relieved when she was offered a seat.

"I liked your letter." Miss MacGill remained standing, but she leaned back against her desk, facing Dash. "Tell me more about yourself. I saw that you have worked a great deal on automobiles. Do you feel you are qualified to translate that into airplane engines?"

It took a moment before Dash could find her voice, then she

couldn't stop talking. "I got to know the basics of airplane engines a few years back when I worked with my uncle on his. Granted, that was only a Jenny—I'm sorry, a Curtiss JN-4, not a Hawker Hurricane, but still . . ." She took a breath then dove back in. "Since then, I have read everything I can find on airplane engines, comparing them to automobiles and adding to my knowledge. I'd love to show you what I can do if you'd give me a chance."

"What is it about engines that grips you?"

"To be honest, Miss MacGill, flying is my real passion. I enjoy the challenge of solving mechanical problems, and I'm always happy to get my hands greasy, but working on plane engines brings me closer to flying. I'm keen to help out with test flying, if that opportunity were ever to present itself—in addition to mechanical duties," she quickly added.

"Very interesting. I never learned to fly myself; however, I accompanied pilots on test flights of the aircraft I worked on." Miss MacGill straightened. "Follow me, if you would."

She led Dash through a pair of double doors into a brightly lit hangar that seemed to go on forever. Beneath its towering ceiling was a world unto itself, and Dash was so filled with wonder she could hardly breathe. The air was alive with the *zing!* of electric drills and the growls of riveters, and voices bounced off the floor. Dozens of Hawker Hurricanes were lined up down the middle of the enormous room, and as she walked between their noses, Dash inhaled grease and gas and everything else that she loved. The whole place bustled with men in coveralls.

Her step faltered, and she grinned. Just like she'd read, they weren't just men. Most were *women*, about her age.

At the end of the vast space was a partially disassembled airplane, and Dash's heart lodged in her throat as she recognized the challenge ahead. Until now, she had never seen a real Hurricane up close, but she'd read all about them. When she had told Uncle Bob that she had an interview at CanCar, he had magically produced an orange, thirty-six-page Hawker

Hurricane manual wrangled from a fellow flight instructor. Awed by what she held, she'd studied the pilot's notes in the book, including photographs.

Miss MacGill stopped beside the plane. "Tell me something about this aircraft, if you would."

"Of course," Dash said, swallowing her nerves. "The Hawker Hurricane was originally launched in 1937 and is the primary fighting plane of the Royal Air Force." She gazed up at the cockpit. "And she is absolutely beautiful."

"Specifics, please."

After all her studying, the answer came easily to Dash. "The Hurricane is thirty-two feet long, and her wings stretch forty feet from tip to tip. She has a powerful Rolls Royce Merlin V12 engine that I cannot wait to hear. She can take off carrying eighty-seven hundred pounds and can fly six miles per minute, which is about three-hundred fifty miles per hour. For battle, she carries up to eight Browning guns on her wings, and she can also carry up to four cannons plus a five-hundred-pound bomb."

"Excellent, Miss Wilson. You have done your research. Now, tell me about this engine."

Dash stepped eagerly toward the guts of the machine. "It's a four-cycle, liquid-cooled engine." Her palm skimmed the shiny pistons, each around fifteen pounds. "A V-12 with offset pistons, counter opposed."

"Why would they be like that?"

"Balance," Dash replied. "They're very heavy, and if they all moved at the same time, the weight would overwhelm the airplane."

"What are those?" Miss MacGill asked, indicating machinery farther back in the engine.

Dash didn't miss a beat. "That's a series of air-intake valves, part of the intake manifold. There isn't enough oxygen for a pilot at thirty-six thousand feet, which is the Hurricane's maximum altitude, so the engine compresses the air from the valves with super chargers, which are connected over here, to the drive line, producing greater air intake."

"Very good. Now, what if I were to ask you to change the oil on this airplane?"

"I'd be happy to. Do you use the newer mesh filters or fabric? I prefer the mesh, but I would obviously use whatever you prefer."

The corners of Miss MacGill's lips lifted ever so slightly. "I'll tell you what. I like your eagerness and your attention to detail. You're hired. See Miss Rose about the paperwork and arranging accommodation." She winked. "And those test flights you mentioned? Give me some time, and I'll see what I can arrange."

twenty-three

DOT

D ot took her fingers off the dial and scowled at the letters she'd just written, spotting a pattern. She was positive they were the same letters she'd written yesterday and the day before, transmitted over the span of the same three hours, and on the same frequency. This could be a standard greeting, like the one she'd identified at Saint-Hyacinthe, but she had a feeling it was something very different this time.

First of all, it was a mechanical transmission. The rhythm and speed were the exact same every time. Second, though she was there to listen, not decrypt, she had done it anyway, and it translated into a statement that intrigued her. Third, and strangest of all, she sensed another pattern behind it, like an echo of sorts. She hadn't heard anything like that before.

Dot's supervisor, Petty Officer Wren Douglas, was a little older than Dot, and she had not spoken with her at all before now. She glanced over, surprised to see Dot's hand up.

"You need the lavatory?"

"No, thank you." Dot handed over her notes. "I want to show you this."

"'Fear light not sound,'" the woman read quietly, squinting at the print. "What's this?"

"Some sort of code. It's being transmitted by a machine."

"How can you tell?"

"Because the message is perfect every time. The spacing and the lengths." Alice's words drifted onto her lips. "Human beings are never perfect."

"Good work. Treat this as a frequency marker."

Dot had already been doing that, using the transmission as a fixed reference for finding other signals. That was simple enough. She was more concerned about the secondary message she was hearing. It seemed to be quietly tagged onto the first, and done in such a way that they should not have appeared connected. Because of the way they overlapped, and how the patterns wound through each other, Dot did not believe it was by accident.

"I already did that; however, I feel like there's more to it."

The supervisor tutted. "Don't let codebreaking interrupt your work. You are here as a listener only."

Telling Dot to stop puzzling something out was like asking the sun to stop shining. Something inside told her this was important. When she slipped her headphones on again, she searched specifically for the same transmission, feeling confident since she'd heard it three times in the past two hours.

There. The original, and just beyond . . . a different cipher. Dot wrote them both down, then she memorized them for later. She wasn't allowed to take her work back to the dormitory with her, but no one needed to know that her memory was nearly photographic.

After she finished her shift, she headed back to the barracks and grabbed a piece of stationery. She flopped onto her bed, and her pencil immediately recalled every letter she'd memorized.

"Coming to supper?" Alice asked, breezing past her on the way to the mess hall.

"Bring me a roll, if you would," Dot said, not looking up.

"What's that?"

Dot slapped her hand over the paper. She didn't want anyone

knowing she'd brought her work outside of the hut. Not even Alice. That would be a major offence. "Nothing."

Alice looked intrigued. "Must be a pretty important letter home. All right. I'll see what I can smuggle back here for you."

Three hours later, Dot bolted upright. The paper was covered from corner to corner with hundreds of letters that would have appeared random to anyone else. Just when she'd been about to quit, the letters had given up their secret, lifting magically from the page and settling into perfect alignment. And now she knew. She checked her watch. It was an hour before lights out, but this message could not wait until tomorrow. She got out of bed, pulled on her shoes, and stuffed the paper inside her blouse.

"Eat," Alice barked from her bunk. "I brought you a perfectly good roll hours ago. You'll turn into a skeleton if you don't eat something." She narrowed her eyes. "A skeleton who looks like she's hiding something."

Dot had been so focused on her work she hadn't noticed Alice deliver the bread. "Thanks, Alice. You're a sport."

Eating the roll as she went, Dot ran out of the dormitory and over to the Administration Building, where a few lights were still on. She made a beeline for Chief Wren Alder's office.

"Dot! This is a surprise," the chief Wren exclaimed, rising from behind her desk. "I thought you'd be fast asleep by now."

"No, ma'am. Um, I . . ."

It struck her suddenly that she shouldn't be here. In her excitement at breaking the cipher, she'd forgotten the rules.

Whatever happened in the hut stayed in the hut.

Chief Wren Alder saw right through her. "What is it, Dot? What have you done?"

"I, uh, figured something out. And I thought you should see it before morning."

"Are you talking about something you heard today? Because that should have been passed along through your supervisor. You know you're not permitted to tell me about it."

Dot couldn't stop now. She reached into the neck of her blouse and retrieved the folded piece of paper.

"It's . . . it's a cipher. I did speak with Petty Officer Wren Douglas in the hut. I told her that there was a mechanically produced cipher and that I had decrypted it. She told me to use it as a frequency marker, and I did. But there was a second, nonmechanical message camouflaged behind the first. It was barely audible, but it overlapped and was very specific. I decrypted it as well, and . . . and I'm sorry I didn't follow protocol, and I know I'm not supposed to be a codebreaker, but the message is important. From the way they tried to disguise it, I knew it would be, and it is."

Chief Wren Alder held her gaze for a full thirty seconds, then nodded. "Show me."

Dot set out the paper and began to explain how she had decoded the messages, and the chief Wren watched closely, following every stroke of her pencil. The carefully crafted code within a code spelled out very clearly that the Germans were planning an aggressive blockade to target a convoy of the Canadian Merchant Navy on the St. Lawrence River. It was planned for one week from that day.

Dot was not privy to how many ships would have been in that convoy, but based on history she had overheard, it could be a dozen or so. The food, supplies, equipment, and personnel they would be carrying was worth its weight in gold to the Allied forces waiting across the ocean. The urgency had come from Dot recognizing that a German "blockade" suggested a German "attack," which meant torpedoes. The SS *Caribou* by Port aux Basques had also been part of a convoy, and Dot had never forgotten that tragedy. If this blockade was allowed to occur, it could claim hundreds of lives.

After a pause, the Chief Wren picked up the paper. "May I?"

"Of course."

She folded the page neatly back into its original shape. "Do you understand why you were not supposed to bring this work outside of the hut?"

Beads of sweat popped up on Dot's brow, reminding her that she hadn't put on her hat before she'd sped to the chief Wren's office. Working on codes outside of the office, sharing work secrets, running around out of uniform . . . she had a sinking feeling she'd really done it this time. And yet it was impossible to feel guilty about the message she had brought. By breaking the rules, she might have stopped an attack.

When had Dot become the kind of woman who saw the justification behind breaking rules?

She exhaled. "Yes, Chief Wren. All of this is top secret, and by taking it from my desk, I could have exposed it to others. The truth is, no one could have seen it. The code was in my head. I can still see it plain as day. I've always been able to do that. And the page you're holding, well, I . . ." She blushed. "I carried it in my brassiere. No one would ever think to check there."

Chief Wren Alder's shoe tapped on the floor as she regarded Dot. "Do you enjoy this work, Petty Officer Wren Wilson?"

"Oh, yes, ma'am! I can't imagine anything I'd be better suited for. Listening, playing with ciphers when I have an opportunity, oh, I could never tire of it." She twisted her mouth to the side, concerned. "I hope I haven't just messed everything up. Have I?"

Her superior's expression relaxed. "You have not. You broke a number of rules, but it appears you had a very good reason for doing it. You went above and beyond your job description, and this vital act will not go unnoticed, I guarantee you. I will bring this to those in charge tonight, just as you did." She reached out and cupped Dot's elbow. "Dot, you should know that with this message, you may have saved many, many lives."

Dot was not prepared for the wave of emotion that washed over her in that moment. For so long, she had tried not to think too hard about the individual people who could be harmed or killed because of the messages she heard transmitted every day. The Freds and Guses she would never see.

Now she stood tall and recalled the conversation she'd had with her father on the day she'd decided to sign up. How his expression had lit up, remembering that he had done some good. Dot had just experienced the pride he'd felt, up there in the sky, signaling the enemy's whereabouts. She loved that she could share that emotion with him.

If only she could tell him about it.

Not everything about working at HMCS Coverdale was ideal. Even Dot could admit that. It was difficult, being stuck for hours in a cold room with no input from the outside world. The work—though she loved it—was draining, the hours demanding. On the bright side, the food was all right, the accommodations better than they'd had at Saint-Hyacinthe, and the more confident she became with all her successes, the more friends she made.

But it came at a very steep price. With all her heart, she wanted to share these special moments with her family. With Dash. With Gus. Because as rewarding as this experience was on her own, their approval and encouragement would have made everything so much more meaningful.

The next day at lunch, Alice joined Dot in the mess hall. "So? Are you going to tell me about last night's secret?"

"Can't," Dot said, swallowing a spoonful of soup.

Alice narrowed her eyes, but Dot didn't mind. Everyone understood the secrecy surrounding their jobs. Alice wouldn't force her to say anything.

Just then, Joyce, one of Alice's friends, entered with a bag slung over her arm. "Mail's here!"

All the mail sent to and from Coverdale, as well as other secret offices—Dot assumed theirs wasn't the only one—was sent to a common central address in Toronto: 25 King Street, Room 1145. Anyone could write to Dot there, but the letters were redirected after that, so no one knew where she really was.

Joyce pulled out a few envelopes. "Alice, your boyfriend wrote . . . Dot, here's one from your sister, and something from command . . ."

Every time Dot received a letter from Dash, her stomach swirled with both joy and guilt. She still felt the vacuum left behind by her departure, though the pain of missing her had eased over her months of training and working with the Wrens. She lived for Dash's letters and all the news she sent. All of her words were open and honest and brimming with satisfaction in her job. And they told the truth.

Unlike Dot, Dash didn't have to lie to her sister.

For now, Dot set aside her sister's letter and opened the other envelope, which bore a symbol of the WRCNS in the top left corner. Inside was a short directive that made her blood run cold.

Petty Officer Wren D. Wilson to attend Captain J. Powell's office at 0900 tomorrow.

With her pulse hammering, she slipped the paper back into the envelope, not bothering to look at Dash's note. The night before, Chief Wren Alder had said Dot did the right thing, coming to her with the decryption, but they both knew Dot had broken some major rules. The chief Wren then shared Dot's information up the chain, and that would have been impossible to do without revealing the fact that Dot had broken protocol. She'd broken the oath of secrecy, and she'd been warned of the punishment for doing that. In the morning, she would receive her sentence.

twenty-four
DASH

— Fort William, Ontario —

Dash was one of over four thousand people employed at CanCar, of which more than half were women. Some were married and went home at night, but the single gals were boarded in various homes around Fort William. Dash stayed in a little house near the centre of town. Her landlady, Mrs. Simmons, was an old prude. Kind of like Pigeon, but bigger and more obvious. She was always tutting around, shaking her head with disapproval.

"Girls working in a factory. You should be ashamed," she griped that morning as Dash finished her breakfast. "It's wrong. In my day—"

"In your day, there were still horses and buggies on the streets," Dash replied, sipping carefully and observing her landlady over the brim of her cup of tea. "Why shouldn't we be helping to win the war? Please explain this to me. What makes women so special?"

"It's a man's place to fight in a war. Women should be at home. That's the way it's always been, and there's no reason to change it."

"I think it's time you recognized that the world's a different place these days, Mrs. Simmons."

"Don't be cheeky, young lady."

"We should all help in our own way. I mean, you are already."

"What's that supposed to mean?"

"You're letting me rent a room here, which means you're helping me, and by doing that, you're helping CanCar." She bit down on a smile. "See? It's not so bad."

Her landlady's gaze dropped to Dash's navy-blue coveralls. "Ladies do not wear trousers. It's indecent, is what it is."

Dash couldn't resist. "Did I tell you I have flown a plane before? By myself. While wearing trousers." She closed her eyes, remembering Jenny, then she reached for her coat. "It was glorious. Have a nice day, Mrs. Simmons."

Dash took a bus to work. The most interesting part of the ride was squinting at the dark profile of Mount McKay in the distance, but CanCar was the best place to work in the whole world, so she didn't mind. There, she was surrounded by airplanes, she worked with engines, and she learned new skills, like riveting the planes' sheet metal skins. Plus, she got paid better than she ever had before, though still not as much as the men in the factory. Icing on the cake was that she got to work with a lot of smart women, some of whom shared her obsession with planes. She had made friends at Conestoga and had loved being with Ginny and Mary in Toronto, but CanCar was the first place where Dash truly felt she belonged.

Monday to Friday, she joined her crew on the latest project, a Hurricane that was about three quarters done. What a thrill it was to watch an aircraft take shape. When she'd arrived that morning, she had pulled on her welding helmet and wrestled an acetylene torch to solder the frame. In the afternoon she was in a cooler position, attaching canvas to the wings, readying the plane for a dope coat tomorrow. The dope, she had learned, was what protected and sealed the fabric.

"These men, they think they know it all, eh?"

That was Margie, a spunky little mechanic from Quebec. She always had a bone to pick with somebody, and Dash got a kick out of her. Her name was actually Marie Marguerite, but the girls had all decided that was too many syllables. Margie didn't seem to mind the change.

"What happened this time?" Dash asked.

"That McMurtry, he says he can do this better than us."

Stacy glanced over. "Yeah, well, men *don't* know it all, and we don't need them." Stacy reminded Dash a little bit of Ginny, with her nimble fingers and quick one-liners, except Ginny had straight blond hair, and Stacy's was thick and brown. "Don't tell them, though. They'll just mope around like my uncle Harry. That man. If I ever saw him laugh, I've seen a cow fly, too."

Dash peered up from under the wing, a couple of nails squeezed between her lips. Out of the corner of her mouth she said, "We'd better build up this hull if there are cows flying up there."

"This is 'ow you do this, this is 'ow you do that," Margie mimicked, still fuming.

Paulette, the fourth member of Dash's crew, was from New Brunswick, but she'd been living in Ontario for years. "Everybody knows women are steadier at welding," she put in.

"Then there's the fact that we show up for work every day," Dash said. "You ever met a man who shows up to work every day like we do?"

"If they do, they're late," Stacy agreed. She hammered a nail onto the wing, securing the fabric. "Speaking of showing up, are we going dancing tonight?"

"What kind of question is that?" Dash asked. "It's Wednesday night. That's what we do. I hope they bring that band back."

Stacy hit another nail. "Men are lousy to work with, but dancing without them is no fun at all."

After work, and after a quick bowl of Mrs. Simmons' surprisingly delicious tomato soup, Dash stepped into her polka dot skirt and swiped a little red on her lips. Dash loved working on planes, but she might have loved being a girl just a tiny bit more.

The Elks Hall was already hopping by the time the girls arrived, crowded with local mechanics, soldiers, and pilots on leave.

"Looks like the whole town is here tonight," Stacy bellowed into Dash's ear. She pointed at a couple doing a wild jitterbug in the middle of the floor, in front of a band. "Gosh, they're good."

All at once a familiar drumbeat filled the hall, and Dash's black-and-white Oxfords started tapping.

"'Sing! Sing! Sing!' I love this song," Stacy exclaimed, rocking her shoulders to the rhythm. "You gonna show us how it's done, Dash? You sure can dance."

"Depends on who's asking," Dash yelled back.

From out of the crowd emerged a couple of young dandies, their dark hair slicked back. They wore wide legged trousers, button-down shirts, and cocky smiles.

"I bet they're from the No. 102 Army Basic Training Centre here," Stacy said into Dash's ear.

The one with suspenders gave Dash his full attention. "Whadda you say? You two gonna bump gums all night, or are you looking to cut a rug?"

How could she resist?

"Let's see if you can keep up," she sassed.

One hand on his shoulder and the other in his, Dash flew around the room, having a ball. Her dance partner swung her out then spun her back, and her skirt flared in a dazzling polka dot circle. She kicked up her heels until she was dizzy and sweat rolled down her face. When the song ended, he kept one arm cinched around her waist.

"I'm heading out for a cigarette," he said, dark eyes still dancing. "Care to join me?"

She stiffened, then she instantly got annoyed with herself. This was a dance, she reminded herself. The whole point was to meet people and have fun. And yet when she looked at this likable fellow and read the invitation in his eyes, all she thought about was Jim. Dancing was one thing. She wasn't interested in anything else.

"No thanks," she replied with a smile. "But thanks for the dance."

"You sure? Can I buy you a drink then?"

If only she didn't feel this knot tightening in her stomach. He might have been fun. "I'm a dancer, not a dater," she told him, and yet she was aware of her own regret as she said it. "Any time you want to dance like that again, come find me."

Stacy waited for her at the side of the room. She held out a glass. "You look like you could use this."

"What is it?"

"Sidecar. Bartender knows how to make a good one."

While Dash gulped down the icy drink, grateful for the break, she watched a tall young man walk past. His blond hair was razored short, and his uniform was a muddy brown. It was impossible for Dash not to think of Gus. Especially here. Gus loved to dance. He'd written her only once since they'd bumped into each other on that snowy night, then his correspondence had stopped again. Dot hadn't heard from him, either. When Dash had told her she'd seen him just before Christmas, she'd sounded crushed to have missed him.

Dot would never have come to a dance like this, she thought. Too many people, too much noise, too much smoke. Instead, Dash would have found her in their bedroom, reading. Or scribbling in a crossword book.

She hesitated. Or would she? Dot's letters lately, while rather boring overall, had a different tone to them. A confidence she hadn't had before. She wrote about meeting people and making friends, even making them laugh on occasion. Wouldn't it be wonderful if one day she wrote to Dash and boasted that she'd been to a dance?

If Dash walked out the door right now and saw her there, what would their conversation be like? Thinking about that possibility brought on a wave of sadness that she'd been trying to ignore. The truth was, Dash felt separate from her sister these days, and it was more than just distance. Sure, Dot kept up her end of the letter writing, but everything she wrote was very much the same. Her job sounded dull, and Dash felt sorry for her. She deserved so much better. Then again, if Dot spent all day typing, like she said she did, maybe her letters were boring because she was simply tired of writing after a long day. That made sense. If only the two of them could escape for a day and talk like they used to. She imagined Dot craved that, too.

"Hey! Why so blue?" Stacy asked, returning with another sidecar.

Dash gave her head a shake. What was she doing, feeling lonely in this crowd? "Not blue at all. Just thinking."

"Thinking's not allowed here. Didn't anyone tell you that?"

"I thought there weren't any rules."

"Let's find some fellas to dance with," Stacy suggested.

Dash grinned, letting go of any lingering thoughts. "Look at those two gents over there, leaning against the bar. They look like they might know what they're doing. Shall we go see?"

Dash liked the look of them, so she gave one of the men the eye, arching a perfect black brow in a way she knew was irresistible. The men immediately pushed away from the counter and came toward the girls.

"Can we buy you a drink?" one of them asked.

"We wouldn't say no to that," Dash replied, though it was still difficult to mean it.

They had another drink then danced until Dash's voice was gone and her feet were blistered. At the end of the night, they all went their own ways, and when Dash fell into bed, she was smiling with contentment. The only way tonight could have been better was if Gus had been there. And Dot. Even Dot would have danced tonight.

twenty-five
DOT

-•• --- -

— *Moncton, New Brunswick*—

Dot stood at attention, shaking so hard from the top of her cap to the tips of her carefully polished shoes, she was almost dancing. Captain Powell was talking on the telephone, his back to her. When he turned and noticed her there, he waved her toward a seat. Now she sat very still in the hard wooden chair, her knees a foot from the edge of the captain's desk, her damp palms pressed firmly against her thighs.

Everything about this meeting made her apprehensive, from last night's summons to this echoing office with the intimidating caption behind the desk. Captain Powell was a thickset man, probably about fifty, with stubby fingers and strands of silver hair falling over his wide brow. Dot had heard someone say that he had an unpredictable sense of humour, but from the looks of it, he was not amused this morning.

Dot was not only nervous, she was disappointed in herself. She had tried so hard. She had sworn never, ever to fail. And yet she feared that's exactly what she'd done.

At last, the captain hung up the phone. "We simply cannot go forward in this business without obstacles, I have learned. One thing after another."

"Yes, sir."

"All right. Let's see about you." He inhaled through a bulbous nose, then flipped through a stack of papers. "Oh yes. I'm sorry to have kept you waiting. Let's discuss what you brought to your superior's office last night."

"I deeply regret my actions," Dot said, though she didn't at all.

"Do you?"

"Of course, sir. I broke the rules. Before you decide my fate, I would like to point out that I never told anyone anything directly."

The corner of his mouth twitched. "I see. Now, tell me about the rules you broke."

"I brought my work outside of the hut, and I shared it with my superior. Oh, and I ran through the building out of uniform."

"Yes, I did hear you were looking somewhat harried. You were lacking your hat."

Dot felt awful. "Yes, sir."

"I see you have it on this morning. Well done. Now. What about bringing your work out of the hut? How was that done, precisely?"

Was he smiling? He didn't appear angry, at least. "When I returned to my bunk I wrote everything down—"

"You copied it from your notes?"

"Oh no, sir! I would never take paper out of the hut. Everything was in my memory, sir. My mind takes pictures."

"Is that right?"

"Yes, sir. I could read that letter you have on your desk right now and repeat it back without looking."

He looked slightly uncomfortable about that and slid the paper to the side. "I see. Do you memorize everything?"

"That would be a waste of time, if I might say so. No. I memorize what interests me."

"And this transmission did."

"Yes, sir. I could hear the codes. I knew they were important by the way they were transmitted. It was more than a simple code or puzzle. It was a puzzle within another puzzle, then overlapped. It was very intriguing."

"Are you aware that your break in protocol possibly saved hundreds of lives?"

Dot didn't reply. She wasn't sure if this was a trick question. She was being reprimanded, was she not?

Captain Powell stacked several documents together then tapped the bottoms on his desk to straighten them. "I would like to clear something up to put you at ease. You did not technically remove work from your station, and you most definitely did not share information with anyone save your immediate superior. Therefore, no charges will be laid against you."

She gaped. "None? Oh, thank you, sir."

"Petty Officer Wren Wilson," he said, his head slightly tilted, "you are quite unique, aren't you?"

This was very confusing. Was that meant as a compliment, or was she back to elementary school, where she was the strange one? "I suppose, sir."

"Your qualities and capabilities are well documented, as are the glowing reports of your superiors regarding your character." He studied her then appeared to make a decision. "Therefore, I am in agreement with the recommendations of your senior officer. You will be transferred out of here first thing tomorrow."

All the air left her lungs. "Oh, please no, sir. I love it here."

"Yes, well, you misunderstand. You are being promoted to a position in Intelligence. Would that suit you?"

Dot's mouth fell open. "I'm sorry, Captain. I don't understand. Would you mind repeating that?"

"Intelligence. Transfer. Yes?"

She swallowed. "That's what I thought you said. Forgive me, Captain, but are we not already working in Intelligence here?"

"Of course. Listening is an extremely valuable cog in the war machine. Extremely valuable." He steepled his fingers, pinning her in place with his direct gaze. "However, you have been put forward to work in a more specialized position. There is listening involved, but this position will also require other aspects for which I understand you are well qualified. Your superior officer reports that you are a natural codebreaker. Is that correct?"

She nodded, unsure of what to say.

"Excellent. I should probably mention that the position for which you have been recommended is a little different. Less regimented, you could say. A little more . . . hands-on."

"But I will still be listening?" Promotion or not, she didn't want to leave that part of the job.

"Oh yes."

Dot's mind raced. "Will I still live here?"

"No. You will be transferred to Ontario."

"I see." That was good news. Her parents would be delighted if she came to visit, and she was dying to see them. Maybe Dash could get away from CanCar for a couple of days, too. "Would I still be under oath?"

Captain Powell scowled. "I'm surprised you would ask that. You will be working in Intelligence, after all."

"I apologize, Captain."

He checked a paper. "Your ride to the train station will pick you up at oh six ten tomorrow. Your train leaves at oh seven hundred. The journey to the station at Whitby will take two days. Someone will meet you there and take you to your next assignment. Do you have any questions?"

A million, she thought. "No, Captain. No questions. I will be ready in the morning."

"Congratulations, Petty Officer Wren Wilson," the captain said, standing. "I wish you all the very best in your new position. I would also like to offer my personal assistance should you ever have need of it."

"Thank you, sir."

On her brisk march back, Dot's thoughts bounced like ping-pong balls inside her head. She thought of all the steps that had led her here, every challenge she'd faced. She had come a long way from the girl who had stumbled meekly into the recruitment office. She no longer felt the need to hide behind anyone. What would Dash say if she could see her now?

In the barracks, Dot sat Alice down. She'd thought about the best way to tell her then decided on the direct approach. "I am being transferred. I'm sorry, but it's just me this time."

"Oh no, Dot! You can't leave us!" Alice cried, standing. "Girls! They promoted Dot all the way out of here!"

Instantly, Dot was shocked then almost overwhelmed by hugs and the coos of "It won't be the same without you," and many heartfelt wishes for a wonderful life. She knew all these girls, had worked, eaten, and slept alongside them, but until this moment she hadn't understood she was considered one of them. That they were all friends, not just coworkers. Alice's eyes were red from crying, and as sad as that made Dot, it also filled her heart. The only people who had ever cried over her before had been family members.

"You avoided everyone's questions," Alice said, after the rest of the girls returned to their bunks. "Now that they're gone, you can tell me. Where are you being sent?"

"I actually don't know. It was all very hush-hush."

"Oh, come on. You must know something. It's *me*. You can tell me."

"This isn't even the oath," Dot replied sincerely. "I have no idea where I am going, or why. I will try to write to you when I can, though you know I might not be able to tell you much."

"I understand," Alice said, softening. "Oh, Dot. I will miss you so much. I know it sounds silly, but I'm proud of you. When I met you, you were almost too shy to say hello to me. Now look at you!"

It was true, and Dot sucked back tears thinking of it that way. Ever since she and Alice had met on the train to Galt, they'd been close. Alice had slipped quite naturally into the empty space Dash had left, and she had been the driving force behind prying Dot out of her shell.

"You made this possible for me, Alice."

"Nonsense. You were made for this. Wherever you're going, my dear friend, they are very lucky to have you."

"You're the best listener here—"

"Other than you."

"Well, yes," Dot admitted. "But now you'll be the best. And you're the best friend I've ever had. My sister, my friend Gus, and you. I'm going to be lost without you for a while."

"I'll be a little lost without you, too," Alice said quietly. She sniffed. "I wouldn't be nearly the listener I am now without all your help. I know you'll be anxious when you land, but wherever you're going, pretend that I'm there. Just think of me standing behind you, shoving you into the thick of things. Before you know it, you will be the most important person in the place."

───

Dot held on to Alice's words when she boarded the bus the next morning in a darkness that felt like the middle of the night. As they bumped out of the compound, Dot's gaze lingered on the low white buildings of Coverdale. In the distance stood the hut where she had worked, and where a team of girls currently listened and wrote. The building was still guarded by a herd of black cows, but Dot had come to understand they were no threat. She'd carried on the charade only because Alice thought it was such fun.

As the base slipped out of sight, Dot faced forward, resolute. Alice had helped her overcome her shyness, but the truth was, Alice was not responsible for Dot's success. Dot alone had put on those headphones and sorted through all the dits and dahs to find the pattern that counted before she'd even been trained. Only Dot had raised a hand when a convoluted series of letters appeared in her mind, already in a translated form. Alice had been there, but Dot had taken those steps by herself. Whatever mysterious destination lay ahead, and whatever sounds or codes or signals called for her skills, Dot was no longer afraid.

twenty-six
DASH

— Fort William, Ontario —

Dash was giving the starboard side of the completed Hurricane a final buff, bringing the grey-green camouflage to a nice shine against the factory lights, when Miss MacGill approached. She stood back from the fuselage and scanned the length of the plane.

"Your team did a quick job on this one," she said. "Did you do it correctly?"

"Oh yes, ma'am," Dash replied, unconcerned. These days the factory was producing three to four Hurricanes a week, and each one had passed their test flights. "She is going to fly straight and true, I guarantee it. I can hardly wait to see her test flight. Will that be today?"

Miss MacGill lifted one shoulder. "Depends on the pilot. Will you be ready in a half hour?"

Dash could hardly breathe. She had begun to think this would never happen. "I get to fly her?"

"If you'd like. I took the liberty of contacting your reference, Bob Wilson, and his references as well. He is an exemplary instructor, and he was an even better fighter pilot, I understand. He highly recommended you and assured me I have nothing to worry about. Of course, if he's

wrong, I will have lost a valuable airplane and one of my best mechanics."
She frowned. "Could he be wrong?"

"Uncle Bob is never wrong. Just ask him," Dash said, straight-faced.
"Oh, Miss MacGill! I will take such good care of her."

"And report back with all your findings."

"Of course. Thank you, thank you, thank you!"

She was still standing there, wearing a stupid grin, when Stacey
came up beside her. "You have a cat-ate-the-canary look on your face.
What's up?"

"Oh, you know. Just another regular day"—she spun toward her—
"that I get to fly a Hurricane!"

Stacey squealed. "Do you know how?"

"What a silly question," Dash said, running her hand along the wing.
"I know every little thing about her. She and I are going to get on fa-
mously."

A thought occurred, and she rushed back to her locker, looking for
her father's old brass compass. Her fingers closed around it, and she
dropped it in her pocket before heading back to the hangar.

Out on the tarmac, by the hangar's huge open doors, Dash bounced
on her toes and watched the Hurricane be hauled outside. The sunshine
flashed against her powerful wingspan, and Dash was struck by how
sleek she was, compared to a biplane. Jenny had been wonderful to fly
in, but this would be entirely different. Pulse racing, she climbed onto
the wing while all the other girls watched and cheered for her, then at
last, she slid into the dark green cockpit. She could hardly think for the
thrill of it all.

"Miss Wilson," Miss MacGill said, scowling up at her, "it is important
that you understand that this flight must be as boring as possible. Take
off, fly over the airfield, land in one piece, then bring it in for a post-
flight inspection. Calibrate the air speed indicator, check that everything
works. No funny business. Got it?"

"Yes, ma'am," Dash said, grinning as she tugged on her helmet. "I can
be boring."

"I doubt that very much. But I do want you to try your best to achieve that while you're flying my plane. If you do not, I cannot guarantee you will get another chance." Then she smiled. "I hope the flight is as wonderful as you've dreamed."

"I know it will be. Thank you again for this opportunity, Miss MacGill."

"You earned it."

Then Dash was alone in the cockpit, staring at the shiny black instrument panel. Before anything else, she bent down and pulled out the checklist stowed beneath her seat. It didn't matter that she knew the plane inside out, she remembered Uncle Bob's lesson: going over this checklist was possibly the most important part about flying. If one thing wasn't working right, the whole flight could be a disaster. Following the order on the list, she reached down the left side toward the master switch on the bottom and flicked it on. Top left were the switches for the undercarriage lights, which she flicked up and down, making sure they stayed green. To the left of her thigh, she set the throttle, then she pushed the pitch button all the way forward. There were three fuel tanks on the Hurricane, and she turned the dial at the bottom to check her reserve. All good. Moving to the right side, she pulled out the primer lever, then pumped it three times. Finally, she flipped the magneto and electrical switches to the On position.

The overhead canopy was always left open during takeoff and landing, providing both visibility and an easier escape route if needed. Now, the opening allowed Dash to stick out her hand, give everyone a thumbs-up and yell, "Clear!"

"Woo-hoo, Dash!" Margie called. "We'll be watching!"

Dash pressed in the starter, and the big Merlin engine coughed before rumbling to life. The purr grew to a roar, and from the way the plane began to vibrate around her, Dash could sense its power, impatient beneath her hands. Dash felt almost breathless with excitement.

"Keep it boring!" Miss MacGill shouted over the engine.

Primer in and locked. Fuel pump tested. Dash let off the brake and pointed the nose of the Hurricane down the runway. As she rolled toward the end, the airplane hummed all around her, as eager to fly as she was.

"One more pre-takeoff check," she told the plane, her finger skimming down the list.

Main tanks on. Check prop cycle and mags, scan all the dials on the panel for temps and pressure, check the altimeter, slow to check low idle, set brakes and trims and tensions. Check fuel one more time, fuel boost on. Flaps up. Harness tight.

Just one more thing she needed to do. Reaching into the pocket of her coveralls, she drew out her father's old brass compass, which she set on the dash. It glinted cheerfully in the sun, and she imagined how happy he would have been to be flying with her, despite saying he'd had enough of the sky.

At last she was ready, and she laid her palms on the instrument panel, smiling. "All right then. Let's go."

Bracing herself for the force, Dash pressed the throttle all the way, then she released the brakes. Freed at last, the plane sped down the runway, and despite her exhilaration, Dash made a note in her head that the wheels rolled straight, without the slightest wobble. That was a good sign, suggesting the landing should go smoothly as well. The tarmac in front was almost done, and Dash's heart whirred like the propellor, accelerating until the plane's RPMs hit 3000. In that moment, she pulled the stick back hard, elevating the nose, and the plane lifted effortlessly off the runway.

Unconstrained by the earth, the Hurricane tore into the sky, and the thrust shoved Dash back in her seat. In no time at all, she was soaring at five thousand feet and laughing with pure joy, tears in her eyes. Miss MacGill was asking the impossible. How could anyone be bored when they flew this plane? Still, she followed her instructions, banking the plane in a smooth turn, setting it up for a circle over the wide, green airfield, with its forested borders bubbling up in the distance. The two enormous CanCar buildings stretched out behind the runways, two blank white rectangles that contained dozens of fighter planes, and in the distance, Mount MacKay. Dash dropped her gaze to the panel, watching for unusual bumps or vibrations in the dials, scouting for sudden changes in pressure or temperature, but she could find nothing wrong with the plane.

"You are perfect," Dash said out loud.

Pushing the control stick forward then to the side, she leaned the Hurricane in the opposite direction, banking harder this time, and the hungry roar of the engine resonated in her chest.

This! This is everything! she thought, her heart singing. Yes, she loved to laugh and kick up her heels, but up here, thousands of feet above the earth, was where Dash felt the most alive. It was impossible not to think of Uncle Bob and all his lessons. The way that old plane used to wait for her on the field like a friend, calling her to *Hurry up and fly!* Dash could hardly wait to write and tell him all about this.

"Sorry to cheat on you, Jenny," she said aloud, "but this plane has stolen my heart!"

Her second circle was over far too quickly, but Miss MacGill was watching, so Dash didn't dare stay up any longer. Just before preparing to land, she roared over the girls' heads and gave them a saucy tip of the wing, hoping that still existed within the "fly boring" category. After that, she touched down in a smooth, sturdy landing and taxied back to where everyone waited, a smile glued to her face. As she climbed out of the cockpit, still riding a wave of euphoria, her friends surrounded her, cheering. They all knew how the plane worked, but every one of them wanted to know, "What did it *feel* like?"

Dash exhaled, her eyes sweeping over the wings of the plane. She was already impatient to go up again. "It felt like heaven," she told them. "A noisy kind of heaven."

twenty-seven
DOT
-.. --- -

— Whitby, Ontario —

Petty Officer Wren Wilson?"

Dot whirled toward the voice, automatically clutching her purse to her chest. She'd just stepped off the train at Whitby Station without any idea of which direction to go, and now a tall man in a black trench coat stepped out of the night and stood before her, his face shadowed beneath the brim of a fedora.

"I am your driver."

She stared at him, feeling as if she'd just walked into a chapter from one of her mystery novels. Despite her exhaustion from two full days of travel, she automatically thought it through. He knew her name, and she had been told to expect a driver, so she followed him without a word and slipped into the warm car. The stranger didn't say where they were going, but she understood that was part of his character's role. Hers was to wait and see. Settling back, she watched out the window, and they raced along the highway in silence. The moon was bright, making the farmland glow eerily white, and Dot shivered. She should not have been reading a murder mystery on the train. On the other hand, it prompted her to look for clues, and her heart lifted when she spied a familiar sign. They were headed toward Oshawa! She'd be able to see her parents!

After a while, the car slowed then pulled over to the side of long, empty road. There was nothing but fields for miles around them.

Dot jerked upright. "Why did we stop? Is there something wrong?"

"Stay here," the driver said flatly, which did nothing to calm her. He got out and shut the door behind him, walked to the front, and lifted the hood of the car. She couldn't see him, since the hood was shielding him, and her thoughts ran wild. Was he still there? Was someone else out there? Who was he really? Where were they?

She jumped when his door opened and he climbed back in. "Something wrong?"

"This is Thornton Road," he said, as if that explained everything. "Leads directly to the camp. Anyone driving down here has to be sure they haven't been followed. I was checking for other vehicles."

The camp. "And what . . . What if you had seen one?"

"I'd have kept driving and come back later. Everything is closely monitored around here and patrolled twenty-four hours a day. Nobody gets in or out without their knowing."

Wide awake now, she stared as they sped up a gravel driveway, passed a lone sign that declared PROHIBITED AREA, DEPARTMENT OF NATIONAL DEFENCE, then paused at a guardhouse. The man within checked their paperwork, then they continued, eventually turning onto a smaller road lined by apple trees. In the field on her left, Dot noticed a huge array of antennae poking into the air like massive porcupine quills, and her earlier apprehension began to give way to anticipation. Antennae suggested communications. Wireless telegraphs and more.

The driver parked in front of a building but left the engine running. He retrieved her bag from the trunk and set it by the building's entrance.

"Welcome to Camp X," he said, opening her door.

Camp X! What a wonderful name for an Intelligence Department!

"Someone will be waiting for you inside. Good luck." He returned to the front seat, put the car in gear, and rolled away.

Dot watched him disappear into the night, slightly dazed. When she could no longer hear his tires on the gravel, she picked up her bag and entered the building. As she'd been told, a man waited within. He was older, and his dark hair was streaked with grey, well on its way to matching his bushy silver moustache. The smile beneath it was cordial.

"Petty Officer Wren Wilson, I presume. I am Major Nelson, but you may call me Gerald. How shall I address you?"

"Dot."

"Fine. That's just fine." He flashed another smile. "Welcome to Camp X, also known as Spy School."

Dot blinked up at him. "I'm sorry. Spy School?"

"Indeed. Is that a problem?"

"Not at all, sir," she stammered. "It's a bit of a surprise, though, as I wasn't told what to expect. Only that I would be working with intelligence of some kind."

"Ah well. This is most definitely the place to be for intelligence."

She scanned the room for clues. What did they need from her? Where were the radios?

"Before we begin, you are familiar with our strict policy of secrecy, I assume."

"I did sign the Official Secrecy Oath."

"Excellent. As a reminder, any word mentioned about this place or the people in it, including yourself, would be considered treason."

Dot nodded.

"I imagine you're wondering what you've gotten yourself into. In a nutshell, we recruit and train secret agents, saboteurs, fighters, other recruiters, and partisan workers out of promising young people like yourself. Oh, and assassins." He gestured down the corridor. "Shall we?"

All the blood drained from Dot's face. "Assassins, sir?"

"When needs must. It is war, after all. You, Petty Officer Wren Wilson, have been identified as having talents perfectly suited to a clandestine war effort." He raised an eyebrow. "Or were your superiors incorrect?"

"No, sir," she replied, but the urge to bolt pulled at her. Chief Wren Alder and Captain Powell had thought she'd make a good assassin?

"All right. Let's begin our tour. It's a shame it's so late in the evening, but you will get the general idea."

She picked up her suitcase, moving quickly to keep pace. Major Nelson—Gerald—strode down the corridor with his hands clasped behind his back, passing doorways and outlining the bare bones of the camp.

"These are some of the senior offices. Their secretarial assistants sit outside them. If you get lost, those women are a wonderful resource. Down this way are our interrogation—erm, interview rooms, and beyond that, one of our gymnasiums."

It was quite an involved operation, she noticed. And rather obvious, since it stood in the middle of an open field.

"Sir, I understand this is top secret, but what do we say if someone asks? This place is quite large and . . . noticeable."

"Yes, it is. We have about two hundred seventy-five acres here. The people in this area believe that our installation is a part of the Canadian Broadcasting Corporation and that we are extending the radio service for local customers. The antennae outside help with that illusion."

Brilliant, she thought, warming to the camp.

"However, no one will ask you, because you won't be leaving the premises."

"Ever?" she squeaked.

He stopped short. "I'm afraid not. In your position, you will be in possession of top secret material. The only way to leave here would be under very special circumstances, and even then, permission may be denied."

Dot's spirit sank. It didn't matter how close she was to her parents. It was an impossible distance to cross.

"What about letters? Can I still write letters to my family?"

"Of course," he replied. "And in them, you will find new and fascinating ways of describing how ridiculously tedious your life as a clerk truly is. Now, back to the tour." Gerald turned. "As you drove in, you no doubt noticed the Communications Building, where our teletype machines are constantly tapping away. Women work on those machines day and night. Beyond them is our codebreaking room."

"Is that where I will be working?"

"Not quite. We have something planned for you which is a little more involved. I will explain that later. I understand you are fluent in Morse code and quite impressive at decoding as well."

"Yes, sir. Morse code is my second language."

"As I thought. Excellent. Moving along . . ."

"Bang!" someone yelled as they passed an open door, and Dot flinched.

Just inside the room, a man held a pistol near the back of a woman's head. Dot glanced at Gerald, concerned, but her guide was observing with interest.

"Faster!" the man barked. "Come on, Susan. You can do this. Try again."

Gerald entered the room, curling a finger toward Dot. "We'll stay back here," he whispered, "out of the way, but this will be your first lesson in self-defence. Watch. The attacker is about a yard behind her, his gun pointed at her back. At that distance, she has no idea where he is exactly, but as soon as she becomes aware of his presence, she will have to disarm him, or she's dead. You'll learn this when you begin your training."

Someone was going to point a gun at the back of Dot's head?

She watched in stunned silence as Susan failed the next two times. On the third, she saw the woman's jaw tighten with determination. In a blur, she knocked her attacker flat then turned the gun on him. Dot tucked her hands in her armpits to keep from applauding.

The man rolled back to his feet and took the weapon back. "Again."

From there, Gerald led Dot through a classroom. He called it a lecture hall and said she and other prospective agents would learn from the blackboard, the books in the library, and their teachers. They would be tested repeatedly. If they failed after eight weeks, they were not welcome to remain at Camp X.

"Does all of this include me? I'm sorry, sir. I'm afraid I still do not understand my role here."

"Naturally, you will be working in communications. Among other things, you will listen to coded messages from and about our agents, you will send coded transmissions when required, and you will decrypt messages. Generally, you will be working with Hydra."

Her pulse picked up. "Hydra, sir?"

"Yes. We'll get to that. Maybe tomorrow. It's rather dark outside to show you now." He frowned. "I realize that in my rush tonight I forgot to mention something important, and I must clear that up first. You are *not* being trained to become an agent, but you *will* be training alongside them. Eight weeks of training is mandatory."

"Training, sir? Like drills?"

"Oh yes." He smiled, looking temporarily younger despite his silver moustache. "It's quite a lot, actually. Physical training exercises as well as classroom and practical education. Everyone here must be prepared to defend the camp at any time."

Defend the camp. Gun at her head. What in the world?

Wordlessly, she followed him into a room that smelled of wool.

"Uniforms, regalia, weaponry, and various forms of international currency are kept in here. Our agents learn how to handle every item in this room, as will you. Usually it's busier in here, but most have retired for the evening."

Dot caught a glimpse of steel in a glass cabinet. Moving closer, she noticed it was filled with knives of different lengths and widths. One blade had a wraparound handle made of steel knuckles. The sight of it scared her silly. While she was leaning in and scanning the various weapons, a man entered, armed with a measuring tape.

"Ah. There you are," Gerald said to him. "Excellent timing." He indicated an open book on the counter. "You'll need to sign here, Petty Officer Wren. It's for your uniform."

Dot signed then held out her arms while the man used the tape measure on her, but she wobbled suddenly, beyond weary. The train had taken two days, the car ride over an hour, and every minute of it had been driven by adrenaline. Now, her mind spun with new and fascinating information. It was exhausting.

. The man finished measuring, disappeared into the shelves and hangers, then returned with a bundle of clothing for her.

"I imagine you're worn out," Gerald said. "You will have quite a day tomorrow, when you'll meet your five classmates, so we'll head off to the barracks now. Those are the two large buildings located directly behind this one. You will eat, sleep, and share the buildings with everyone else living here at Camp X; however, everyone has a private room with a bed and dresser."

Dot had never had her own room in her life. She could hardly imagine it.

They stepped into the chilly night, and Dot's eye was caught by a tall, wooden structure to their right, about ninety feet high. At the top of it was a shaky-looking platform.

"Sir, what's the tower over—"

The boom of a distant explosion cut her off, and Dot ducked, clutching her uniform against her like a shield. After a couple of frantic heartbeats, she rose cautiously and spotted a cloud of grey smoke rising from a nearby field. Gerald didn't seem to have noticed either the explosion or her shock. He was still walking.

"Sir?"

He glanced back. "Ah. Mortar practice. You will hear quite a bit of that. You cannot easily see it at night, but there is a large physical training area out that way. Our agents also participate in underwater explosives training, which is quite interesting."

She pointed to the tower they had just passed. "And what's that, sir?"

"That's the jump tower. It's where agents learn how to parachute."

She froze midstep and looked up, up, up to the platform, her lifelong fear of heights rolling in her stomach. At its peak, the platform was bare of any railings or gates, and she imagined the wind coming off Lake Ontario could get fierce. Even worse, this was a *practice* tower. "Learning to parachute" meant they planned to eventually jump from much higher.

Blinking up at the tower, Dot remembered another time she'd stood in this position. She and Dash had been eight, and they were playing in the yard on a beautiful summer day. As usual, Dash was fifteen feet over Dot's head, nested in her favourite tree, entertaining herself by dropping rocks into a bucket. Dot had gotten caught up in the rhythms and patterns she heard. Watching and counting, she realized that it didn't matter what size the rocks were, they all landed at the same time. Dash and Gus had teased her about finding puzzles in everything, but it had been interesting to her. Eventually, their father came outside, and Dot had run to him to ask about it.

"That's to do with gravity," he explained to the three children, "the planetary pull of the earth on all things. Gravity is the reason you fall down instead of up if you trip, and it's the reason your sister shouldn't climb so high in that tree."

Dot was intrigued. "What about birds, Daddy? How do they fly if gravity is always pulling them down?"

"Good question. Birds stay aloft because of something called 'lift.' It has to do with the passage of air over the wings versus the air beneath the wings."

"What about airplanes?" Dash wanted to know. "They don't flap their wings."

"No, they certainly do not."

"And they're very heavy."

"Yes, they are, but their propellers help them move very quickly. Planes are something altogether different. They use something called 'thrust.' It works along with the specific angle of the wings to keep them in the air. Think of how your hand feels if you hold it outside of the car window while we're driving. It feels easier or harder to go through the wind depending on what angle you're holding it at."

Now, as Dot peered at the ghostly profile of the parachuting platform, with its rickety, windy staircase and its open platform on top, she couldn't help but think of gravity—and of her sister.

Looks like fun, Dash would have said. *Watch me fly.*

Dot's throat constricted in her sister's absence. How she missed that voice. That spirit. Dash would climb that awful thing without a second thought, and Dot would watch her, filled with both dread and wonder. Dash had been the one who always wanted to fly, not Dot.

twenty-eight
DASH

—— March 1943 ——
Fort William, Ontario

The morning sun streamed through the window far too early, and Dash dug deeper into her blankets. She'd overdone it at the dance last night, and everything hurt.

Mrs. Simmons rapped on her door. "Miss Wilson," she chirped. "There's a message for you."

"Thank you," Dash groaned. Today was Saturday, wasn't it? Why would she get a message on a Saturday? "I'm going to sleep a little longer, then I'll—"

"I did knock a couple of hours ago, but you were dead to the world. Then I got busy. It's from Miss MacGill."

Dash sat up, the curls from last night tumbling over her face. "Miss MacGill?"

"I know you were out late, missy. I don't support that sort of behaviour, and you know it. Well, it's come back to bite you this time, hasn't it? I wouldn't be putting this off if I were you."

Dash struggled to her feet, hand on the wall for balance, and staggered to the door. Shoving her hair off her face, she reached for the door handle, and Mrs. Simmons withdrew dramatically, fanning at her nose due to Dash's apparent odour. Dash snatched the envelope, nodded a thank-you, then closed the door again.

Dash's boss had been cordial ever since Dash had started, but she had never sent a personal note before. Nothing good could arrive in a Saturday morning note, could it? She opened the envelope and recognized Miss MacGill's handwriting right away.

Miss Wilson,
  Please come to my office Saturday at 11:30 in the
  morning.
-Elsie MacGill

Dash dropped onto the pile of clothes she'd left out the night before—or rather, early this morning—and dug through, searching for her watch. When she found it, she squinted at the tiny hands and gasped: 11:00. She had half an hour to make herself look presentable, then actually present herself.

She hastily washed and dressed. Pinning her long, dark hair into a makeshift roll, she raced out the door and caught the bus just as it was pulling away. She disembarked at her normal stop, a block from the Can-Car factory, and kept running. When she arrived at last, she checked her watch again: 11:28.

No one could accuse her of being late, she congratulated herself, gasping for breath. She stepped through the entrance then paused outside Miss MacGill's office to collect herself. A moment later, Miss Rose opened the office door, surprising Dash. Did everyone in the offices work on Saturdays? Thank heavens Dash was just a worker bee. She'd have missed her Friday night fun too much.

"Take a seat in here, please. Miss MacGill will join you momentarily," Miss Rose said, then she saw herself out.

Dash sat on the edge of her chair, hands clasped on her lap, her feet jiggling. Her eyes burned from all the cigarette smoke clogging the Elks Hall last night, and her head was killing her. The ticking of the wall clock seemed to get louder by the second. Last night had been a time and a half with her friends, and one she felt she'd earned. Her plan had been to dance all night and sleep all day. Not once had she considered taking it easy, because not once had she imagined being called to Miss MacGill's office the next morning. Was she in trouble after last night? Were the other girls being called in as well? She slumped. If that's what this was about, Dash had just danced her way out of her dream job.

The door opened behind her, and Dash jumped to attention. Miss MacGill entered, her smile tight, and Dash's heart sank. From the look on her employer's face, she was in trouble. Then again, Miss MacGill wasn't one for smiles in general. Maybe . . .

Her boss lowered herself behind her desk then gestured for Dash to sit as well. "Good morning, Miss Wilson."

"Good morning, Miss MacGill. Before we begin," she blurted, "please allow me to apologize profusely for everything you might have heard about last night. I was irresponsible and impulsive, and I deeply regret my actions."

A frown flickered over her boss's face. "Is that right? I am sorry to hear that. From the look of you, Miss Wilson, you had a good time."

Dash made a lame attempt to smile.

"There's nothing to apologize for. Young ladies need to let loose just as men do—to a degree, of course. Everyone here works hard, and they deserve a night off. It is I who should apologize, apparently, for calling this meeting today. It looks like you wish you were still asleep in your bed."

Dash's cheeks burned.

"Miss Wilson, I did not call you here to discuss last night or any other night. I have a very different conversation in mind."

"That's a relief."

Miss MacGill folded her hands on the desk. "You have not been here very long, but you have made a great impact on this company's productivity. I commend you for your hard work and your unexpected skills. You are a problem solver and a leader, and you do not seem to tire easily—today being an unfortunate exception."

Stars coasted through the corner of Dash's vision. "Thank you, Miss MacGill."

"Would you mind telling me what you like best about working here?"

"Oh, Miss MacGill. I couldn't possibly," Dash protested. "I love so much about it."

"Yes, but do you have a favourite aspect?"

"I love the work we do, building these airplanes for the men, and knowing they are the best planes they can be. I work with intelligent women and have made tremendous friends." She swallowed. "Of course, none of it compares to when I am in the air on a test flight. I never dreamed I would be able to do that. Soaring through the sky is magical to me."

Miss MacGill leaned back in her chair. "That's what I thought. Miss Wilson, you remind me very much of myself at your age."

A feather could easily have knocked Dash out of her chair. "Thank you, Miss MacGill. I'm flattered."

"Designing airplanes is for my mind. Flying in them is for my soul." She touched the handle of her cane. "Of course I cannot physically manage an airplane, but I do love to watch you girls up there. You're a very able pilot, Miss Wilson. You should be flying more."

"Oh yes, please!"

Her boss's gaze dropped to the wooden surface of her desk, and she rubbed at an invisible spot with one finger. "This is not a widely known fact, Miss Wilson, and I would appreciate your keeping it under your hat until I choose to speak more openly about it with the rest of the personnel. The Canadian Car and Foundry Company has nearly completed our contract with the Royal Air Force, having built over fourteen hundred Hawker Hurricanes. We have been negotiating with a new group for a different contract, but there are aspects to that project which give me pause. I would be happy to keep you on here, Miss Wilson; however, I believe I have a direction that would suit you better." She reached for a paper on the corner of her desk. "Are you familiar with the Air Transport Auxiliary?"

"No, ma'am."

"The ATA is a civilian organization in which new and repaired aircraft, as well as men, supplies, and much-needed parts, are ferried between factories, assembly plants, and other destinations. In 1940, I was pleased to hear they had welcomed a small number of women pilots to their ranks. Since then, those numbers have increased.

"I find it encouraging that men are finally beginning to understand how useful women are and how much they are needed in this war. In fact, the ATA recently raised the wages of women pilots so they are equal to those of their male counterparts." She handed the paper to Dash. "Anyhow, I thought you might like to consider working for them. If you are interested, I can speak with one of the people in charge and recommend you."

It took a second before Dash could find words. She didn't even glance at the paper in her hand. "I could fly for a living?"

"You would be working out of the White Waltham Airfield, in Berkshire." She frowned when Dash didn't respond. "Is that a problem?"

"I— I'm not familiar with that airport."

"It's in England. Shall I contact them on your behalf?"

The room was silent for a few very rapid heartbeats. "England? So you're saying . . . Oh yes, please!" Dash breathed. "If it's not too much of an inconvenience, I mean. I am—" She touched the edge of her boss's desk. "Oh, Miss MacGill. I don't know what to say."

"In my opinion, the ATA would be lucky to have you." She gave Dash a conspiratorial smile. "If you do this, you know what they will call you?"

"No, ma'am."

"Folks call them the 'ATA-girls,'" she said, pronouncing it as one word: *attagirls*. "And knowing your personality as I do, that label suits you as well as the job does. I'm very pleased you want to do this."

A week later, Miss MacGill called Dash back to give her the paperwork she needed to submit. After that, all Dash could do was wait. If the Air Transport Auxiliary wrote back and invited Miss Margaret Wilson to pack her bags, Dash would soon be going to war.

twenty-nine
DOT

-•• --- -

— Camp X —

D ot rushed out of the dormitory, buttoning her new khaki coat. "Oh!" she cried, mortified, as she crashed into another woman. "I am so sorry. It's my first day here, and I'm rather nervous, I'm afraid. I wasn't watching where I was going."

The heavily freckled woman barely appeared to have noticed. "I'm Ruby." She gave Dot a wide, closed-mouth smile. "Glad to meet you. It's my first day, too."

Ruby had pinned her light brown curls into a roll, but Dot could tell it had no plans to stay in place. She touched her own hair reflexively, checking it was still as she'd arranged it.

"Shall we go to breakfast together?" Dot suggested.

Ruby nodded. "I'm from Brandon, Manitoba," she informed Dot as they strode across the yard then inside the main building. "Someone told me there are six of us, and only one other girl in the class. You and I should stick together."

"Good idea. I'm Dot. I'm from Oshawa, Ontario, but uh, I'm not sure what else we're allowed to say to one another."

Ruby laughed. "I figure it's all right to talk about where we've come from, just not where we're going." She pointed across the mess hall toward a young man with soft brown hair and a tight jaw. "That's Gordon. He's one of us. He's a radio operator."

Dot regarded him with interest as she reached for a meal tray. "I'm familiar with radios."

"He's smart, but he barely says anything. His brother was killed in Germany, so he can't wait to get over there and get his hands dirty, if you know what I mean."

A radio operator who was also an operative. "I think I do," Dot said.

"Where do you hope to end up? France? Maybe Poland?"

Dot followed her to a table and sat. "I didn't know we had a choice."

"Oh, I don't think we do," Ruby replied, digging into her scrambled eggs. "I just like to think about travelling. I've never been out of Canada."

"Me neither, but I won't get that chance. I'll be staying at the Camp X base, as far as I know."

Ruby's eyes narrowed. "You're not training to be an agent? That means you're what?"

"I'm in communications," Dot said. "I don't know any more than that yet."

Across the room, Gordon stood and carried his empty meal tray to the front. He gave the girls a tentative smile as he passed.

"Guess we should go," Ruby said, shoveling what remained of her breakfast into her mouth. "Lecture hall, right? Not my favourite."

Dot didn't mention that it was hers. She could feel the fragile threads of a new friendship possibly forming, and she didn't want to mess it up by appearing overly keen.

When they walked into the hall and saw what was written on the blackboard, Ruby stopped short. "Explosives? This is going to be fun!"

Before that morning, Dot hadn't known there were almost two dozen different types of explosives, all based on combinations of ammonium picrate, TNT, pentaerythritol tetranitrate, RDX, and powdered aluminum. She wasn't sure if she would ever need to use any of that knowledge in the future, but it was interesting learning how it all fit together. Ruby peered over, looking impressed by Dot's detailed notes, so Dot helped her spell the chemical names properly. After that, they had a brief lesson on pistol shooting. Dot dutifully sketched all the diagrams on the board and added notes from the lesson.

Then their short, wiry instructor closed his book. "Let's put these lessons into action. Back field. On the double."

Dot glanced at Ruby, who was practically in raptures at this news. She supposed she shouldn't have been surprised that this was their next step. It only made sense that they'd be testing out their new knowledge. But explosives? Guns?

"You have learned the basics of explosive theory," the instructor said, stopping in a field by a melting pile of blackened snow. Beside him was a small black box. "Now you will witness what they do."

He reached down, pushed a button on the box, and the earth exploded about forty feet away. Dot dropped. It was a few seconds before Ruby could coax her out of her panicked crouch. Next time she swore she would be better prepared. And she would cover her ears.

How on earth had she ended up in a place where they'd expect her to fire explosives?

On to the next part of this morning's lecture: the six trainees marched to a different section of the field, where a younger, stony-faced instructor put a pistol in Dot's trembling hands. The metal felt cold and unfamiliar, and she didn't like it at all. She wanted to hand it back, but the knees of her uniform still bore mud stains from the explosives' demonstration, and she refused to embarrass herself again.

One by one, the students stood and were taught what to do. Quiet Gordon, the radio operator, went first. He took the gun, fired, and hit the target as if it was the easiest thing in the world. The next two boys each attempted it a few times before they were successful. Ruby and the last boy took a few tries, and they eventually got it. Dot observed everyone, mentally breaking down positioning, posture, speed, and whatever else she could see so that she could shoot as naturally as Gordon had.

When it was her turn, she stood beside the trainer and let him force the fingers of both her hands into the right position around the weapon. His boots nudged hers so her feet were set apart.

"Hold the pistol in front, and grip it tight. Picture your shoulders and your hands in an isosceles triangle. Do you remember that shape from math class?"

"I remember everything from math class," she told him flatly.

"All right. That's your target." He pointed. "Look straight at it, squeeze the trigger slowly, and brace yourself for the kick."

Dot squinted down the field about sixty feet and saw a large paper target. At least she assumed it was large. The fact that she was supposed to hit it made it seem impossibly small. Following instructions, she loaded the gun, took off the safety, aimed, then pulled the trigger. Two things happened. The first was the kick that he'd warned her about, which knocked her back a step. The second was a rush of disappointment that she hadn't hit anything remotely near the target. She aimed and fired again and again, reminding herself that this was just physics. She could master this if only she thought through it logically. The instructor encouraged her, angling the pistol this way and that, checking her grip, and assuring her that every shot fired brought her a little closer. That wasn't enough for Dot. She worked at it without ceasing for the rest of the hour, increasingly frustrated, but in the end she walked away a failure. She had not hit the target even once.

After a quick lunch, the class headed back outside where they met yet another instructor. This one was probably about thirty, with slicked-back gold hair that was thinning on top. He cheerfully introduced himself as Mr. Turner, then indicated the running track.

"I, ladies and gentlemen, am in charge of torturing you." He gave them a bright smile. "Time to sweat. Let's go. If you stop, you drop and give me ten push-ups."

Dot stepped onto the track, aware that this was going to hurt. She hadn't run laps since her training at Saint-Hyacinthe. After a few rounds, every muscle in her body burned, but she refused to be the only one to slow to a walk. Failing now would be beyond humiliating, and after the firing-range fiasco, she doubted her fellow Camp X trainees would let her live it down. Ignoring her screaming muscles, Dot focused on the loose streams of curls bouncing against Ruby's back, and she managed to match her friend's pace. When they finally left the field, Dot could barely walk, but she wasn't the only one. Even the men staggered alongside her, their hair and clothing dark with sweat.

"What's next?" Dot whispered to Ruby.

"Bed?"

That made Dot smile. "It's only two o'clock."

"Okay!" Mr. Turner said, walking backward in front of them. "Now we have something really fun for you."

Behind him loomed the parachute tower. Behind the rest of them, one of the other trainees threw up. Dot felt her own stomach roll.

Mr. Turner grinned. "Well done. Now, I need a volunteer . . ."

"Petty Officer Wren Wilson?" a voice called.

She spun toward it. "Major Nelson!"

"Interested in meeting Hydra?" He glanced up at the tower. "Or would you rather . . ."

Her whole body relaxed, and she trotted over to him. "Hydra, please, sir."

As they walked away, he chuckled. "Oh, did I not tell you? You are exempt from this aspect of the training. We need you in one piece."

Giddy with relief, Dot accompanied Gerald to the series of antennae she'd noticed on the drive in. Beside those stood a building with a large entrance and very high windows. With the antennae so close, she knew that building had to contain communications equipment. Just the thought of seeing radios again had her fingers tingling with anticipation.

Gerald stopped before the building, arm outstretched. "This is where Hydra lives. Hydra is a fifteen-megahertz shortwave transmitter/receiver."

"Fifteen megahertz, sir? I have never heard of anything like that."

"That is because it is the only one of its kind in the entire world." He faced her. "Hydra will be your domain."

"M-mine?"

"Well, not entirely yours, but this will be your main station. One person is always inside, since the transmitter is manned twenty-four hours a day, three-hundred sixty-five days a year. You will rotate in eight-hour shifts. In addition, you will also work in the office with me when I require an assistant." He pushed open the large door. "Shall we?"

Dot walked slowly into the room, taking it all in. One wall was occupied by floor-to-ceiling radios and another held different technical systems. A man sat with his back to the door, headphones on, and she longed to listen in. The specialized equipment before her, with its precise dials—most of which bumped periodically with intercepted signals— was so much more than she'd ever imagined. Hydra was a different realm, capturing voices that cried out all over the world. Now she understood the reason for the high, unreachable windows: no peeking allowed.

"You will be training with Bill Hardcastle, the genius behind Hydra," Gerald said. "Unfortunately, he isn't here at the moment. I am mostly thumbs when it comes to this, but I can give you an overview, anyway." The young, bookish-looking man with the headphones glanced up, acknowledged them, then returned to his work. "We will keep out of the way of young Thomas here."

"How was this built? The components don't all match."

"That's the sweetest part of our Hydra," Gerald said, sounding a bit like a proud father. "It was basically 'jerry built,' made up of bits and pieces of radio equipment collected from amateur radio operators across Canada. Everything arrived in pieces, and Bill put them together again. Over here is the work schedule—you'll see I've taken the liberty of including your name, though you will still be training, of course. These are the drafting prints of the radio design in case anything should require adjustments."

For now, Dot looked past the papers posted on the walls and leaned in, reading the dials, excited to see words and letters she knew.

"Your records show your exemplary talent in receiving messages, but also in simultaneously breaking codes. You'll share some shifts with the codebreakers, but your primary role will be transmitting. For example, messages from the White House as well as captured German codes will be transmitted from Hydra to London."

"So far? How?"

He gestured beyond the windows. "You've seen our rather unique antenna system, I gather. We call those 'rhombic' antennae. Three of them are strung between four telephone poles, which were donated by Ontario Hydro. The rhombic design is new. It's very effective at covering the greatest number of frequencies possible. It can communicate through Morse code with Ottawa, New York, Washington, and London, delivering messages in less than a minute. Bill will show you everything when he returns. Any questions before then?"

"Yes, but I can't think of them all right now. Oh wait. I do have one." She pointed at the headphones. "How soon can I start?"

thirty

DASH

— May 1943 —
Fort William, Ontario

Dash sat at the table in CanCar's dining room—which sounded so much more elegant than just calling it a mess hall—staring into space. The other girls had all gone home, but just as she was grabbing her coat, Dash had been called into Miss MacGill's office. There, her smiling boss had presented her with her acceptance letter and invitation from the Air Transport Auxiliary.

Now, Dash's pen hovered over a blank piece of paper. Her news felt too good to be true. As if it belonged to someone else. She had the strangest fear that if she wrote it down, it might not happen.

So much had changed since Dash had joined the Wrens, planning to be the best, but having no idea what to expect. In a way, some of what she'd learned had made her feel inadequate for the first time in her life, but she'd worked harder to make up for that. Then she'd been sent to the garage in the city where she'd been surrounded by men who didn't want her there. Not as a mechanic, anyway.

Her experience there had been frightening, and it had shattered her confidence for a while. She'd never really understood Dot's timid nature before then. To her shame, there had been times when Dash had thought of Dot's shyness as a weakness, but that had changed. Dash had learned the wisdom of being cautious. The importance of protecting oneself rather than simply charging in.

From her despair, she had dared to dream about working at CanCar under the brilliant Miss Elsie MacGill. When she had boarded the train to Fort William, she'd been hopeful, but thanks to her incident at Eisen's garage, more anxious than she'd ever been. What if she couldn't handle the job? But she had. And she'd done it so well that Miss MacGill had personally referred her to the ATA.

And yet, now that she stared at the paper, wondering how to tell Dot about everything, apprehension had returned. Dash had been good at what she did at CanCar, but what about this next opportunity? What if she got there and discovered she wasn't as good as she used to be?

If she was here, Dot would know what to say. She had gotten through more obstacles than Dash ever had. Simply leaving home had been a major accomplishment for her. She might be stuck in a dull office job now, but she'd surprised even herself by mastering that job and making friends while she was at it.

Dot would know.

Dash bent over the paper and began to write.

Hold on to your hat, Dot, because I have news! I have been accepted by the Air Transport Auxiliary! Can you believe it? I will be flying planes in the war! No, not in combat, silly. My job will be bringing planes to where they need to go, replacing downed ones and broken ones, I guess. I will learn more soon, because I am heading to England in a few weeks to start training! Are you able to come see me when I am home, packing?

She shook her head, reading her own words again. England. Flying. The war. Dash was about to do everything she never dreamed possible. The only thing she regretted was that once again, she would have to leave so many friends behind. When she was done with Dot's letter, she wrote to Ginny, who would share everything with Mary, she knew. As for Margie, Paulette, and Stacy at CanCar, Dash would sit them all down in the morning and give them the news in person. Would she ever see these girls again? It felt a bit like school, where all the children were herded into one place, expected to make friends with whomever they could, then set free again. Where were those friends now? She promised herself she would make an effort to see them again someday. Unlike Gus, she was determined to keep in touch and talk with them again after this was over. Because the war *would* be over someday. And that reunion would make all the waiting worthwhile.

Her last letter was to her parents. They'd be excited for her, but concerned, and they were probably right to be. They had accepted that Dash was a pilot, but becoming an actual part of the war would be beyond their imaginings. It was beyond Dash's too, she thought, smiling from the inside out. Yes, she was scared, but she wasn't truly afraid. She'd created this opportunity through her hard work and determination, and now it was time to test herself again. She took a deep breath, reminding herself of everything she'd already done, then she imagined everything ahead. Soon she would travel across the Atlantic and start over in a whole different world. What a ride that would be.

thirty-one

DOT

-. .. --- -

— Camp X —

The grass squished under Dot's shoes as she ran laps with the others, but she barely noticed. The Camp X trainees had settled into a daily morning routine of two hours of blackboard theory in the lecture hall followed by two hours of fitness. After lunch, they headed outside to work on explosives, the firing range, and survival techniques. When the others went to the parachute tower, that was Dot's cue to disappear into Hydra, which she loved.

For now, she just had to keep moving, one foot in front of the other. To her surprise, Dot had actually started to enjoy running. After weeks of doing it every day, the exercise had become almost meditative. The more she ran, the more peaceful she felt, and when her anxieties eased, she thought more clearly. Today, as she followed Ruby, she let her mind wander to yesterday's letter from Dash. She had a lot to think about.

It appeared Dot wasn't the only one traveling from post to post. Dash was moving on as well, and in a very big way. She couldn't help noticing that every time the sisters switched jobs, things became more interesting, but they also got more dangerous. Dash was about to sail to England and fulfill her dreams by flying airplanes in the war. Meanwhile, Dot was learning how to kill people with her bare hands.

"Pick it up, Ruby!" Mr. Turner yelled, and Dot pushed herself to stay on her friend's tail.

Before heading out on her transatlantic sail, Dash would return to Oshawa, less than an hour from where Dot was presently sweating. It broke her heart that she wouldn't be able to leave Camp X to see Dash, even for a few hours. Even if she could, she would have had to lie to her family about everything, so she supposed the silver lining was that she wouldn't have to do that. But she wanted so badly to look Dash in the eye and tell her how thrilled she was for her—despite the fact that the very idea of Dash flying in a war zone terrified her. Dangerous or not, Dash was on her way to achieving her dreams. More than anything else, Dot wanted to hug her and wish her safe travels, safe flight, or whatever it was one said to a pilot in times of war.

She loved how full her sister's letters were, speaking openly about her job at CanCar, her friends, and all the fun they had. Dot tried to see past her sister's complaints that her own letters were boring, because there was nothing Dot could do about that. Dash had been sympathetic at first, encouraging Dot to seek a more stimulating post, but she had eventually given up and accepted that Dot was satisfied. If only she could tell Dash what was really going on. She knew her sister would be astonished, and in a good way.

As she began her last lap, Dot's mind returned to the importance of today. Now that she and the others had finished their training, the instructors were following them around with clipboards, marking test scores. They'd all worked so hard, and with each day their confidence had grown.

Ruby could parachute without screaming.

Gordon could take down three men with his bare hands.

Dot could break a code and an attacker's fingers in a minute flat. She'd mastered all the blackboard theory, including explosives. Anything about Morse code and codebreaking was simple, of course. She could keep up with Ruby on all the physical exercises, though she could never catch up to Gordon or the other men. She had learned basic hand-to-hand combat moves so that she could outmaneuver an attacker much larger than she was, bring him to his knees, and render him helpless. A most satisfying result, though she couldn't see herself actually using it in real life.

The same went for the lessons she'd been taught on defying German interrogation.

"Camp X is conveniently located near Camp 30 in Bowmanville," their instructor, Mr. Marsh, had told them when those classes began halfway through their training. "Many German POWs are being held there, including officers. The proximity gives us a unique advantage."

He opened the door to a small room. Inside was a desk and two chairs, one behind and one in front. A stiff, older man sat behind the desk, eyeing Mr. Marsh but not speaking. A metal disk hung like an unlit lamp over the empty chair.

"Camp X," Mr. Marsh continued, "is the only place in the world where we have ready access to German officers. This is Heinrich Huber, an English-speaking German naval officer. Nice to see you, Herr Huber." He turned back to his students, who stared at the German with a kind of horrified fascination. "I had him summoned, and he arrived here within thirty minutes. Quite convenient."

"Why would we want him here?" Ruby asked, echoing Dot's thoughts.

"Fair question. This man, and others like him, are useful in our training. Many have been involved in German interrogations of Allied prisoners, so they are well versed in the techniques used. We extract their knowledge, and they teach us how to survive a German interrogation. Important knowledge, should any of you ever have the misfortune of being captured." Mr. Marsh surveyed the ashen faces before him. "Now, who would like to volunteer? Gordon?"

Gordon dutifully entered the room, looking more than a little nervous. Mr. Marsh instructed him to sit up straight in the chair and stare down at the surface of the table. He then cuffed Gordon's wrists behind him.

"The first exercise today is one where you will not move a muscle. Stay completely still. That is vital. Do not move your head, your hands, your feet, or anything else. Think of it as a game of sorts. The goal is that no matter what our man here says or does, you will not move a muscle. Simple enough?"

With that, Mr. Marsh and the others left the room so they could observe through a window in the door. Dot squinted at Herr Huber's mouth, trying to read his lips, but she could not make anything out. Gordon was glaring at the table, looking ready to burst.

"What you see here," Mr. Marsh said, "is our friend Gordon believing this test will not be a problem for him. He is a serious, quiet student, and he is prepared to resist anything Herr Huber throws at him. But the fact is, he is not ready at all."

The German said something, and Gordon lifted his head to glare at him. In that second, his entire body shook violently, and his eyes bulged.

Dot stared at Gordon in shock, paralyzed by what she'd just seen.

"What's happening?" Ruby cried, her hands pressed against the window. "What did he do?"

"Gordon did not pay attention to the instructions," Mr. Marsh explained calmly. "I imagine he wanted to stare down his interrogator, who continues to antagonize him, but when he lifted his head, he received an electrical shock from the charged plate above him. What did I tell him? That he was to remain completely still. What will he do after this?"

Gordon had returned to sitting straight and staring at the desk, unmoving, but his face was a sick grey colour, and rivulets of sweat trickled down his cheeks.

Mr. Marsh opened the door slightly. "*Fragen Sie ihn nach seinem Bruder*," he said. Ask him about his brother.

Dot gasped, sickened by Mr. Marsh's order. How dare he antagonize Gordon by introducing something so deeply hurtful?

"How could you?" she cried, but Mr. Marsh only smiled.

"Watch what happens, Miss Wilson. Gordon has learned his lesson once. Now the challenge is greater. Will he master his anger? Remember, if this was an actual interview, Herr Huber would be doing much worse than simply hurling insults. Hardening ourselves to mind games as well as physical violence is very important."

Dot turned back to watch Gordon, tears blurring her vision. She couldn't imagine the struggle he was going through in there. But Gordon was still as a statue. The only movement she could see came from his eyes, which rolled furiously up at the German officer. The German continued to taunt him, but Gordon did not move. Eventually, he returned his gaze to the table, controlling himself completely. No more electric shocks were necessary. And no one in the rest of the group ever, *ever* took their eyes off the desk when it was their turn.

Much less painful were the lessons taught on how to become nearly invisible. Dot had been an expert at hide-and-seek all her life, finding the best hiding spots and staying put, no matter how long it took for Dash or Gus to find her. One time she'd remained tangled in the bushes behind her father's workshop until after it got dark. She was a little afraid, so she'd rustled the branches when she heard voices. It was Gus who found her at last.

At Camp X, she was taught to dress unremarkably, meaning no bright colours, no eye-catching neckline or hem. That was easy. If she felt someone might be watching, she was supposed to change something subtle about herself, like adding a limp she didn't have. She should never speak unless necessary, and when she did, she should be neither loud nor soft. And she should never reveal her language proficiency, her instructor cautioned her specifically. One never knew when one might happen upon valuable information spoken in another tongue when the enemy felt safe.

Now, after all the training, Dot came to the end of her ten laps without so much as a stitch in her side. But the day was not done. One test remained: hitting a target with a bullet. As she followed the others to the range, Dot's confidence began to crumble.

"You'll hit it this time," Ruby assured her.

But she hadn't so far. Not once in eight weeks. It might have started with poor aim. Maybe it had to do with the quickness of the firing, or being apprehensive about the startling noise it made. Whatever the reason, by the end of their training, Dot had come to believe that firing a gun was something she would never master. If only the others wouldn't regard her with so much sympathy. It was bad enough that she couldn't hit the target. It was so much worse when she could feel her classmates' pity.

She sank onto the grass to await her turn. "Why should today be any different?"

Her friend rubbed her back. "Because today's a new day. You never know."

One by one, the trainees rose from where they were sitting and approached the line, pistols in hand. Gordon's turn came two before Dot, and he did not hesitate. The second his gun was at eye level, he fired. As he had every single time, he hit the target dead centre. Dot lowered her gaze to the grass. She was certain she would graduate. She was too strong in every other subject to fail overall. But she wanted this particular success so badly she could taste it.

Once he was done, Gordon left the firing line and settled on the grass beside Dot. "I heard you tell Ruby that your cousin was shot down and killed by a German."

She glanced at him, surprised. Gordon rarely initiated conversations with anyone, though she'd seen Ruby corner him on occasion and bully a few words out of him. Maybe he was like Dot, reticent to reach out.

"That's right."

"What was his name?"

Dot hadn't thought about Fred in a while. She'd only mentioned him once to Ruby when she'd told Dot that she had ten cousins fighting in Europe. Now she pictured Fred's face clearly: his thick black hair falling over one eye, and his goofy, lopsided smile.

"Fred," she whispered.

"I want you to think about something," Gordon said quietly so only she could hear. He gestured toward the target with his chin. "That target is the German pilot who killed Fred. All you gotta do is remember that, then really believe it. When it's your turn, move slowly, like you don't want to scare him off. Lift the gun to your eye, picture a German uniform on the target, then line it up in the sights. Before you shoot, take a deep breath, hold it, and think of Fred. Remember that you are aiming at his killer, not just a paper target. Then squeeze the trigger." He cleared his throat. "I think of my brother every time."

Dot rose unsteadily to her feet, wondering if that's all it was. As with everything else, she'd approached this exercise as a technical lesson, but she knew it was not about that. Firing a gun was about actually wounding, if not killing, another person, and the idea of doing that felt like a punch to her gut. She could not imagine a possible moment in her future when she might resort to doing that. She'd heard too many dying voices through her headphones, too many men crying out to God in different languages, begging for forgiveness, for rescue . . . No, she couldn't end someone's life. If that was why she kept missing the mark, Dot would have to accept that successfully hitting a target would never be a part of her arsenal.

She stepped toward the line, acutely aware of the pistol in her hand. As always, her mind went to the absurdity of the situation. Who would ever have imagined Dot the Dormouse firing a gun? She felt slightly ridiculous, and knowing everyone was watching didn't help. It was like being called to the blackboard to demonstrate to the class that she knew nothing about engines.

Months ago, when Dot had first been forced to step out of Dash's shadow, she hadn't known much about failure. If there had been a chance of failing at something, she simply would not try. She would not go to dances; she would not climb a tree. Since then, she had done so many things that had scared her at first, but without any choice, she had simply worked at them until she was comfortable. Not here, though. Here at the range, when she missed a shot, she took another, having already accepted it would not hit the target. She was confident in her inability. Having recognized that, she felt awful.

Now, garnered by Gordon's words, she shoved her old instincts down. He was right. This wasn't a technical or personal challenge; it was a rehearsal for reality. For revenge, even. Fred had been a fun, happy, nutty boy. He'd become a pilot because his dad had been a pilot. He'd joined the war along with so many others because he wanted to defeat a common enemy, and because all his friends were going. Maybe he'd even dreamed of someday becoming a hero, like his dad. He hadn't deserved to die.

Still, the idea of killing anyone, even the enemy, felt wrong to Dot. When she looked across the field, all she saw was a paper target, and she knew she would miss again.

Then Dash appeared in her imagination. She was flying one of those warplanes she never stopped talking about, oblivious to the dangers Dot heard every day. Her beautiful sister's eyes sparkled with joy, and she was laughing.

Dash's plane suddenly burst into flames, and the target changed before Dot's eyes.

She lifted the gun and put a German uniform on the target, just as Gordon had suggested. Still thinking of the fire, Dot forced herself to believe to her core that the invisible attacker had killed Dash. Now there was no question in Dot's mind. He deserved to die. She shifted the uniform slightly in her mind so the centre of the target was exactly where the man's heart would be, and she heard Dash call her name. Blinking away tears so she could see clearly, she squeezed the trigger again and again.

Bull's-eye.

———

Graduation was an understated affair. There were no certificates or awards of any kind given out. To the rest of the world, Camp X did not exist, and no one here needed to see proof that they had successfully completed the training. If they hadn't, they wouldn't be here.

Nevertheless, Gerald called the group of six into his office to officially welcome them to Camp X as graduates.

"Camp X is known by a few names," he began, surprising Dot. After all they'd been taught over the past two months, she was impressed he still had information to share. "To the Royal Canadian Mounted Police, we are S25-1-1. To the Canadian military we are Project J. The Special Operations Executive, a branch of Britain's MI-6, calls us STS-103. Whatever the name, we are the organization that everyone—and no one—is talking about. We came into existence December 6, 1941, because of a request made by Sir Winston Churchill to the chief of the British Security Co-ordination, William Stephenson, a Canadian from Winnipeg. Churchill's exact words to Stephenson were that he wanted him to create 'the clenched fist that would provide the knockout blow' to the Axis powers."

With a flourish, Gerald raised his closed fist and met the eyes of each graduate for a heartbeat. "Ladies and gentlemen, that is who we are. We are that closed fist. Welcome to the team."

thirty-two
DASH

—June 1943 —
Fort William, Ontario

Dash stared at the envelope she had just taken from Mrs. Simmons's pudgy fingers, dread pooling in her stomach. Telegrams, Dash had a feeling, were mostly used for bad news. She had never received one. Not until today.

Who would have sent her a telegram? Could it be Gus? Was he all right? But if something had happened to him, Dash wouldn't be the one receiving a notification. Where would they send it? Likely to her parents. Then who? Sick to her stomach, Dash tore the envelope open and felt her heart stop.

DAD IS ILL NOT MUCH TIME
COME HOME STOP MOM

"Dad."

Dash gaped at the wall, trying to think straight. She had to go home. Today. Had to tell Miss MacGill she was leaving. Had to get to the train station and buy a ticket . . .

She lunged for her suitcase, half buried beneath her clothes, and threw everything in. Then she pulled on a skirt and sweater, rushed to clean her teeth and brush her hair. That done, she screwed on her hat—aware that she was barely presentable—and tore out of the house.

What was wrong with her father? Her mother had never mentioned anything in earlier letters. Oh, how could she have sent such a cryptic telegram? Not much time? It couldn't possibly be something *that* bad, could it?

Dash took the bus to CanCar, suitcase gripped in her sweating hand, then she threw back her head and uttered a silent scream, frustrated with the bus's labouring progress. Was it always this slow? Once she spoke to Miss MacGill, there would be a long train ride home, and she already knew that every second in that train would be spent worrying that she was too late. If only she could leap into one of the Hurricanes and fly home.

By the time the factory opened on Monday, Dash would be back home with her parents. She knew Miss MacGill would understand once she heard what had happened, but Dash couldn't just up and leave without any explanation. It broke her heart that she wouldn't be able to say goodbye to her friends, but they'd understand. They were expecting her to leave soon for England anyway. And what about the ATA girls? Would they still take her after she abandoned her post like this?

At the office, she yanked on the front door, almost pulling her shoulder out of its socket. The door was locked. Of course. *Saturday.* Wasn't Miss Rose here at least? She banged on the door, but no one came.

Dash pounded on the door again, her stomach clenched. "Is anyone in there?"

No one answered. Crushed, she leaned back against the door, imagining her father as she'd last seen him, because she couldn't bear to think of him in any other condition.

She'd failed at Eisens, today she would run off from Miss MacGill without telling her why, and now she might lose her only chance to fly in the war. None of that mattered. Dash would *not* fail her father. She would be there for him, her mother, and Dot. Family was the most important thing of all. *Hang on, Dad! I'm coming!*

"Miss Wilson?"

A small door down the building had opened, and a familiar face peered out.

"Charlie! Oh, thank goodness!" She wiped away her tears. "I need to see Miss MacGill!"

"She isn't here today."

"No! She has to be!"

She launched into her story, and the sweet, patient boy nodded as she explained everything in a flurry of words that even Dot probably couldn't have kept up with. In the end, he not only promised to pass the message along to Miss MacGill, but he insisted on driving Dash to the train station and waiting with her until it came.

As her train finally pulled out, Dash watched Charlie and the car slide past the window, feeling wretched. *This isn't fair*, she thought, tears streaming down her cheeks. She was supposed to ship out and report for duty with the Air Transport Auxiliary in two weeks. She should be packing and laughing and looking up friends to say farewell. She was so proud of herself. So proud, and so happy. And now . . .

None of it mattered anymore. She had to get home.

thirty-three
DOT
-.. .. --- -

— *Camp X* —

Dot's favourite part of every day, bar none, was when she had Hydra to herself. To no one's apparent surprise, she had caught on quickly. As soon as she entered the building, she felt in full control of everything going on around her.

Sometimes, as she listened to the rest of the world, far away, she thought of the freezing cold hut at Coverdale and wondered about her friends. Did Alice or Sally think of her at all? She imagined they might have wondered about her for the first while, then moved on. They'd be as busy as ever, hunting U-boats and scribbling out messages. Did the Menace still taunt them?

Now that Dot was officially a part of Camp X, assigned with the dual roles of working with Hydra and manning a desk in headquarters, she was able to see more of the big picture. Before, she had been trying to assemble a puzzle with at least half the pieces missing. Here, she felt great satisfaction, seeing more things play out. The intercepted codes from her friends at Coverdale and from other listener stations across Canada, as well as those intercepted at Camp X, were usually sent to Ottawa, and sometimes to the United States. The most urgent of them were sent to Bletchley Park in England. Dot didn't know much about Bletchley, but from what she could figure out, it was the last stop for codebreakers. After Bletchley decrypted the messages, London made decisions about what actions to take, if any.

I could work there, she dared think. She never mentioned that aspiration to anyone, but she knew it to be true. Her abilities to break codes were getting sharper by the day. Sometimes she joined the women with their heads down in the codebreaking room, craving the mental stimulation and the satisfaction of solving something new, but her favourite job was still picking up on those tiny, almost inaudible dits and dahs through Hydra. And now she had the authority—in certain cases—to transmit some of those herself. She was no longer restricted to listening, here at Camp X. It felt like so long ago that Alice had asked her what she might say to the enemy if she could transmit. Now she could.

The day after she graduated, the camp suddenly teemed with agents returning from around the world, and Dot was struck by how regular the incoming men and women appeared. If she hadn't worked there herself, she never would have guessed who they really were. Now she saw agents on a daily basis as they passed through on their way to being debriefed in one of the back rooms. From there, the senior secretaries typed up their reports. Dot never saw any of their notes, and while she understood the reason for the secrecy, she couldn't help being a little disappointed. She was so close to their adventures, and yet so far.

As the previous agents flowed in, the new group flowed out. Dot stood at the main door, bidding her friends goodbye as they embarked on their first jobs in the field.

"It's not goodbye, silly," Ruby said, giving Dot a hug. "I'll bring you something from France when I'm back. Cheese? Oh, wait. That's Switzerland. Chocolate? Switzerland again. How about a croissant?"

Gordon looked like he didn't know whether to shake Dot's hand or not, so Dot took the initiative and hugged him instead. "We listeners don't say good luck. We say 'good hunting,'" she told him. "I hope you hunt them all down."

"We will," he assured her. "We may not be able to tell you anything about it, but you'll know we did well when you see us again."

It was difficult to say goodbye. Especially when the future was so unknown. Nothing in this world, Dot had discovered, was guaranteed.

After dinner, she passed Frances, Gerald's secretary, sitting at her desk. Frances was a tiny little thing with a bubbly smile that might encourage a stranger to underestimate her. But above her deep dimples, Frances's eyes were steel with intelligence. Dot had recognized that right away and stayed firmly on the woman's good side, which was easy. She was a lovely girl, and Dot was in awe of her efficiency. If someone asked Frances for directions to China, she'd have a map in her hand within seconds, Dot was sure.

"Oh, Dot! There's a telegram for you," Frances said, holding it out. Dot opened it right away.

DAD IS ILL NOT MUCH TIME
COME HOME STOP MOM

Breathless, she pressed the note to her heart, too stunned to move, and felt the walls closing in on her. Her hands were suddenly cold with sweat. Not much time? What could be wrong? Her mother's letters had mentioned his headaches were increasing, but she'd never suggested they were serious. Were they to do with his illness?

"Dot?"

Her mind went to Dash, who she imagined was already packing for the long trip from Fort William. Getting home would take a couple of days. Oh, how lost her mother must feel, all on her own! Dot had to go home right now, to tend her father and help her mother. She would leave first thing in the morning. First, she had to talk to Gerald.

"Dot? Are you all right?"

She glanced at Frances, off balance. "I . . . I need to speak with Gerald."

Frances quickly brought her in, and Dot stood stiffly in front of his desk until he gestured for her to sit.

"Dot," he said with a broad smile, "I have been meaning to commend you on the superior work you've been doing."

"Thank you, sir," she said, her fists bunched at her sides. "Unfortunately, I am here on a personal matter." She thrust the telegram into his hand. "This just arrived. I have no time to waste, sir."

He frowned at the note, then he slowly passed it back. "I'm sorry to see this. Truly."

"I need to go home and take care of him, sir. Right away. Dash will already be on a train."

"And Dash is . . . ?"

"My sister, sir. She's been building Hurricanes at CanCar, but she'll soon be going to England to join the ATA."

"Ah. Your parents had a sense of humour with names," he observed.

"Yes, sir. About my father, sir?"

He laced his fingers together and looked her straight in the eye. "We talked about this when you first arrived. I am afraid I cannot permit you off the base at this time."

Her throat knotted with panic. "But, sir, you said that if there were special circumstances—"

"I did. And these would be considered special circumstances, of course; however, at this time, we have too many operations going on. I simply cannot allow you to leave."

"But, sir! It's my father! Please."

His expression was sympathetic. "I am very sorry."

"My mother would never have sent this if it wasn't urgent. I fear he is dying. How can I tell my family that I cannot join them at his side?" She knew it was unprofessional, but she couldn't stop tears from coming to her eyes. "My poor mother and my sister . . . They think I'm a clerk, sir! They won't understand!"

He let out a long breath, and Dot wished with everything that she had that he would change his mind. Then he reached inside his coat for his handkerchief and handed it to her, and she knew her cause was lost.

"I suggest you tell your family that you are working on a top-secret file that requires a report, which is being written for the office of the prime minister. It is due on his desk in Ottawa right away, but it has only this morning been started. It will take a while to pull it all together."

She dabbed her eyes with his handkerchief. "Am I?"

"Not precisely."

"My father might be dying, and I must lie to my family?"

"I am afraid so, Petty Officer Wren Wilson."

She didn't miss the fact that he used her rank this time. He was officially serious. There was no way she could leave the camp.

"Again, I am terribly sorry." He gestured to the door. "Please see yourself out."

In a daze, Dot stood, clutching his desk for support, then she left his office on shaky legs. She craved her bed, where she could be alone to cry, but it was time for her shift. Mute, she took up her post by Hydra and put on the headphones, still warm from Thomas's previous shift. She sat and closed her eyes, waiting for the secret sounds of war to travel through the air, but her mind refused to settle. Instead, it gathered her up and carried her home to her family's arms. Home to her father's bedside, where he would be holding Dash's hand but not hers. Dash never would have let Dot suffer alone with him, but Dot was doing exactly that, leaving all the pain to Dash, her mother, and her poor father. She was letting down everyone she loved.

What would Dash do in this situation? If she was forbidden to leave and confined to the oath, would she find a way around it?

From the corner of her eye, she was aware of the door opening and a man stepping into the room. Moments later, she felt a touch on her arm. She looked up into the compassionate gaze of Bill Hardcastle, the original genius behind the creation of Hydra, and Dot's teacher. Ever since her arrival at Camp X, he had quietly and expertly taught her the secrets of Hydra, and she'd come to understand that he was the kind of man who preferred to speak with radios over people.

Bill calmly informed her that she was dismissed from Hydra for now. He suggested she take some time to sort out her thoughts—while remaining on the base—then return to her post the following morning. Dot left without a word and returned to the main building. Somehow, she kept her emotions under control until someone bid her a cheery good day, then she shattered. With her hand over her mouth, she quick-walked down the corridor, looking straight ahead as tears rolled down her face. At the end of the hall, she turned into a seldom-used office and collapsed onto a chair.

How was she supposed to tell her family that she couldn't come? That she was sworn to secrecy, even from them? Dash would hate her for it, and Dot couldn't blame her. If her father's illness was as bad as she feared, Dot might never see him again. Was he asking for her right now? Waiting for her? Brief, panicked thoughts of fleeing the camp flashed through her mind, but that was impossible. Running from Camp X would be considered as bad as treason.

"Miss? I'm sorry to intrude, but are you all right?"

The voice was familiar. Dot jerked upright, wiping her face, then her jaw dropped.

"Gus?"

thirty-four
DASH

— *Oshawa, Ontario* —

The house was very still when Dash barged in on a gust of wind, and the silence frightened her. She stopped short.

"Mom?" she called softly.

"I'm in here." Her mother's voice came from the second floor, so Dash tiptoed upstairs.

Her father was sleeping, his mouth slack against the pillow, his breathing shallow. Her mother sat on a chair at his side, knitting calmly, just as Dash remembered her doing all her life. But she didn't look the same. Dash read the exhaustion on her face. And the resignation in her eyes.

"I'm so glad to see you."

Dash knelt at her side. "What's happened?"

She set aside her knitting then laid her cool hands on Dash's. "It's a tumour, Margaret. In his brain. There's nothing to be done."

Dash couldn't move. "No. There has to be something they can do. An operation? Some kind of medicine?"

"I . . ." Her eyes closed briefly. "Your father has been sick for many years, Margaret. We both knew about it, and though the doctors tried every avenue, we have known the truth all along. The tumour is simply too big."

"His headaches? All this time?"

It had been right there in front of her all along. Those days when he couldn't bear the light, when he couldn't move from his chair. She had thought nothing of it. Just a headache, he'd said. Probably just something in my head, he'd joked. No wonder he was always so pale.

"But why didn't we—"

"He didn't want anyone to know. He kept it secret for everyone's sake. He is so proud of you both and everything you are accomplishing. He didn't want to get in the way of that."

Dash faced the slight figure on the bed, tears streaming down her cheeks. "What now?"

"All they can do is give him pain relief. It helps him sleep." Her fingers skimmed her husband's pale brow. "He sleeps most of the time now."

He looked shrunken, his black eyelashes stark against the paleness of his face. Even sleeping, she could see the strain in his expression as he battled the pain. Dash leaned in to kiss his cheek. He didn't react.

"When is Dot coming? She must be devastated. She and Dad . . ." She didn't need to say anything more. They both knew Dash's sister and father were closer than anyone else.

"I imagine she will be all right eventually."

Her mother's hesitation made Dash's skin itch. "You imagine?"

"She sent a telegram saying she can't come home."

"I don't understand."

"She isn't allowed to leave her work."

Dash drew back, aghast. "That's ridiculous! There has to be a way. I mean, Dad is . . ." The words pounded against her skull. *He's dying.* "Did you write back to her?"

"I only just heard from her this morning. I haven't had an opportunity." She glanced at the bed, then whispered, "She can't, Margaret. That's all there is to it. I wrote to Gus as well, but he hasn't replied. It's you and me now. And Uncle Bob and Aunt Lou, of course. They have been wonderful. They come every day. They'll be here tonight."

"Does Dot have a telephone we could call at least?"

"I was never told of one. I don't know how to reach her except by sending letters, and it's a central mailing address. I have no idea where she really is."

In the living room by the front door, the grandfather clock gave a tired *Bong! Bong! Bong!* then returned to its endless counting. Endless, that is, if her mother remembered to wind it. The old clock had been her father's responsibility, but now her mother would have to keep the time. What a weight to bear alone.

"Mom, please go and sleep in my bed for a while."

Her mother looked startled. "Oh no, I couldn't. What if he wakes up?"

"If he wakes up, he'll see me. Let me take care of him for a bit. Please."

Dash nearly cried fresh tears, seeing the gratitude in her mother's eyes. She watched her go, then she studied her father's sleeping face, wishing he would open his eyes. She needed to speak with him. She needed to hear his voice. If only she could make him laugh in that careful, measured way. If only she could walk through the kitchen and see him bent over a crossword puzzle with Dot, not looking old at all. Not in pain. How lucky Dot had been, to have spent so much of her time with him. To understand him the way she did. Dash had never felt envious of her sister until now.

All the years Dash had wasted. When her father and Dot had sat quietly together, she had chosen instead to play outside or go out with her friends. She'd never considered there might come a day when he wouldn't be there. She needed to make up for so much lost time, but she didn't know how much was left.

She felt suffocated in the dark room, so she opened the curtains to let the sunshine in. If he woke and it hurt his head, she would close them in a blink, but for now she needed the brightness of day. She needed a glimpse of the blue sky, laced like the curtains in thin white strands.

Was it true, what they said about people rising to heaven after they died? When Dash flew in the wide-open sky, above the birds and the cares of everyday people, there was so much quiet—outside of engine noise, that is. She felt alone up there, free, weightless, able to drift through the clouds, to bank on a sunbeam. The sky was Dash's idea of heaven. If she died, she'd want to be up there. So she hoped it was true.

There was a softness to her father's cheeks she had never noticed before. A thickness to his black hair, which was like hers, though his sparkled with silver strands. A fist twisted her heart as she realized that she would never know him as someone whose hair turned grey.

At last, those dark lashes lifted, and his eyes pulled into focus. She opened her mouth to speak, then closed it. They were already communicating. She might not have sat with him over puzzles or tapped Morse code with him for fun, but she knew that pale gaze all the way to her soul. Dot might be his twin in that sense, but Dash was just as much his daughter. She knew how much he loved her, because she had seen it in his expression since she could remember.

"Are you in pain?" she finally asked. Her mother had shown her where the pills were. They both hoped she wouldn't have to give him any. Not for a bit.

"I'm all right for now." His voice was raspy. "I am so happy to see you, Margaret."

"I came as soon as I could," she said, and her mind flew to her sister. "I wish Dot was here."

"As do I," he whispered on a breath, then he drifted back to sleep.

thirty-five
DOT

-· ·· --- -

— Camp X —

Dot's burning eyes took in the Gus she knew so well, needing to convince herself he was real. All her life, he'd been her protector, and here he was in her hour of need. He was regarding her with the same kind of wonder she felt rushing through her, then he seemed to come to his senses. He stepped forward and gathered her in his arms before either of them could say anything else. Only when she believed she could contain her emotions did she release him.

"What are you doing here?" she asked, but he spoke at the same time.

"What's wrong? I've never seen you cry before."

She started to explain, but her words came quickly, too quickly.

He handed her a handkerchief from his pocket. "Try again. Slowly, Dot."

Instead, she gave him the telegram, and shock darkened his features, followed by understanding. "You can't go," he said softly.

"How am I supposed to tell them?" she cried. "They'll never believe me."

"They'll have to. You don't have a choice, unless you want to go to jail, or worse."

Oh, the pain in her heart! "You have to go, Gus. Tell them something. You'll think of something."

He shook his head. "I can't go, either."

"Even if it's for a day, just to give Mom a hug. A couple of hours."

"No, really. I can't go."

"Why not?"

"Because I work here, too."

———

For the third night in a row, Dot lay awake in her bed, hours after her shift ended, staring at the ceiling. She felt as if she hadn't slept at all. Or maybe she did. Perhaps she slept and dreamed of waking. She couldn't be sure. All she knew was her father was dying, and she had let her family down. And the reason why she couldn't be with them was a secret she must keep for forty years.

Thank goodness Gus had been there. What an impossible coincidence that had been! To see him at that moment, she had felt like a drowning woman being thrown a life preserver. She couldn't imagine having gone through the initial shock alone, and from the look on his face, she knew he felt the same. Her family was his family, after all. But she hadn't seen him since then, and she was on her own again.

On the first night, they had stayed up late, their conversation flowing from her father to memories from their childhood. Her father had always been in the background, quietly observing, or else he was teaching them: physics, mathematics, science. She saw his expression fall when they spoke of Dash, and how she might be feeling right now, wondering where they were. She knew it must hurt him terribly not to be there with her. He had always been closer to Dash than herself. They had more in common. But now, incredibly, he was here, far from Dash. It was selfish, she knew, but Dot was privately pleased to have him to herself for a change.

Since they were both stationed at Camp X, they were able to share the basics of their jobs with each other, just not specifics. After he'd voiced their shared amazement that they both had ended up there, he admitted he wasn't surprised to hear she was working with Hydra. He told her he was an operative, often working in Europe, tasked with sabotaging the enemy as well as recruiting and training agents to join the French Resistance. When he said that he spent more time over there than he did at Camp X, she tried not to show her disappointment.

From an early age, Dot had been captivated by Gus. As a boy in her house, he'd been a novelty, and the fact that he could not only keep up to but exceed Dash in her fearlessness had enthralled her. The two of them were strong and energetic, teasing and laughing, competing all the time. But as connected as they were, they always included Dot by checking that she felt content and included. And she had, until she turned fourteen. Then something changed. Dash kept on playing rough games with Gus and the other boys at school, but a strange new jealousy had begun to burn Dot's chest.

It wasn't about Dash's confidence. Dot admired that. It wasn't that she got to play with the boys and Dot chose not to. It was the sight of Gus's hand resting casually on her sister's shoulder that pinched Dot into awareness. The way Dash jumped into his arms for a hug after she hit a home run. Dot craved that closeness. She wanted Gus to look at her that way, with those pale blue eyes and that warm smile. She wanted to be the one to make him laugh.

After the shock of the telegram, as they spoke for hours in her tiny bedroom, her gaze had taken in the light stubble on his cheeks. Uninterrupted, and in such a vulnerable space, she'd noticed the movement of his throat, even the softness of his lips. When he couldn't possibly detect her interest, she studied the line of his shoulders beneath his loose white shirt. She was here with him, alone. All this was new, and she was so ashamed.

After he left for his own room, Dot sat a while, staring at her stationery. She had meant to write a letter to Dash and her mother, but after everything, her mind was blank. She would write in the morning. She would labour over every line, but in the end it wouldn't matter. They would only see the one that said she was not coming home.

She didn't know where Gus had been for the past forty-eight hours, and a part of her felt plagued with guilt. He'd been there for her, and she had needed him. But another—very secret—part of her had *wanted* him. His absence suggested that he had probably noticed.

There was nothing she could do about any of it. Tomorrow was another day. No one, including Gerald, would accept her putting in less effort than she always did. She closed her eyes, exhausted. She should at least try to sleep.

She was startled by a faint knock on her door. No one should be walking around the building this late. "Who is it?"

There was no answer save another tentative knock. She reached for her robe, wrapping it around herself. "Who's there?"

"Open up, Dot," Gus whispered.

She pulled the door open and yanked him inside, out of sight. "What on earth are you doing here?"

"Let's go see your dad."

"What?! Are you crazy?"

"Yeah. Put on something warm. And dark."

"Right now?"

"It has to be tonight. I leave for Europe in the morning."

She stared at him, confused. "But how—"

"Are you going to stand there asking questions, or do you want to go? There's no time to waste."

She grabbed a shirt from her dresser and held it up. "Dark enough?"

"No, not your uniform. Yes, wear your boots." He turned around, giving her privacy. "Hurry."

She'd never dressed so quickly in her life. "Done."

"Here. Put this on."

It was a black wool cap just like the one he was wearing, and she understood what he wanted right away. While he watched, she rolled her blond hair into a bun then tucked all the ends under the hat.

"Good?"

He smiled. "Perfect. Let's go."

He didn't need to tell her that everything depended on keeping quiet and moving fast, so she bit her tongue. She trusted Gus. Even more so, now that he was a fully trained agent. He snuck around for a living. Still, her pulse thumped like a bass drum in her ears as he led the way down the pitch-black corridor. She stuck to him like a second skin, every hair on her body raised, her fingertips skimming the wall for reference. The hinges on the exit door barely made a sound when he pushed it open. When they stepped out into the chill of the night, Dot paused on the doorstop, shivering. She didn't think she'd ever been out this late in her life. It felt almost dreamlike.

He leaned in close so he could keep his voice down. "You okay?"

It struck her that because of the moon, the night was brighter outside than in. She could see his face clearly; the blue of his eyes looked grey. She nodded, willing herself to stop shaking.

"It's a bit of a walk. If we go fast, you'll warm up. Just hang on to me."

He took her hand and led her along the dormitory wall, staying hidden as much as possible. It occurred to her that she didn't need to hold his hand, and that they might be able to run a little faster if she didn't, but it was reassuring being connected to him. When she slipped on a little dip in the grass, he swooped in, an arm around her waist for balance.

"You all right?"

"I'm fine. This is crazy, Gus. What are we doing?"

She saw his grin through the darkness. "We're on an adventure. I know that's not usually your thing, but in this case—"

A dog barked in the distance, and Gus was instantly alert. He grabbed her hand again, and they sprinted across the field toward a line of trees blocking the starry sky. They didn't slow until they were into the thick of the forest, then he let go so she could better navigate the twisted twigs and weeds at their feet. He was a dark figure to follow, but every now and then he paused to make sure she was still with him. She was. During her training she'd become agile and strong, and she trusted her own abilities.

She couldn't tell how long they walked, maybe a half hour of winding through the trees before they began to thin. The flat grey line of a road materialized before them.

"Where are we?" she asked.

"Thornton Road."

Remembering her driver's words that first day, she looked both ways. "We have to make sure no one sees us. Can't let anyone find the camp."

"True. We're all right. I checked. How'd you know that?"

She told him about her driver. "He said if there was anybody in view, he'd keep on driving."

Gus went to a large pile of branches on the side of the road and started throwing them to the side. Just like in their childhood days, she copied him without question. Then she caught a glimpse of metal beneath, and she almost laughed. He'd hidden a car. Seeing it, she cleared the brush off even faster.

Gus turned, watching her pitch the heavy branches.

"What?"

"No more Dot the Dormouse for you."

She warmed all the way through. The Wrens had changed her. Camp X even more. Dot never wanted to be that person again.

"After all the training I've had since Conestoga, I should hope not," she replied. "Where did you get the car?"

He wiggled his eyebrows like he had when they were kids. "I have my ways. Get in."

"What happens if we get caught?" she asked after they were on the road. She noticed he hadn't turned on his headlights.

"We won't."

"How do you know?"

"Because I don't want to think about what would happen."

She sank back into her seat, watching the unfamiliar landscape transform into something she had known forever. She'd forgotten just how close Camp X was to Oshawa and how disappointed she had been, learning she wouldn't be able to visit her family. Her mother's telegram had brought it rushing back.

"I understand why they don't want me to leave Camp X." She gazed out the window, feeling a little sad. "But they know me by now. They know I'd never spill a drop of a secret. I'm as loyal as they come."

Gus peered sideways at her, one hand on the wheel. "Yet here you are, on a covert midnight rendezvous."

"Under extraordinary circumstances. I still wouldn't tell any secrets," she muttered.

"Did you know that if you did get to go out, you'd be followed by the Mounties? They'd write down everything you said, ate, and did, then give their notes to Camp X HQ. You'd be quizzed on everything."

That didn't sound so bad, if she could see her family once in a while.

Gus put his hand on hers. "This will be worth it, Dot. Even if the worst happens. Which it won't."

He turned his lights on when they got into town, because driving without might be suspicious. It didn't make any difference. The streets were empty. They passed the elementary school, and Dot briefly wondered about her students. Were they still learning French? One or two might be in high school by now. Did they ever think about the lessons? Did they ever think about her?

When they reached their street, Gus exhaled. "Here we go."

It hit her full force. She was going to see her father. She was going to say goodbye. Gus glanced at her as they passed the familiar houses, and she knew he was feeling the same as she was—anticipation that would soon be smothered by grief. It was her turn to squeeze his hand.

He parked the car a half a block away. "We can't see your mother. You know that, right? Or Dash. We can't see anyone but him. I'll climb up and peek through the window, but if there's anyone else in there, we have to turn around and go right back."

Her heart sank. Surely someone would be sitting at his bedside. "I understand."

She practically jogged along the road in her haste to get home. When the familiar white house came into view, her gaze slid to the maple tree at the side. It looked so much smaller than she remembered. They paused behind the neighbour's fence, out of sight of anyone passing by, collecting their thoughts, and Gus looked up at the tree, too. Was he remembering Dash up there, teasing them both? Did he see the big yard where he and

Dash had played catch so often, their leather gloves making a soft *thwack!* whenever they caught the ball?

Dot remembered it all. She had been there too, on the ground or on the stump, listening to them laugh, and though they spoke to her while they played, she had always felt a bit forgotten, being on the outside. It was no one's fault but her own. She'd been self-conscious, fearing that if she tried, she'd drop the ball more than she caught it, embarrassed to admit—even to the two of them—that she didn't know how to throw a ball.

Did he remember getting older and going out at night with Dash and some of the other kids, always trying—and usually failing—to convince Dot to come? Dot did. She remembered feeling so disappointed in herself every time she sent them off without her.

If she could go back in time, things would be different. Now that she knew so much more about herself and what she was capable of, she would have joined them, and she might have been surprised at how well she did. After all, she wasn't bad with a pistol and a target these days. If she could go back, she would laugh more, try new things. It was so hard to think of all the time she'd wasted.

"You know what I remember most?" Gus asked quietly.

"Dash," she said out of reflex.

He glanced at her with surprise. "Not Dash. You. Sitting on that tire swing your dad made. I was pushing you, and you kept making me solve math problems."

That's what came back to him? Not the fact that Dot had never really done anything fun? "They were easy problems," she teased. "If you'd gotten one wrong, we would have switched places. Why didn't you just make a mistake?"

"I liked pushing you on that swing. I could have done it all day."

He held her eyes for a heartbeat, looking as though he had more to say, then he lifted his gaze up toward her parents' window.

"I'll go up the tree and see if he's alone. I'll come down and get you if he is. Otherwise, we're leaving."

She nodded, feeling divided. Someone should be with her father. Someone should be taking care of him, making sure he had everything he needed. He shouldn't be alone. But with all her heart, she hoped he was.

thirty-six
DASH

— *Oshawa, Ontario* —

Dash had mustered a show of strength for her family, but she could feel it giving way. She tended to her father, comforted her mother, and did whatever shopping, cooking, and cleaning needed doing, all while fearing she might completely fall apart.

Her father came and went, going in and out with the medications, riding the pain then floating above its absence, with brief stretches of clarity in between. When he was lucid, she took full advantage, soaking in all she could.

"I'm sure there's a good reason," he said when Dash mentioned her sister again. "If she cannot come, I want you to forgive her."

"I don't think I can."

His eyes were sunken into his skull, surrounded by tired black circles, and the whiteness of his skin appeared ashen in contrast to his black moustache. When she touched his hand, his skin was cold, smooth, and as soft as an old man's—not the skin of a forty-year-old.

"It's the only thing I will ask of you, my beautiful girl. Open your heart to your sister. Welcome her back. She would not have stayed away if she'd had any choice. You know that in your heart. Please, Margaret. Forgive her."

Dash couldn't see that happening. Ever. Dot had abandoned her family, not just her father. She had abandoned *her*.

Instead of responding, she asked, "Is the light hurting your eyes? Should I close the curtains?"

"In a minute. I want to see you. You are looking so well. You must really enjoy your job. And what's all this about England?"

She was glad to talk about CanCar for a while. He smiled when she described joking around with her coworkers or how it felt to build, then fly a Hurricane. She told him everything she knew about the ATA and how incredible it was, just knowing they wanted her there, but she didn't mention the decision she'd made. He never would have allowed it. Dash had agonized over it for days, but in the end it had been simple. After her father was gone, Dash would give up her dream of flying with the ATA. Her mother needed her here.

Her father dozed, and Dash stopped talking. A hole had begun to form in her heart, thinking of her life. All the adventures, all the laughter and dreams she'd had, they seemed so shallow now. Fly? Why should she care about flying, when her father could no longer drink water on his own? Why was it important for her to reach the sky when he would never stand again?

"Proud of you, Margaret," he whispered, his eyes still closed. "So very proud. Live your life to the fullest."

She felt a collapse coming, building in her throat and burning behind her nose. She could no more prevent its arrival than stop a train with her bare hands. He heard her little sob and opened his eyes.

"Margaret."

Her tears burst through, and she struggled to get words past them. "I don't know how to handle this. I don't know what to say or do or think anymore. I feel so lost. Please, Dad, there has to be something we can do to make you well again. This can't be happening. Not to you. What will I do without you?"

In response, he drew her hand to his lips and kissed the back of it. His eyes shone. "I will always be with you, Margaret. You know I could never really leave any of you."

The next day was Aunt Lou's birthday. In the evening they celebrated it quietly in Dash's father's room so he could be included. Dash snuggled up close to him, listening to him sing a little when her mother entered, carrying the spice cake—that same spice cake she remembered from her childhood. After taking a tiny nibble, he'd drifted off to sleep. At least he had been there, still with them.

Uncle Bob seemed so much older than he'd been last December, when Dash had seen him last. Back then, he'd cheered her on despite her misery after Eisen's, encouraging her to write to Miss MacGill. He'd changed Dash's life by doing that, just like he'd changed it years before by letting her fly with him. But he'd lost his son, and now he was losing his brother. She worried about him. He'd gotten almost skinny since she'd been at CanCar. Poor Aunt Lou looked completely worn out.

After her aunt and uncle headed home, Dash sat at the kitchen table with her mother, the remnants of the cake and a solitary candle flickering between them. As she watched the halo of the flame, she thought about heaven again.

"I want you to go to England," her mother said, breaking the silence. "After."

Dash hadn't expected that. "No, Mom. I'll stay with you."

"I want you to go." Her voice was calm. "And I want lots of letters. I want to hear all about your life over there. I always wanted to go to England, you know. Not during a war, obviously, but . . ." She smiled. "I know what you're thinking, Dash, but you're wrong. I'm stronger than you think. This is the chance of a lifetime for you, and your father knows it as well. He and I have spoken about it."

"You've spoken about . . . after?"

"Of course." Her gaze went to the candle. "You can't really avoid that discussion when you spend your whole life with someone. He's made me promise that you'll go, and I told him I had already planned to send you on your way."

She'd thought she was all out of tears. She'd been wrong. "How can I?"

"There is nothing for you here, Dash. You aren't made for living a quiet life at home. Your future is up there, in the clouds. Your heart is built for adventure. Quite frankly, I think you'd drive me crazy if you stayed."

"Mom."

"I mean it."

Her father had basically said the same thing. *Live your life to the fullest.*

"I don't know, Mom. I haven't decided yet."

She went to her room and curled into a ball on her bed, her head so crammed with feelings she could hardly think. Needing comfort, she grabbed Dot's blanket and bundled herself in the soft material. Out of habit, she buried her nose in it, but her sister's scent was long gone, and anger shot to the top of her emotions. Dash shouldn't have had to go through this on her own. Dot was supposed to be her other half, not an empty space at their father's bedside. And what about Gus? Where was he? He hadn't even replied to her mother's telegram.

Her poor mother. She wanted Dash to go on and live her own life. She insisted that Dash should sail across the Atlantic and fly airplanes in the war, because she knew as well as anyone else that that was all Dash had ever wanted.

But everything had changed. Right now, all Dash wanted was family. Her mother and father. Her sister. Gus.

Tears trickled from the corners of her eyes as she drifted off to sleep. She woke a little later, thinking she'd heard something. A branch of her maple tree hitting the wall outside, perhaps. Or the boards of the old house creaking. A soft thump and scrape, like a window opening. She'd been away for so long she'd forgotten the old sounds. They were reassuring, bringing back memories of happier times. She could almost imagine peering across and seeing her sister sleeping peacefully through the night. Dash closed her eyes again, soothed by the little noises, too tired to let her emotions rise up again. Slowly, she breathed in, breathed out, listening to the sounds and remembering.

thirty-seven
DOT

- •• - - - -

— *Oshawa, Ontario* —

Dot held her breath, hidden in the shadows beneath her parents' bedroom window. Gus swung onto the first branch as if he were a gymnast then shimmied up to the next, higher than even Dash had ever gone. It bowed as he sidestepped along its length, then there was a sharp *crack!* followed by her own gasp. Dot covered her mouth, worried they had woken the entire neighbourhood, but other than a hound baying a warning down the street, everything seemed the same. Gus kept moving as if nothing had happened. When he was close enough, he pressed his face to the window. Dot held her breath.

"He's alone for now." He started climbing down. "I'm coming for you."

There was no need. Dot knew how to scale this tree. She'd watched her sister do it a hundred times, and since then Dot had trained hard. She was strong, and that knowledge gave her the confidence to grab the lowest branch. She pulled herself up, got her feet under her, then reached for the next.

From his perch above, Gus observed her, not saying a word. She read the delight in his expression and couldn't help smiling to herself.

"No more Dormouse," he said when she reached him. "You amaze me more and more."

He jimmied open the window then turned back and urged Dot along the branch ahead of him. The next step would be for her to vault off the tree and through the window. Peering down at the nighttime grass twenty feet below, she almost lost her nerve. Then she felt Gus's hands on her waist, anchoring her to safety, and she knew with certainty that he would never, ever let her fall. She leaned forward and gripped the top of the window frame, then she kicked off the branch and hung halfway inside the window, just over the edge. As she had practiced in training, she tucked her chin to her chest, pushed forward, and somersaulted into the darkened room.

Gus followed, landing with cat's feet behind her.

The room had a damp smell. She pictured her mother spending all day here, pressing cool cloths to her father's brow and helping him sip water. Barely breathing, Dot tiptoed toward the bed, blinking through the darkness as she sought him out. When she made out the shape of his head on the pillow, she was shocked by how diminished he was. This specter in the bed couldn't be her father, she thought desperately, a lump in her throat. She'd known he was ill, but seeing him now— He looked barely there.

Gus's arm brushed hers as he came to her side, and though she longed to bury herself in his arms and escape this nightmare, she did not glance at him. She was determined not to cry. If there was ever a time when Dot needed to be strong, it was now. Her father needed her. She would not let him down. She knelt, pulling the black cap off her head so that her hair tumbled loose, then she touched the back of her father's hand. His skin felt brittle, like paper, but she didn't pull away.

"Dad," she whispered. "Dad, it's me."

She feared he might not wake up, but his eyelids opened slowly, sluggish from pain, sleep, medications, she didn't know. As soon as he saw her, his eyes filled with tears.

"I knew you'd come," he exhaled.

The tears she had fought broke free, and she hugged him, soaking the collar of his pyjamas. She felt the sharpness of his shoulders—those shoulders she'd ridden on so many years before—and the weakness of his hands on her back.

"Oh, Dad," she whimpered. "I am so sorry I wasn't here. All this time."

"I knew you'd come," he said again.

The corners of his mouth twitched, and she was so glad she was there to witness it. And she was so, so grateful to Gus. Without him, she was certain she'd never have seen her father's little smile ever again.

"Does it hurt?"

"Medicine helps," he said huskily. "How are you?"

"I'm fine, Dad. I'm . . ." She glanced up at Gus, seeking guidance. What could she say?

"Gus, my boy," her father said, seeing him there.

Gus's eyes shone. "Mr. Wilson, I'm so sorry . . ."

"It's all right," her father told them. "It will be all right now that you've come."

Now came the hardest part. "Dad, we cannot stay. And you can't tell anyone that we were here. Not Mom, not Dash. No one."

Creases formed across his brow, catching the faint moonlight. "People are looking for you both."

She couldn't take her gaze from the lines of his face. They held her, carried her back. They had been there on those cool Sunday mornings at the kitchen table when they frowned at the crossword. Not even the sun had been awake on some of those mornings, just the two of them. When one solved a question, the other would nod, impressed. They would jot down the answer then sip at the cup of hot water they substituted for coffee, pretending to be satisfied.

Those same wrinkles had formed other times as well. Like whenever he removed his glasses and rubbed the bridge of his nose, trying to ease the pain she had never understood. How long had it plagued him? How long had he suffered silently? *Why didn't you tell us?*

"Your mother hasn't been able to reach you. She misses you terribly. Please stay and help her."

"I can't, Dad. This is the only time we will be able to come here."

"I don't understand. Why the secrecy? Why are you here in the middle of the night?" When neither of them answered, his eyes widened and went to her abdomen. "Are you in trouble? Has something happened?"

She almost laughed. Was he suggesting she might be "in trouble" because of Gus? "No, Dad. It's nothing like that." Beside her, Gus smiled but said nothing. "It's just something we can't talk about."

From downstairs Dot heard the old grandfather clock strike one, slightly muffled by the ceiling. Time was running out for all of them.

"Does it . . . have to do with the war?"

Of course he'd keep asking, and of course he would try to figure it out. As would she, in his place. All she could do was refuse to answer, and that was getting more difficult by the second.

"Dad, I—"

Gus put his hand on her shoulder for reassurance, then he crouched beside her, his expression set in stone. "Mr. Wilson, Dot and I work for a secret government agency."

Her heart stopped, hearing him say the forbidden facts out loud. Was he trying to get them both killed?

"Dot is a miracle worker when it comes to codebreaking and intercepting enemy signals, and I am a field agent who trains resistance groups in France, among other things." She saw his throat move as he swallowed. "We both signed oaths of secrecy, sir, which is why we need you to never say a word of our visit to anyone. By telling you this, and by being here without permission, we risk placing ourselves in front of a firing squad."

Gus turned to her, his face no longer hard. His eyes were dark with sorrow, and his grief hit her all at once. He believed her father would take their secrets with him to the grave, and very soon. She looked down at her father in anguish. This couldn't be happening. Her father couldn't simply be gone. Except it was, and he would be.

And when he is gone, she thought reluctantly, his pain will go as well.

A hint of a smile returned to her father's dry lips. "Heroes. You are both heroes. I knew all three of you would do big things. I could not be more proud." He looked at Gus, then back at Dot. "Your secret is safe with me. Now that I've sworn my own secrecy oath, can you tell me about your life?"

She'd kept everything inside her for so long it was difficult to get going, but Gus made a comment about how the Intelligence Department was fortunate to have Dot, and that helped her open up. She tried to sum up the past year, going into a little bit of extra detail about the codebreaking work, then she gave him a brief insight into the magic that was Hydra. Despite their weariness, his eyes lit up at the things she said, as if he could see his treasured puzzles once more.

When her stories ended, his gaze returned to Gus. "Young man, there's something I have always wanted to say to you, and I'm ashamed I never did. I want you to know that taking you into our home was our greatest decision. It has been our privilege to raise you to be the man you are today. Secret agent, indeed! Your father would have been so proud. Thank you for coming tonight, and for bringing my daughter."

Gus's jaw set against showing emotion. "You were the father I never had."

"And I know your weakness." A crafty grin spread across her father's face, astonishing her. "I have trouble seeing you as a spy, Gus. You were always a terrible liar."

"I'm better at it now," Gus said, his own smile shy.

"Perhaps. But I still see it."

Dot frowned. "See what, Dad?"

He winked, looking pleased with himself. "Ask him."

Dot and Gus exchanged a glance, then Gus looked away. She frowned at them both, puzzled, but her father's eyes suddenly opened wide.

"There's someone on the stairs," he whispered urgently. He squeezed Dot's hand, and though it was weak, it meant so much. "Thank you for coming. Tonight was the greatest gift you could have given me. I love you both with all my heart. Now go."

Gus drew her away when she couldn't move, and they crept soundlessly toward the window. For a heartbeat, she stood in confusion, feeling lost. When she glanced at the bed, she tried to imagine a peace settling over her father, but she couldn't see him in the dark. Everything in her ached to rush back and check, but Gus gently took her elbow, then he helped her through the window and onto the branch.

Along with the cool night air came moonlight and a sense of panic. Nothing felt real anymore. Seeking clarity, she tried to label all that she felt. Loss. Dread. Guilt. A need to push past Gus and go back in, to be with her father.

But Gus slipped the window closed then moved ahead of her on the branch. "Keep moving. We have to get out of view."

"I can't. How can I leave him?"

"Climb down, Dot. Follow me."

She knew he was right. It would do no one any good if they were to end up in front of a firing squad. Except . . . She looked back at the window, visualizing her father—

"Dot."

Gus was on the ground now, reaching for her. He had taken care of both sisters for as long as they had known him, and they trusted him with their lives. She had always followed him without a second thought. But this, this was the most difficult moment she had ever faced. She needed one more minute.

From the corner of her eye, she caught movement in the room. She ducked out of sight, but in that second she saw who was with her father, and she understood why she had needed that extra time. Dash's face glowed above the candle she carried then placed it on the bedside table. Then she sank onto the chair beside him, her back to Dot.

Dash was there. Dash was with him. Now Dot could go. It would be all right.

She moved slowly, testing every branch before putting her weight on it. Climbing up had felt easy; this was harder. On the last step, Gus clasped his hands around her waist to help her down. Once on solid ground, she looked up at him, still in disbelief.

"I will never forget what you did for me tonight."

She wrapped her arms around him so that his head rested on hers.

When his hold loosened, she stretched onto her toes and gave him a peck on the cheek. The light stubble brushing her lips was unfamiliar, and unexpectedly enticing. His eyes were closed, his lashes impossibly long. Something low in her belly tightened. On impulse, she kissed him again, this time on his lips.

He pulled away, startled, his eyes reading hers. Then he bent down and kissed her back the same way.

She moved back. What on earth had she just done? "I'm sorry," she blustered. "I— I don't know what I was thinking."

"It's all right, Dot. I've wanted to kiss you for a long time."

He was teasing, and she thought that cruel. Then again, after what she'd just done, maybe she deserved it. All along, he'd laughed at Dash's jokes, followed her lead, and taken her dancing on those nights Dot chose to stay home. Dash was the beauty between the two of them, and there had never been a question about Gus being a man who drew every girl's eye. Dot had always imagined the two of them together, though she'd never said anything.

Her lips tingled from the warmth of his. "That's not true."

He chuckled. "That's not something I'd lie about."

"Well, even if it is true, I couldn't do that to Dash. I have already hurt her enough."

He frowned. "What does this have to do with Dash?"

This. What was "this"? She retreated another step. "You and she . . ."

A sheepish smile rose to his mouth. "Your dad's right. I'm a lousy liar, and he guessed my secret. As great as you are with puzzles, you're terrible at seeing what's right in front of you. Of course I love Dash." His smile faded. "But it's always been you, Dot."

thirty-eight
DASH

— Oshawa, Ontario —

After a week in her parents' home, it had become obvious to Dash and everyone else that her father was fading fast. He barely spoke anymore, and when he did, the words often made no sense. The tumour was causing hallucinations, and it frightened Dash to see him tortured this way. From the slits of his eyes, she sensed how much pain he was in. She wanted that to end, but she never wanted him to go.

Thank goodness for Aunt Lou, who had singlehandedly taken over caring for everyone in the house. Perhaps that was how she eased her grief, Dash thought, accepting yet another casserole from her aunt. Now she sat with her in the kitchen while Uncle Bob spoke with his brother. At Dash's insistence, her mother was napping upstairs. She would need strength to deal with everything once it was all over. There was no longer a question that that moment would come soon. Dash had been here only a short while and she already felt wrung out like a dishrag, physically, mentally, and emotionally.

And Dot, well, Dot had broken her heart in a whole different way. Just the other day, her mother had received a letter from her. As far as Dash could see, it was one giant, unacceptable excuse.

I'm so sorry, Mom. It's a really important report. They tell me it will be shared between Prime Minister King and Churchill himself. I know you are in an impossible place, and it's a lot for me to ask, but I beg you to understand. This is not my choice. I am not allowed to go. I would be with you all if I could. Please tell Dash I'm sorry. And please tell Dad I love him . . .

Dash had crumpled the letter into a ball and dropped it in the trash. How could she do this to the family? To Dash? Even to herself? If it had been her, Dash would have stormed out of the office with a nice loud "I quit!," and that would have been the end of it.

After that, there were no more letters from Dot. Her sister had said she would not be there, and she was not.

She was not there when their father took his last breath.

She was not there to hold her weeping mother after he was gone.

She was not there to arrange the funeral and help her mother find a black dress to wear.

Dash was there for all of it.

On the morning of the funeral, Dash sat by her bedroom window, remembering. Her father had been a quiet man. She'd have called him solitary, if not for their family, and she knew he was more content away from people's scrutiny. She couldn't help comparing the way he had lived to his job in the last war, out of sight within the fragile belly of a surveillance plane.

And yet, when they arrived at the church for the funeral service, it was full. By coincidence, it had been scheduled on the same day as the town's big party, celebrating the 500,000th military vehicle built in General Motors' plant. She'd assumed most people would be at the celebration along with the reporters, but every pew was filled. Many in attendance were strangers to Dash; some were people she vaguely recalled from her past. A few were the girls' schoolteachers. She assumed they had come to see what the twins were up to. When the service was over, Dash approached Mr. Martin, her former mathematics teacher, now much rounder in the middle than she remembered. He greeted her sympathetically.

"I'm very sorry for your loss, Margaret. Your father was a true hero. It's a loss for the whole community."

Dash hesitated, unsure of what he was talking about. Her father had rarely joined in community activities. She credited the comment to the fact that her teacher had always been a little absentminded— was that how it was with mathematicians? She knew he meant well, so she thanked him. He went on to tell her how impressed he was by her working at CanCar, and he applauded her for joining the Air Transport Auxiliary.

"I knew you'd make a mark," he said. "You and your sister were always on top of things, though I think you'll agree that your sister enjoyed my class much more than you did."

"Oh no, Mr. Martin. Your classes were very interesting."

He chuckled. "Come now. It's nice of you to cheer up an old man, but the truth is that not everyone enjoys math. Very few people connected to it like your sister did." He peered around. "Where is she, by the way? I would like to say hello."

"Dot isn't here," she said and left it at that. "Thank you for coming. I must go check on my mother now."

"Take care of yourself." He leaned in conspiratorially. "Give 'em hell over there!"

"I will do what I can, sir."

Her mother was speaking with a few women in the marble vestibule of the church. One was Dash's Sunday School teacher, Mrs. Olson.

"Margaret! Oh my dear," she said. "We are so sorry about your father. The community won't be the same without him."

"Thank you, Mrs. Olson," she said. "It's nice to see you here."

"Oh, we never would have missed it. Your father was far too important to all of us for that."

Dash glanced at her mother, a question on her face. "Later, Margaret," she said quietly, then she turned to another guest.

One after another, people came to offer their condolences, and Dash grew more and more perplexed. Who was this man they kept talking about?

Eventually, she felt Aunt Lou slip her hand through her elbow. "You're confused, aren't you?"

"I'm wondering if they are mixing Dad up with someone else," Dash admitted.

"Come with me, away from the chatter, and I'll tell you something you never knew."

Aunt Lou pushed open the door of the church, and sunshine streamed in, blinding them briefly. When she could, Dash blinked wistfully at the sky.

"Do you remember what your father said he did during the war?"

"Sure," she said, still looking up. "He transmitted the locations of German munitions buildings from planes."

"He did. Also the locations of troops, enemy ships, whatever he saw. Your father saved a lot of lives with his work." She patted Dash's hand. "Mr. Olson, Mr. Martin's brother, and Mr. Jeffreys from the bakery are three of them."

Dash looked back at the church. "What do you mean?"

"The story goes that your father was flying one day—well, you know what I mean. He was observing and sending messages while someone else flew the plane. Anyway, he got the requested information, then he moved to sit with the pilot up front. Just before the pilot turned back to base, your father spied something on the horizon. On the ocean. Neither could tell what it was, so he asked the pilot to fly a little closer. The pilot was concerned about not having enough fuel to get back, but your father convinced him. When they got closer, he identified a German battle cruiser surrounded by other, smaller ships, all of them sailing toward where he knew the Canadian forces to be.

"He took all the technical measurements and whatever else he needed as quickly as he could and began relaying them right away, but the ship spotted them and fired on his surveillance plane. The pilot tried to avoid the guns, but there was a lot coming at them, so he turned back. Your father kept typing in the coordinates the whole time, knowing that what he was sending was far more vital than what he'd been tasked to report on. You see, Dash, without his observations, all those men in the Germans' path could have died."

Dash stared at her in disbelief. "Dad saw combat?"

"He never wanted to talk about it. He knew how it upset your mother."

"Why? That's so heroic!"

"Because that isn't all there was to the story. As they flew away from the ship, something hit a wing, and the plane spun out of control. Your father kept transmitting the whole time."

Dash stared openly at her. Why on earth hadn't he told them?

"Oh, it was terrible," her aunt continued. "The plane crashed into a forest and burst into flames. The pilot was badly injured, and your father—even though he'd broken his arm—was able to pull him out in time. The radio had been damaged on impact, but since your father had sent the coordinates in advance, the military was able to send a rescue to find them. Still, with everything going on, it took two days for the team to get there. Somehow, your father navigated his way out of there and carried the pilot to an area where they could be rescued, all the while watching for the enemy. He kept that pilot alive."

My compass, Dash thought with wonder.

"Your father never wanted to talk about what happened, but the pilot did. He told the newspapers, and the news travelled here and made it into our small paper." Aunt Lou chuckled. "You should have seen your mother's face. He hadn't even had a chance to write her a letter before the news broke, and she showed up at my door in hysterics. By reporting the German ships, he had saved dozens of our troops, including those three local men. At one point, the town talked about putting up a statue, but your mother and Uncle Bob put a quick stop to that. Your father would have hated it."

Dash scanned the crowd as it departed the church, seeking Mr. Olson and Mr. Martin. Nearby, she spotted the town's baker, Mr. Jeffreys, though he was harder to recognize without his flour-dusted apron. All of them, she realized, her heart twisting with grief, were alive because of her father.

"I wish I had known."

Her aunt's smile was warm. "Would it have made you love him any more than you did?"

"Of course not. But why wouldn't he have told us?"

"Sometimes in war, secrets are necessary. Some are for reasons of national security, but others are personal. So many men came back different after that war, and a lot never spoke of their experiences ever again. Your father didn't want to remember the war. He wasn't like your uncle. Your father was good at his job, but he'd never wanted to be a hero."

Outside the church, people in black gathered in groups, their voices conversational. They'd said their goodbyes to the dead; now it was time to greet the living.

"I'll give you a bit of insight into your other parent, now." Aunt Lou smiled, motioning toward Dash's mother, who was speaking with a few neighbours. "Your mother is a hero as well, just a different sort. She did so much for the people here who had been left behind during the war. She organized monthly get-togethers for the wives so we could feel normal for a little while. We needed that, and she knew it. Oh, and she threw a big party at the church after Mr. Davey's house caught fire. Everyone donated something. He had been sent home from Europe after he lost his leg, and I'm sure he had given up all hope, but that party was something else. People brought quilts and food, and so much else, including supplies and muscle to help rebuild." She tilted her head. "And then there was Gus."

Dash couldn't speak while it all sank in. "And then there was Gus," she whispered.

She hadn't known her parents at all.

"I feel like I've been asleep my whole life. I feel . . . selfish."

"No, no, dear. Never selfish. Your father was a quiet man, and even quieter when he returned from the war. He never boasted, so there's no reason you should know. If anything, it was your mother who spoke for him. When you and Dot were born, well, I'd never seen him happier. You two filled his heart."

Her eyes twinkled in the sunlight. "One episode in a person's life does not define who they are, Dash. You knew everything that was important about him. You knew he loved you and your sister, and that's all he needed you to know. He was so, so proud of you both. He always said you would do more important things than he ever did. He was thrilled to see you making your dream come true. Did you know he had your mother frame that photo you sent of you beside the Hurricane?"

Dash's grief surged up again at the thought. She glanced back at her mother, seeing her in an entirely new light. Not fragile at all. Rather, someone to be admired.

"But Dash, I need to say one more thing. It's about your sister."

Tension gripped Dash's jaw. "There's nothing to talk about. She didn't come."

"Your father wanted you to forgive her. We all know, especially him, that she would have been here if there was any way. He knew how much she loved him. The two of them were so similar, weren't they? There was no way she would abandon him in his final hours without a very good reason. You know that, Dash."

Dash stepped back, feeling overwhelmed. "I don't know what I know anymore. Dot has always been my best friend. My other half. We used to know what each other was thinking without even trying. The truth is, I don't know what I'll say to her when I see her again. I don't know anything. I feel sick over it."

"Think of your father." She moved closer and rubbed circles on Dash's back with her palm. "Think of the love in his heart, and the forgiveness. What is one goodbye when you've spent your whole life sharing everything? We will miss him awfully. Your uncle is a disaster, I'll tell you that. Your sister must be devastated. She needs you. Dash, I want you to look deep into your heart, beyond all this hurt."

While others were still talking in the churchyard, Dash headed home, memories crowding her mind. When she reached the tree at the side of the house, she didn't pause. It was the same as it had always been, just a few years older, and she loved that about it. Every nook and cranny in the bark felt familiar against her fingers. She easily climbed to the Y amid the branches, reaching the little nest that no one had ever sat in but her. If she listened hard, she could still hear her sister's giggles coming from the ground below. Back then, this spot had been a fun place. Now it was a place where she could grieve alone. Where she could curl up and miss her father without witnesses.

Except it wasn't just her father that she missed. She missed her mother's warm laughter, and the way she looked at her father when he said something funny. She longed to see again the bond he had shared with Uncle Bob, with the two of them joking across the dinner table. Most of all, she ached to see the love in Dot's eyes when the two were together and they didn't know Dash was watching.

One man had left behind so many.

After a while, she climbed down the tree and shut herself in her bedroom. Just before falling asleep, she looked at the empty bed across from her. The pillow where Dot's shining blond hair splayed out while she slept sat plump and untouched. The spot where Dot's face had turned toward her own, sharing all their secrets in the dark, held nothing now.

The sadness and loss that had stewed in Dash all day hardened to anger once more. Dot should have been there, on that little bed next to hers.

Two days after the funeral, Dash woke up to a miserable, rainy morning that reflected her mood. After breakfast, she sat at the kitchen table with her mother and aunt, sipping boiled water.

"I want you to go to England," her mother said, bringing up the conversation again.

Dash's heart was already broken. This talk would only make it worse. "I already told you. I can't, Mom. I can't leave you alone."

Her mother gave Aunt Lou a small smile. "I'm not alone. If you're concerned about me, please don't be. I know what you're considering, and I absolutely forbid it. Your father would be distraught if he knew you were giving up your dream because of him. I want you to go. He did, too. Live your own life. Please, Dash."

So many tears had been shed, Dash was surprised she still had any left. They lodged in her throat now, hearing her mother call her by her nickname for the first time.

And so it was settled. Dash went through her dresser, deciding what to pack, but everything felt different now. The exhilaration she'd felt, knowing she was heading overseas to fly, was weighted by regrets and grief. And doubt. What should she pack? No one knew how long the war would last, and Dash had no idea what the weather was like in England. Dot would have known. She would have planned out exactly what should be folded and how.

How could you do this to me, Dot?

She was placing a sweater in her suitcase when she bumped something small and hard in the back corner. Her fingers closed around her father's old, dented compass, and she sat back on her bed, holding the treasure and pointing the magnetic needle due north out of habit. She remembered the old scavenger hunts her father had created for them, teaching her to use the compass, and she remembered how the glass had shone when she'd placed it on the Hurricane's dash. She'd always wanted him to fly with her, so by bringing it, he had in a way, she thought fondly. The brass case was tarnished, and she noticed a tiny crack in the glass. Had that happened on that awful day when he'd saved so many lives and nearly lost his? Her thumb skimmed over the tiny fissure, and she wondered how many times he had done the same.

"All right, Dad," she whispered. She kissed the little glass circle before tucking it safely back into her suitcase. The compass would be with her on every flight she took from now on.

A couple of days after that, Uncle Bob drove Dash, her mother, and Aunt Lou to Union Station. He was weary, she could see, but he was also practically jumping out of his skin with excitement for her.

"You'll have to tell me all about your flights," he kept saying. "Where you're flying, what you're flying, I want to hear it all."

When they reached the station, he went with her to the ticket booth, and she reached into her purse.

"One to Halifax, please."

Before she could fish out her wallet, her uncle placed an envelope of cash on the counter. "It's from me and your dad. I'd give anything for him to be here to give it to you himself." He exhaled. "We are all so proud of you, Dash. Where you're headed, it's where you're meant to be."

She stared at the envelope, overwhelmed once again, then she reached for her uncle before she could give in to tears. "Thank you, Uncle Bob. I wish he was here, too, but I'm so glad you are."

At last it was time to board, so she hugged everyone again.

Her mother held on to her a little longer, and Dash never wanted to let go. "Mom," she whispered into her ear.

"This is the right thing for you," her mother said back. Dash sensed the sob she held in her throat, the one battling to escape. "Your father knew you would do something truly amazing with your life, and here you are." She pulled back to look in her daughter's eyes. "I love you so, so much. I am so proud. There's just one thing I need to ask of you now."

Dash waited, her tears flowing freely now.

Her mother's hands tightened around Dash's arms. "I need you to promise me that you'll be safe out there. I know you'll have a wonderful time in those planes you love, but please, please promise me you'll be smart. Be safe. I need you to come home in one piece when this is all over."

"I promise, Mom."

After a final hug that terrified Dash to her core, she stepped away from her family and looked up at the big black beast in front of her: Locomotive No. 6213, one of the newest trains in the world. Just the first of so many adventures, she thought, her heart thrumming in consort with the train's idling engine.

She climbed the stairs and searched for a seat, still feeling miserable. How she wanted to celebrate this moment. She should be jumping up and down, grinning and calling for champagne. But after all that had happened, everything felt anticlimactic.

It wasn't until she'd settled by the window, her bag stowed on the rack over her head, that she felt herself awaken to what was really happening. It began slowly, like the first turns of an airplane's propeller. Like the wheels of the train as it left the station. Slowly, tentatively, building the strength needed to steam ahead. Or the power to roar into the sky.

Soon the train was well on its way, and there was nothing Dash could do but sit back and watch the passing view. Why wasn't she bubbling over with anticipation?

Guilt, she supposed. Grief, regret, anger, all of it.

Live your life to the fullest, her father had whispered.

Live your own life, her mother had urged.

But this feeling was like an anchor, wrapped around her throat and dragging her under. She closed her eyes and pictured her parents, knowing they were right. It was time to move forward, and no one could do that for her. With every bump she let the tension ease a little more. Miles on, she spotted a gull out the window, swooping from side to side like an airplane. Like *her* airplane. *I'm going to fly*, she reminded herself. *I'm going to fly, Dad.*

Dash believed in heaven. She couldn't fathom a life simply ending and having nowhere to go, but she wasn't convinced that a universe of angels existed beyond the clouds. She'd been up there, and other than pure, open freedom, nothing suggested the idea was more than symbolic. Still, it didn't hurt, she reasoned, to hold out hope. If her father was up there somewhere, and she happened to be flying nearby one day, she would be watching.

thirty-nine
DOT

— July 1943 —
Camp X

Gus would be halfway across the Atlantic by now. Dot stared into her cup of tea, miserable. Was he asleep? Was he thinking of her? Was he furious? He had every right to be.

She hadn't slept at all. After leaving her parents' house, they had driven back to Whitby in silence. Somehow they'd escaped their childhood neighbourhood without incident, though she noted Gus constantly scouting their surroundings. He also glanced to the side occasionally, checking on her, but Dot burned with embarrassment the whole way. She'd kissed Gus. Instead of giving him a sweet, chaste thank-you kiss, she had flung open the door to the desire she'd felt for so long, and she'd rushed through it.

Dot was a horrible person. First Dash would hate her for abandoning their family in their hour of need. Then she would discover that Dot had stolen Gus from her. Who had she become?

Before they got to the camp, Gus pulled over and turned off the engine.

"Dot. Talk to me."

She bit her lower lip, wishing she could disappear.

"Hey." His fingers touched her chin. "Look at me, Dot. It's just me."

So she did, feeling sick with guilt. "I shouldn't have kissed you."

"I kissed you back."

The intensity of his expression was too much. She turned away. "This is wrong. It feels wrong. I can't. I'm sorry I started it."

"Are you?"

"I am."

"Are you sure?"

"Yes. What if it isn't what you think it is? What if it doesn't work out and I lose your friendship as a result? I can't do that, Gus. I need you too much."

"You'd never lose me, no matter what," he assured her. "You're stuck with me."

"I will never forget what you did, taking me to see Dad tonight, and I know how much it meant to you as well. So thank you, Gus. Thank you for doing that for me. But I need you to stop thinking about . . . us. I kissed you because I was excited, I was grateful, and I was emotional. I shouldn't have. I regret it."

"You regret it?" His eyes narrowed slightly. She recognized a flicker of anger in them. "I'm disappointed, Dot. I thought you never lied."

He drove the rest of the way to the camp without saying a word, and she flushed with shame. Of course he knew how she felt deep down. He could read her so well. Saying she regretted what had happened was far from the truth, and they both knew it. But if lying about how she felt was the only way to make sure it never happened again, she was glad she'd done it.

At camp, he brought her safely to her room, barely even looking at her, and she'd slipped inside without speaking. When he was gone, she curled up on her bed, feeling miserable. She couldn't do anything right. By kissing Gus, she'd struck out on a new path without a map, following an impulse she should have ignored. By letting him go, she felt lost. Now she didn't know which way to turn. Somehow she'd ended up more alone than ever.

forty
DASH

— *Halifax, Nova Scotia* —

The train ride to Halifax took two days of little sleep, but when Dash finally walked into the misty Nova Scotia fog, anticipation whirled around her. She tightened her scarf and inhaled the unfamiliar smell of seaweed and salt water. That's when it hit her that she was truly leaving, not just Ontario, but *Canada*, and she was about to sail across the ocean on the famous *Queen Mary*. For heaven's sake, Bob Hope had been on that ship! She could only imagine what Mary and Ginny would have to say about that. If only they were with her. She'd write them all about it, and they'd gasp and giggle over every detail.

Even from the train station, she could see the massive ship looming over the harbour, its three big steam funnels on top. Her father had taken a similar journey almost thirty years before, though she didn't think he'd ever sailed on the *Queen Mary*. Her mother had been so envious when Dash told her she'd be on this particular ship. She'd write to her, too.

Good thing she had a lot of stationery. The only person Dash was not going to write to was Dot.

Following a line of fellow travelers, Dash hauled her suitcase across the street toward the Halifax pier, then hesitated, unsure where to go for her ticket. The crowds of men around her were a little intimidating, but she worked up the nerve to approach a couple of redheaded men speaking to each other.

"Excuse me. I wonder if you can help me," she said.

They turned to face her, and she did a double take. One wore a navy uniform, and the other was dressed in civilian clothing, but there was no mistaking that they were twins. The only difference she could see was a rather dramatic scar across the face of the one not in uniform.

"Of course we can," said the one in uniform. "What do you need?"

She glanced between them, wondering if she should tell them she was a twin as well. "I'm . . . I'm not from here, and I'm wondering where to go for a ticket."

"Normally Pier 21," he replied, jabbing a thumb over his shoulder.

"But there was a fire a while back," said the brother with the scar. "Second storey is gone. There's a detour that way."

She squinted and spotted a wooden sign where they indicated. "Pickford and Black's Wharf?"

"It's a temporary departure site."

She couldn't stop looking at the men. "I'm so sorry. It's just that—"

"Let me guess. You've never seen twins before," said the first.

She had to laugh at that. "I *am* a twin. I've just never met any others."

They both grinned, almost like a mirror with a crack in it. "I'm Eugene. This is Harry. Nice to meet you."

"Twins are lucky," Harry said. "We always have our other half to back us up."

She felt a sharp emptiness where Dot was supposed to be. "You're right about that," she said, moving on. "It's really nice to meet you. Thank you so much."

She followed their directions to the temporary wharf and found the ticket desk. The spectacled man at the counter scowled as he stamped her ticket for the *Queen Mary*.

"Traveling alone? This is not a pleasure cruise, young lady."

"I shouldn't think so," she replied. "I'm going to serve my country in the war, sir."

"Is that right?" His eyes narrowed. "The *Queen Mary* has been reoutfitted mostly for troop transport. No matter why you're going over there, you will be required to stay in your room as much as possible with the other ladies." He slipped her ticket under the window and pointed out the print. "There are six women on board. You will be sharing two rooms. These are the room numbers."

Giving the man an exaggerated thank-you, Dash collected her ticket, left the building, and was instantly enveloped in a fog thicker than she'd believed possible. When it briefly cleared, she stared up in awe. The renowned ship stood like a mountain before her. The first thing she noticed, other than its sheer size, was the anchor hanging from the side of the bow. When she matched it up to the rows of portholes dotting the sides, she calculated the anchor had to be four storeys high. And that was only the part of the ship she could see, not the underwater decks keeping them afloat. She hoped she didn't get lost in all the space.

Men in uniform dominated the area, many of whom she assumed were lined up to board. It felt overwhelming to be in the middle of the throng, let alone be the subject of dozens of admiring glances. When she spotted a small group of five women about her age standing off to one side, all wearing matching blue capes, Dash rushed over to introduce herself.

"You've no idea how pleased I am to meet you," she said to the others. "I'm Dash."

A blond woman held out her hand. "Nice to meet you. I'm June. Are you with the nurses?"

"I'm afraid not." She scanned the others. "You're all nurses? What courage you have. I haven't the stomach for that. No, I'm going to be a pilot."

"A pilot!"

She tried to look nonchalant. "Yes, I'll be with the Air Transport Auxiliary, ferrying replacement planes. I'm very excited."

The women exchanged a startled glance, but June gave her a wide smile. "I should say so! Flying an airplane all on your own? How extraordinary!"

On the first night, Dash tucked into a top bunk, excited to watch their departure through the room's porthole. Unfortunately, she soon learned that all the ship's portholes had been blacked out for the sake of safety. She understood the reason, but it was disappointing nevertheless. Still, what an adventure this was. None of the women had ever been on the ocean before, and Dash agreed that they weren't about to miss out on the experience just because they were female. If the six of them snuck out together, she was sure they'd be allowed to watch some of the goings-on.

Escaping the segregation rules was easier than she'd hoped. In the morning they went for breakfast and were assigned to two tables in the corner of the room. From her menu, Dot ordered a simple meal of a soft-boiled egg and toast with a cup of coffee. One of the girls had gotten awfully sick the night before, and Dash wasn't entirely sure yet how her stomach would fare with the ups and downs of the ship's movements, so she decided to be safe rather than sorry.

Following the meal, their waiter approached the table and handed Dash an envelope with their room numbers written on it in elegant handwriting.

"Go ahead," June said, leaning in. "Tell us what it says."

"It's from the captain," Dash gushed. "Oh my goodness. Ladies, I hope you have a nice dress with you, because he just invited us to dinner and a concert tonight. You'll never guess who is on this ship."

"Well? Tell us!"

"Mr. Bing Crosby! He's on board with us! Can you imagine? He's going overseas to entertain the troops!"

The rest of the day the girls were caught up in anticipation. When the magical hour arrived, a porter came to their rooms to escort them to the captain's table, where Dash practically vibrated in her seat. If seeing Bing Crosby wasn't enough, the menu was something out of a dream. Dash chose the rack of lamb with asparagus, boiled new potatoes, and a vanilla ice with butterscotch sauce for dessert. Apparently rations did not apply to the *Queen Mary*.

"I think I've died and gone to heaven," she hummed after the meal.

Bing Crosby soon came onto the stage, charming as could be. Almost like a real person, not a star. In her head, Dash was already composing a letter to Mary and Ginny, describing every little thing about him. In that smooth voice of his, he thanked the captain for giving him the opportunity to acknowledge all the troops in the room in his own small way. Dash held her breath when he nodded to the piano player seated behind him.

"I know we are headed in entirely the opposite direction," Mr. Crosby said to the audience, "but I thought it might be nice to imagine we're in the Pacific, instead of shivering over here."

He began to sing "Blue Hawaii," and Dash fell in love, just like Mary had said. A couple of the girls sat with their elbows on the table, their faces resting in their hands, blinking with big, sleepy eyes. At one point he sang, "Embraceable You," and he smiled at the girls the whole time. Dash knew it wasn't personal, but she had never felt more beautiful in her life. He ended the performance with "Danny Boy," and Dash pressed her fists against her cheeks, trying not to cry at the pleading melody. From her seat at the side of the room, she could see he held all the sailors and soldiers spellbound as well.

And then, well! Mr. Crosby came to thank the captain in person! Dash practically swooned when he went around the table and shook the girls' hands.

"This was the most wonderful night of my life," she told him. She felt silly, but she couldn't do anything about that.

He tilted his head, those ice-blue eyes soft. "I'm awfully glad to hear that. It was pretty special for me, too. I hope you have a lovely voyage."

They didn't see him for the rest of the journey, but that was all right. Dash would never forget that evening. She and the others sailed on, enjoying sunny days on the deck and exquisite nights under the stars.

But there were dark moments as well. One cold, dark night, when banks of clouds covered any hope of stars, Dash pinned herself to the rail, paralyzed by concern and awe. In the distance, explosions painted the pitch-black sea and sky with raging flashes of orange. Though she could not hear any screams, Dash knew what she was watching. Everyone was aware of the risks of being on a ship at this time. Even this one, with its legendary size and history, wasn't truly safe, despite its being part of a large convoy. How far away was the battle happening? How far could a torpedo be fired from a U-boat? The opportunity to sink a ship carrying thousands of troops would have been almost irresistible to the Germans, she thought with a shudder. Fortunately, the convoy continued without a loss, but the dread that had held her captive that night never completely went away.

At last they sailed into Portsmouth, England, and Dash joined the others on deck, scrutinizing the approaching port over the water. Halifax was the only harbour she'd ever seen, and it had been blanketed in fog. Here, the harbour was awash in sunshine, with foaming lines of white sparkling off ripples in the sea. Gulls shrieked and dove by the dozens, and Dash gawked beyond them, seeing what war had destroyed. Stark, broken walls along the docks as well as bombed-out buildings beyond provided a clear reminder that there was no peace on this side of the ocean.

Despite everything, Dash wished Dot was here. If nothing had changed between them, her sister would have been pressed against her side, pointing out every detail she saw—a ship here, a crumbled building over there—and Dash would have been caught up in her excitement. Or maybe it would be the other way around, with Dash elbowing her again and again, needing to show her something she'd seen. Either way, she couldn't help wishing they were together. That's the way it had always been, and she supposed it always would be. Thinking of that made her feel unsteady, as if there was something left unfinished. Someday the war would end, and when it did, she would go home and deal with what she'd left behind. Maybe the hurt would fade over time. Maybe this experience would help her stand on her own again, possibly even stronger because of Dot's abandonment. And maybe, she thought, inhaling the salty air, they would all heal over time.

The ship gave a mighty blast, jolting her heart into overdrive, and the docks swarmed with workers preparing for their arrival. She could hear men below and on deck yelling to each other as they saw to their duties, and the activity cheered her. Like them, Dash would soon have a job to do. She was about to become an ATA girl. Before too long, she would roar down a runway then soar into the clouds, doing her part to end the war. She could hardly wait. Up high, in the freedom of the sky, she could leave all her regrets behind.

forty-one
DOT

-•• --- -

— *Camp X* —

Morse code. Crossword puzzles. Books and more books. Hot water that could never really be coffee, but felt close enough. Quiet, loving eyes that understood her. Had always understood her, even when no one else did. All this and so much more, suddenly gone. It hadn't been her fault, but Dot didn't think she would ever forgive herself for not being with her family during this horrible time. She knew Dash never would.

As she crossed the Camp X grounds toward Hydra, her thoughts were on the short note she had received from her mother following the funeral. She heard her voice through her elegant handwriting, but her tone had felt hollow. In the letter, she reminded Dot of how much her father had loved her, and how proud he was of both of his daughters. She said that he had supported her the entire time, telling everyone around him that Dot must have had a good reason for not being there. She said that he did not want Dot to ever apologize for her absence.

He hadn't told a soul about their midnight visit. She wasn't surprised, but it was a relief.

It was also one more secret kept from the people she loved.

She never heard from Dash, but her mother had tried to smooth out what Dot imagined her sister had said. *We all need time to accept what has happened. Margaret left this morning for England. She didn't want to leave me, but you are both adults now. You have your own lives to lead. Please don't worry, Dorothy. I am stronger than you think.*

Dot found it difficult to reply. Her mind, usually so busy, felt blank. In the end, she wrote something brief about sorrow, love, grief . . . but she didn't go into the memories. Those would have to wait until she was stronger. Anything she wrote now would read as empty as she felt.

forty-two
DASH

Dash rubbed at the kink in her neck, but the ache didn't ease. The bus from Portsmouth to Hamble Airfield was slowly skidding along a road somewhere, and now it hit a hole. It happened so frequently, three of the larger male passengers had gotten used to getting up and rocking the bus out of the ruts.

"Just another crater!" the lady bus driver called cheerfully.

Dash wished she wasn't so tired. She'd had trouble sleeping on the ship, partially because of the unfamiliar movement, but mostly because she had a lot on her mind. And though she had been determined to leave her grief behind, once in a while her father appeared in her memories. She'd had a few good cries, keeping as quiet as she could by snuffling into her pillow, and she wondered how long the terrible sadness would last. It was exhausting on so many levels.

England's landscape, or what she'd seen of it so far, was shocking. The devastation at the docks continued unabated inland. The Germans must have attacked here a few times to clear out ships in the harbour, then they'd taken out the town behind it. At one point, Dash spotted a charming, undamaged little cottage with cheerful red shutters, and she leaned forward to admire it. As the bus bounced past, her delight evaporated. The other side of the cottage was missing. She could see right into the front room, where the furniture was covered in rubble.

The bus lumbered out of the crater and back onto the road. After another hour or so, they pulled up outside the main building of Hamble Airfield. By the time they stopped, Dash was already on her feet.

"You'll want to go into that building, dearie," the bus driver said, pointing. "That's where the pilots meet."

Dash's heart raced as she stepped inside the smoke-filled room, bag in hand. All conversations stopped, and she blinked nervously at the dozen or so ladies inside.

"Welcome!" one called, then she pointed toward a closed door outside of the room. "Go see Mrs. Farnham in the office there. She'll sort you out."

Mrs. Farnham was middle-aged and portly, and her eagerness to help practically bubbled over. She looked up Dash on the lists, welcomed her again, then started setting out papers.

"This is the address where you'll be living, and this will be your landlady, Mrs. Pemberton. I've put you in with Stella Rodgers. You'll like Stella, I should think. She's rather . . . straightforward." She reached into her pocket and retrieved a package of cigarettes, which she gave to Dash. "Here. You'll make an excellent first impression if you offer her a cigarette right off the hop." She handed Dash another page entitled "Training." "Training to become an ATA pilot is rather detailed, but of course it needs to be. You will have all sorts of interesting lessons over the next three months. After that, you'll be ready to fly."

Dash had known about the classes, and even though they would delay her getting in the air, she was looking forward to them. She knew car engines and Hurricanes inside and out, but she'd heard there were more than a hundred different types of planes over here, and she might be flying different kinds. She wanted to be well prepared.

"The rules are posted in the common room, where all the ladies are. That is sort of the clubhouse, if you will." Mrs. Farnham beamed. "Oh, you'll make wonderful friends here. I'll introduce you now, then you can come back here later to pick up your uniform. I'll get it all laid out for you. Let's go say hello, shall we?"

This time when Dash walked into the main room, she didn't raise as many eyebrows. Mrs. Farnham pointed out different women and smiled proudly, clucking like a mother hen over all her chicks. She led Dash to two women sitting in a cloud of smoke, laughing at something, then waited for an opportunity to speak.

"Mrs. Farnham," one of them said, glancing up. "Who do we have here?"

"Stella, this is Dash Wilson, your new roommate. She's come all the way from Canada, she has. Dash, this is Stella and Violet. They're fast friends, aren't you, dears?"

Getting to their feet, they shook Dash's hand.

"Good to meet you," Violet said. She was shorter than Dash, with curly black hair cropped close as a boy's and dimples in both cheeks. "You have a brilliant name. Have you any flying hours?"

"About two hundred," Dash said, including every time she'd gone up with Uncle Bob.

"That will do nicely," Stella said, towering over them. She was slim and handsome, with hooded eyes that seemed to be enjoying an inside joke. "Thank you, Mrs. Farnham. We shall take it from here."

"Lovely to meet you, Dash. Ta-ta for now." Mrs. Farnham pointed to the wall behind Stella, where a white sign hung, painted with stark black lettering. "Don't forget the rules."

AIR TRANSPORT AUXILIARY RULES

Bad weather flying is strictly prohibited.

Competition between pilots is strictly prohibited. The idea that if A gets through and B does not, this is a reflection on B, is quite erroneous.

No flight shall be commenced unless at the place of departure the cloud base is at least 800 feet, and the horizontal visibility at least 2,000 yards.

Dash noticed Stella studying her, so she reached into her pocket and produced a flimsy little box. "Care for a cigarette?"

Stella's smile was appreciative as she took one and slipped it between her lips. "Do sit, Miss Dash. I believe you will do very well here."

As Stella lit the cigarette, Dash sat and scanned the room. Some of the women were wearing the heavy, fur-lined flying suits provided by the ATA. Dash could hardly wait to have one of her own. A few, like Stella, had kicked off their furry black boots. On the tables were scattered helmets and goggles.

Stella exhaled a stream of smoke. "Well, Miss Dash, one of the first things you need to know is that boys don't want us around here."

"That's not true, Stella," Violet scolded. "Don't frighten the new girl. Only some of them don't, Dash, and I think they're mostly just sour because we get paid the same as they do. Most of them are thrilled to see girls in jumpsuits." Violet placed the back of her hand against her brow and fell dramatically back into her chair. "'A woman pilot! My heart!'"

"I don't know about that," Stella scoffed. "I've heard a lot more of the old 'women belong in the home, not in the sky' refrain."

That sounded uncomfortably familiar to Dash, like Mrs. Pidgett and the men at Eisen's Garage.

"There are an awful lot of men piloting," Violet explained. "I think they outnumber us ten to one."

"Ah," Dash said with a smile. She'd done a good bit of reading on the voyage across the ocean. "You're talking about the ATA-boys. The 'Ancient and Tattered Airmen.'"

The original Air Transport Auxiliary members, she'd learned, were mostly retired pilots from the first war. Some had come with their own challenges—missing limbs and eyes—and that had resulted in their somewhat derogatory label. No one had planned for the war to still be going in 1941, and by then the people in charge of the ATA realized they wouldn't be able to keep up the pace without a lot more pilots. At last, they'd made the leap and brought women into their ranks. The *reluctant* leap.

"To be fair, when they added women, they renamed it the 'Always

Terrified Airwomen,'" Stella said, inhaling. "You know what else they say about ATA-girls? That we're either loose women looking for attention, or that our lessons were paid for by men."

"And we're all filthy rich," Violet added.

She knew it wasn't true, but Dash could see why people thought that way. After all, a single one-hour lesson cost about the same as what Dash had earned at CanCar in two weeks. She'd never be able to pay Uncle Bob back for all he'd given her. She glanced around. "So where are the men?"

"Hamble is our base, not theirs," Violet said.

"This is a women's-only airfield?" Dash asked, heartened.

"Other than mechanics and such. Hamble and Cosford are the only two bases with change rooms."

Stella stubbed out her cigarette in an overflowing ashtray. "They're slowly coming around to the fact that they need us, but they still don't like it. Show her the magazine, Vi."

"I don't happen to have a copy handy," Violet replied, rolling her eyes. "So, Dash. Where are you—"

"There's always a copy under the table. I'll get it," Stella said.

Dash watched her tread, catlike, across the room. "Magazine?"

Violet sighed. "She's determined to show you this, so we might as well let her get it out of her system. Every time Stella feels slighted, she likes to bring it up. Keep in mind that it's from last year, so it's a little dated. We've changed a lot of minds since then."

"Here we are."

Stella placed a copy of *Aeroplane* magazine on the table in front of Dash. It fell open to a spread with ragged edges.

"Read this and tell me they want us here." She resumed her seat and lit another cigarette. "Go ahead, Dash. Read it aloud. Who's it by?"

Dash picked up the magazine. "C. G. Grey. The editor."

"That's right. He ought to know a thing or two about airplanes and pilots, don't you think?

"Just let her read, Stella."

Stella waved her cigarette in Dash's direction. "Go on." Dash cleared her throat and started to read. "Skip ahead, dear. To the part that's out-lined at the bottom."

Dash dropped her eyes to the indicated passage. "'There are millions of women in the country who could do useful jobs in war. But the trouble is that so many of them insist on wanting to do jobs which they are quite incapable of doing. The menace is the woman who thinks that she ought to be flying a high-speed bomber when she really has not the intelligence to scrub the floor of a hospital properly—'" She looked up, aghast.

"Keep going."

"'—she really has not the intelligence to scrub the floor of a hospital properly or who wants to nose round as an Air Raid Warden and yet can't cook her husband's dinner.'"

Stella's eyes danced with mirth. "See?"

"That's an insult to everyone in here. How can he actually write this?" Dash tossed the magazine back on the table. "It's awful."

"He's still the editor there, I believe," Violet said quietly.

Dash was stunned. Here was a well-respected man spouting lies, and readers were eating them up, she assumed, since he still worked at the magazine. That meant that others believed the same as he did, just like back in the garage. Not one of those other mechanics had lifted a finger to help Dash out of her situation. Not one had told Jim to back off, though they'd heard her say no to him many times.

Stella was eyeing her, waiting for a reaction. Yes, Dash was angry. And yes, she was still living through those horrible moments when Jim's arm had been jammed against her neck. She'd had those bruises for days.

"I can hardly wait to run into that ignorant little man one day," Dash declared, flashing the big, irresistible smile that had once made her the talk of the town. "I'll be sweet as apple pie, and I'll invite him to fly with me. We could do a few barrel rolls, and maybe his seat belt's a little loose . . ."

Both girls' jaws dropped, seeing her transformation from a shy new-comer to one of them, then Stella let out a low chuckle. "Oh yes, Dash Wilson. You are going to fit in just fine."

forty-three
DOT

-•• --- -

— Camp X —

Dot was up before the sun. Since the funeral, she had felt weak and broken, heavy with guilt, and running laps was the only way she could get her thoughts back on track. It helped her remember that she simply had no time for emotion. Her priority now had to be this job. For months, Dot had been involved in preparations for Operation Husky, a major landing the Allied forces were planning for the southern coast of Italy. This would be an important battle, and it fascinated Dot on many levels. Mostly, the fact that this piece of the puzzle fit so strategically well with others.

The first piece had been placed in May. After three long years of fighting, the Allies had claimed their first major victory by defeating the Germans and Italians in North Africa. By doing so, the Allies took control of the eastern Mediterranean.

Now the second piece of the puzzle: Operation Husky, also known as the Battle of Sicily, would—they hoped—result in a second major victory: the defeat of the Fascists in Sicily. That piece would clear more of the Mediterranean, increase Allied shipping, and open the door to an invasion of the rest of Europe.

This was the most important project Dot had ever participated in, and she was part of the communication strategy. Like her, Gus had a role to play. His job was to go behind enemy lines and sabotage enemy communication posts in the lead-up to the invasion.

Gus. Her stomach knotted with the hurt she'd caused them both. She had to stop thinking about him. She had work to do.

Last night, while she had been sleeping, the Battle of Sicily had begun. Today was going to be busy. After she finished her run, Dot cleaned up, got into her uniform, then went to Hydra. Early July was setting the bar for a hot summer, and the fields were as green as could be. Out by the firing range, trees had tripled in size and their leaves were in full glory, but there was no breeze to stir them. Dot wiped the perspiration from her brow, watching birds lit from branches to the wires outside Hydra's building.

Inside, Bill Hardcastle drooped slightly at his post. He had been on duty all last night, and Dot was set to relieve him. She would be here for the next eight hours, until four p.m. Before she started, she picked up the logbook and read through the events of last night.

"Oh dear," she murmured, taking in the bad news.

To prepare for the main seaborne invasion, which would begin today, the Allies had sent transport planes and 147 gliders with parachutists into Axis airspace over Sicily. The plan was to drop the parachutists, who would quietly take possession of a strategically important bridge before the Italians could destroy it. But a windstorm had blown in, tossing and destroying planes, and then the Italians' searchlights and antiaircraft guns had added to the chaos. In the end, only a dozen of the gliders arrived on target. The planned attack had been almost a complete failure.

Bill rose with an impressive stretch toward the ceiling and bid her a good morning on his way out the door. "Happy hunting. I hope your day is better than my night."

"Thank you, Bill. Have a good sleep."

Despite the disastrous events of the night before, the seaborne invasion would begin soon, and that was Dot's focus. Her job was to hunt for nearby enemy ships that might threaten the operation while ensuring the transport of Allied troops went without a hitch. For this battle, the Canadians were part of the British Eighth Army and would attack from the Brits' left flank. The Americans would come in from the other side. Over a hundred and fifty thousand troops—including twenty-six thousand Canadians—were involved in Operation Husky, along with three thousand ships and four thousand tanks.

Dot swore to herself that no enemy ships would get past her. Her fingers rested on the dial, slowly turning it as she listened for the frequency she wanted. The ships would be nearing the coastline by now, so Allied communication was being kept to a minimum to avoid interception. So far, Hydra's sensitive antennae had picked up nothing. All Dot heard was background static.

But there was something out there. She could feel it. She closed her eyes and let her brain sink into the empty sound, blocking out any other thoughts.

Dot lived for moments like this.

The moment the beep sounded, she was on it, the hair on her forearms standing to attention.

There. Deep in the warm waters of the Mediterranean Sea, north of Malta, lurked a lone U-boat. As far as Dot could reckon, the Allied ships drawing near the coast of Sicily hadn't spotted it. The closest vessel to the sub, from her figuring, was the ship carrying the men of the 1st Canadian Infantry Division, among others. She touched the dial again, locating the boat exactly, then she hesitated. Protocol dictated she should get this information to Gerald as quickly as possible; however, she knew he was in meetings. This could not wait. She had not been given permission to transmit a message like the one playing in her head, but this could not wait.

Men could die. She could prevent those deaths. What choice did she have? Dot placed the tip of her middle finger on the curved surface of the tapper and began to transmit.

BE AWARE UBOAT 409 Position 36°12'20.4"N 13°40'54.7"E

Then she held her breath and waited. No sound came from the ship or from anywhere else.

Come on, come on, come on . . . she thought. Had they not heard? Should she type it again? She risked being overheard by the U-boat, but if the ship had not—

Dit-dah-dit dit dah-dit-dah-dit dit dit-dit dit-dit-dit-dah dit dah-dit-dit

.-. . -.-. . .. ...- . -..

Received

She exhaled and threw her arms into the air, silently triumphant. Here she sat, alone in a little room, thousands of miles from the war, and she'd just had a say in the lives of all those men. Because of her message, the Allied ships would either alter their course or chase down the submarine. Dot had forgotten the sense of elation that she felt now.

"Did you hear that, Dad?" she whispered, heart singing. "I did it."

Her thoughts went to Gus, and she tried to imagine his reaction to what she'd just done, breaking the rules like that. He would be so proud. Her jubilation faded a little, wondering where he was. Was he all right? Was he safe? Would he come back to her? And what then?

She forced herself to clear her mind and focus. The chatter in her headphones had picked up, and it was thrilling to listen to the updates now coming through the wires. When the landing happened, the Italians on shore witnessed tens of thousands of Allied troops roaring toward them, and from what Dot was hearing, most enemy troops had panicked and withdrawn. The rest put up a token fight, but in the end the Italians and a spattering of Germans had been forced to flee. Victory belonged to the Allies. They still had a difficult operation ahead of them, but as of today, the good guys were one step closer to ending the war. And Dot was part of it all.

forty-four
DASH

Dash sat in the lecture room, twiddling with her pencil and staring out the window at the airfield while she waited for the instructor to join the class. Before she'd arrived in England, she had been confident she could bear the wait time before she was allowed to fly, but on her first day of training at Hamble, she'd watched all the experienced ATA women climb into planes, and her chest had ached with envy. Thankfully, she had a lot of distractions. Over the next ninety days, Dash and the others would squeeze in three years of learning. It was a lot, but Dash was determined.

Miss Tallis, their instructor, finally hustled into the classroom, heels clacking on the wood floor. She was tall and slim, with thick glasses that made her eyes look like an owl's. Miss Tallis was not interested in wasting time.

"Workbooks open, ladies. Eyes up here. Today's lesson will focus on navigation, map reading, course plotting, and meteorology. Quickly, someone tell me why you need to learn about these things."

"So you know where you're going," one girl volunteered.

"Precisely. It is easy to get lost, especially because ATA pilots fly with neither maps nor radios. Now, pay close attention."

When it came to classes on mechanics, Dash felt confident. She had learned from Uncle Bob and then Elsie MacGill. But these classes were more in depth in every category: hydraulics, automatic boost, and carburetors, which she'd thought she already knew. The new details were fascinating, and she soaked everything up.

Dash and her classmates had a number of instructors. One was pilot Robert Lister, a jolly Australian fellow, with thinning white curls, rosy cheeks, and a bit of a limp. At his first class with them, he had pointed out his eye patch before anyone could ask, then claimed to have misplaced an eye while flying over France fifteen years before.

"I hope you ladies can manage to keep both of yours," he said, closing the subject. "Now, today, you will think back to every lesson you've been taught up to now, which I'm certain you've all memorized . . ." He peered around, eyebrow raised when some of the girls looked guilty. "If you have not, you will do that later tonight. For those who have, let's teach the others what I'm talking about when I begin a preflight check."

He led them out to a hangar to watch him demonstrate a preflight checkup on a Tiger Moth. Dash smiled, seeing the plane there. The Tiger Moth was almost identical to Uncle Bob's Jenny. She watched and listened, feeling pleased with herself. Nothing new here. She'd performed this test many times before.

"Right," Lister said. "Got it? Good. Let's do it again." He repeated the lesson. Then he did it again and again, making it clear that the tests were to be done every single time any of them got into an airplane. It was the same lesson Uncle Bob had taught her so long before.

"How are we going to remember all those things?" one of the girls asked, looking lost.

"I'm glad you asked. All you need to do is remember this: Hot Tempered MP Fancies Girls."

"Beg your pardon?"

"HTTMPFGG." He held up his hands then dropped one finger at a time. "Stands for Hydraulics, Trim, Tension, Mixture, Pitch, Petrol,

Flaps, Gills, and Gauges. Of course there's more, but I find the Hot Tempered MP helps."

Then Lister led them to a Hurricane, with its beautiful single wing, and he began to talk about its engine. He invited them to ask him anything they didn't know, and a dozen hands shot up. Dash stepped back. After her time at CanCar, she could have *taught* that class.

At the end of their busy days, Dash usually joined the others in the Hamble common room. The comradery she found there was like nothing she'd ever known. Rude magazine editors might call the girls inept, and disbelieving people might call them spoiled and rich, but the truth was that the ATA-girls were like Dash: impossible to label. They'd come from all over the world—Australia, New Zealand, Poland, Holland, Chile, South Africa, and Canada—for no reason other than a desire to help end the war. Some had flying experience of a year or more, one had been part of an aerobatics team with her husband, and others were starting from scratch. A few had never even driven a car.

Stella, Dash's friend and roommate, had flown with the ATA for two years already. She was a fountain of sarcastic information. This morning, as they entered the common room at Hamble, Stella tilted her head to the side and gave Dash a wink and a smile.

"I heard what you and the other rookies are doing this morning. You're gonna love it."

"Running laps? What?"

"Patience, little one. All I can tell you is the actual exercise is even more fun than the instructor, Jack Reimer. And that's saying a lot." She puffed on her cigarette then picked up her chit at the front desk. "While you're doing that, I'll be flying a Spitfire to Scotland."

With a pang of envy, Dash watched her friend head out to the airfield. Every morning, those chits told the pilots what they were flying and where. Every day, Dash got closer to joining Stella and the others, but not today. With a sigh, she filed into the gymnasium behind a dozen new friends, prepared to work hard.

The morning began as the others had, with grueling physical training.

Every day they ran laps until some of them lost their breakfasts. They did push-ups, climbed ropes, and learned to somersault by rolling over one shoulder in preparation for jumping out of a plane with a parachute. Dash had no trouble with any of it. She'd do whatever it took to fly, with or without a plane. Whatever it took to get her up in a Spitfire, just like Stella.

"Over here, ladies!"

Wiping the sweat from her eye, Dash and the others jogged to the side of the track and were introduced to former RAF pilot Jack Reimer. He was a sharp-looking Brit. Not Dash's type, but she could certainly see why Stella liked him.

"I'm here to teach you about parachutes," Jack told the group. He looked them over then pointed at Dash. "You. Come here, please."

Dash joined him and faced the class. Beside her, Jack lifted a large grey pack for everyone to see. "This is your parachute. It weighs about fourteen kilos. For those of you living outside of civilization, that is about thirty pounds. We try very hard to keep planes in one piece; however, keeping the pilot intact is always the priority. This is how we do that."

He turned to Dash with a cocky smile, and she blinked, surprised by the directness of his gaze. He wasn't even pretending not to be flirting.

"First step is to put the straps on like a coat," he said, handing it to her. "Here you go."

Dash almost dropped the pack, and he chuckled. "Heavier than it looks. Try again. That's it. One arm at a time."

Yes, yes, you're strong and handsome, Dash thought facetiously. He stepped in front of her, and Dash frowned down at her chest as he connected her straps in the centre, tight like a corset.

"Would you mind setting your feet apart, please?"

She kept an eye on him as he drew the strap up between her legs then linked it to the right side of her hip. He did the same on the left.

"If you are ever flying without the comfort of an airplane, this is what holds you together." He pressed a smaller pack against Dash's stomach then clasped it to the main harness. "This is your reserve chute."

He moved behind her, his hands curled unnecessarily on her waist. "You feel secure?"

Dash rolled her eyes for the girls, and they hid their smiles behind their hands. "Nice and snug, thanks."

"Good," Reimer said. "Now we'll learn how to use it. Over to the tower, please."

While the other girls headed off, Reimer blocked Dash. "Interested in dinner sometime?"

What was it with men and dinner? "I appreciate the personalized lesson, sir, but no, thank you. Nothing personal, but I am not at all interested in anything like that."

Reimer gave her a nod and stepped away. On her way to the tower, Dash smiled to herself. She supposed he'd meant to be slightly intimidating, but she hadn't been afraid of him. And by holding her own, she'd earned his respect.

The girls initially practiced jumping from the tower with their chute connected to a complicated wiring system overhead. The thrill for Dash came when it was disconnected, and she was on her own, flying with the chute.

"Well done," Reimer said after she landed, rolling flawlessly over one shoulder and popping up as she'd been taught. "Make sure you keep your feet together."

"Yes, sir."

"Feeling confident?"

"Ask me anything," Dash replied smugly.

"What's the lowest altitude that is safe enough for you to open your chute?"

"Twenty-five hundred feet."

"Excellent work, Wilson. Back in line. Do it again."

———

As they moved into the final month of training, the instructors started talking about the various airplanes the women would be flying. Finally,

Lister led them onto the tarmac and to a Gypsy Moth, which was practically identical to a Tiger Moth.

"Here is your first ATA transport. We begin flying today."

Dash bit her tongue to keep from cheering.

"We're flying that?" one girl asked. She wrinkled her nose. "Open cockpits are so dreadfully cold."

Dash didn't mind the Gypsy Moth. Thanks to Uncle Bob, she already knew the basic maneuvers. As soon as it was her turn, she did all the checks then took off, flew over the airfield, shut off her engine in midair to demonstrate dead-stick landings, then made a perfect landing. Lister noticed her skill and moved her ahead to the next leg of the training: thirty solo cross-country flights following specific routes of railway lines, rivers, and Roman roads. The point was to get the overall aerial picture of England, since she would eventually fly without the guidance of radios or maps. If an airfield was nowhere in sight, she would have to judge the direction and wind speed by watching smoke rise from chimneys, then she'd follow rail lines to fields where she could find a safe place to land.

When Dash graduated from biplanes to monoplanes, she felt a spring come back to her step. What a thrill to be behind the controls of a big, bold engine again, and feel the power and the speed. She was pleasantly aware of the other girls and Lister watching her zipping confidently past them in a Hurricane, and she wondered if she might have been one of the mechanics who had built this beauty.

At last, training came to an end. On the morning of Dash's graduation ceremony, she let Stella make a fuss over her.

"You have to wear the wedge cap off to the side, like this," she said, making sure Dash's navy uniform was spotless. "It looks more plucky."

Later that day, under Miss Tallis's guidance, the girls were sent by train then bus to White Waltham Airfield, the Air Transport Auxiliary's headquarters. It was a beautiful journey through rolling land and summer forests, and Dash enjoyed seeing it from the ground for a change. *Dot would love this*, she thought, surprising herself. She hadn't thought about her sister much during her training, which was odd, she realized. Before

The Secret Keeper   295

all this, the sisters couldn't have imagined life apart. Now Dash had trouble remembering the last time they'd corresponded.

For a while after the funeral, Dot had written, but Dash had never responded. After that, the letters stopped. That had made their division feel final. Sometimes Dash missed her sister so much she almost forgot why she wasn't talking to her, then it all came rushing back. Her father's deathbed, and Dot's inexplicable abandonment. How could she ever forget that?

A temporary stage and a couple dozen chairs had been set up on the lawn outside the headquarters building, and the graduating students, both male and female, milled around, chatting. Some of them had family living nearby, so they'd come to watch the ceremony. After a little while, Miss Tallis asked everyone to take their seats, then a man in a stiff navy uniform strode to the front.

"I am Captain Holbourne, one of the instructors here at White Waltham, and it is my privilege to make these presentations. Today, we celebrate the official moment when our pilots become certified members of the Air Transport Auxiliary. We've brought you here to receive your stripes, and to welcome you to a small luncheon in your honour."

When it was Dash's turn to be presented, Captain Holbourne shook her hand then placed the prized gold shoulder stripe in her palm. He moved to shake the next girl's hand, and Dash returned to her seat. The stripe declared that Dash was qualified to fly with the ATA. Her next goal was the prized second stripe that would make her a first officer, which meant she could fly any kind of plane on the tarmac—and there were dozens to choose from.

In the beginning, Dash had been a bit intimidated by that idea. How could she possibly fly so many different planes? Stella had put her fears to rest by showing her the Ferry Pilots' Notes, a pocket-sized notebook kept under each plane's seat. Inside was the small, neat handwriting of dozens of women, each of them contributing their thoughts and advice for flying that particular plane. When Dash discovered that every aircraft had one of those notebooks, she was full speed ahead. For now, she was limited to specific types of airplanes, but that was all right. She would fly anything just to be a part of this. Tomorrow morning, after Dash picked up her chit and learned which plane she would be ferrying on her first official day as an ATA-girl, she'd be doing something she'd never thought possible.

After the ceremony, she glanced at the other girls, happily speaking around the luncheon table, and she was struck by a wave of melancholy. That annoyed her, because today was supposed to be a happy day. Tomorrow would be even happier. But not today. Dash walked toward a nearby tree, skimming her thumb over the gold material of the stripe, thinking. What she really wanted was to share this moment with her family. To burst into her childhood home and show *both* parents the stripe. She wanted to rush to Uncle Bob's and tell him all about her experience. She wanted to boast to Gus. And she wanted to share her joy with Dot. Instead, she was on her own.

"Hey, Dash." She turned to see one of the girls approaching, a plate of sandwiches in her hand. "You should come over. There are chicken salad sandwiches. They're delicious."

Dash had seen the girl only a couple of times before, and while it was obvious she was from Australia, Dash couldn't remember her name. She used to know everyone. She used to be the life of the party. What had changed?

"Thanks, but I'm not really hungry."

She thought the other girl would leave, but instead she put the plate down and embraced Dash. "I know you miss your family. I do, too. We have to make do with each other for now. We're our own family."

"You're right," Dash said, hugging her back. "Thank you. Maybe I will come have something to eat."

"You should. It's much better than mess hall food."

Dash pasted a smile on, and after a little while it came more naturally. But as the girls rode the train back to Hamble, Dash found herself sinking back into despondency. Despite everything, she wanted Dot beside her. She wanted to feel her sister's love and pride. The irony was that Dash could fix all of it simply by forgiving Dot. If she did, her heart would lighten and everything would be all right between the sisters. But to do that, Dash would have to dig up a world of sadness and regret that she'd already buried. She wasn't ready.

Maybe someday, she thought, gazing out the window. But not today.

forty-five
DOT

-.. .. --- -

D ot perched on a stiff black chair outside Gerald's office as two muted male voices droned on from the other side of the door, and she wondered vaguely what she was missing. She'd been waiting for ten minutes, and her knee bounced with impatience. She understood Gerald was busy with many operations, but having been at Camp X for almost a year, Dot was also handling multiple things. She couldn't afford to be idle. The days were too short to waste sitting around.

"They'll be done soon, I'm sure," Frances said from her desk.

At last, the door opened, and Gerald emerged with an officer whose expression was tense. As he strode away, Gerald turned to Dot. Her boss looked tired, she thought, but not overly so. She supposed she wasn't the only one who could do with a little more sleep.

"Ah, Dot. Thank you for joining me. Please, come in." She took her seat, and he did the same. "All right. Let's get right to it. No time for small talk, as I'm sure you agree."

"Yes, sir."

"Firstly, I want to commend you officially for the work you have been doing. Bill Hardcastle and I were discussing your contributions, both your superior listening skills and your uncanny ability to spot ciphers. Your reports are faultless and thorough. Exactly what we need."

"I appreciate that, sir, but there's no reason to thank me. I'm just doing my job." Except his words meant the world to her. She was painfully aware that her cheeks had gone bright red, and she was so grateful that he knew better than to comment on that.

"You arrived at Camp X about a year ago—"

"Eleven months, sir."

Gerald smiled. "I stand corrected. Eleven months."

After she'd successfully signaled to that ship about the U-boat threat during Operation Husky eight months ago, Dot had a whole new understanding of her purpose. No one knew how long this war would go on, but she was in it every step of the way. She was here to save lives. To defeat the enemy. To win the war. Nothing else mattered.

And she was not the only one. Somewhere out there, Dash risked her life by flying through the war, and Gus, well, that was simple. He put his life on the line every time he went to Europe.

She hadn't seen him much lately. Ever since their disastrous night at her father's bedside, he'd spent as little time as possible near her, either training or doing his job in Europe. To distract herself, Dot had focused fully on her job. She had made herself into the most valuable tool she could be. That's what mattered.

"Anyhow," Gerald was saying, "I knew when we met that you would be up for the challenge, but recently you have gone beyond. You have stepped into a leadership role, filling in when people need help, volunteering to work with the decrypting girls more often, all with exemplary confidence."

"Thank you." She cleared her throat. "Thank you, sir."

"Operation Husky was your first major operation. You conducted yourself professionally and exceeded expectations. I especially appreciated your initiative. Notifying an Allied convoy about the presence of a German U-boat without clearance from me was not protocol, but it was exactly what needed doing. Sometimes in war we cannot afford to delay."

"No, sir," she replied flatly, but inside she was elated. How gratifying that he remembered what she'd done.

"Right. On to the matter at hand. Overall, I believe we can agree that, while we wish it was done with entirely, the war is going relatively well for our side. Well enough that I feel safe in suggesting there might be an end in sight. With help from Allied bombers, the Red Army is forcing the Germans to retreat from Ukraine, and they continue to march toward Romania. Our Soviet allies have liberated Crimea. We have basically won the Battle of the Atlantic. Of course, the Japanese continue to be a source of annoyance, but let's manage one enemy at a time." He exhaled. "Still, despite the gains, the world is in disarray."

That's an understatement, Dot thought.

"However, in the midst of that—possibly *because* of that—I am very pleased to tell you that we have found opportunity. For the past year, a new plan has been in the making, and this one, to be frank, will make Operation Husky look like a walk in the park."

She settled back, intrigued.

"The plan is, in simple terms, all about intimidation. The goal is to divide enemy forces and weaken them. They will see our troops massing everywhere, and as a result they will feel pressured and alarmed by the sheer magnitude of our presence." He reached behind him for a thick, weathered binder. "The trouble is, Dot, we have neither the manpower nor the weaponry required to worry them in the slightest. Right now, we can barely muster six divisions, and we are critically low on landing craft."

She waited expectantly for him to share the strategy, but he appeared to have lost himself flipping through the binder.

"Sir," she said after a moment, "I don't understand. Without the necessary manpower or weaponry, what is the solution?"

He smiled, holding her gaze. "We fake it."

"Sir?"

He set the binder on his desk, and she noted the label on the front. OPERATION FORTITUDE. Fortitude. *Standhaftigkeit* in German. *Coraggio* in Italian. *Courage* in French.

"Operation Fortitude is a campaign entirely based on deception," Gerald said. "Its existence relies upon total secrecy. You, Dot, will play a vital role."

Adrenaline shot through Dot's fingers. Her role would be *vital*. "Yes, sir. Whatever you need."

"Operation Fortitude's mission is to flood Europe with leaked information; however, everything the enemy hears will be riddled with *mis*information." He turned to a map of Europe in the binder and rotated it toward her. "Through your efforts on the wireless, the work of double agents on the ground, and the rest of our forces, the enemy will be fed specific, false information over the next few months. It will confuse them and force their command to make a decision that will ultimately split them." He tapped Scotland, then Calais. "The enemy will think we are planning to invade using one of these two entry points, and we will encourage them to believe that Scotland will be the starting point for an invasion of Norway. We will also convince them that we plan to land at Calais and take back France."

She hesitated. "But we're not doing either of those things?"

"No. As I said, we are not equipped for anything of the sort, but the enemy doesn't know that." He flipped a page. "They will believe what they hear, and they will send forces to block us."

"I see. The goal is to confuse the enemy and break them down to more manageable sizes." Dot read the notes, interpreting some of the plans. She set her finger on one. "Sir, the British Fourth Army? I may be mistaken, but I do not believe that unit exists."

"You are not mistaken, and this is exactly what I am talking about. I would say that the British Fourth Army exists technically, but not officially. We do have troops on the ground there, but far fewer than what is noted here. To accommodate the plan, each man wears various uniforms representing different forces."

The fog began to lift. "The enemy will have no idea."

"Exactly. It will be your task to transmit broadly, albeit in a vein of secrecy, about an increase in bombers around the Scotland area. Those will, of course, not exist. You will also whisper about multiple landing craft and ships near Calais, which are not real. I have full confidence that you will convince them, Dot."

"Of course, sir." She paused. "They will have surveillance planes, so they will study the areas from above. That means transmitting messages will not be enough. May I ask how this will be handled?"

"It's quite an impressive operation on that front. First of all, we are in the process of hauling damaged ships to the Calais area. Those have been cosmetically repaired so that they will appear to be in working order. The enemy surveillance planes will report tanks in both Scotland and Calais; however, those are being made of inflatable rubber and papier-mâché. We are currently building a fuel depot at Dover and will purposely leak photos of troops using the base. As with the British Fourth, those photos will be retaken multiple times using the same men wearing different uniforms." He looked amused. "I will admit, there have been some issues, as there always are. The imitation landing crafts, for example. They are made mostly of wood and canvas materials, which has proven to be too light. In a breeze, some have flipped over entirely. And the tanks at Calais, well, just last week I saw a private photograph of a soldier balancing one over his head. Of course we've put a stop to those shenanigans, but it would be amusing if it wasn't life or death."

Incredulity filled Dot. "The entire thing is a ruse."

"Precisely. Operation Fortitude is made up of a multitude of big lies and even more little ones. But it is all based on one truth: there *will* be an Allied invasion." His finger slid to the south of France. "The invasion is planned for June 5 on the beaches of Normandy, barring any unforeseen obstacles. The event will be called Operation Overlord, and it will be the largest invasion the world has ever seen."

forty-six
DASH

—

— April 1944 —
Southampton, England

The Air Transport Auxiliary was everything Dash had ever dreamed it might be, and more. Their motto was "Anything to Anywhere," and they meant it. In her first month as an ATA-girl, Dash had flown fifteen different types of aircraft, including Hurricanes, Barracudas, and Wildcats. Eventually, she was promoted to first officer and began flying twin engines, including the big Wellingtons, Tempests, and even a Lancaster bomber. Over the past eight months, she had landed on dozens of airstrips and a couple of open fields when things got tough. At the end of the day, if Dash couldn't get a flight home, she slept overnight wherever she was, or she climbed aboard a train and chugged back to base.

This morning, Dash had three planes written on her chit. The first, she read, was a Ventura V FN957, which she would ferry from Hamble to High Ercall. From there, she'd fly a Barracuda to the next stop. Then she would take—

At last. "I finally get a Spitfire!"

Dash had been dying to fly a Spitfire ever since she first saw one soar over the airfield, its powerful Rolls-Royce Merlin engine growling gloriously. The other girls all raved about them. She could hardly wait to get to that last stop on her chit and see what all the fuss was about.

"Now, remember," Stella coached, "if you spend the whole trip doing victory rolls, you'll never get there."

Dash flew all morning and early afternoon. Her second-to-last flight was an Anson taxi, and she dropped off two passengers at Reading. She gave them her usual forced smile when they told her how surprised they were to have a woman as a pilot, and then to learn that—incredibly!—she actually knew what she was doing.

"Have a nice evening," she said, waving them away. She glanced around the field, looking for her final flight of the day, then she caught sight of her, shining in the sun across the tarmac. "Oh hey! There you are."

forty-seven
DOT
‒ •• ‒‒‒ ‒

— Camp X —

The day had finally arrived for Dot to begin playing her role in Operation Fortitude. To the left of her radio, she kept a thick black book with Gerald's orders for sending misleading information, including transmission dates and times. Those lists included her own translations into German, then the coded versions. Gerald had left the coding itself to Dot and Bill. Between the two of them, they decided to introduce their broadcast with a key Dot had recently come across, and one that any German decoder would recognize: POWER. Using that word as a key, the receiver could decode Dot's message and feel confident that the transmission had come from a reputable German source.

Now it was all up to Dot.

"All right," she said, her finger hovering over the tapper. "Let's see who is listening."

‒‒ •‒ ‒•‒• •••• ‒ / ‒••• •‒•• •• ‒ •• •••• ‒•‒• ••••• • / •••‒ •• •• •‒•• ‒ • / •‒ ‒•‒ ‒‒ •• / •••‒ •• •‒•
••• •‒ ‒‒ ‒‒ • •‒•• ‒ / ••• •• ‒•‒• ••••

MACHT BRITISCHE VIERTE ARMEE VERSAMMELT SICH

Power British Fourth Army assembling, she'd transmitted in German, followed by the coordinates for Edinburgh.

Holding her breath, Dot slid the tapper away and put her headphones on. This was her first contribution to Operation Fortitude, her first hook dropped into the water. How long would it take for the enemy to bite, then send a reaction or response? One minute later, she sent it again.

-- .- -.-. .... - / -... .-. .. - .. ... -.-. ..... / ...- .. . .-. - / .- .-. -- . . / ...- . .-.
... .- -- -- . .-.. - / ... .. -.-. ....

MACHT BRITISCHE VIERTE ARMEE VERSAMMELT SICH

A crackle in her headphones, then:

. .. -. --. . --. .- -. --. . -.

EINGEGANGEN

Received. She squealed with excitement. She'd done it. An hour later, she changed frequencies and reminded them with a slightly different message.

-- .- -.-. .... - / -... .-. .. - .. ... -.-. ..... / ...- .. . .-. - / .- .-. -- . . / .- .-
..-. ... - . .-.. .-.. ..- -. --.

MACHT BRITISCHE VIERTE ARMEE AUFSTELLUNG

Power British Fourth Army muster, then Edinburgh's coordinates. The response was quicker this time.

. .. -. --. . --. .- -. --. . -.

EINGEGANGEN

Received. From that moment on, she wrote down every action she could track over the next two hours based on her counterfeit warning, then she knocked on Gerald's door. He looked up expectantly.

"Well?"

"They bought it."

forty-eight
DASH

—————

— *Berkshire, England* —

Dash headed quickly toward her very first Spitfire, anticipation building. When she was done with her first check, she climbed into the cockpit and reached under the seat for the pilots' notes. She scanned them—saw nothing of concern—then began her preliminary check, her body comfortably snug.

Undercarriage lever set to "down"; indicator shows "down"; green light on light indicator; flaps lever set to "up"; thirty-seven gallons of fuel in the lower tank . . .

With the throttle lever opened to half an inch, Dash primed the ki-glass a few times to pressurize the fuel pumps. She switched on the ignition, lifted the flaps, and pressed the starter and booster buttons; the Spitfire purred to life. The plane's power vibrated through her chest.

"Clear!" she called to the ground crew, then she taxied down the runway, idling briefly at the end while she awaited her turn. Finally, the planes ahead were gone, and the runway was clear.

The Spitfire seemed as impatient as Dash, and the noise of its engine built to an impatient roar. When at last she set it free, they tore down the runway, adrenaline pumping through Dash's veins. She held her breath when the dial hit 3000 RPMs, anticipating the magical point of separation from earth to sky, then it happened, and her heart flipped in the most delicious way. Airborne at last, the Spitfire surged upward with effortless, breathtaking speed, hugging Dash tight against the back of the seat as they rose above the few low clouds. She banked right, and the plane's smooth manoeuvre held her as close as a lover. She turned in the other direction, a little steeper this time, and the plane gave her a perfect circle. She wasn't quite ready to try a victory roll, but someday she would, and she already knew it would take her breath away. Levelling out, she laughed aloud, thrilled to be sitting in this cockpit, doing what she loved most in the world.

The other women had been right. The Spitfire was the most beautiful plane she had ever flown.

It felt like no time had passed when she found herself soaring over the long, wide airfield at Christchurch, near the south edge of England. She aimed reluctantly at the runway and pulled the overhead canopy open, sorry the flight was already done. She could have flown this plane for hours and never gotten tired. Right on cue, the Spitfire's landing gear rolled into place then she touched down with the smoothest of landings.

As she taxied in, Dash spotted a couple of men in RAF uniforms standing outside the main hangar. They looked up, hearing the Spitfire's distinctive rumble, and she pulled to a stop in front of them. Still glowing from the flight, she unbuckled the harness, slipped off her helmet, then climbed out of the cockpit.

"Whoa!" one of the men cried, jogging over to lend a hand. He was a little taller than her, with short black hair and a well-fitting uniform. "I did not expect to see *you* climb out of that aircraft."

She set a hand on her hip. "What's the matter? Never seen a woman pilot before?"

He gave her a crooked smile that cut a dimple in his right cheek. "I've seen a couple, but not one that looked like you."

She laughed, letting him put his hands on her waist to help her off the wing. As soon as she had her feet on the ground, she looked up at him with a challenge.

"Now that we've danced, you owe me your name."

"Master Corporal Pete Clark, at your service."

"Petty Officer Wren and ATA First Officer Dash Wilson."

"I must say, you are a breath of fresh air. How was the flight?"

His buddy laughed. "Let the lady catch her own breath, yeah? She's barely out of the cockpit."

Dash had said no to a lot of boys after Eisen's garage. She'd left any connections at harmless flirting, but she liked the look of Pete, and she very much liked the twinkle she saw in his eye. Some of the girls talked about having "a man at every port," and Dash didn't even have one. Maybe she ought to think about trying a bit of that.

"Oh, it was fine, thanks." How far did she dare push it? "I'm just hungry. It's been a long day."

"Awright then," Pete's friend said, slapping him on the shoulder. "Wife will be asking where I am, so I'm off. See you in a couple of weeks?"

"Sure," Pete replied, his eyes glued to Dash.

"You got a wife waiting for you, too?"

He shook his head. "Free as a bird." He stuck out his arm in invitation. "Dinner?"

Her arm fit snugly in his. "That sounds good."

"With an ocean view?"

"Delightful."

"This way, then," he said and they headed down the gravel roadway, away from the parked planes. "I hope you like fish. This fellow makes delicious fried fish. He calls his recipes different names, but it's all the same thing, really. It's a twenty-minute walk or so. You all right with that?"

Dash couldn't remember the last time she'd been on a date. She didn't count the dances at CanCar, because those had only been fun frolics to let off steam. There was something about this man, with his enticing British accent and confident smile. Or maybe it was the timing. Maybe she was still higher than a kite after the Spitfire, and Master Corporal Pete Clark was in the right place at the right time.

"That was my first Spitfire," she told him, grinning.

"Ah yes? And what is your opinion?"

"She lives up to her reputation and then some."

"Have you flown a lot?"

For some reason, that question was the key. As they walked, she told him about learning to fly with Uncle Bob. Pete was a good listener, asking questions so he could see the whole picture. He encouraged her to keep talking, so she did, telling him about Dot and Gus and how inseparable the three of them had been. She tried to focus on her life prewar, but the conversation inevitably wound around to her father and everything that had happened with Dot.

"There must have been a reason," he said. "She would never have chosen to do something like that, from what you've told me about her."

"That's what people keep telling me."

"You have to trust her. You know her better than anyone."

"And yet apparently I don't," she snapped, annoyed that Dot had interfered in her lovely evening. "Let's talk about something else."

He nodded thoughtfully, then pointed ahead. "Up there's the restaurant I was telling you about. That's Southbourne Beach."

She'd been so deeply immersed in their conversation she'd missed her surroundings, and now the sight nearly stopped her short. An explosion of melting sunshine spread over the calmest of seas, a rippling mirror of reds, oranges, and purples. At its base stretched a long beach, empty but for a small building with crumbling walls and tables outside. She glanced around, looking for other people, but she could see no one else. This spectacle was for the two of them alone.

She saw the corners of his mouth draw up. "Glorious, isn't it?"

All she could do was smile. When they reached the beach, she took off her boots so she could feel the sand between her toes.

"Too cold for me," he said. "I've heard Canadians are a different breed."

"We're pretty tough," she agreed.

"Well, you're pretty, anyway." He raised his voice. "Tony! Tony, are you open? I've brought a date for supper."

"I've never seen a restaurant that looks like this."

"Technically, it's his house, but he likes to cook, so he made it his restaurant."

An old man, bald and bent, shuffled out to greet them. "Pete, my lad. First customer I've seen in weeks, you is." He turned to Dash. "And look at you!"

"Tony," Pete chuckled.

"Pete never brings nobody here, miss, so this 'ere's an occasion. I'll cook you something special, mate."

Pete gave Dash a wink. "Your fish is always special, Tony."

"Find yourselves a table," Tony said, gesturing toward two that were still intact, then he disappeared into the house.

Instead of sitting across the table from her, Pete chose the seat beside her.

"So I can enjoy the view, too," he said, his arm brushing hers, and Dash wondered if he meant the ocean or her. It was a line that might have made her roll her eyes coming from anyone else, but with Pete, she felt instantly at ease. She couldn't remember the last time that had happened with someone outside of her family. She was always good with people, but sometimes she put on a show to impress them. It didn't feel necessary with Pete.

Before long, Tony reappeared and placed two glasses of beer in front of them.

"Beer! Where have you been hiding these, mate?" Pete exclaimed.

"Special occasions," his friend said, leaving them again.

Pete held up his glass and gazed in Dash's eyes. His were the most captivating shade of deep blue.

"Cheers," he said.

She tapped her glass against his.

"It's your turn to tell me about yourself," she said after they had taken a sip.

"All right," he said, peering into his drink. "Here's the story. I grew up nearby. My parents live about a half hour from here. Haven't seen them in a while."

"Tell me about little Pete."

"He was a right genius on the piano, little Pete was. Not the brightest star when it came to mathematics or spelling, but hum a tune and that fella could play it for you."

"I'll have to be on the lookout for a piano," she said. "What about flying? When did you start?"

Like her, he'd wanted to fly his whole life, but unlike her, he hadn't had a kindly uncle to teach him. Lessons were too pricey until the war came up, he said, and his family had never had any money. When the RAF needed more pilots, Pete was first in line.

As they spoke, Tony brought out their meals, but they were both so engaged in conversation they barely noticed him. There was something about the way Pete smiled, the way he gave little self-deprecating shrugs that were all made in fun, the way he lifted his dark eyebrows when he was interested. The candid way he spoke, and the way he looked at her. She was spellbound, and it wasn't just the beer. He reminded Dash to eat before the meal got cold, but it was too late. She ate it anyway, pretending not to notice, as he told her more about his family, and his younger brother, an army man who had recently been killed.

The very idea of losing Dot was too painful for her to consider. "I'm so awfully sorry."

His eyes softened, and she caught a glimpse of his broken heart. "They gave me a week off after that." He didn't want to dwell on that, she could see. "So you steamed here from Canada? From where?"

"Halifax. In Nova Scotia, on the East Coast."

"What's it like there?"

She shrugged.

"Why would you shrug? It's where you live. You should be able to tell me more than that."

"I'm not from Nova Scotia," she told him. "Canada's a bit bigger than that. I'm from west of there."

"On the Pacific?"

"Somewhere in between." She sat back in the old chair and teased him with an admonishing look. "You need a geography lesson, Master Corporal."

He folded his arms, matching her. "Is that right? Where's Maidstone, then? Or Folkestone?"

She grinned. "I don't know where any of those stones are. I know where the airfields are, and that's all that matters."

After supper, they walked along the beach and watched the sun go down. Their conversation became more thoughtful as the fading pinks turned to deep purples, but even the occasional silences felt comfortable. Only once did they touch on the subject of war.

"I saw the strangest thing the other day when I was flying into Edinburgh," she said. "There were a dozen planes lined up on the airfield, but when I landed, I couldn't believe what I was looking at. They were rubber, Pete. Rubber fighter planes."

He frowned. "What? Why?"

"I have no idea. I asked when I checked in, but no one would tell me anything."

"Sounds mysterious," he said, wiggling his eyebrows. "I love mysteries, don't you?"

"You sound like my sister."

"Is that a good thing?"

That made her laugh. "Let's talk about something else."

"Like what?"

She thought about that. "Does flying ever scare you?"

"Sometimes. Not usually." He studied the sand beneath them, and his steps slowed. "But when you're under fire, everything's scary. I'm glad they can't fire on you in the ATA."

They stopped walking. It had been a beautiful day, but she wasn't ready for the sun to set so quickly, and she shivered in the chill. Reading her, he took off his coat and set it on her shoulders. Shadows darkened his face, hiding the dimple in his cheek, and she resisted the urge to touch it.

"Well, 'can't' isn't exactly right," she said. "If they see us, they assume we're you, I suppose. I've been all right, but I have some friends who have narrowly avoided the ack-acks when they've flown over France."

He chuckled at the expression. "The ack-acks?"

"Antiaircraft guns. You know them, I'm sure."

"I do, unfortunately. I just haven't heard that term."

At some point, he'd taken her hand. Every part of her felt warm now. Above, a dim scattering of stars flickered into view. This was the moment, she knew. He'd been waiting for just the right one, as had she. And here it was.

"I wish I were your wingman, Dash Wilson. I'd never let anyone hurt you."

Ingrid Bergman, she thought. Those beautiful grey eyes, twinkling under the lights, then filling with disbelieving tears as the man she loved sent her away. The way Bogart had looked at her, determined to sacrifice everything in his heart so he could keep her safe. Until now, Dash had never truly believed that delicious tension, that kind of romance could exist outside of *Casablanca*, beneath the lights and cameras. And yet, here it was.

So when Master Corporal Pete Clark moved just that little bit closer, she did, too. He kissed her softly, whispering her name with a kind of wonder, and her arms went around his neck, drawing him in for more. He took her breath away, this man. She'd never felt quite so light before, like she would float if she only kicked off the ground. His hands circled her waist, his breath caressed her face, and she wanted more of everything. She knew. She already knew.

forty-nine
DOT

‾.. ‾‾‾ ‾

— May 1944 —
Camp X

Operation Fortitude, Dot had decided, was similar in many
ways to the dozens of murder mysteries she had read in the
past. She revelled in the opportunity to be the one planting false clues
and leaving tidbits of misleading evidence. As long as the people listening weren't as smart as Miss Marple, she felt safe in what she was
doing. The trick was to be sharper than any of them. Dot believed
she was.

This morning's transmission was different from what she usually
sent. She loved tapping it in.

.. ‾. ...‾ .‾. ‾. ‾ .‾ .‾. ‾....‾ .‾ ‾. ..‾. .‾. .‾ .‾ ‾‾. .

INVENTAR-ANFRAGE

Inventory request. Immediately following, she listed items of warm
clothing, including hats, gloves, and winter boots. She added skis, snow-
shoes, and instruction manuals for engine maintenance in extremely cold
weather. The enemy would wonder at her requests, but then they would
add them to their growing list of information about the impending Allied attack on Norway through Scotland.

Or rather, their growing list of *mis*information.

Hours later, after her shift on Hydra ended, Dot reported to Gerald. He had put in place daily meetings with her ever since he'd introduced her to Operation Fortitude.

"The Germans have communicated that they know of more than eighty Allied divisions ready to attack at Calais," she told him, consulting her notes.

"Excellent. You should soon be hearing about the fifty imaginary divisions we will be sending from America. They're all headed to Calais."

"Quite a force, sir. Enemy won't stand a chance."

"Right you are," he said with a knowing smile. "I need your help with something, if you have an hour."

"Of course."

"Frances is out sick today, and she was supposed to be paired with Gus this morning. He is debriefing a captured German officer." He wrinkled his nose. "Major Karl Böhm. Quite a monster. Would you mind taking notes on their meeting? It will be conducted in English this time."

She hesitated. How long had it been since she'd spoken with Gus? For the last eight months he had been in and out of Camp X, traveling to Europe more and more. She'd barely seen him other than a few times passing in the corridors. She wasn't sure how it would feel to sit in the same room with him, but she was positive it would be uncomfortable. All she had to do was take notes, she reminded herself. Nothing personal. She could handle that.

"Of course," she said to Gerald.

Half an hour later, she sat in the corner of the debriefing room, taking shorthand while Gus questioned the captured German officer across the table from him. From the moment she walked into the room, she'd felt the tension between them. He'd glanced her way only once and shown her absolutely nothing of what was going on in his head, and that broke her heart. She forced herself to keep her eyes on her paper and off of Gus, but it was impossible to look away the whole time. His hair had grown in a bit since they'd last spoken, curling the slightest bit under his ears.

She liked it; he looked a little less severe. Her gaze went to his neck and shoulders, saw the muscles flex under his shirt when he reached for something, and her thoughts drifted to that night outside her father's window. As if he felt her watching, he glanced over, and she dropped her eyes, her cheeks blazing.

Concentrate, Dot. Focus.

Gus's subtle questions to the German revolved around Operation Fortitude, probing how much Major Böhm knew about it as well as about the locations of specific German officers. From the major's few admissions, Gus could determine which enemy troops were advancing where, and he could get a general picture of how Operation Fortitude was doing.

Both men were cool but cordial, respectful yet wary. A calculated tail-sniffing of two pack leaders, Dot mused. Böhm observed Gus through narrowed, caustic eyes. In contrast, Gus's expression was relaxed. Entertained, even. If Böhm imagined Gus was a weak adversary, he was making a grave mistake. She recognized the little tic in Gus's jaw that signaled that he was very, very aware. If Böhm was wise, he would not underestimate him.

Major Karl Böhm was a fiend. Gerald had shown her his file beforehand. He looked decent, even handsome, with his confident smile and silver temples and educated German accent, but he was the worst kind of man. Two months before, he had sent soldiers to a small French village and ordered them to hang a local priest in front of the townspeople. It was rumoured the priest had been helping Jewish children escape Nazi clutches. Böhm had not permitted the parishioners to cut their priest's body down for three full days.

Sometimes, Dot noticed, the tiniest hint of Gus's native language snuck back in when he spoke with other Germans. *This is* was closer to *Das ist.* His *w* sounds hardened to *v.* Gus was the reason that she had learned German to begin with, and he'd learned a great deal of his English from the girls. He had been the only German child in their school. Anti-German sentiments had still been strong after the first war, so they taught each other their native tongue, then they had agreed to stick with English.

Listening to him now, the crisp German syllables sharpening his words, it was almost as if he became a different person. Slightly separate from her. And something about that observation prompted butterflies to flutter in Dot's chest.

After a while, Gus stood to grab a coffee for them both. That was Dot's cue to join him outside the office in two minutes. She made no sign that she understood, merely kept her head down and pretended to write.

"*Bist du nicht ein hübsches kleines Ding,*" the man said quietly after Gus was gone. Aren't you a pretty little thing.

Heat shot up Dot's neck, but Camp X had trained her how to be invisible even in cases like this. She tilted her head so he could only see the crown and made no sign that she had understood what he said.

"*So weiche weiße Haut. Er hätte dich nicht mit mir allein lassen sollen. Frauen finden mich unwiderstehlich, weißt du.*"

Alarm prickled through Dot at his suggestion that Gus shouldn't have left her and her "soft white skin" alone with him, but really, what was there to be afraid of? His wrists were shackled. Nothing could hurt her here, in the middle of Camp X. He was just a bully. She'd learned long ago from Gus that if he wasn't around to protect her, bullies were best ignored.

When Böhm informed her that women found him irresistible, Dot wished she could tell him she found him repulsive.

"*Kann ich eine Zigarette haben?*" He cleared his throat. "Pardon me, *Fräulein.* Can I have *Zigarette?*"

Dot glanced up, a meek smile on her face. "I will ask and be right back."

It was time she went out to talk with Gus anyway. She gathered up her notes then got to her feet, relieved to escape this man's vulgar attentions.

Two steps from the door she heard him move behind her, then she felt a quick rush of air as his bound hands went over her head. He pulled back and his forearm blocked her throat, choking her, but Dot didn't panic. She had trained for a moment just like this one, she'd just never imagined using the skill. In one swift motion, she reached up and grabbed his arm with both hands. At the same time, she dropped low and brought her left leg back so her calf pressed against his. Pushing off with her right leg, she spun 180 degrees, swept her left leg even farther to unbalance him, then she bent and threw him onto his back, still holding his arm. He landed with a crash, then she gave his wrist an extra twist and pushed down, pinning him in place. He was completely helpless now. And it had all happened in under five seconds.

"*Wie gefällt dir jetzt meine weiche weiße Haut?*" she said, a sense of power filling her veins. How do you like my soft white skin now?

The door flew open, and Gus burst in, eyes wide.

She blinked coyly at him. "*Können Sie mir bitte helfen? Ich werfe nur den Müll raus.*" Would you help me, please? I'm just taking out the garbage.

Gus jerked the man to his feet then shoved him out of the room. "I guess you preferred your cell," she heard him say in German.

Moments later, Gus returned. She sensed his guardedness. He didn't know what to expect from her anymore. Neither did she. Oh, if only she'd never kissed him.

"I thought you said you'd never have to use those skills," he said.

"I have been known to make a mistake on occasion." She grinned. "That felt good."

"I bet you worked up an appetite." He put both hands on his hips, fortifying himself. "Want to go for lunch? We haven't talked in too long."

She shouldn't. She'd done so well at holding him at arm's length, pretending nothing had happened. It was safer that way. Less complicated. But she felt so lonely without him. She nodded, grabbed her bag, and they walked down the corridor toward the mess hall.

"I don't know what to talk about," she admitted as they reached the entrance.

The air in the mess hall was thick with beef stew, which wasn't Dot's favourite, but she was hungry. Gus moved into the line behind her. "Let's talk about Dash. That's pretty safe."

She gave him a sideways glance. "*Du denkst, es ist sicher, über sie zu sprechen?*"

"Of course it's safe to talk about her. Dash is not a dangerous subject, Dot."

"No?"

As much as she missed Dash, she didn't want to talk about her sister, but she didn't want to discuss that fateful night between her and Gus even more.

At the counter, she put a bowl of stew, a roll, and a cup of tea on her tray. Gus did the same, then they went to a quiet corner. He sat across from her, seeming as reluctant as she to start the conversation, even though it had been his idea. She watched him dip his spoon into the steaming hot stew then swallow it right down. Dot pushed her spoon around to cool her meal first.

"I don't know what to say about her," Dot began quietly. "I haven't heard from her in months. She's still so angry at me about Dad, and she has every right to be."

"It's not your fault," he said through a mouthful.

"I never dreamed I might keep secrets from Dash or anyone else. You know me. I don't lie."

He lifted an eyebrow, and she flushed, remembering their conversation on that dark, empty road. She'd said she didn't care for him in a romantic sense, but he knew better.

"You keep secrets for a living now. Better get used to it," he said, tearing into his roll. "You said she's in England?"

"Yes. She's been flying with the Air Transport Auxiliary since March, I think. I wish I knew more. Gosh, I'd love to know more." She tried the stew. "I've written so many times, but she never answers. The only reason I know that she joined the ATA is from Mom. I won't be hearing from Dash anymore, I don't think."

"You should write to her again."

She shook her head. "She doesn't want to hear from me."

"How do you know? You know, one day this war will end. Then we will all go home to . . . what? Come on, Dot. She's your sister. She can be tough, but we both love her for that. Try again. Someday she'll understand."

"In forty years maybe, but not until then."

"Don't give up. She hasn't. She loves you too much to just stop."

"What about you? Why did you stop writing to her?"

"We're not talking about me."

"We are now."

He took a long time inspecting what was left of his roll, then even longer to take a bite and chew. After he swallowed, he said, "I don't have a good excuse. I'm just more chicken than you. I couldn't lie to her."

"But I could?"

"Well, you did, right?"

"So much for solidarity."

He stared at his empty bowl. "I should have written, but I didn't have the answers to the questions I knew she'd ask. I chose the easy way and just didn't say anything. Of course it's worse now, since it's both of us lying to her." He lifted his gaze. "You know it's never been our fault, right? We didn't keep secrets from her on purpose. I didn't know where you were or what you were doing, just like you didn't know where I was. I never thought about your taking the oath. I guess I should have. You were always way too smart to settle for a desk job."

She threw his words back at him. "We're not talking about me."

"I am, Dot." He pushed his meal tray to the side. "Let's talk about the elephant in the room. Let's talk about you and me."

"It feels wrong, Gus," she whispered, her cheeks burning. "Sneaky. Like we're keeping another secret from her."

"It's not about her."

"Plus, it feels like it's you and me without her, and that's not how it should be. We all belong together."

He hesitated. "Are you so naive that you really believe that? Do you imagine the three of us will live happily ever after as friends? That we'll get old together playing bridge or something? Because I don't see it wind-ing up that way, Dot. I see it very differently."

For so many years, she'd envied her sister his attentions. Dash was vivacious and exciting. He was handsome and courageous. Her sister and Gus belonged together. They always had.

"What would Dash say?" she asked.

"Does it matter?"

She couldn't answer. It did, but it didn't.

"I always loved you both as sisters," he said. "I've never loved anyone as much as I love the two of you. You know that. But things change. You looked at me a certain way a while back, and it was as if a light went on in my brain. Everything kind of shifted in my head."

"A while back?"

He shrugged. "About five years ago."

"Five years!" she exclaimed. She dropped her voice. "Five years! And you never said anything?"

His blue eyes met hers, and he looked so much younger in that mo-ment. Vulnerable in a way she hadn't seen in years. Her heart did a little somersault.

"I'm saying it now. I tried not to. I was afraid you didn't feel the same way, and I'd wreck everything. Besides, there's a war on, and my job is dangerous, so I decided not to tell you. I figured if I was killed, you could remember me as just a friend, and that's all. As a brother. If I didn't make it back, it might be less painful in the long run."

His words stopped her heart. "If you were killed," she said softly, "nei-ther Dash nor I would ever recover. You are a part of us just as we are of each other. It's always been that way. We love you. I don't think that if I thought of you . . . romantically, it would be any more or less painful." She picked up her spoon, poked at a chunk of beef in the stew, then set it down. She'd lost her appetite. "Honestly, I don't know how I feel. A part of me is screaming that Dash loves you, and I would never ever take you from her. I couldn't. But you're saying it's not like that between the two of you, and I . . . Even if I allowed myself to feel that way . . ."

"Allow yourself?"

"You and I are tangled up in so many secrets and lies, I don't know how we'll ever straighten things out. Like you said, this war won't last forever. It can't. Then what?"

"Then I want to be with you." He reached for her hand, and his fingers closed around hers. "Listen, Dot. If you don't feel the same way about me, I'll let it go. I will never do anything to make you unhappy or uncomfortable. I'll follow your lead."

Her heart squeezed with regret, and she pulled her hand away. "I can't think about it right now, Gus. It's about more than you and me. You're not the only one with a dangerous job. Dash is out there flying in a war, never hearing from either of us. What if she thinks we don't care anymore? What if the unthinkable happens, and she never understands why we abandoned her?"

One of the training techniques Camp X used to toughen their agents up was to have them stand in front of a sheet of bulletproof glass. They were not permitted to flinch when someone shot directly at them. Dot had gone through that exercise. It had terrified her the first time, but after that, something inside her had hardened. Cheating death made her feel as unbreakable as the bulletproof glass itself. It was such an alien feeling that laughter had bubbled up from deep inside. The instructor had ordered her to stop. He wanted no reaction from her. No reaction at all.

To anyone else, it would have appeared that Gus hadn't reacted to what Dot had just said. He didn't flinch, and nothing on his face showed the slightest change. But Dot wasn't anyone else. The pain she saw flash behind his eyes cut right through her. She'd frightened him. She didn't think she'd ever seen that before.

"Then we'll write to her," he decided. "Both of us, separately. And I'll tell her how I feel about you."

Neither spoke for a moment.

"Whether you write to her or not," Gus said, "I'm going to."

"She probably won't write back."

"That doesn't matter. Not to me. I'm doing what I can. The rest is up to her."

He was right. Dot drew in a breath. "Don't tell her about . . . about you and me, okay?"

"Is there a you and me, Dot?"

Everything was so much easier when she didn't think about him or about Dash. She thrived when her energy went into the work, not her feelings. This was too much, sitting with him, trying to sort through all the mess in her heart.

"I don't know," she admitted. "I have so much to think about."

He looked so defeated that she almost cried, but he managed a smile. "I guess that will have to do for now." He rose. "Listen, I get it. It's something different for both of us. Whatever you decide, I'm glad we're talking again, Dot. Our friendship means everything to me."

"Me, too, Gus. I'm sorry I've stayed away."

She watched him take their trays to the front then walk out of the mess hall, feeling the distance between them stretch like an elastic band. She couldn't turn away from him any more than she could turn from her sister. Except she had given up on Dash, hadn't she?

Guilt tore at her for the next twenty-four hours until she couldn't take it anymore. For the first time in a long time, she brought out her stationery and wrote her sister's name at the top of the page. *The rest is up to her*, Gus had said. She took a deep breath then began to write, hoping she was strong enough to face the possibility of never hearing back.

fifty
DASH

—— Southampton, England ——

Dash strode across the tarmac toward the common room, feeling sad. It made no sense, really, because she'd just landed after a heavenly flight. When she'd been up there she'd forgotten about everything else in her life, but now that her boots were on the ground, it all came back. She'd just enjoyed the most wonderful two weeks of her life. Now that they were over, she felt very much alone.

Her fingertips brushed the two pieces of paper in her pocket. One was a long-awaited letter from Gus. She took it out and read through it again, reminding herself that in all her misery, she still had a friend.

Dear Dash,

I'm just going to say it: I hope you're still speaking to me. I am a louse, not writing to you for so long, even with my rotten handwriting. You can go ahead and remind me of that when—if—you write back to me. In fact I encourage you to tell me exactly how angry you are. Anything, as long as you write back.

It's not that I haven't been thinking of you. I hope you know that. You and your sister have been my family my whole life, and you'll never know how much that matters to me. I owe you more than this one very late letter. My excuse is the war is keeping me busy, but I know that doesn't count because it's keeping everyone busy. Still, I am sticking to that.

Speaking of the war, I wanted to tell you that when I heard you were out there flying, I was so proud. You got what you always wanted, and I hope you are happy. You deserve it.

Dash, I know about your dad and everything you went through. I cannot imagine how hard that was. Especially without Dot. I'm going to say something now that I know only I can get away with: it must have been horrible for Dot, too. You know how they were, she and your dad. Thick as thieves. To be stuck somewhere, unable to see any of you, it must have torn her apart.

There was a reason for it, Dash. You have to trust in that.

You may never forgive me for being the worst letter writer there ever was, but I am still going to beg you for one thing. Write to your sister. Forgive her. Neither of you is complete without the other. And, selfishly, I need you both.

Fondly,
Gus

P.S. I would love to hear about the planes you're flying, if you feel inclined to tell me.

Gus's letter had been a relief, though she was a little curious about how he knew about her father and Dot. He must have written to her mother for her address, and she would have told him about all that, she guessed. The important thing was that he was fine. Hearing from him after so long eased her anger. She wrote back to him right away.

As she tucked Gus's letter back in her pocket, she pulled out the other, much shorter note.

Can't stop thinking about you. Yours, Pete

She touched his handwriting, thinking how surprisingly elegant it was for a man.

She missed Pete terribly. She missed the way he made her feel like the only woman on earth.

Dash had always assumed she would do the right thing and wait until she was married before she shared a bed with a man, but with Pete, one thing had evolved so naturally into the next, she'd never felt the slightest hint of shame. He was gentle with her but sure, self-assured and strong, but never to the point where she was afraid. His desire for her delighted her, as did the lines and curves of his smooth skin under her hands. Falling asleep in his arms was the safest, most comforting place on earth, and she wished they could stay like that forever. She belonged there.

After that first night, they'd seen each other as often as they could, staying in a small inn near the sea, but there had always been an end in sight. He and his squadron had two weeks' leave, but those had sped past. They'd taken advantage of every minute they could. Dash had swapped flights with anyone going to Christchurch, and she'd even asked Stella to call in sick for her a couple of times. The last two days of his leave were Dash's official two days off, and they had clung to each other, unwilling to say goodbye. She never said so, but she had the most horrible feeling that she might never see him again.

"I'll try to fly in to see you this week," he promised. She sat on his lap on the innkeeper's overstuffed armchair, which technically had room for only one. She had him hypnotized, her fingernails etching featherlight circles over his stubbled cheek and beneath his chin. "I'll have to. I cannot possibly be expected to go a week without you."

"You're a very important RAF pilot." She sank her nose into his hair, wanting to keep his scent close. "You can't play with assignments like I can."

"You're a very important pilot, too. Don't sell yourself short."

"I wish we could go away somewhere," she mused. "Just you and me. No deadlines, no rules."

"Where would you like to go?"

She smiled to herself, wondering if this was what love felt like. Real love, like between her mother and father. A love that could withstand years of uncertainty and pain while still being filled with joy simply because they were together. He moved a lock of her hair behind her ear, and she wondered if he was pondering the same thing. Did he love her? Would he always?

"Tell me where, Dash. I will be there for you."

"Paris," she said on impulse. "I've heard it's the most romantic place in the world. Or at least it used to be, before the war."

"Personally, I think this is the most romantic place in the world. Right now, at least." The dimple on his cheek deepened when he smiled. "Anywhere, as long as I'm with you. But I'll take you to Paris, my beautiful girl. I'll fly you there, all right? Or you can fly me there."

He was right; the most romantic place of all was wherever they were together, and when they returned to the bed, they reminded each other of that.

A little while later she awoke, sluggish from a sweet doze. With her head still on the pillow, she watched him sleep, taking in the line of his jaw, the dusting of eyelashes on his cheeks. How had this happened? How had she ended up the luckiest girl in the world, flying airplanes and being loved by the most wonderful man? What had she done to deserve all this?

"I feel you watching me," he murmured, smiling despite his closed eyes.

"I don't know what you're talking about," she teased. "I'm still asleep."

"Liar," he said, gazing at her.

Time stood still. The only thing Dash could hear was the wind outside, stirring the shutters. She never wanted to move.

"Have you a photograph?" he asked, skimming a finger over the curve of her cheek. "If I can't have you in my arms, I'd at least like to keep you where I can see you. On my instrument panel, I was thinking."

It was a reminder that today was the end of their blissful holiday, and it pushed her out of bed. The only photograph Dash had with her was one with Dot. The worn paper was soft as cloth between her fingers. Despite everything, she'd always carried it, though she'd folded it in half in her angriest moments. When she was frightened or sad, she'd found herself touching it for security.

"I have this one."

"So this is Dot," he said quietly, unfolding the picture. "She's lovely."

Dash tucked in beside him so their faces were side by side. "She is. She has no idea, though. She's a funny duck. Dot never sees beyond puzzles and mystery books. I never once saw her swoon over a man."

She hesitated. That wasn't entirely true. Dot had always watched Gus, though they both knew he was something else entirely. Dash loved him to pieces, but he wasn't the kind of boy she went for. He certainly wasn't Pete. When they were little, she and Dot had been curious about how Gus would fit into the family. Dash had been prepared to send him back where he came from on day one, but Dot had argued. She liked having him around, she'd said.

"I imagine her typing all day then digging into her books all night. She's too smart for the job they've given her, whatever it is." She sighed, missing the smile on Dot's face in the photograph. Dash had loved making her sister laugh. No one else could do that quite as well as she did.

"Maybe you should write to her."

"It's too late," she told him. "I can't."

"There's nothing you can't do, Dash Wilson."

She looked at him, a bittersweet memory sweeping through her heart.

You've never failed at anything you've done, her father had said so long ago, as she was leaving to join the Wrens. She would never forget that.

"I stopped writing to her a long time ago."

"Because you were angry. And you still are."

"I am." Her throat tightened. "Even so, I wish I knew what she's doing, and if she's okay. She's the most important person in my life. Well, she was. Before you came along."

He kissed her lightly on the mouth. "You know you'll have to forgive her, right? Someday."

Something made her pause. "Pete, promise me something?"

"Whatever you want."

"If anything ever happens to me, you have to find her."

He drew back. "What's this? You planning something I should know about?"

"Don't be silly. I just . . . I don't know. It's war. Things happen. She's the smartest person on earth. She would know what to do."

"Well, I'm glad to hear that," he said, drawing her toward him. "Because I wouldn't have any idea. I don't think I'd be able to think straight if anything happened to you. So now you must make me a promise. Do be careful, darling."

fifty-one
DOT

-.. --- -

— Camp X —

Operation Fortitude was all anyone at Camp X could think about, including Dot. It was all building toward Operation Overlord, the campaign Gerald had heralded as "the largest invasion the world has ever seen." The countdown had begun. It was set to happen June 5, three weeks from today.

Dot took constant notes of the chatter streaming through the airwaves, making sure there was enough misinformation circulating. All their plans hinged on Germany being so focused on a possible attack on either Calais or Norway that they'd never think to move their forces to Normandy. According to Hydra, the enemy had sighted Allied landing crafts in ports and tanks positioned around likely embarkation points around southeastern England. All those German transmissions came with reports of heavy Allied troop activity.

Of course, most of what they reported was fake, built of wood or rubber. The troops were, in large number, small groups of men masquerading as a bigger force. And yet, from everything Dot had read, heard, and shared with Gerald, the Germans had taken the bait and made a decision. Tens of thousands of troops were gathering, preparing for a massive battle—at Calais.

Dot was staring into her supper, thinking about her latest meeting with Gerald, when Gus slid in beside her. He didn't say a word, just settled in like he belonged there, which he always had, of course. She glanced at his plate and frowned. Usually it was piled high with meat, potatoes, gravy, and whatever else was on the menu. One potato and a couple of thin slices of beef were not going to hold him.

"What's up with you?" she asked.

"Nothing."

"Gus," she scolded.

He reached into his coat pocket and pulled out a piece of paper. He unfolded it with a dramatic flourish then set it in front of her. "I heard back from Dash."

Her first reaction was envy. After all the letters she'd written after their father's death, Dot had never received a response. Maybe hers hadn't meant as much to Dash as Gus's had.

"What does it say?" she asked quietly. "Read it."

Dear Gus,

I could never stay angry at you for long. And you're right: you do have appalling handwriting.

You're choosing not to mention it, but I'm sure you know I was furious with you, too. You should have come to see my father. You should at least have come to the funeral. The army lets men off on leave, don't they? So I may forgive you for not writing, but I'm still stewing on that part.

I miss Dot so much. I have no idea where she is, what she's doing, or anything about her life. She may have broken my heart into a million pieces, but she still makes up most of it. I told her I would never forgive her. I was in pain, and I was angry. I never should have said all those horrible things. Now I fear she will never forgive me. I've been afraid to write to her. I should have done what you and she always told me to do: think logically. I should have calmed down and thought it through and trusted that, like everyone kept telling me, there had to be a reason. But that's not me, is it? Gus, I've never been so sad as I was watching my father die. I needed my sister, and she wasn't there. That had never happened to me before.

Maybe you've given me the push I need, writing like this after so long. Maybe it's a wake-up call for me. I will think about what to say, then I will write to her.

I have news I need to tell her, and I suppose I should tell you as well. I'm in love, Gus. I have fallen madly, deeply, irreparably in love with a British flyboy, and he loves me, too. I need to talk with her about it.

Thank you for writing to me, and for so much more. I love you, Gus. Always will.

Dash

P.S. I'll tell you all about the planes another time. I'm too tired tonight. But that should cheer you up, because it's a promise that I will write back—as long as you do as well.

"She's in love," Dot said softly, her hand over her heart. "And she's afraid I'll never forgive her. How can she think that?"

He leaned sideways into her, arm to arm. "It's time for you to try again. Write to her."

"I already did," she admitted. "I didn't tell her about you and me." She blushed, then hurried on. "That you and I are both here together in the same place is what I meant. Not that we are, uh, you know, together."

One corner of his mouth curled up. "Uh-huh. Are we?"

Her entire face felt like it was on fire.

"I'm just teasing, Dot."

She heard the amusement in his voice, but she knew he was serious. He wanted to mend this bridge because he was afraid he was the one who had broken it. But it was all her fault.

"I know you're uncomfortable," he said, his voice soothing. How many times had he calmed her in their lives? She had always felt safer with Gus than with anyone else, including Dash. "I don't want that. I'm leaving for Europe in the morning. That will give you lots of time to think about things."

She scoffed. "Lots of time."

Gus wasn't the only one going to Europe. Operation Fortitude was almost over, and after that, the door would swing open for Operation Overlord. On the eve of June 5, eighteen thousand British and American paratroopers would be dropped behind enemy lines to create havoc and take out any remaining means of German communication, though many of those would already have been destroyed by local resistance and men like Gus. Once that was done, the focus would shift to the tens of thousands of British, Canadian, and American troops already waiting, strategically hidden from surveillance planes for the next three weeks.

If the grand deception of Operation Fortitude worked like they hoped, so should Overlord. The Allies would land on then capture Normandy's long string of beaches, then they would proceed inland, on the road to defeating Hitler at last. Then the war would be over, and they'd all go home. But to what?

"I'm sorry," Dot said. "I don't know what to do about what I'm feeling. I feel so stupid."

Gus straddled the bench to face her. "You're not stupid. You can't study for this, Dot. You can't puzzle through it, because there's no real answer. There's no absolute right or wrong. I can't describe to you how I feel when I look at you, but I know what it is."

She looked away, sick with confusion.

"I'll be gone in the morning," he reminded her.

She already knew that. She'd been the one to type out the orders. He would sail to England, then get on a plane and drop over Germany, hanging like bait from a parachute. If the weather didn't sabotage him first, he would land behind enemy lines and become both the hunter and the hunted. She hated to think about any of it. What if the worst were to happen?

He placed his palm against her cheek, warm and reassuring, and she leaned into it, her eyes closed. "There's a lot going on right now," he said. "If there was ever a time for me to admit how I feel about you, I think this is it."

The sadness in his voice seemed to come from his longing for her to understand. But she didn't. For so many years, she'd buried her feelings for him so deep she didn't even remember they were there most of the time. She hadn't expected them to bloom that night, and she didn't know why they held her captive now. Dot needed logic, and it wasn't coming to her.

"You have to know, Dot, how I feel. How I've always felt. Please. Look at me."

She feared she might break apart from the sheer force of emotions rising to the surface. Like the explosives she'd learned about so long ago.

"What are you thinking about?" he asked.

"You," she confessed, risking a glance into his pale blue eyes.

"And?"

She couldn't let him leave without solving this between them. He deserved an answer. She bit her lip, summoning the courage she could only seem to find when she functioned alone in the darkness, listening and tapping into the unknown. She couldn't afford to be afraid this time, because she finally understood. What mattered most was what she felt in her heart.

She got up, her heart beating with purpose. "Come with me."

"Where are we going?"

"Shh. Just come with me."

She took him by the hand and led him outside, behind Hydra, where they could have a private space to themselves.

"You asked what I was thinking." She took a deep breath and watched his expression closely. "I was thinking that if something were to happen to you out there, you'd never know how I felt, because I've been too afraid to tell you. It's like when you used to ask me to play, and I'd hide in my room. Just like then, you've given me every opportunity, and I've panicked. You look at me that way, and I turn back into that dumb old dormouse and run away."

She stepped closer to him, daring herself to ignore her head for once, and to embrace what her heart craved instead. Holding his gaze, she placed her hands flat on his chest. "The truth is, I don't want you to go. I need you to stay here with me. But since you have no choice, I want you to go with my promise in your heart, and my kiss on your lips."

Her arms went around his neck, and when her lips met his, the smell of him filled her senses. She felt his arms tightening around her and melted into them. *This*, he'd called it. *This* was something beyond her, beyond any reason, and she needed it more than she'd ever needed anything before.

"I never believed I was good enough," she whispered. "You and Dash—"

"Are best friends," he finished for her. "It's not the same. I love you, Dot."

She kissed him again, and all her doubts disintegrated like the smoke from the bombs she'd lit during training. It was she who had caught fire now.

"I love you, too, Gus. I always have."

She'd never seen him smile like that before. Open and honest, of course, but also . . . amazed. Like a child receiving a coveted gift at Christmas that he'd never dared ask for.

They spent the next few hours hidden away together, trying not to think about the possibility that they could be their last. When the sun went down, they walked side by side under a glorious full moon, then he held her in his arms beneath the parachute tower. At the end of the night, he walked her to her door and asked her not to come see him in the morning.

"Kiss me goodbye tonight," he said. "Otherwise, it will be too hard to go."

"Come back to me," she whispered, her lips on his.

"I promise," he said.

She accepted that without question. Gus never broke a promise.

The sun rose over Camp X without him in it. The day began for Dot like any other, but unlike any day in her life before last night. He loved her. She'd finally found the courage to understand that, and to tell him she felt the same. He would come back. He had promised. Until then, her heart would wait.

fifty-two
DASH

—June 1944—
Southampton, England

Through the window, Dash scanned the airfield and the half-dozen airplanes awaiting pilots. She was dying to fly. She *needed* to fly. The tarmac was wet from an earlier storm, and it looked like it might rain again soon, but the weather wasn't the reason she couldn't go.

No one was flying. Hamble's common room was so hushed it felt like a tomb. Dash tiptoed past sober conversations and subdued card games toward the food counter for a cup of coffee, then she turned back to the room, mug in hand.

All the ATA girls had come here to be together. Most, like Dash, were dressed in their dark navy uniforms, not having been aware of the tragedy before they arrived. Before leaving the house, she had pulled on her fur-lined jumpsuit and boots, secured the knife she always strapped to her calf, then grabbed the bag carrying her helmet, goggles, and her father's compass.

She'd dropped everything on the floor of the common room when she learned what had happened.

There had been so many flights lately, everyone was exhausted. Two weeks ago, Dash had flown six flights in one day, four the next. Nobody ever told the ATA pilots anything, but they had all noticed the recent uptick. Something big was happening out there.

Yesterday, for Stella's last flight of the day, she had flown a Mosquito Mk. VI through miserable visibility to the temporary airfield of B-10 Plumetôt. Every one of them had done a trip like that. Nothing to it. Dash could almost picture Stella in that cockpit, impatient to land. Dying to light up a cigarette, eager to climb onto a train that would bring her back to Hamble and her bed at last. But the plane had crash-landed on the tarmac. No one would ever know if mechanical issues, weather problems, or pilot error was to blame.

Stella had died on impact.

Not one of the women had been left untouched by the tragedy. And no one wanted to talk about it. Especially with Dash or Violet.

Dash's gaze went to Stella's best friend, pale and diminished on the couch across the room. Violet glanced up at Dash, and they exchanged the same grim smile Dash had seen on her mother's face at her father's funeral. Publicly, Violet was so strong. But when she returned to work tomorrow and climbed into her plane, she would be on her own. When she pushed in the throttle then burst into the sky, grief would hit her like a fist. The clouds floating past would be reminders of Stella's cigarette smoke, the atmospheric blue the same as her friend's irises. The freedom whistling past her wings would be the loss, screaming through her heart, then gone.

Someone lit a cigarette, and Dash was carried back in time. Stella had an ingenious method to time her flights. After years of chain-smoking, she claimed to go through a cigarette in seven minutes flat. If she finished four cigarettes through the duration of her flight, well then, she landed twenty-eight minutes after takeoff.

Would Dash spend the rest of her life thinking of Stella every time someone lit a cigarette?

She let herself think about Pete, and about the promise she'd forced out of him on that final morning together. It had seemed a strange request to both of them, insisting that he find Dot if anything ever happened to her. Dash hadn't known where that idea had come from, but there it was, and she was glad it was out there. Because now, standing in the hushed common room, grieving Stella, she understood. Things really did happen. Awful things.

Every girl in the Air Transport Auxiliary sensed the empty seat in the room. It was a stinging reminder that no matter how many planes they'd flown, or how high they flew, they were not indestructible. A similar ending could be waiting for any of them, just an airfield away.

Mrs. Farnham, Hamble Airfield's house mother of sorts, walked in at that moment and cleared her throat. "I find it extremely distasteful that I am forced to ask at a time like this," she said, "but I have no choice. I need a pilot to go to France right away."

The room was still. Everyone was staring at Mrs. Farnham, but no one knew what to do.

Dash stepped forward. "I'll go."

She grabbed the chit from Mrs. Farnham's hand, then her coat from a hook on the wall. She wasn't sure why she'd volunteered, but it made her feel better. The common room was claustrophobic with grief. Dash needed fresh air. Wind in her hair. Freedom. There was only one place she was going to find all that, and it wasn't on the ground. She glanced at the chit and managed a smile. She'd be flying a Spitfire.

As she reached for the door, it burst open, and a soaking wet mailman stomped inside. She stepped to the side to let him in, then walked past. She couldn't get to that plane fast enough.

"Oh, Miss Wilson!" the mailman called, catching her sleeve. "I have a letter for you."

"Thank you."

She tucked the envelope into her flight suit's inside pocket and promptly forgot about it. She was not in the mood to read anything. She'd get to it after landing.

The tarmac was shiny from the earlier rain. Dash dodged as many puddles as she could without checking her stride, wary of an incoming bank of clouds. Her destination was B-21, a temporary landing ground in France in a location called Sainte-Honorine, which was interesting to her. Dash hadn't crossed the English Channel before, but she had flown over the coast. Out of necessity, the ATA sometimes ferried replacement planes into occupied countries, but that could get dodgy, with all the ack-acks. Temporary airfields popped up around France and Belgium out of necessity, basic facilities with steel plank–surfaced runways, but they closed just as quickly. Violet had flown into one just last week, but when she'd arrived, the squadron that had requested the plane had already moved on. She'd been forced to keep flying to the next temporary airfield on the list. Until recently, only male ATA pilots had been sent on those flights. Other than Stella and Violet, Dash knew only a few women who had flown into either France or Belgium.

Dash climbed into the cockpit then went through the checklist, oblivious to the rain that had begun pattering overhead. She felt it as soon as she pushed the canopy back for takeoff, and she pulled down her goggles to see better. A little rain wasn't going to stop her, though she'd have to be surefooted upon landing. She hit the throttle, impatient to get away from all this sadness. As the Spitfire left the pavement behind, she left her miseries, loosening the strain in her chest. In the sky was where she needed to be. Up here on her own, away from grief. The sky, like her maple tree when she was a child, was the place where she went to heal.

From way up high, she could see the blocks of grey in Portsmouth, the war ships loading and unloading troops and supplies. Much more activity than usual these days. Farther west of her line was Bournemouth, and she smiled as her thoughts went to Pete. She wondered if he was flying today. Wouldn't it be wonderful to pass each other in the sky?

Soon she was over the Channel, that long, unforgiving body of water that intimidated all the girls. If they ever got in trouble over the water, there would be no chance of finding an emergency landing field. Through the rain, Dash saw the coast of France, and she breathed a little easier. She was almost past the danger zone. The land ahead was covered in fog, and she thought back to the map in her head, trying to pinpoint the location of the landing strip at Sainte-Honorine. It was a pretty name, she thought. She wondered if the village was, too, or if it had been destroyed by the war, like so many other things.

She was forced to pay close attention to her location now, because the rain had closed in alarmingly fast, coming hard, carried by troublesome winds. It was soon too dark for her to feel comfortable, and she flinched at flashes of lightning. Before long, the rain smashing against her canopy was so loud, she wouldn't have heard someone if they yelled in her ear. Wrapped in the darkness and buffeted by rising winds, real concern spread in Dash's chest. She had no lights, no maps, no radio, and now that she was engulfed in storm clouds, she could barely see the ground.

Instinctively, she pushed open the throttle and pulled the control stick back, climbing steeply so she could fly above the storm. Maybe she'd find an escape route from up there. The engine of the Spitfire rumbled agreeably as she rose to two thousand, three . . . she burst into blinding sunlight above the clouds and levelled out at four thousand feet. She breathed easy for a moment, then dread set in. The silhouette of the Spitfire drifted across the forbidding grey surface beneath her, seeking out any possible break but finding none. Even from up here, she couldn't see any way to get away from the storm—the entire horizon was blanketed by clouds. Bursts of lightning came more often now, lighting the clouds below like giant fireflies.

She had to be getting close to her destination, but she'd never be able to see anything from up here. Her only option was to descend and hope for some sort of window. Bracing, Dash lowered the Spitfire's nose back into the rain clouds and jumped when lightning struck nearby. Lower and lower she flew, nearing the three thousand feet mark, scouting for an opening while she monitored her altimeter and fuel gauge. At that altitude, the wind tossed the plane like a plaything.

Then lightning struck, and Dash's world flashed a violent, brilliant white. A deafening crack snapped one wing, throwing the Spitfire into a sharp turn, and she grasped the stick, hanging on for all she was worth. With adrenaline flooding through her, she pulled back hard, levelling out the plane as well as she could, but the wings teetered perilously. The engine burst into flame, snapping fire backward toward the windshield, and then it stalled completely. Breathing hard, Dash hauled the nose up again, but without power, the plane kept sinking. She watched the altimeter needle spin faster and faster as she fell helplessly through the sky.

The earth suddenly opened up below her and she checked the dials. *Two thousand feet,* her mind reported. *Too low, too fast.* A thick carpet of trees and rocks streaked beneath her wings, but she could see no possible landing strip. She was going to crash. She was going to die.

"No, I'm not!" she screamed. She still had one option. "All right, Margaret Wilson. Let's see if you're as tough as you pretend to be."

Her parachute was snug, connected exactly as it should be across her chest, with the straps secured around her thighs. She knew she was too low. She clearly remembered telling Jack Reimer that twenty-five hundred feet was the minimum, and she was now barely hanging on to two thousand. She twisted to see behind her, but when she moved, the plane angled again, and the pull of a spiral began. She'd seen enough to know that if she bailed from this angle, she risked hitting the tail on the way out. There had to be another way.

In a moment of clarity, Dash rolled the Spitfire upside down so the canopy and the forest were directly beneath her head. Before she could change her mind, she jerked the lever to jettison the canopy, and the wind blasted into her face like a wall. The plane wanted to dive, but Dash gritted her teeth and struggled with the steering, forcing the nose upward and level. Upside down, she clung to the sharp restraint of the safety belt across her hips and shoulder for as long as she dared. Then all it took was a quick release of the buckle.

She dropped into a chaos of nothing, plunging toward the earth, riding the most exhilarating and terrifying thrill of her life. Immediately, she yanked the strap of her parachute then counted *One thousand, two thousand, three thou—* The chute opened in a glorious white above her—*Thank you, Jack Reimer!*—jerked her up like a gasp, then started drifting down, down, down on the exhale. Everywhere, trees reached up to meet her. She hauled desperately on the chute's control lines, steering as she had been taught, but there wasn't enough time to slow her descent. The tops of the trees whipped at her feet, then her legs, faster and faster and faster, and she started to scream.

fifty-three
DOT

-•• --- -

— Camp X —

Dot woke with a gasp, struggling from the grip of a nightmare. In it, Dash had been climbing the tree in their yard, higher and higher until she was miles above the earth and waving at Dot from the clouds. Dot shouted, telling her to *please come down*, but Dash stood on the edge of a branch, laughing at the whole world. Then the branch snapped—

Dot patted her cheek, forcing herself awake. She had no time to waste thinking about a dream. She glanced at her watch, which she'd left on her bedside table, and winced. Noon. After her midnight-to-eight shift, she had fallen into bed, determined to sleep a full seven or eight hours, but four would have to do. There was no way she would be able to sleep again after that.

She needed all her wits about her, because today was June 4. Operation Overlord was set for tomorrow, except they were six hours ahead over there, which meant the mobilization had already begun. As she brushed her teeth, she thought through the chain of events about to occur. Thousands of ships and landing crafts would soon begin crossing the English Channel to France. Airplanes would prepare to defend the troops after gliders dropped parachutists behind enemy lines.

So many things were about to happen. So many already had. Dot felt as if she was running late.

Gus had been gone for three weeks. She knew vaguely what he was doing now as part of Fortitude, because she had sent out some of the directives, indicating target locations. Since that final night together, when she had said what she'd been wanting to say for years, things had changed. It was no longer a simple task for her to send him into life-threatening situations.

The plans she'd sent out to Gus and the other teams were quite specific. Plan *Vert* was about setting explosives to sabotage railway stations, while Plan *Tortue* focused on destroying roads. Telephone and power lines were being cut through Plan *Violet* and Plan *Bleu*. Gus's assignments tended to revolve around the three colours she least liked to think about: *rouge*, *noir*, and *jaune*, which ordered attacks on German ammunition dumps, fuel depots, and command posts. The risk terrified her.

Still, she couldn't have been prouder of him. Over one hundred thousand resistance fighters were in Europe right now, many of whom had been trained by Gus and others like him from Camp X. Each one was a thorn in the side of the Nazis, sabotaging factories, cutting telephone lines, derailing trains, blowing up bridges and fuel dumps, capturing thousands of prisoners, and killing when necessary. And just as Dot's father had done in the first war, they reported German army movements and potential bombing targets for the Allies.

Occasionally, she knew, Gus would have cause to use his marksmanship skills, and, worse, his ability to kill. He had never admitted to her that he'd done that before, but she knew he had. She could see it in his eyes.

She splashed cool water over her face then threw on her uniform and headed out. The rest of the camp was awake and busy, and she was immediately caught up in the action. The first person she saw was Frances, Gerald's secretary, who told her shocking news. U.S. General Eisenhower had postponed the invasion to the following day, June 6, following his meteorologist's strong warning that the weather on June 5 would be terrible.

"One day's grace," Frances said. "Oh, hey, Dot, I have a telegram for you from last night. Let me get it."

When she handed the envelope to her, Dot scowled. "I hate telegrams."

Frances nodded. "Understandably."

PETTY OFFICER WREN DOROTHY WILSON TORONTO TYPING POOL—ADDRESS UNKNOWN
URGENT

She frowned at the little envelope, trying to puzzle through what it meant. The sender knew she was a Wren who had attained the rank of Petty Officer, and they knew she was somewhere near Toronto. Regardless, the most important part was the bottom line. She tore the envelope open and her knees gave way.

DASH MISSING TWO DAYS
CONTACT PETE CLARK RAF A7293169

Two days? Where? Dot could hardly think, her heart beat so fast. Visions of Dash—alone in the middle of Europe, hurt, maybe worse— filled her frantic thoughts. As panic rushed through her body, the calm, collected part of her mind ran to Hydra, searching for a way to find her sister.

But how?

She read the telegram again, though it tore her apart to do it. Pete Clark. Who was this man? What did he know? How had he located Dot then gotten this message to Camp X? Pete Clark. RAF. Royal Air Force. Was that his service number?

Pete Clark, RAF.

I have fallen madly, deeply, irreparably in love with a British flyboy, and he loves me, too.

Was this him? Whether he was or not, Dot had no choice but to trust this message and find him somehow. If she had to swim across the Atlantic to save her sister, she'd do it.

She should speak with Gerald. She should show him the telegram, tell him what she needed. He was smart, he was trustworthy, and he was ingenious when it came to figuring out next steps. He would know all the direct contact names and numbers.

He was also loyal to the war effort above all else. To defeating the enemy. To Operation Fortitude and to Camp X. As he should be. Dash could never be Gerald's priority. Realistically, Dot's sister should not be *anyone's* priority right now. Despite her rank as a Wren, Dash was now an ATA pilot, which meant she was considered a civilian. That put her very low on the scale. With everything else going on—Dot had never seen this place busier—no one had a free moment to search for a lost girl.

But there was another, more personal reason she did not tell Gerald about the telegram. She would never forget that Gerald had banned her from going to her father's deathbed. She already knew he would not let her take time from her valuable military assignment to help her sister. She decided not to ask. She was on her own.

But that didn't mean she couldn't seek out help wherever possible.

"I hope it's not bad news," Frances said kindly, glancing up from her typewriter.

Dot had forgotten she was even there. "It's . . ." she began, then an idea formed. Dot tamped down her racing pulse as she folded the telegram and stuffed it in her pocket. "Oh, it's nothing." She kept her voice light. "Frances, I must say. How you keep track of everything and everyone in this place absolutely amazes me."

"Well, you amaze me with all you do." Frances tilted her head, birdlike. "Do you need something from me?"

Dot dropped her smile, aiming to look businesslike. "I need to track down a specific RAF pilot. It's, uh, in reference to a decryption I worked on last night."

"RAF? Those brave lads. You're not looking for one of our boys? We have a lot flying with the RAF, as you know."

"Yes, I know. This one, however, is British."

"All right. What do you need?"

"The message I intercepted was personal. It's important for me to contact him directly."

Frances's smile wavered. Maybe Dot should have said that differently. But Frances was already digging in the filing cabinet behind her. She had worked at Camp X a long time. She knew better than to ask Dot for any more information than what she'd already been given.

"I believe I have some contact information in here somewhere. RAF ... RAF ... Aha!" She spun to face Dot, a file in hand. "There are multiple avenues we could pursue for this. I'm afraid it may take some time to sort through." She gestured to her desk. "I have a lot of important things I need to take care of today."

"May I help you? I have hours before my shift starts."

"Pull up a chair."

It didn't take long after all. The files were slightly out of order to Dot's way of thinking, so she rearranged them, and that pulled the contact information for the RAF to the top.

"You're good at that," Frances said while Dot hastily copied down the information. "If Hydra ever bores you, you're always welcome here."

Dot grinned at her. "Thanks for the invitation, but Hydra is the least boring place on earth."

"Maybe for you."

"Um, Frances, I have another favour to ask. Could I possibly use your telephone?"

It rang at just that moment, and Frances shrugged apologetically as she answered. She held up a finger, asking Dot to wait, then she knocked on Gerald's door.

"Your two o'clock appointment is in the front lobby," she told him, then she returned to her desk. "My telephone is probably going to be tied up. But I'll do you one better. Come with me."

Dot hadn't even known the little room at the end of the hall existed. It was almost small enough to be a closet. In fact, she'd always assumed it was a closet.

"For personal calls," Frances explained. She studied Dot a moment. If Frances decided Dot was doing something untoward, she could ruin everything, but Frances gave her a wink. "If you need help, I know where a lot of things are."

Dot started by dialing the first entry on her list of contact numbers. It was a dead end. The next number she called had no idea who Pete Clark was, but they suggested another telephone number. Dot circled it on her list then called it next.

"It was recommended that I contact your office directly," she told the woman who picked up the phone. "They said you might have a record of him."

"Is he still in service?"

A cold, impersonal question. Yes, Pete was still alive, or at least he had been when he'd sent that telegram last night.

"I believe so."

"Do you know his rank?"

"I'm afraid not."

"Hmm. You said you are telephoning from Canada? And you're a Wren?"

"Yes, ma'am. Petty Officer Wren Dorothy Wilson."

"All right." The woman sounded harried, but she also seemed interested in helping. "There are a few of our pilots listed here. Please give me that service number again?" After she did, she could hear the woman flipping pages. "There he is. Master Corporal Peter Clark. From the Christchurch area. What do you need?"

"I need to speak with him directly," Dot said. "It's a matter of some personal urgency."

"Please hold on a moment while I see where he is."

"Come on, come on, come on," Dot whispered, sitting on pins and needles. "Where are you, Pete?"

"You're in luck," the woman said a moment later. "He is here on base. I will put out a call for him then have him telephone you back. Your number, please?"

How could she be so stupid? She should have asked Frances that question. It wasn't as if someone would have—

There it was, written on a card beside the telephone. She gave the number, then sat back to wait.

Twenty minutes later, the phone rang.

fitty-four
DASH

The darkness was complete. It didn't shift when Dash cracked her eye-lids open, and fear rippled through her. She was afraid to move, but the only way she could sense what was happening was if she could shift her body. Just a little. Just enough. The greatest pressure, she realized, was around her torso, as if she were restrained. Needing to understand, she inhaled, expanding her chest as much as she could, and she felt movement beneath her. Just a bit. Her feet. Her legs. She was dangling.

Dread rushed in as she recalled the lightning, then the terrible angle of the plane plunging to earth, and the moment when she understood she was mortal after all. Her throat clogged with a new sort of panic. Where was she? What was it she couldn't remember?

The tree! The shuddering impact, then nothing. Suddenly, she realized she hung from branches, kept alive by a tree, the suspension lines of the parachute, and possibly the chute itself.

A new pain, a burning, throbbing agony shot through her left arm. It felt as if a blade twisted from her shoulder to her elbow. Gritting her teeth, Dash moved her other hand across to find the source. Her left arm was hot, swollen, and tacky to her touch, and it . . . Her stomach rolled as her fingertips closed around a small branch, maybe a half inch thick, that had broken off the tree when she'd collided with it. The branch had passed all the way through her arm, back to front, leaving a splintered end sticking out either side.

Dash brought her right hand back where it belonged, thinking hard. She had to assume she was in France or Belgium, which put her in enemy territory. Someone might have seen her plane going down, and the bright white of her parachute would be a dead giveaway. She had no idea if anyone had heard the crash. All she heard was her own ragged breathing. Even the rain had stopped.

How long had she been unconscious? Long enough for the blood on her arm to have become sticky. The branch was blocking the flow. She wondered how badly it would bleed if she somehow managed to pull herself free of it.

If only she could think clearly.

Be smart, her mother had said, saying goodbye at Union Station.

Dash had never been good at that, she thought miserably.

Except that wasn't entirely true. She was smart. It was just that her brain operated differently than Dot's. The two had always relied on each other to make up for their weak points, to protect each other. What would Dot do in this situation? The question was laughable. Dot never would have gotten herself into it in the first place.

Dash's eyes were adjusting to the night, softening the blackness so she could differentiate between the shadows, but she could not see the forest floor. How tall was this tree? Was she at the top of it? Was it forty feet? Fifteen? That made a big difference. If she cut herself loose, the discrepancy meant either a painful landing or a deadly one.

Count, she heard Dot say in her memory. Dash let her mind go back to that sunny day when they were so small, and Dot had timed the passage of rocks as Dash tossed them into a bucket. Afterward, Dot had asked their father how high the roof of the house was. Thirty-five feet, he had told her.

"And how tall is Dash's tree?"

He squinted out the window, calculating. "I'd say the tree is about twenty feet, and she normally climbs about fifteen feet up." He glanced sideways at Dash. "Which is, as your mother so rightly says, far too high for a little girl to be."

Turning away from him, Dot had told Dash what she wanted her to do. Without questioning her, Dash dragged some boxes from her father's shed so she could climb up to the window, then to the peak of the house. From there, she dropped a stone while Dot counted. She still remembered: the roof at thirty-five feet had gotten a *One-one-one-one Two-two*.

The restraints around her chest dug in as she filled her lungs. She was cold, and the pain in her arm was so bad, so sharp, but she refused to cry. *Figure this out now, cry later.*

Her father had told them that Dash's spot in her favourite tree was about fifteen feet off the ground, and she remembered Dot counting *one-one-one-one* from there—about a half second less than the rooftop.

Trying to ignore the pain, Dash reached around all the suspension lines looping down from the parachute then dug into her kit for her water bottle, still half full. She let out a breath, then she dropped it.

One-one-one-one—

Fifteen feet, give or take. She smiled, despite it all. It was hard not to appreciate the irony that she presently hung from the same height she'd always climbed to in her tree. It wasn't great news, though. One time she had climbed down to about ten feet then jumped, with her mother's coat flung out like wings, and she'd broken her arm. Another time she'd landed on top of a very young Gus.

Be smart.

Fifteen feet above the ground, maybe a little more. It was too high to drop, but closer than she'd initially feared. Maybe she'd be all right. If she curled herself into a ball she might not break anything.

First, she'd have to deal with the injury. Sweat rolled from her brow into her eyes, and Dash ran her hand carefully along the stick poking out of her arm, checking to see how strong it was. It didn't bend; it was an old, dead branch. A thick twig, really, and it was long enough that it could catch on something as she fell. It needed to be shortened. It would snap, given enough pressure. She grit her teeth, then pushed down on it. Pain exploded up her arm as she broke off the excess, and she stifled a cry. Her injured arm screamed in protest when she hugged it against her chest, and she froze, waiting for the shock to lessen. She had no time to waste on feeling sorry for herself.

When she felt a little more under control, she reached for the knife she kept strapped to her leg, then she moved the blade toward the suspension lines tethering her to the parachute.

Let's see if I can fly without either plane or parachute, she thought.

Then her mother's voice again: *Be smart*.

She drew her hand back, thinking. There had to be a different way.

Dot's favourite words whispered in her ear: *It's a puzzle*.

Dash just had to solve it. She pointed her toes, stretching down as far as she could, seeking a branch that could hold her weight. There. She felt it knock against her boots. Next, she considered the parachute. Its suspension lines hung slackly around her, and when she tugged on one, it came to her willingly, to a point. An idea swirled in her mind. Every suspension line on a parachute was twenty feet long. She remembered that from her classes with the ATA. With that in mind, she reached up and sawed one-handed through the rope at her back. There was a disconcerting release, but she landed safely on the branch below, and she could breathe more easily once the pressure around her ribs was gone. A little braver, she looped the twenty feet of rope over the branch so ten feet hung on either side. She wrapped the ends around her then carefully used both hands to secure them onto her harness. Moving very slowly, she lowered herself so one leg hung on either side of the branch, like she was riding bareback. Then she cut all the remaining lines.

Nothing happened.

She exhaled. She'd been right about that, at least. Now it was up to the branch, the rope, and her sweaty, shaking hands.

She held the handle of her knife between her teeth while she lifted one leg over the branch to join the other. For a couple of heartbeats, she sat perfectly still, sick with fear. The next step was terrifying, but she reminded herself that she could die just as easily up here as she could getting down, it would just take longer. She couldn't wait.

Twisting so her stomach was on the branch, she let her legs dangle over one side, and she clutched the rope with her good arm. Hanging tight, she began to descend. The forest seemed to get darker the lower she went, sheltered from the sky by so many trees, but her vision adjusted. She could see the outlines of the trees now, though still not the ground.

Quite suddenly, she ran out of rope. That meant she had been right; her initial position was about fifteen feet above the ground. The parachute cord was twenty, but she had folded it in half, making ten feet of climbing. If her math was even close to being correct, she'd only fall about five or six feet from here. She could do that. With her entire body shaking from stress, she took the knife handle out of her mouth and sawed at the strap until it snapped.

The fall was immediate, and a sharp flash of pain shot through her on impact. She cried out then bit back the noise, allowing herself only a whimper. Had anyone heard her?

When she could manage, she edged backward to lean against the tree. The air burned her injury, seeping into the torn nerves. When she reached for the source, her hand came back slick with blood, as black as the night itself. She could only hope the bleeding would stop on its own. There was nothing she could do.

She couldn't stay here. Whether she was in France or Belgium, she was not safe. Someone would spot either her plane, her parachute, or her. Gingerly, she peeled off what remained of her harness and stuffed as much as she could under a mound of shrubs next to the tree. Her kit was still slung over her back, and she pulled it around so she could fish inside for her father's compass. Since she'd come to England, Dash had never flown without it. It was too dark to see which way the needle pointed, but she needed to feel her father with her.

Something touched her, and she flinched. Rain. It was starting up again and building fast. She had to find shelter. Before long she was caught in a deluge, but she had no idea which way to turn. Then lightning flashed, and she caught a glimpse of her surroundings. When it happened again, she spotted a pine tree, large enough to provide an umbrella. The tree could be struck, but she had to bank on the odds. It had made it this long, so it should last through the night. She staggered to the tree then curled in tight beneath its branches, her chin tucked in the top of her flight suit. She'd hide until the sun rose. Maybe then she could figure out what to do.

fifty-five
DOT

-•• --- -

— *Camp X* —

Dot stared at the ringing phone, paralyzed. Was it him? What if this man was not who she hoped? What if, by doing this, she was somehow betraying Camp X?

But she was doing this for Dash. She had to try. She picked up the headset. "Petty Officer Wren Wilson."

"*Dot* Wilson?"

"Yes?"

"Ah. Brilliant. You received my message." She heard the relief in his voice. And the urgency. "I'm very sorry, but Dash is missing."

Her hand was tight on the handset. "Who are you? Why are you contacting me directly?"

"I'm— I'm sorry. Of course you wouldn't know about me." His voice was deep, with a charming accent. She tried to imagine the face behind it. "You and Dash aren't in regular communication, I gather. My name's Pete. I am, well, I suppose in Canada you would call me Dash's boyfriend. She told me that if anything were to ever happen to her, I should find you."

"You're him," Dot said softly, loosening her grip on the telephone.

"I beg your pardon? I'm afraid this isn't the best connection."

"How did you find me?"

"Frankly, I went a little mad, trying to think what to do. I am about to fly on assignment, and I wanted to see her first, so I went against orders to Hamble, the airfield where she's based. They told me they hadn't seen her in two days, and that she hadn't reached her destination. They were quite frantic, but with everything going on, they had no way to search for her." He exhaled. "I want to believe she's all right, but I simply have no idea, and I cannot go to look for her."

Maybe you can't, Dot was thinking, but I can. "Tell me what you know, Pete. Her destination? The code for the airfield?"

"There's a Mrs. Farnham at Hamble," he said, sounding a little more positive. "She told me Dash was headed to B-21, a temporary airfield in Sainte-Honorine, France. That was two days ago, but with the terrible weather I was unable to get there. I'm fairly certain the airfield's no longer there."

Dot's mind was already ticking, racing around the map in her head, trying to locate the tiny area. Why was there no map in this room? There should be maps in every room, she thought, frustrated. At least she had a starting point.

"How can I reach you?"

"I'm afraid you won't be able to. I'm here for now, but then I am flying."

Operation Overlord, she realized. He'd be involved in the invasion. Despite everything, she still hadn't gotten used to the human part of what she did. The fact that those planes plunging from the sky were manned by actual men. Men like Gus. And Fred. And now Pete. *Please be safe*, she thought.

For a heartbeat, all she heard was the empty crackle of the long-distance telephone line.

When he spoke again, his voice was somber. "I wish I could offer something else, Dot. I . . . your sister is an incredible woman, and she loves you very much. I don't know if I'll ever meet you in person, but after all she's told me, I'd have liked to say hello."

"Pete, you and I will meet one day," Dot assured him. "If Dash is alive, I will find her."

She fled the room, her mind scanning every face she passed, searching for someone—anyone—who could help her. She worked with *spies*, for crying out loud. There must be someone. But everyone else was doing their duty, telling lies, spreading misinformation, sending the Germans on a wild-goose chase, far from the beaches of Normandy.

A map. She needed a map. From the corner of her vision, she spotted a large one of Europe, practically waving to her from the corridor. She found the location of B-21, Sainte-Honorine, right away, six hours northwest of Paris. The area would likely be teeming with Germans. She skimmed her finger toward Calais and dared to think that it might not be quite as bad. The enemy forces were on the move *past* Paris, heading northeast instead, on their way to what they believed would be a major battle at Calais.

Gus had parachuted in behind enemy lines, hoping to land near Düsseldorf. He would have carried out his orders on the German-Belgian border, then he and his operatives would have continued toward the sea, tasked with slowing the Germans on every front. But that was weeks ago. Maybe he was closer to France by now. Realistically, he could be anywhere, but Dot held on to the sliver of possibility that he and his fighters were somewhere near B-21. She had to believe in that. She had to find him.

Hydra.

Rushing from the main building, she burst into the late-day sunshine. Dash was in trouble. She could die. She might be dead already. And Dot could stand in front of a firing squad just for trying to find her.

"Doesn't matter," she whispered, walking purposefully toward Hydra.

Bill Hardcastle was sitting outside the door as he often did, letting the radios receive and transmit while he took a well-earned break, and she was briefly tempted to turn back. Never in her life had Dot considered sneaking around or breaking rules—except for that one night when Gus had taken her to see her father. Now her squeaky-clean reputation was a thing of the past. Dot had been trained for deception, and she figured this was as good a time as any to put that into effect. The trouble was, she wasn't sure she could outwit Bill.

Pulse hammering in her temples, Dot approached as if nothing was out of the ordinary and stopped beside him. "Hello, Bill."

"Good afternoon, Dot. Lovely day."

Every nerve in Dot's body strained toward the transmitters. "It certainly is. June sunshine, I have always thought, is the most hopeful."

He tilted his head. "I like that. I'll keep it in mind when I'm working through all the dark hours on Overlord."

"At least there's one extra day. I hope the weather cooperates this time."

"It'll be a mess if it doesn't," he agreed. "Ah well. Weather will do what it will do. Rather large consequences in this case, however."

It struck her then, that if anyone would know how to look for help, it would be Bill. But if he didn't want to help, if he decided to report her ...

"Bill," she began. "I need your help."

His dark eyebrows lifted. "From the look in your eye and the tone of your voice, I imagine this is not something that Gerald has authorized."

She shook her head. "It's not. It's ... it's personal."

"Oh!" He chuckled. "Well, in that case, take a seat. I don't know much I can help with personal issues, but it's a nice day for a chat."

"No, uh, it's something personal that I am hoping you and Hydra can help me with."

His guard rose instantly. "Aha. I had hoped you wouldn't say that. What's this about?"

"I need to find someone. One of our agents in Europe. It's a matter of life or death."

"Isn't everything these days." He tugged at his collar. "I don't know, Dot. You're asking a lot."

"I know, but it's nothing bad. It's just ... I need to find this agent."

"Who?"

"Gus."

He shot her a sharp glance. "Young lady, I am not going to break radio silence for the sake of romance."

"What?" She flushed. She hadn't thought anyone had noticed them together. "No, no. It's not that. It's ... it's my sister. She's a pilot with the Air Transport Auxiliary, and she's missing. I know where she was headed, but no one has heard from her in two days. The temporary airfield she was aiming for was near Sainte-Honorine, northwest of Paris. I'm hoping he might be somewhere near there."

"He may be slightly busy, Dot. We do have a few things going on, in case you haven't noticed."

"I have to try."

He exhaled. "I cannot guarantee anything when it comes to Hydra. You know that."

"I do. But if there's a chance . . ." She held his gaze, needing him to believe that she meant no harm. "She's my sister."

He studied her, not blinking. Every second he spent analyzing her felt like an hour, but she'd stand there as long as it took to get his help.

"Dot, I haven't mentioned it in a while, but you've been doing excellent work here." He was still regarding her, but now he was nodding as he spoke. She had to assume this was part of his thinking process. "You're catching a lot, and many of those messages have gone straight to London, saving lives." He offered a reluctant smile. "You may be a bit of a rebel, but I appreciate having you on the team."

She smiled inwardly at the thought that she was any kind of rebel. "Thank you, sir. So you'll help me?"

"Hydra is not a personal telephone, Dot." He was stern again. She had pushed too hard. "Hydra is a unique, extremely valuable piece of machinery. The only one of its kind. And at present, it is quite pre-occupied with global issues."

"Yes. I understand, and I would never dream of interrupting any of that."

His eyes narrowed. "You have a different plan."

"I'm trying to come up with one, to be honest."

"Gerald would not be pleased if I agreed to this."

She knew of Bill's loyalty to Camp X and to Gerald. She lifted her chin with a confidence she did not feel, knowing this was her last chance. "I already know what his answer would be, Bill. The thing is, I believe there must be a way for me to seek Gus while not interfering with what is going on. I don't think Gerald understands all the different facets of Hydra, but you do. So I have come to you, and I'm begging for your help."

Something in Bill's expression changed, and she gathered he was thinking through how to accomplish what she was asking. After a moment, he stood, and she followed him inside.

"As you know, all our teams carry radios," he told her, "and they are required to check in to update their status as long as it is safe to do so." He gestured for her to sit, then he pulled over another chair and reached for the headphones. "I do have access to their general locations and frequencies, so hypothetically, we should be able to find them. Then again, there is rather an important operation stirring everyone up at the moment. They might be otherwise occupied."

He picked up a small blue book then flipped through the pages until he found what he wanted. "I'll put out a general call." He held the book open with his left hand while his other reached for the key and began to tap.

Dot leaned back in her chair and closed her eyes, listening. She never tired of the patterns, of the communication that could be accomplished with two simple percussive sounds, one long, one short.

... . . -.- .. -. --. / --. / -... . -.-. -.- . .-. / .-. -..... ---.. ----- .---- --.../ -.-. .-
.-.. .-.. / .... --- -- .

Seeking G Becker R67257 Call home

He tapped it out four more times, then he faced her. "I'll try again on the hour. I'll let you know if I hear anything."

"Thank you, Bill," she said weakly. "Thank you so much."

"Seems harmless enough," he replied with a sigh. "I just hope it doesn't muck anything up with Gus's timing. He's on a difficult schedule over there, destroying everything he can get his hands on."

She liked imagining Gus like that, cutting wires, blowing up railway tracks, all while knowing in his heart that he was making a difference. In her own way, she was doing the same.

"Would it be all right if I stayed here with you?" she asked. "My shift's not until eight. That way I could reach out to Gus myself. I still need to figure out a plan for after he responds, so I could just sit here and tap out the same general call again later."

"I don't see why not. Let's hope he gets back to us soon, for your sister's sake."

fifty-six
DASH

— *Somewhere near Sainte-Honorine, Northwest France* —

Dash jolted awake, startled by the sound of men talking. Their voices were faint, but they traveled with the breeze. She lay as still as she could on the wet floor of the forest, listening.

Despite her injury, she had eventually slept a short while beneath the pine tree, her body squeezed tight into a ball, her arm protected. Even with her fur-lined coat and flight suit, she shook from the cold. The rain, the crash, the fall . . .

Her arm was so swollen her sleeve felt noose-tight. It was sensitive to her touch and what she could see of it was black with dried blood. She wiggled her hand, but her fingers didn't move; they were hot and fat like sausages. Bile pushed up the back of her throat just looking at it.

Above her, the sun sparkled through wet pine needles like stars. Whether the men she heard were friend or foe, they would find her here unless she found a better place. All around her, pine trees dragged their branches over brown carpets of needles, but none offered refuge. Dash's eyes lit on what was left of an old deciduous tree, long dead and split, about twenty feet away. A rotted cavity yawned in its side. From her vantage point, Dash thought she might be able to fit inside that hole.

The voices were getting closer; she made out two or three men speaking in . . . It wasn't English. She listened for the smooth curves of French, even though many of the Frenchmen around here had been turned for the Germans. No, it was not French. Her stomach tightened as guttural German syllables cut through the air.

"*Sie sagten, das Flugzeug sei hier abgestürzt.*"

"*Ich sehe keinen Fallschirm.*"

Dash had no idea what they were saying. If only she'd listened to Dot and Gus when they'd tried to teach her. Cautiously, she edged out from under the canopy to see how close they were. At first she saw nothing, then fifty feet away she spied movement. A black uniform, then two more, headed in her direction. She took another look at the open-mouthed tree, uneasy. Could she fit in there? She scanned the area looking for something better, *anything* better, but it was all the same.

With her arm tucked against her torso, Dash wound between the trees as quietly as she could, grateful that her muddy brown flight suit camouflaged her. When she reached the tree, she realized the hole was deep, but not that wide. Smaller than she'd thought. And the bark looked fragile. What if she managed to climb inside but the whole thing splintered?

One of the men laughed, and she judged that they were maybe thirty feet away. She had no choice. Dash lowered one foot then the other into the tree's cavernous trunk and crouched, curving the rest of her body beneath the top edge as she squeezed her torso in. The movement jarred her injured arm, and through a sheen of tears, she watched fresh blood flow to the surface.

Then the men were there. Three of them. They had their backs to her, and they were pointing toward where she had landed.

"*Ich glaube, ich sehe es. Siehe? Der Schein von der Sonne.*"

"*Das muss weh getan haben. Wo ist der Pilot?*"

Dash couldn't miss that last word. They were searching for her.

Hide and seek, Dot! Am I getting warmer?

She burrowed deep into the collar of her coat, trying to be invisible.

"*Er ist irgendwo hier. Schau dir den Weg an.*" The tallest of the three stepped away, moving toward her crash site.

There was a snap of sulphur and a curl of smoke as one of the remaining men lit a cigarette. The other turned to light his own, facing the first while they spoke. He coughed to the side, and he saw her.

"*Schau dir dieses lustige Eichhörnchen an.*"

The other man turned around, and Dash's heart stopped. They took a step toward her, both smiling.

"*Es ist ein Eichhörnchenmädchen.*" The corner of his mouth lifted, and he crooked a finger at her. "*Komm her, kleines Eichhörnchen.*"

Dash put up her hands and started to cry. *Goodbye, Pete. Goodbye, Dot.* "Please, no. I'm not important. I'm not in the air force. I'm just a girl flying planes. Please—"

In a blur, two dark figures leapt out from behind the Germans, hooked their arms around the men's necks, then slit them open while Dash stared in shock. They dropped the bodies, and when the tall German rushed back for his friends, they shot him in the centre of his forehead.

Everything happened so fast. Dash thrust her empty hands outside of the tree, even as her left arm screamed in pain. "Please don't kill me! Please don't kill me!"

"This is your lucky day." It was a woman. The other was a man. She could see the outline of a beard above his black turtleneck. "What's your name?"

"M-Margaret Wilson. I'm . . . I'm a transport pilot. I'm a civilian." She sucked in her tears. "I just want to go home."

The woman gave one of the German bodies a nudge with her boot. "They called you a squirrel."

The man approached Dash to help her out of the tree, and when he accidentally bumped her arm, she shrieked. She hissed in a breath as he inspected her wound, but she was no longer afraid. She could feel his tenderness.

"That doesn't look good," he said to his partner. "We can't wait."

"We'll meet up with the others then we'll all go," she replied. "Where are you from? You're not British."

"Canada," Dash blurted. "I ferry planes with the ATA."

"Well, you're in the right hands," the woman said brightly. "I'm Ruby. I'm from Manitoba. This is Gordon, and he's from Ontario. We're going to take you home."

fifty-seven
DOT

−.. −−− −

—Camp X—

A few hours of sitting beside Bill at Hydra turned into Dot's next graveyard shift. She was working on four hours of sleep over the past twenty-four hours, but there was no way she would leave her post.

Midnight in Toronto was six o'clock in the morning over there. Operation Overlord was well underway. The largest amphibious invasion in history had begun before sunrise. Over one hundred fifty thousand Allied troops had landed, or were in the process of landing, on the beaches of Normandy, including more than fourteen thousand Canadians. Dot leaned closer to Hydra and let her brain soak in the sounds of war. She knew the Allied fighters were emerging from the sea and diving from the sky, and while thousands fell to the sand, never to get up, their friends roared past, pushing against the German machine, finding the worst and best parts of themselves in their courage. If only she knew whether Gus was safe among them.

There would be little communication for her to hear between their own troops. Everyone had a job to do, and no one would be asking or answering questions about it. Not until afterward.

But she did hear much more. German messages resonated through her headphones, including messages of surprise and shock at the intensity of the invasion. Occasionally, she caught a voice wavering over the miles and miles of sea, and her heart squeezed. She remembered almost two years ago, talking with Alice about the people on the other end, like the Menace. They'd thought about the Germans, Americans, Canadians, British, and others trying to survive. All those voices.

Fear sounds the same in any language.

Dot copied every transmission she heard until her hand ached. Whenever there was a break, she called for Gus. No one replied.

He'd been wounded.

He'd been captured.

He'd been killed.

She couldn't bear to imagine any of it, but she could think of nothing else. And while she loved Gus terribly, she also knew that if any of those awful things happened to him, Dash would be left behind. There was no one else in the entire world that Dot could count on.

Many hours before, when Bill had still been in the building, an ache had started between her shoulders. Now it had traveled up to her neck. She scrubbed her forehead, trying to ease a persistent headache. She should have gone for supper, but it was too late now. She'd have to wait. The only part of her that had moved in all that time was her right hand as she tapped into the transmitter, adjusted the dial, or wrote down incoming messages. When she could bear the muscle cramps no longer, she stood and stretched her back.

Between bursts of Morse code, Dot's gaze returned to the transmitter, like a magnet to steel. For the hundredth time that evening, she started tapping again.

... . . -.- .. -. --. / --. / -... . -.-. -.- . .-. / -.-. .- .- .-.. .-.. / .... --- -- .
Seeking G Becker Call home

... . . -.- .. -. --. / --. / -... . -.-. -.- . .-. / -.-. .- .- .-.. .-.. / .... --- -- .
Seeking G Becker Call home

A crackling broke up the static, and Dot held her breath as a reply came through.

-. --- - / -.-- . - / .-.. --- -.-. .- - . -..
Not yet located

Dot bit her lower lip, fighting tears. She had to keep trying, but exhaustion was taking over. Her head drooped and her eyes closed.

"Excuse me, Dot? Are you still in there? Your shift's done."

She startled awake and saw Thomas at the door. "Sorry. I didn't hear you come in."

"Not to worry. You've been busy, I imagine. I'll go through the posts. You need to go to bed. It's going to be a long couple of days."

"No, I . . ." What if Gus replied? What if he answered and she wasn't there? But she couldn't tell Thomas what was happening. It was bad enough that Bill was in on it. She had no choice but to go. "I suppose you're right," she said.

"I imagine things will calm down and get into a rhythm later this week. By tomorrow afternoon we'll have a clearer idea of where everyone is."

He had no idea how much those words meant to her. "Yes. We will know where they are by then. Thank you, Thomas. Happy hunting."

———

When she awoke hours later, she quickly dressed, impatient to call for Gus again. On her way to Hydra, she spotted a world of news headlines on Frances's desk.

"Allies Land in France. Canadians in Spearhead, Eisenhower Announces," proclaimed *The Globe and Mail.* "Canadians in Thick of It as Allies Smash Inland," read the Saskatchewan's *Leader Post.* "Canadian Troops Lead Great Commando Raid," declared the *Hamilton Spectator.* And further down the front page of the same paper: "Mighty Allied Forces Land, Shatter Path into France."

They had done it, Dot realized.

"Excellent work, Dot," Gerald said, striding past. "Your contribution was critical to this success. You should be proud."

"I am, sir. Proud of all of us. I have reports of over nine hundred acts of sabotage. Gus and his fighters have been working overtime."

"As have we all," he agreed. "I feel cautiously optimistic in saying we have them on the run at last."

She flipped through more reports, her heart swelling with pride and grief for the tens of thousands of men who had fought and would not come home, for those who still fought, and for those operating behind the scenes. History would remember the beaches, but she and so many others would keep the secrets that had made it all possible.

fifty-eight
DASH

— *Somewhere in Northwest France* —

Dash dreamed of a bear gnawing on her arm, his breath hot as acid. Trapped in the murk of sleep, she could only lie back and watch it happen, because the rest of her limbs were too heavy to move. When the talons of a giant eagle latched on to her arm and tried to rip her from the bear's jaws, she forced herself to the surface.

No bears, no birds. Just Ruby and Gordon and a man carrying a brown leather bag. He shook his head at the two of them then glanced back at Dash. Seeing she was awake, he reached for his coat, and Gordon walked him to the door.

"How are you feeling?" Ruby asked.

"Hot," Dash mumbled, "and dizzy."

"The doctor says you have a bad infection. Not a surprise. You've been sleeping for days."

Dash remembered this feeling from being sick as a child. The doctor coming and going from her parents' house, speaking quietly behind closed doors. But she had survived that. She would survive this. Back then she hadn't had a bear and eagle battling over her arm.

She hadn't been in such luxury, either. From the comfort of a large bed, she studied the room she was in. The moon shone through the tallest windows Dash had ever seen, washing the lavish bedroom an eerie shade of white. A pair of dark, embroidered armchairs stood at the foot of the bed, near a solid wood cabinet. The ceiling was at least ten feet high, and the walls were liberally covered by gold-framed mirrors and paintings.

"Where are we?" she asked.

"Safe apartment in Paris," Ruby said.

Dash must have heard her wrong. "Paris? Isn't Paris a beehive of Nazis?"

"It's also the base of one of our most active underground networks." Ruby pressed the back of her cold hand against Dash's forehead and grimaced. "You gotta work on getting better so we can send you home."

"How long have we been here?"

"Two days. Too long. We're waiting for instructions."

"From whom?"

She jabbed her thumb toward the door. "Gordon has the radio."

A half hour later, Dash was shivering violently. Ruby wrapped her in a blanket, but the cold was within her, battling the fever. All night her body alternated between sweltering hot and frozen, but in the morning, she felt some relief. Ruby helped her sit, and between them they moved her to one of the armchairs. Once she was settled, Dash got a good look at her arm for the first time. The stick had been removed. The wound had been cleaned and bandaged. Her arm was still swollen but not as much. To her relief, her fingers moved independently once more. Her flight suit was gone, she saw. She wore someone's clean shirt and trousers.

"My compass," she said. "Did you find an old compass?"

Ruby dug it out of a small trunk. "You didn't want to give me this," she said, studying the banged-up old thing. She handed it to Dash. "Must be something special."

"My dad's."

Gordon brought her a bowl of soup, but Dash could barely taste it. Still, the warmth felt good, and she swallowed as much as she could.

"You gotta eat more, Margaret." Ruby was scowling at her. "You never know when you'll eat again."

Across the room, Gordon's radio sparked to life, but Dash was too groggy to translate the Morse code.

"They're waiting for us at the meetup point," he told Ruby. "We have to go now. It's too dangerous here. They've spotted enemy forces in the area."

Ruby immediately started packing things up around the room, then the radio began beeping again.

"They're still looking for him," Gordon muttered. "Apparently the one place he isn't, is near a radio. Last I saw him was in Düsseldorf two weeks ago. He could be anywhere."

"He always shows up," Ruby said. "We have to go."

"I'm ready," Dash said, getting to her feet, but she staggered, light-headed.

"You're not coming," Ruby said. "You'll slow us down. But you'll be safe here until we can come back with more help."

"Well, not exactly *here*," Gordon said from the other room.

Ruby's mouth twisted. "Not quite as comfortable as here, no. But you'll be safe. Come on. I'll show you."

Dash leaned against Ruby as they made their way through the apartment. They stopped beside a tall shelving unit populated by the faded spines of books, and to Dash's surprise, Gordon shoved it aside, revealing a wall in its wake, unbleached by sunlight. He squatted and slid his fingers along the bottom of the wall, then Dash heard a tiny *click!* When he gave it a push, it opened into what appeared to be a hidden room.

"You get her settled," Gordon said quietly. "I'll get the room fixed up."

"This wall does not open from the inside," Ruby informed Dash, helping her into the little space.

No one had been here in a while. The corners of the room were inhabited by cobwebs. The wood floor was old and cracked, and a musty odour clung to the air. There was a small cot, and on the floor by its head, Dash spied a couple of well-thumbed books in French.

Her arm throbbed, but worse was the swell of apprehension building in her. "Where's Gordon going?"

"He's going to make the place look like we were never here, then he'll go outside to keep watch. I'm sorry to leave you here," Ruby said, "but we have no choice. You'd be a liability in this condition. We'll come back when we have reinforcements."

"How long?" Dash asked, trying not to sound afraid, but she already felt claustrophobic. "How long do I have to stay here?"

"I wish I could tell you. So many things are going on right now. Big things. The good guys are winning, but we're still fighting fierce battles. The fact is, Margaret, you are not our most important mission. We will let our leader know you're here, and he will pass the information on, but we can't promise anything."

From her pack, Ruby produced a canvas bag, which she handed to Dash. Inside was a short length of dried sausage, a roll, and a container of water.

"That's all I have. We didn't plan on having you with us, so we put our own rations in here for you. Drink and eat sparingly."

"Is there a candle for light?"

She shook her head. "No one can know you're here. You'll have to live in the dark for a bit."

Why did she have to hide? "Who might look for me? Is someone coming?"

"No, no. It's just in case."

Dash's stomach fell. "Please don't leave. I'm scared."

"You fall out of the sky, crash into a tree, get tracked down by Nazis, and *now* you're scared?" Ruby chuckled. "You're safe here. We use this place all the time. If all goes well, you will soon be tucked into your safe little bed back home. We will do our best."

Dash wanted to grab her, insist that she let her come, because she couldn't stand the idea of staying here alone. But they were right. Until she was healthy, Dash would slow them down. Her body needed to heal.

Ruby ducked under the hidden entrance, then she turned back. "I almost forgot. This was in your flight suit, which we had to burn, I'm afraid."

She handed Dash an envelope, and somewhere in her memory she recalled the mail boy giving it to her in the pilots' room at Hamble. Dash was about to thank Ruby, but the wall was already closing behind her. It shut with a click, leaving Dash in the darkness. She heard the cabinet sliding back and then Ruby's receding footsteps.

There was no light in Dash's world save a sliver leaking from beneath the bottom of the wall. It was too dark to read the letter, so Dash hugged it to her chest as she waited for her eyes to adjust to her tiny refuge: the shapes of a small sack of food and water, a cot, and two books. That was all.

Her throat burned with tears, but she forced them away. There was nothing to be afraid of. A dark room was nothing. She was safe here. They would come back for her.

Outside, someone pounded on the front door of the apartment. The creaking of the floorboards told Dash that Ruby was moving swiftly, and a window scraped open. All at once, she heard a smash, then two men were shouting in German, demanding, accusing . . . Ruby replied in that same language, sounding reasonable, but there was a tremor in her voice that made Dash's blood run cold. A shot cut through the room. Something heavy fell to the floor, and the two men said something to each other.

Ruby.

Dash didn't move. Her fist was jammed so hard against her mouth she could barely breathe, and still she feared she might be heard. The Germans' boot heels crossed the room to the open window and returned a moment later. Evidently they had seen nothing of interest below. One of them grunted, and Dash pictured him throwing Ruby over his shoulder like a rucksack. Then they were gone.

Ruby.

For two full minutes, Dash stood in place, not moving a muscle.

"Someone will come," she whispered at last, sinking onto the cot. It smelled of mould and old sawdust, further clouding the whirlwind in her mind. "Someone will come for me."

She had to think clearly. That's what Dot would say. Think logically and an answer will come. Dash slowed her breathing, and she remembered Gordon had left before the Germans had arrived. Had he been able to send a message to headquarters in time, or had the Germans been waiting for him?

Did anyone know she was in here?

She lay down on the cot, still clutching the letter, aware that her arm was hot and pulsing again. She closed her eyes, cheering herself with the thought that this letter, whoever it was from, had come from home.

"Can you hear me, Dot?" she whispered across the world. It felt a little silly, but sometimes they'd sensed each other as children. If only she could go back to that simple time.

"If you can hear me, Dot, I need you."

———

In the morning, the fever was back. Her eyes burned when she opened them, and her arm was on fire. Seeing a hint of light, she sat up slowly, the letter still curled in her hand from the night before. She carefully opened the envelope.

Dear Dash,

She burst into tears. Had her sister heard her plea the night before? Because here she was, Dash's light in the darkness.

Dear Dash,

I miss you more than you'll ever understand. I feel lost, not hearing your voice, even if you were yelling at me. I know I am to blame for all that has come between us, and I understand your anger. I am afraid you hate me, and that is the worst pain of all.

I stopped writing before because I knew you didn't want to hear from me, but I can't hold back any longer. Please, Dash. Even if you never forgive me, at least tell me in your own words.

I have said a thousand times that I would have been with you if I could, and I know that you believe me, deep down. Please let me be with you again, Dash. I love you so much.

Your sister forever,
Dot

fifty-nine
DOT

-·· --- -

— Camp X —

Dot set her elbows on the table and pressed Hydra's headphones against her head, holding herself upright. She was nearing the end of her shift, and her right hand was worn out from all the messages she'd sent and received. Part of the plan for Operation Overlord was to keep the misinformation going even after the invasion; they wanted the Germans to believe more attacks were imminent so they wouldn't send reinforcements to Normandy. It was up to Dot and the others to convince the Germans that June 6 had been a minor battle compared to what was coming. There was a lot to put out on the airwaves and even more to take in.

It had been six days since Pete had first contacted her. Since then, Dot had heard nothing from or about Gus. Where was he? Where was Dash?

After her shift, she stepped into the chilly evening and walked to the main building. She had been summoned to Gerald's office, which she thought was odd, since she reported to him every day. When she entered, Gerald was sitting behind his desk, squinting through cigar smoke. He did not invite her to sit down as he always did. Ill at ease now, she stood tall as she'd been taught back at HMCS Conestoga: chin up, heels together at a forty-five-degree angle, thumbs lined against her seams, eyes front.

"Correct me if I'm wrong, Dot, but I thought you understood that

Camp X was not your own private playground, to be used for personal missions."

She should have known he'd find out. It was practically impossible to lie successfully to a spy.

"You are not wrong, sir."

"And yet that is exactly what you did."

"Yes, sir."

He puffed on his cigar, and she knew he was weighing his options.

"Please don't have me arrested, sir. Or shot."

"I could."

"Yes, sir. I am aware. I am hoping you will exercise compassion."

"Give me an excuse to do that."

She cleared her throat. "Sir, I have not allowed this mission to impede or affect my work. I have gone above and beyond what has been asked of me on both Operation Fortitude and Operation Overlord, just as I do with every operation. I have never shared knowledge or secrets with anyone. I believe my service record stands for itself."

"I am aware of your exemplary service." He pointed the smoking end of the cigar at her. "But you used our personnel and resources, and you did not discuss it with me first. I have already spoken with Bill about this, in case you are wondering."

Her face burned. "Please do not blame him, sir."

"I do not, though he should have known better. Back to you. Tell me why you used our resources for personal reasons."

"I used Hydra because that was where I was already working, and it was the only way I could think of to achieve my goal," she said, staring straight ahead and speaking to the wall instead of him. "I was able to do my job and my personal mission simultaneously, with neither interfering with the other. With regard to the agent you mentioned, I have not heard back from him. He does not know I am trying to reach him. I . . . still hold out hope that he will reply."

"At ease, Dot."

Her feet automatically separated, her hands going behind her back, and she lowered her gaze to watch the major.

"You should not have done this."

"No, sir," she agreed, unflinching. "But I had to."

"Explain."

"My twin sister has gone missing." It was that simple. "She is a Wren, and she is also a civilian, flying with the Air Transport Auxiliary. She has been performing essential military support by ferrying airplanes around Europe."

"I see."

"Pardon me, but I'm not sure you do. Because of her contribution to the Allied forces in this conflict, I feel she should be regarded as equally important to a serviceman. In fact, I might even suggest that the military owes my sister a debt of thanks for all that she has done in her civilian role. But I am aware my feelings on this matter have no bearing on reality."

She did not often speak so plainly with him, and she wondered if her manner had been out of place. But it was too late to stop now.

"Sir, I could not possibly ignore what was happening and leave her out there. Especially if I had the means to try to find her. And I did not ask you because I knew you would say no."

His eyes had softened, watching her. "Is your mission complete?"

"No, sir." Dot stepped closer to his desk. "I love my job, sir. I love what we do. But I love my sister more than anything in the world, and Dash is in trouble. I first heard she was missing on June 4, after she was assigned to ferry a plane to a military designation in France. I have heard nothing since then. I am petrified about what that might mean." She gritted her teeth and squeezed her hands tight. "But Camp X is the clenched fist that will provide the knockout blow, sir, and I work within the brain of the centre for Intelligence. If she is out there, I will find her."

There was a beat while he considered her speech, and though she wasn't great at reading people, she thought he looked impressed. Then again, she had come on a little strong. Maybe he was laughing at her. She couldn't tell for sure.

"You are communicating entirely by radio, am I correct? Trying to reach someone on the ground to help find her. Specifically, Agent Gus Becker."

She nodded.

Another beat. "This is not interfering either with your job or with Hydra itself."

"No, sir."

There was a knock on the door, which he ignored. He closed his eyes and let out a long sigh of resignation. "Fine. Go ahead. Find your sister. But Dot, I do not want you sneaking around anymore."

Her knees weakened with relief. "No, sir. Thank you, sir."

The knock came again.

"Come in," Gerald called, rising.

Frances entered, looking sober. "This just arrived, sir."

Gerald picked up the page, and Dot watched the lines of his face fall as he read. Her gut tightened instinctively.

"Thank you, Frances. Have a seat, Dot."

She rushed forward. "What is it? Is it Gus? Please, sir. What does it say?"

"It's not Gus, but you do need to hear this." He cleared his throat then looked directly at her. "It's your classmate, Ruby. She and Gordon have been in France, as you know."

She stared at her boss, taken by surprise. Did she see tears in his eyes?

"They were ambushed last night," he said. "I regret to inform you that Ruby was killed."

Dot sank into the chair, numb with disbelief.

"A terrible loss," he said gruffly. He passed her his handkerchief. "Everyone here knows what we signed up for. Especially with a war on. We know what can happen. But this kind of news never gets any easier. Ruby was a crackerjack agent, and I know she was your friend. I'm very sorry, Dot."

Dot stared at the note on his desk. She saw Ruby's wide grin again, the way she could never wait to get to the explosives field, and those bouncing brown curls Dot had watched while she ran laps around the track. *I'll bring you something from France when I'm back.*

She looked at Gerald helplessly.

"She told me you were one of her inspirations for getting through this programme, Dot. Did you know that?"

Dot blinked, and tears rolled down her cheeks.

"Give it time," he said gently. Then he tapped the note. "On a brighter note, this was sent by Gordon two hours ago. Here's the frequency. Find him. Gordon will find Gus."

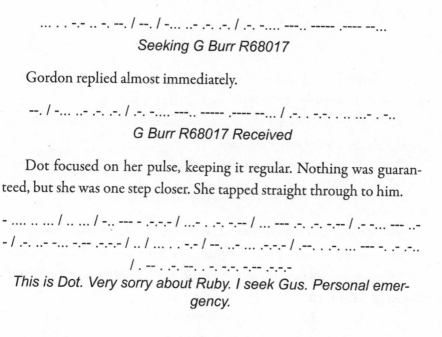

... .. .-.- .. -. --. / --. / -... .. -.- .-. / .-. -.... ---.. ----- .---- --...
Seeking G Burr R68017

Gordon replied almost immediately.

--. / -... .. .-. .-. / .-. -.... ---.. ----- .---- --... / .-. . .-.. . .. .- . -..
G Burr R68017 Received

Dot focused on her pulse, keeping it regular. Nothing was guaranteed, but she was one step closer. She tapped straight through to him.

- .... / .. ... / -.. --- - .-.-.- / ...- . .-. -.-- / ... --- .-. .-. -.-- / .- -... --- ..-
- / .-. .. .- -... -.-- .-.-.- / .. / ... . . -.- / --. ..- ... .-.-.- / .-. . .-. ... --- -. .- .-..
/ . -- . .-. --. . -. -.-. -.-- .-.-.-
This is Dot. Very sorry about Ruby. I seek Gus. Personal emergency.

.... --- .-.. -.. / --- -.
Hold on

--. ..- ... / .... . .-. . / --. --- / -.. --- -
Gus here. Go Dot

At first, she couldn't breathe, then she almost sobbed with relief. It was almost like hearing his voice, and she longed to talk with him without the dots and dashes between them. *Thank God you're alive!* she wanted to say, but there was no time.

She tapped her message through: *Dash missing since June 4. Honorine area.*

There was a beat, then:

-- .. .. -. --. ..--..

Missing?

As she prepared to answer, a stream of sound came through.

- --- --- / .-.. .- - . / - --- -. .. --. .... - .-.-.- / .-- .. .-.. .-.. / ..-. .. -. -.. / .... . .-. / - --- -- --- .-. .-. --- .-- .-.-.-

Too late tonight. Will find her tomorrow.

She wanted to tap *Tomorrow might be too late!* but what else could he do? It was the middle of the night over there. He was right.

She had not yet tapped a reply. He would sense she was afraid. A moment later, he sent another message.

.-- .. .-.. .-.. / .-. . - .-. .. . ...- . / .. ..-. / .. - / -.- .. .-.. .-.. ... / -- .

Will retrieve if it kills me

A cry caught in her throat. *No, Gus. Don't say that. Never say that. Come home.* But that was exactly what she needed him to do, wasn't it?

She tapped *Received*, then she took off her headphones, put her head down, and wept.

sixty
DASH

— Paris, France —

Dash chewed the last of the remaining sausage, though the dried meat turned to leather in her mouth. She couldn't taste it, didn't want to eat it, but she was already so weak. Without it she would have no strength at all. She had gotten worse. Her arm smelled rank with infection, and she could no longer lift it on its own. Her fingers looked like sausages. The night before, she'd hallucinated that she stuck a pin in her arm and all the infection spilled out, easing the pain, but even with her fever raging, she understood that was not an option. She feared the doctors would probably amputate her arm when she was rescued.

If she was rescued. The truth was, she had no idea if anyone was coming. Ruby was dead, and Gordon was gone. Did anyone know she was here? Did it matter anymore?

When she wasn't drowning in sweat from fever and nightmares, Dash daydreamed. She imagined Dot with her, sharing this dismal space. Dot being there changed everything. Dash no longer lived in a cage, but in an observation post. Dot counted the boards beneath the cot then the nails in the wall. She remarked on the patterns covering the walls and ceiling. Throughout the fantasy, Dot never apologized for what had happened between them with their father, and Dash never felt the need to hear it.

She was just relieved to have her there, beside her, where she should have been all along.

Where was Pete? she wondered. Flying overhead? Waiting for her on the beach? Did he know she was lost? Would she ever see him again?

Where was Gus? Safe somewhere, she hoped. Warm and dry. Could he hear the guns? The planes roaring overhead? Did he ever look up and imagine her in one of the cockpits?

Her mother. Aunt Lou and Uncle Bob. How she missed them all. She yearned for home. A quiet night with Dad and Dot doing a puzzle at the table.

She started at the sound of the apartment door creaking open, then the latch closing. She opened her mouth to call out then swallowed her words when she heard German voices. A woman and a man. Dash couldn't understand a word, and she didn't recognize either voice. The woman sounded angry. The man sounded apologetic.

Their boots clacked on the floor as they headed deeper into the rooms. Moments later, the pair returned and spoke a few words that sounded like confirmation. They exchanged a sharp *Heil Hitler!* and the man left. She heard the woman meandering through the apartment, picking things up and setting them back down. Eventually, she receded toward the bedroom.

In the silence that followed, Dash tried to think straight. She couldn't afford to panic; she was too weak for that. All she knew was that there was no escape from this little box where she lived. *This wall does not open from the inside*, Ruby had said, but Dash had tried everything she could to get out that first day. She'd pinched her fingertips under the wall to lift or slide it. She'd thrown her body at the wood, again and again. It had not budged. When she was no longer able to stand, she gave up.

Time passed.

Someone knocked on the door to the apartment. A man, evidently expected. The woman purred a welcome, giggling as she led him down the hall, away from Dash's hearing.

He left. An hour after that, a different man knocked and received the same warm reception. It happened twice more after that. Dash came to the foggy conclusion that her new roommate was a prostitute. She was also a pretty good cook, filling the air of the apartment with the aroma of fried onions and potatoes in butter, and Dash's mouth with saliva. Who had butter these days? This woman was being kept in style.

All this came to Dash in a hazy sort of dream that she knew to be true. Hollowed out by hunger and weak with fear, she lay motionless on the cot.

She wasn't the first to have existed here in this strange, suffocating purgatory. There were old bloodstains on the cot, and someone named *Steven Murphy, Sheffield, Army* had signed his name on the wall. He had left behind the nub of a pencil, rolled under the cot. Dash pressed the rounded tip against the wall, near his name. Her hand shook so badly it was hard to hold the pencil.

Dash Wilson, she wrote as neatly as she could. *Canada, Pilot.*

She was so sick that she began to wonder if she could simply close her eyes and just stop breathing. End the agony. But her body was more stubborn than she thought, and the torture continued.

———

By the third morning in the room, there was nothing left to eat or drink. How long could a person survive without water? Dash had probably read it somewhere long ago, but she couldn't remember now. She didn't care.

Another knock at the door. Dash listened idly, long past caring who came or went. A man spoke.

"*Guten Nachmittag. Ich bin Polizeiinspektor Braun.*" Dash heard: Police inspector.

The woman's tone was wary, which made Dash think the inspector had not been expected. Despite her lethargy, she was intrigued. Why was he here, and why did her housemate sound upset? With all the strength she had, Dash crawled off the cot and pressed her ear to the wall. The man was still speaking, but he was farther away now. Then she heard another sound, just beyond the wall. A second man was walking slowly through the room, tapping a cane on the floor. The floorboards creaked under his weight. She closed her eyes, dreaming of a hammer hitting nails. The canvas wing of a Hurricane taking shape.

A light flickered in the darkness of her mind, and it registered that the tapping sounded like a pattern. Morse code, she mused. With all she had left, she focused her straying thoughts on translating it.

--. ..- ...

Gus

Dash gasped. Gus? It had to be another fever dream. They felt so real, it was hard to tell.

--. ..- ...

Gus

But it *was* real. He was here. Why? How? He had to be looking for her, didn't he? Dizzy with disbelief, she set her hands against the wall and pushed, as if she might somehow break through to him. So close. So close. He knew she was here, so—no, wait. He was still tapping his name, looking for her. He needed her help.

She tapped with her knuckle:

-.. .- ... .

Dash

An audible exhalation came through the wall, then the bookshelf slid, just a little, and she spotted something beneath: a scrap of paper, wiggling as it was forced through the crack. Dash grabbed it.

I will come for you tonight. Be ready. It will be loud.

G

"Gus!" she cried softly, but the woman's agitated voice was approaching, joined by the inspector's. Through the thin wall, she heard Gus walk away. *Gus, Gus, Gus, Gus! Come back! Please, Gus!* She gulped back tears as the apartment door opened then closed. Alone once more, she lay on the floor, lacking the energy to cross the few feet between her and the cot. He would come for her tonight.

She had no idea if she could wait that long.

―――――――

Hours later, an explosion shuddered through the walls, but Dash barely felt it. In the next room shards of broken glass tinkled like bells as they littered the floor. She dozed, then was woken again by a staccato burst of gunfire. She smelled smoke, heard panicked screams from the street below. Beyond Dash's thin prison wall, the woman was shrieking.

Dash heard it all from far, far away. The floor beneath her felt like syrup, rising and falling in thick waves, beckoning. She drifted off to sleep again.

Someone pounded on the apartment door. "Fräulein Köhler!"

The woman cried out with relief. She yanked the door open and escaped.

I'm here, too, Dash thought vaguely. *I need to leave, too.*

But no one was coming. She closed her eyes again, and she let herself go.

―――――――

Hands, warm and gentle. Strong. Touching her back. Her arm was grazed, then everything went black.

Arms under her, around her. That voice. "It's all right now. I have you." She knew that voice. Her body lifted off the floor, floating, drifting . . .

"Dash? Talk to me."

"Gus," she croaked, dragging herself to the surface. His cheek felt cool against hers.

"My God. You're on fire." His arms tightened around her. "I've got you, Dash. I'll get you out."

Gus. She wished, oh, she wished she could hold on to him, but her body was limp. Her arms felt pinned to her sides, her head heavy on her neck.

"You found me," she whispered.

"Hide and seek. Just like old times." He tilted a canteen against her lips. "Drink."

She sipped, savouring every drop. When she opened her eyes, his gaze had wandered past her, toward the wall where she had written her name.

His lips brushed her brow. "I'm sorry it took me so long. Let's go home."

In one motion, he rose, shifting his hold so she lay against his chest like a child, and carried her down flights of stairs that felt endless, then into the night. Another explosion, more screams, peppering gunfire, and so, so cold. She shook, helpless against it all, but he held her securely.

"I've got you," he said again.

Someone whistled, and Gus ran in that direction. She gave in to the exhaustion, safe with Gus. Her whole life, always safe with Gus.

When she awoke next, she was on the ground, wrapped in a blanket, her head cushioned on someone's coat. She felt a strangeness on her arm. Someone had changed the bandage. The stink was gone, at least for now. She rolled her head to the side and saw Gus standing about six feet away, his chin down as he listened to the people around him. He said something she couldn't hear, then someone brought him what looked like Gordon's radio. The grass swished quietly as his boots came toward her. He unpacked the radio then held the headphones to one ear. Subconsciously, she translated as he tapped in the Morse code.

.--. .- -.-. -.- .- --. . / .... . -.-. .-- .-. . -.. .-.-.- / .--. .. -.-. -.- .. .--. / -----

....- ----- -----

Package secured. Pickup 0400

A crackling sound escaped the headphones, then more beeps.

- .- -..- .. / .-- .- .. - .. -. --.

Taxi waiting

"Am I the package?" Her voice sounded funny to her own ears. Lazy. As if she'd been drinking too much alcohol. Too many sidecars with Stacy. Too much dancing.

He dropped beside her and unscrewed the top of his canteen. He held it to her mouth again. "You heard that? I thought you'd forgotten Morse code."

"How could I, with you and Dot hammering away all the time?"

He pulled out a piece of bread and tore off smaller bits for her. She ate, appreciating the softness of the bread. Between bites and sips of water, her head began to clear, and yet nothing made sense.

"Why are you here?"

His fingers swept across her brow. "You caught me. I'm a tourist, exploring the wilds of France."

Her gaze dropped to the pistol in his belt. "With guns and radios?"

"It's the latest thing in tourism. There's a truck coming to get us, Dash, then we have a long drive. You can sleep the whole way."

"I have been sleeping for days."

"You need it. By the way, the ATA wants their Spitfire back."

She winced, remembering that night. "I'll build them a new one." She gazed up at him, so, so happy he was there. "I should have done what Dot did and got a safe little desk job. All I ever wanted to do was fly planes, not get involved in all this."

A smile touched his lips. "But you're not Dot."

"She always was the smart one."

"You're both smart."

They turned toward the sound of approaching tires on gravel, and one of the men with Gus stepped out from behind a tree to inspect the vehicle as it slowed. Like Gus, he held a gun. He turned his face into the light and nodded to Gus, and she recognized Gordon.

"Can you walk?" Gus asked.

She nodded but was unsure. Gus kept his arm around her as they moved to the car, where Gordon waited like a shadow. He was quiet as before, but she sensed a new sadness in him.

"I'm sorry about Ruby," she said.

He glanced away. "I'm sorry for leaving you."

"Climb in and get comfortable," Gus said, opening the rear door. "Let's go home."

Home. An unexpected sadness lurched in Dash's chest. The war was over for her. She would have to leave the Spitfires and the Hurricanes behind. Her fellow pilots would continue their precious duty, but she would not. Would she ever fly again? Did she want to? After those final terrifying moments in the Spitfire, she had trouble imagining herself finding the courage to sit in a cockpit again.

"We'll get you flying again someday," Gus said, reading her mind.

The drive was pitch black and quiet. Even the car they were in had its lights off. Gus sat beside her, and when he bundled up his coat on his lap, she laid her head on it. What was left of her anxiety melted away.

Some time later, he woke her. She blinked, trying to sort the images coming through the dark. Gordon had parked on the side of a road edged by trees. Ahead, a large field. Gus opened her door then wrapped his coat around her.

"Come on," he said, supporting her every step. "We have to be quick. We're not alone out here."

A light blazed across the field then shut off just as quickly. Gus picked up his pace, forcing her to almost run to keep up with him. Then an engine started, catching at last, and Dash's pulse took off. She knew the sound of a Mosquito, that twin engine, two-seater, night fighter she'd flown so many times. She stopped ten feet from the plane's shiny nose, suddenly afraid.

"What do you think?" Gus asked.

He looked so proud, and she realized he was somehow responsible. She could only imagine everything he'd gone through, coming here for her.

Humiliation swept through her. "I don't think I can fly it. I . . . The crash, it . . ."

Gus squeezed her hand. "It's okay." She was confused by the smile in his voice. Then she heard the canopy open. "We brought you a pilot."

She peered into the darkness. Could it be one of the girls? That would be so nice. Violet would have come if he'd asked, and it would be good to see her again. Any of the girls, really. But no. From where she stood, she could see the profile belonged to a man.

"You said you wanted to go to Paris," he said. "My mistake. I thought you meant *after* the war."

All the air left Dash's lungs. "Pete?"

He hopped off the wing and reached for her. "I missed you awfully," he said, then he kissed her in a way that showed her he meant it. "What do you say we postpone Paris for a while?"

She turned to Gus. "You brought him here, didn't you?"

"This flyboy reported you missing. Only seemed right that he get the grand finale."

Pete kissed her again, and all the little pockets of emptiness in Dash's heart filled with his warmth. Almost all, anyway.

"You're not coming?"

Gus had moved away from the plane. "I'll be back, but I have things to do here first."

"Oh, please come with me."

"I have to save the world," he teased. "Besides, it's only a two-seater. Listen, when you get back, do me a favour? Be kind to your sister. She needs you."

"I don't know how to find her. That's been a big part of the problem all along."

"I have a feeling she will find you," he said. Gordon made a sharp motion from his spot behind them, and Gus tensed, on alert. "Time to go."

"Let's get you in the air before we have too much company," Pete said, helping her onto the wing.

She'd worried the cockpit would be too much for her, but with Pete beside her, she wasn't afraid at all. He buckled her in, taking special care with her bandaged arm, then he wrapped an extra blanket around her. She watched him start up the twin engines, thinking how perfect it was that she'd be flying with him.

Suddenly there was a metallic *ping!* that she didn't recognize, and Pete pushed in the throttle.

"Go!" Gus shouted, waving wildly at them. "Get her out of here!"

"What's—"

Too late, she recognized them as gunshots. As the Mosquito roared across the field, she spotted a dozen or so black uniforms charging toward Gus and Gordon. The two returned fire, but they were vastly outnumbered. As the plane lifted from the earth, Dash saw Gus stagger backward.

"No!" she screamed, squirming in her seat. She had to get to him. "Gus! Go back, Pete! Go back!"

"Hang on, darling," Pete said, banking hard so that he came back toward the airfield from the other direction.

Gordon had rushed out to Gus and was dragging him out of the way, but the Germans were still approaching, still shooting.

Tears streamed down Dash's face. "No, no, no! Gus! No! Pete! We have to go back!"

His expression was tender, but firm. "You've flown a lot of fighters, Dash, but you've never flown with a fighter *pilot*. Hang on."

That's when he opened up the Mosquito's four .303-calibre machine guns and took the black uniforms down. At the end of the field, he nosed back up into the sky, pulling Dash's stomach into her chest, then he reached for her hand and kissed the back of it.

"He'll be all right." His eyes shone with tears. "God, Dash. It is good to see you."

Dash twisted backward, desperate for one more glance, but the wing blocked her view. Pete pushed the plane higher, but the night was too dark. She saw no movement at all.

sixty-one
DOT

-•• --- -

—July 1944 —
Oshawa, Ontario

Dot stood at the door of her mother's house, hat in hand. Other than the night she crept in through the window, this was the first time she'd been home in nearly two years, when she'd first joined the Wrens and headed to HMCS Conestoga. Her whole world had changed since then.

Never before had she been so eager or so nervous to see her sister. She knew from Dash's earlier letter to Gus that she missed her, but she still worried. No matter the reception, things would continue to be difficult between them because of the unavoidable secrets. Secrets that would remain in place for the next thirty-nine years. All she could do was hope Dash would let it go.

Gerald had taken very little persuasion this time when Dot requested a week off work. After everything she'd done with Hydra during Operations Fortitude and Overlord while simultaneously coordinating the search and rescue of her sister, even managing to bring in a charming RAF pilot to fly her out of danger, he couldn't really say no. Especially now. Since that night, no one had heard anything from or about Gus or Gordon. Dot had transmitted to them again and again, refusing to give up, but over the entire month, she had received no response. No one knew where they were or if they were even alive. The only person who might know anything was Dash.

Dot wasn't sure what she would do if Gus never came home.

Dash had arrived in Halifax a couple of days ago on a hospital ship, where she'd been fed and treated for her infection before she boarded a train to Union Station in Toronto. Dot knew the hour she was arriving, and she could swear she felt the air change when Dash stepped out of the train. This morning, her mom, Uncle Bob, and Aunt Lou had gone to pick her up. Now she was here, mere feet away, on the other side of this door. Dot was so afraid, she was shaking.

But Dash must have seen her walk past the victory garden, because there she was, flinging the door open and wrapping Dot in a one-armed hug that they both wanted to last forever. Dash's other arm was trapped in a sling against her chest.

"I'm so sorry," Dot blubbered.

Dash squeezed her tight. "So am I. We have so much to talk about. I missed you so much. Come on. Let's go to our room."

The house smelled like heaven to Dot. The aroma of her mother's roast chicken mingled with the perfection of Aunt Lou's freshly baked apple pie, and though both girls' stomachs grumbled, they needed to catch up by themselves. Dash told her about her work at the ATA, and Dot sat on her bed, knees hugged to her chest, taking in the miracle that was her sister.

"What happened the night you went missing?" Dot prompted, eager for the full story.

She only knew about what had happened after Pete had first contacted her. Dot had handled the search through Hydra, but she'd never received any kind of report from either Gus or Gordon because they had gone missing.

"I haven't even told Mom yet. Let's wait until dinner," Dash said, then she patted Dot's knee. "Tell me about you. I haven't heard about you in so long."

"I don't want to talk about me," Dot replied, even as she felt the heat of her little white lie creeping up her neck. More than anything, she wished she could share the truth with Dash, but she defaulted to her Camp X training. "All I do at work is type and think of you, so just let me listen, all right?"

"If you insist," Dash said, though she didn't quite look like she believed her. "But let me look at you at least. You look different. Stronger somehow. Happy. You may just be typing, but those must be great memos. You look . . . is there a man in your life, Dot?"

"What? Don't be ridiculous." Her cheeks bloomed, and this time she knew her sister saw it. "But now that we're on the subject, please, tell me about your Englishman. When are we going to meet him?"

"Not soon enough for me," Dash said with a weary smile.

Their mother called them for dinner, and Dot followed her sister to the door. Before she stepped through, she paused and turned back. She took in the little dolls on the vanity and the overloaded bookshelf her father had made. The room and everything in it looked smaller than she remembered. And so much simpler.

"Gosh, it's good to be home."

Dash was already halfway down the stairs. "It sure is. Come on. Let's go eat."

They sat around the table Dot had missed so terribly, and she filled her heart with the sound of Dash's voice and the sight of her loved ones. As if nothing had changed, Dot stayed quiet, listening rather than speaking, but her mind drifted beyond Dash's tales of flying. Their father's chair remained at the table, and she couldn't stop thinking of that night. Of the relief she'd seen in his eyes. *I knew you'd come.* But she almost hadn't. If it hadn't been for Gus, she never would have made it.

Uncle Bob asked Dash something about plane engines, and Dash jumped in with information that had everyone except Dot fascinated. Dot knew nothing about mechanics, though she was in contact with pilots and sailors and soldiers every single day. She longed to share the adventures she'd witnessed through her headphones, maybe even boast a little about the lives that she had saved, but she never could. In the beginning, there had been something exciting in knowing she held secrets so important they could never be shared, but that novelty had gotten old very quickly. It would be thirty-nine more years before her stories would be told. Who at this table might be gone by then?

"Tell us about the happy ending," Aunt Lou said.

"Well, it certainly didn't start happily," Dash said. "I flew into a thunderstorm, and . . ."

Dot listened as she described the crash, the Germans in the forest, and then waking up in the Paris apartment. Her heart ached when Dash told them about the horrible little room where she'd waited after Ruby had been killed. Then, with a wonderful flourish, Dash revealed that it had been Gus who rescued her. Dot did her best to look as shocked as the rest of her family.

"Gus!" her mother exclaimed. "How on earth did that happen?"

"Honestly, I don't know." A sneaky little smile appeared. "I think—now, he never told me specifically, but I think he's one of those secret agent guys. You know? Like a spy? He had a radio and a gun, and he looked like he was in control of everybody."

Dot forced out a laugh, her training kicking in. "Gus, a spy? He's a soldier, that's all. There has to be another reason he was there."

"No, you have no idea, Dot. He was amazing! Somehow he found me, then he carried me out, and we drove forever. I slept the whole way. But then—oh, I will *never* know how he accomplished this—he somehow managed to get Pete, the RAF pilot I told you about, to fly in and take me away!"

Dot fought the impulse to jump in: *I did that! I found Pete after he found me, and it wasn't easy, but we got him there . . .* but she couldn't. She'd reveal too much, and she had sworn Pete to secrecy. Dash might never know.

Instead, she leaned in and asked what she really needed to know. "What happened to Gus?"

Dash's expression fell. "Right when we were taking off, we heard shots." Her eyes filled with tears. "I saw him fall."

"What?" Dot cried, and a shiver raced down her spine.

"The Germans came across the field, and they shot Gus. Pete roared in and took all the Germans down, but I have no idea what happened to Gus after that."

Dot couldn't breathe.

"No. That can't be," she whispered, feeling lost. "He promised that he would come home."

sixty-two
DASH

— Oshawa, Ontario —

Dash lay on her side, watching her sister sleep. With everything that had happened overseas, then the ship back and the anticipation of finally seeing Dot again, Dash had thought she'd sleep a whole year. But to her surprise, she'd slept poorly. In a way, she was glad, because it gave her the opportunity to watch her sister sleep.

Dot had changed. There was no more fear behind her eyes, though there was pain. Had she fallen in love? Dash hoped so. She needed her sister to feel that sense of happiness. Of oneness. After all this time, after the rift between them, after being an ocean apart and having their lives go in different directions, Dash was fascinated by how right it felt to be together again. She still had things to say to Dot, things to ask her, but her old anger had been replaced with a calmness that had not been there for a very long time.

She knew when Dot was waking. She knew her breathing patterns as well as she knew her own.

"Good morning," she said softly.

Dot's eyes opened, and Dash felt the love in them like a touch. "Good morning, Dash."

She was also aware of the moment when Dot's guard went up.

"What?" Dot asked.

Dash kept her voice relaxed. She didn't want to fight. "You know what. Why weren't you there?"

"I thought you'd forgiven me."

"I have. But I still need to know why. It makes no sense."

Dot swallowed hard. "I still can't tell you, Dash. Can you please just leave it at that?"

"Did you do something bad, Dot?"

That surprised her. "No! I just can't . . . it's the war. There are secrets in war."

"That you can't even share with me?"

"That I can't even share with you."

Dash frowned, recalling Aunt Lou's words at the funeral. She'd told Dash about her father, and of the secret life he'd led in the first war. Of the things he'd left unsaid. *Sometimes in war, secrets are necessary*, her aunt had said. Then Dash thought about her days at GECO when she'd had to take an oath of secrecy before she could fill munition shells with explosives. She supposed Aunt Lou was right. She couldn't tell Dot about that job, either.

"Did you know Dad was a hero?"

Dot propped her head up on her hand, her hair tousled by the pillow. "What?"

"Aunt Lou told me. At the funeral."

Dot's gaze faltered at the mention of the funeral, but Dash pressed on, telling Dot how he had saved Mr. Olson, Mr. Martin's brother, and Mr. Jeffreys. "He saved a lot of lives, but he never told us."

Dot had gone very pale. "Mr. Jeffreys from the bakery? I had no idea."

Dash nodded. "He didn't want to talk about it, ever. The whole town knows, but they respected his wish to keep it quiet. Dad was a hero." She copied Dot, lifting her head and meeting Dot's eyes. "Are you a hero, Dot?"

Dot wiped away a tear. "No, Dash. I'm no hero. I just typed memos. I just did my job."

Except there was something different in Dot's expression now. Regret? What was it she wasn't saying? Her sister took a deep breath then exhaled.

"Gus was a hero," Dot said softly.

sixty-three
DOT

-.. --- -

— May 1945 —
Camp X

Dot had feared Camp X would close after the war, but Hydra had proven itself to be the foremost communication tool in the world, and there was no reason to shut it down. So Dot stayed on after VE Day, at least temporarily, to continue exchanging messages with London, Washington, and Ottawa. She was glad of it. She couldn't imagine how she could ever go back to a regular life after all this.

After her shift one Tuesday, she passed Frances's desk and picked up her mail. She stood awhile, talking with her friend, then headed back to the dormitory and the quiet of her room. As she walked, she sifted through the mail, then she froze in place, seeing familiar, dreadful handwriting on one of the envelopes. With trembling hands, she tore it open and unfolded the letter. Reading the salutation, she fell to her knees in the spring grass, weeping.

Gus was alive.

She and everyone else had given up on him months ago. After what Dash had told them, they were convinced he had been killed that night in France. Her heart had shattered into a million pieces, though she tried not to let her suffering show. No one knew that the two of them had become so much more than friends. No one could understand her loss. As a family, they grieved him and tried to move on, but Dot knew she never would.

This letter, this fragile piece of paper in her shaking hands, changed everything. In it, he told her that he and Gordon had been captured on the night Dash was saved. They had spent the last eleven months as POWs in Stalag VII-A in Germany. They were now on their way home.

Delirious with happiness, she rushed back to Gerald's office to tell him.

"Wonderful news," Gerald said, smiling wide as he took the letter from her. Gerald had softened over the past year, and while he was still her boss, he was more like a friend now.

"But why didn't we know this?" she demanded. "Why were we, the best ruddy spy camp in the world, completely in the dark about Gus and Gordon?"

Gerald read the letter, his face falling. "Stalag VII-A," he said slowly. "The commander of that camp is known to us, Dot. He was a submarine captain in the first war, and according to our notes, he did not stand with the Geneva Convention. That would explain why we did not receive notification that our men were being held there. From reports I've read, that was a rather brutal camp. They may be a little broken when they get back." He held her gaze as he returned the letter to her. "Gus will need you, Dot."

Dot was prepared. She could fix whatever needed fixing. She just needed him back.

When his train arrived in Toronto, Dot was waiting. Heart pounding, she peered between the throngs of people on the platform until she spotted him, scanning the crowd for her.

"Gus!" she cried, then she rushed forward, dodging other travelers. When he saw her, the happiness in his expression filled her with so much joy she could have flown to him. He was here. He was really here.

He dropped his duffel as she flung herself at him, and he held her like a drowning sailor would hold a life ring, and that was right, because she would save him. He had suffered, but now he was home. All those years when he'd stood up for her, taken care of her, now it was her turn. All those years when he'd loved her, but she'd been oblivious, now he would see that her love for him was boundless.

His cheek pressed against hers, and he uttered a quiet sound of relief. It was a moment before their grips loosened, then she looked up and saw the tears in his eyes, just like hers. His fingers shook when they went to the sides of her face, and she thought she might die of happiness. Oh, she wanted to kiss him, to laugh out loud out of sheer pleasure, but he held her in place, the blue of his eyes achingly beautiful.

"Just let me look at you," he whispered. "God, I have dreamed of you."

That's when she let herself see the pronounced bones of his face and feel the sharpness of his shoulders. He was so awfully thin. Even his soft blond hair, now grown well below his ears, looked thin. The blue of his eyes had paled, their glow washed away by his imprisonment. It was as if he had aged forty years.

Finally, he drew her in, and his kiss stole her breath. It felt urgent, as if it was now or never, as if he was afraid she was only in his dreams and might vanish into nothing.

She pulled back. "Gus," she said softly. "It's all right. You're home, and I'm here with you. Everything is going to be better now."

With Gerald's help, Dot had paid in advance for a room at the Royal York Hotel. They could have gone straight home, she knew, but she'd thought he might need a little quiet first. When she told him that, he had seemed glad of it. She had no romantic plans for the hotel room, only knew she needed a safe, quiet place where they could be alone. Gus was back. She needed to hear his words, and they had to be spoken in a private place. The room was expensive, but it was practical, and with the hotel's underground tunnel from Union Station, it was close.

He barely spoke as she hustled him from the station to the Royal York, so she made up for it in frantic babble, trying to hold his attention. When they reached the hotel, she was momentarily distracted by the opulence of the lobby and couldn't stop staring as she went to the front counter. She'd read up on the hotel, with its ten elevators, twelve-bed hospital, twelve-thousand-book library, and its very own concert hall, and she'd wondered fleetingly if she and Gus would get a chance to explore. But Gus barely seemed to register their surroundings. He didn't say a word as they ascended to the eighth floor.

Inside the elegant room, he sat on the edge of the bed, but it was as if he didn't know to lie down. She helped him onto his side then pulled a blanket over him. He promptly fell asleep.

She had understood it would take a while for him to breathe freely again, to relax and come to terms with what he had experienced, whatever it was. What she hadn't expected was how lost he would appear. How fragile. She thought she'd been prepared, but seeing him like this was so difficult. He would need much more time than she'd planned. While he slept, she went down to the front desk and rented the room for an entire week, though it was far more than she could afford. Feeling a little sheepish, she telephoned Gerald and explained what was happening. He told her not to worry about a thing, and he said he would cover both the room and room service for the entire time they stayed. He also sent over some clean clothes for Gus.

The next morning, Gus got up and took a shower. She set the new clothes outside the bathroom door, then she phoned downstairs and ordered breakfast, which arrived before Gus was done getting dressed. When he was ready, he sat with her at the little table in their room. She encouraged him to eat and she could tell he was a little stronger after he finished his eggs and toast.

Then he looked at her. It was the first time his eyes had really focused. "Dot, thank—"

"Please don't thank me." The words rushed out. She needed him to know that she would always do anything for him. He never had to thank her. "But I need to thank you."

He frowned, confused.

"Dash," she said, and he smiled.

"She's okay?"

"She's fine."

"I was worried about her when I found her. She'd been through a rough time. You know, you were amazing, finding me like that."

She shrugged lightly. "I knew you were my only hope." She sucked in an unexpected sob. "But then I didn't hear from you, and no one knew anything..."

He stared at the cup of steaming coffee on the table, uncertain. Dot knew the sound of voices, the dots and dashes of hidden messages being sent into the unknown. After all she'd heard, she knew what those voices needed. What Gus needed.

"You don't have to tell me anything." She took his hand. "Either way, I'm right here."

"It's not a nice story, but I do need to tell it. I suppose you should get Gerald to debrief me."

So she telephoned Gerald, and he was in their room within a half hour, welcoming Gus back with open arms.

"This girl refused to give up on you. It was either you or the entire Allied military forces, you know."

"I never had to choose," she said.

"No, because you managed both," Gus replied, smiling softly.

"And she did it behind my back."

Gus grinned. "You have to give her credit for that." He cleared his throat. "All right. Ready?"

"Ready," Gerald said, sitting back.

Dot pulled out a pen and paper. "I'm listening," she said.

Gus took a deep breath, and his eyes lost their focus. "I was kept in solitary at first. For questioning. Gordon was in another cell. I was trained never to say a word, so I didn't."

What Gus wasn't saying was that he'd been tortured. They all knew it. Dot felt sick, but she didn't interrupt.

"Keeping quiet didn't work, so I asked the Germans what they wanted me to say. That made them *really* mad." He drew down the neckline of his shirt and showed her an ugly round scar on his shoulder, trapped in raised webbing. "The bullet from that night with Dash is still there. They cauterized it inside me when I wouldn't say anything."

"We'll get that looked at," Gerald muttered.

Dot noticed Gus's two fingers slightly parted in a V. "Gus, do you want a cigarette?"

He gazed past her, through the window. She turned and grabbed a pack off the table. She'd bought it just in case and tried not to cough as she lit one for him.

"The camp was real big," he said, inhaling the cigarette, long and deep. Smoke seeped out of his nose and lips. "Thousands of us were in there. I'd heard of POW camps before, but when I first saw those men, it was hard to believe. They were skeletons. I tried to talk with them about escape, but they weren't listening. They were past believing it was possible, and soon I was, too. In the winter, there was hardly any food. Ironically, I knew a lot of the shortage was because of what I'd done with my teams. We'd cut their supply lines."

As soon as she'd received his letter, Dot had researched what she could of Stalag VII-A in Bavaria. It had been built to hold ten thousand Allied prisoners, but by the time Gus had been liberated, the *New York Times* reported over one hundred ten thousand men had been there. Most were French, Polish, and Russian. She was glad Gus at least spoke French and German. It might have helped him along the way.

The tip of his cigarette burned hot when he inhaled. "One morning, Stinson came to see me. Sergeant Major Stinson. He was called a 'man of confidence' for the Canadians in the camp. A representative, I guess. He told me the Red Cross had thousands of care packages but no way to deliver them. He needed volunteer drivers and mechanics. I jumped into a driver's seat before he could get the question out of his mouth." He shook his head, looking bemused. "We Canadians manned three convoys of relief trucks and drove all over Germany. Sometimes we drove for forty-eight hours straight just to deliver the boxes of food. By that point, the Germans didn't care about us. We were more concerned about the Allies shooting us or hijacking the trucks."

His voice changed slightly, becoming a little weaker. "Last month, my trucks and I were sent north for a prisoner exchange instead of a delivery. Three hundred women from the Ravensbrück camp were being traded for a bunch of German civilians in France. Our assignment was to get the women out, take them across the hellscape of Germany, and deliver them to Switzerland. I figured I'd just deliver the rest of us to Switzerland, too, and get the hell out of there."

Ravensbrück. Dot shuddered inwardly, thinking of the research she'd done on the concentration camps. Ravensbrück had been the largest concentration camp in Germany, second in size only to Auschwitz, in German-annexed Poland. It was almost exclusively for women, who had been subjected to horrific conditions and torture, including starvation, forced labour, medical experiments, and sterilization. When the camp had been liberated just a month ago by the Soviets, there were more than fifty thousand women trapped there. Dot had seen a few photos and would never forget them. She couldn't imagine how Gus had felt, being there in person.

He gnawed on his lower lip. She was seeing so many new mannerisms. A twitch, a wandering gaze. What had they done to him?

He set the cigarette in the ashtray and stared at the smoke twisting upward.

"It was Easter," he said softly. "Or somewhere around then. We pulled onto the side of the road outside Ravensbrück's gates the night before, staying out of the way of an air raid. When the sun came up, we sat in our trucks and waited for the women to come out."

He was back there, she could see, and he didn't want to be. In his hardened jaw and parted lips, she watched him relive that morning.

"They didn't look like women. If they hadn't been standing, we might have thought they were dead already. Their bones... They'd been beaten, some of them mutilated. I kept reminding myself that those women were the strongest of the thousands within the camp. If they'd been too weak to stand, they would have been killed ahead of time.

"Nothing about that morning felt real. We were gaping like idiots, and those poor, brave women just stared at us. I didn't even know I was crying at first. Then someone started yelling in German, and I jumped out of the driver's seat and ran to the gate. The others came with me. When I came face-to-face with one of the women, I held out my hand. She looked at me like she was a child, like she wasn't believing what was in front of her." He took a shaky breath. "Then she touched my hand and said, 'You're real.'"

Dot closed her eyes against the tears that threatened. What horrors those women must have survived.

"She collapsed into my arms," he said. "I carried her to the truck. All sixty pounds of her, maybe. Her bones were sharp. I remember trying not to cry as I went back and carried more of them. Some were able to walk, but they were so weak."

Forgotten in the ashtray, most of his cigarette had become an inch-long cylinder of grey ash. Dot lit a second one and replaced the first. He didn't notice.

"One of the women kept saying how lucky she was. She said five hundred women had been gassed just that morning before we arrived." Again, that gnawing on his lip. "My truck blew a tire after a bit, and two of the women dropped out of the back and went to it." He stared at Dot, incredulous. "They thought we would make them fix it!"

His voice cracked, and Gerald looked away. A part of Dot broke, hearing the fragility in his words. It was almost like hearing human voices interrupting the Morse code in her headphones. She didn't know how much more of his pain she could take, but just like at Hydra, she would never stop listening.

"We ran out of gas in Hof, a little Bavarian town. We all slept on straw for a couple of nights, then we left again. Everything was bombed out. The whole country looked like rubble. We took the women to Switzerland, but I couldn't escape like I'd planned. None of us could, because so many people were counting on us. We went back to the trucks and started making deliveries again."

A tear escaped her eye, and she wiped it away. She shouldn't be crying. It was his story, not hers. Except knowing that he hurt made it hers as well.

"After another month or so of driving all night, I parked in a ditch and fell asleep. In the morning, there were American soldiers standing all around the truck. They told me my job was done, and they sent me home."

The second cigarette was turning to ash in his fingers. Gus stubbed it out and the three of them sat in silence for a full minute.

"Anything else?" Gerald asked.

Gus shook his head, and Gerald looked between them. "I'll go back to the office then. Give you two some time. Thanks, Gus. And welcome home. We missed you."

They both showed him to the door, then Gus faced Dot. He looked completely defeated.

"I'm not sure what to do now, Dot. I had a purpose, now I don't."

"But you do," she said. "You need to be here with me." She put her arms around him. "Thank you for coming home."

He leaned down and kissed her, slow and soft. "I promised you I would, didn't I?"

epilogue
DASH

—1982—
Oshawa, Ontario

Thirty-six years. That's how long Dot had been married to Gus. A marriage Dash never could have expected, and yet one that had made so much sense. The first time Dot had told her that she and Gus were together, Dash had been stunned.

"You two have been keeping secrets!" she had teased, but when she really thought about the two of them, it felt right, and it made her heart happy.

They were happy, too, though it had not been an easy path for either. After the POW camp, Gus had been plagued by illness. Dot was with him every step of the way, and he had been determined to live through it all. Stubborn to the end, Gus had died a month ago, when his body finally gave in to the malnourishment and sickness that had destroyed his organs. Sixty years was pretty good, she reasoned, considering everything he'd been through. Then she exhaled, feeling empty. No, she thought again. It wasn't nearly enough.

Dot had dealt with Gus's death in her own quiet way, but Dash never could have suffered in silence. Gus had been their best friend. He'd been their brother, and somehow he had saved Dash's life. He and Pete.

Neither one of the men had ever said anything more about that day, no matter how much she pushed them, and it had always made her curious. She wondered if that's why they did it. To tease her. She didn't really mind. She'd rather not think about that time in her life anyway.

Gus had been the quiet but funny uncle to Dash and Pete's four children. He was also the father of two blond angels, and grandfather to three more. But more than anything else, he had been Dot's world.

Shortly after they'd married, with Dash and Pete standing as witnesses, their mother had died. Again, far too young. Dot and Gus had moved into the old house and never left.

Today was their birthday, and the girls sat together on Dot's old tree trunk. A lot had changed in the yard—Gus had updated the tire swing for the grandchildren, planted Dot a flower garden, and built a front porch—but the tree was still there.

"Happy birthday," Dash said. "Feels weird, being fifty-eight. I don't feel that old."

"You don't look that old, either." Dot laid her head on her sister's shoulder. "I have a gift for you."

"Oh no! I didn't get you anything," Dash exclaimed. "I didn't think we were exchanging anymore."

"It's not like that. It's something I've wanted to give you for a very long time, but I had to wait. It's a story." Dot gazed up at the old tree, thoughts flickering behind her eyes. "It's about the first time I kissed Gus. That night was the first and only time I climbed this tree."

"*You* climbed it?" Dash exclaimed, shocked.

She chuckled. "By myself. Gus was up top, waiting for me."

"When was that?"

"It was the night I came to say goodbye to Dad."

Dash stared, her heart constricting.

"Yes, I came, Dash. But it was complicated. I couldn't tell you. Gus and I were both working at a place not too far from here, near Whitby, called Camp X. It was a top-secret Intelligence base. When you said you thought he was a spy, you were actually pretty close." She took a deep breath. "When I got Mom's telegram about Dad, I wasn't allowed to go. Gus knew that would practically kill me, so he snuck me out. He put us both at risk, but he made sure I saw Dad one last time."

Dash breathed silently through the knot in her throat, her whole world opening wide.

"I kissed him that night, and he kissed me back. He said he'd wanted to do that for a very long time," Dot said, still sounding amazed after all this time. "I didn't believe it. I thought if anyone, he loved you. But . . . no. It was me."

"Why didn't you tell me?"

"Oh, Dash. I am so happy that I get to tell you at last." Dot took her sister's hands, and her face was radiant. "Gus and I had both sworn an oath of secrecy. We couldn't tell a soul anything about where we were or what we were doing for the next forty years. If we did, we would have been charged with treason and could have faced a firing squad. We couldn't even tell anyone that we'd signed an oath." She gave Dash a sly smile. "And if I'd said anything about the two of us being together, well, you'd have wanted to know how and when that happened, wouldn't you?" Her smile widened. "Did you really believe I was just typing all that time?"

Dash's throat swelled. *I'm sure there's a good reason*, her father had said. *If she cannot come, I want you to forgive her.*

"You want to know the best part about turning fifty-eight?" Dot went on.

"Tell me."

"It's been forty years since I signed that oath. It's done."

Dash burst into tears, finally understanding her sister's terrible burden. *At last. At last.*

Dot blinked through glassy eyes. "Now I can tell you everything. It's going to feel so good. Ready, Dash? It's the wildest story you've ever heard. You'll never believe it was mine." She bit her lip briefly then gave Dash a tremulous smile. "But first, you asked me something once, and I didn't tell you the truth. Now, after forty years, I can. The answer to your questions is yes. I guess I was a hero after all."

A Note to Readers

Where do you get your ideas? That's probably the number one question I'm asked by readers. My answer is that since I write historical fiction, the basis for a story is already there. Really, there are infinite stories to be told from history. The challenge is to find the right one.

On the flip side, the trouble with history is that it is over before you know it. Who hasn't lamented the fact that we didn't ask our ancestors enough about their lives when we had the chance? Either we were too young to understand the importance of their history, or the stories were kept secret from us. In the latter case, perhaps the person was trying to avoid reliving a painful experience, but what about those who were simply not *allowed* to tell?

Think about the countless secrets that have been kept over time. All the things we were never supposed to know. The very idea of classified information opens a world of possibilities when it comes to writing a novel. *Secret agents, codes, half-truths, misinformation . . .*

The history behind *The Secret Keeper* was irresistible.

Most of the pieces fell into place one day as I perused the internet for information about Canadian women during World War II. It began with a YouTube video entitled "Canadian Women Share Stories of Their Efforts to Help Win WWII" (CBC), about a particular branch of the Women's Royal Canadian Services (WRCNS, also known as the Wrens). Through these services, Canadian women officially served in the military for the first time, assuming traditionally male jobs so they could "free a man to serve."

Despite opposition, tens of thousands of women rose to the challenge. By mid-1942, three military service organizations were open to Canadian women between the ages of eighteen and forty-five: the CWAC (Canadian Women's Army Corps), the Women's Division (WD) of the Royal Canadian Air Force (RCAF), and the Royal Canadian Navy (Wrens). Combined, these three organizations were made up of over forty-five thousand members. To be clear, the term "Wren" was originally used for the members of the Women's Royal Navy in the United Kingdom, but for the purposes of this book, I refer only to the Canadian women, the WRCNS. The Canadian Wrens was the smallest of the three Canadian organizations, comprised of 6,783 women.

All Wrens began their training at HMCS Conestoga (also known as HMCS Bytown), which opened in Galt, Ontario, in June 1942. Like HMCS York, where the sisters went for their medical examinations, HMCS Conestoga bore the name of a ship but was on land only: a stone frigate with all the standard room labels, like the mess (meal hall) and the head (washroom). Lieutenant Commander Isabel Macneill, OBE (born in Halifax, Nova Scotia) was the commanding officer of HMCS Conestoga, making her the first woman in the British Commonwealth to hold an independent naval command, either on land or water.

Wrens were paid daily for their work, depending on their station: chief Wren $2.10; petty officer Wren $1.50; leading Wren $1.15; Wren $0.95; probationary Wren $0.90. Each woman was issued both a winter and summer uniform and a grant of $15 to purchase under clothing and toilet accessories; in addition, they were given $3 every three months to stock up on replacement items.

During their three weeks of basic training at HMCS Conestoga, the women were sorted according to their strengths. In all, the Wrens worked in thirty-nine trades, including mechanical positions that suited women like Dash, such as aircraft maintenance and servicing anti-submarine equipment. Communications-related positions like visual signalling, coding, and wireless telegraphing were offered to women like Dot. Those communication positions were always in high demand. Recognizing a need, the WRCNS converted a former army camp in Saint-Hyacinthe, Quebec, into a specialized long-distance communications training ground for both operators and technicians, called HMCS Saint-Hyacinthe.

Communication has evolved in many ways throughout history. For centuries, people relied on fires lit at strategic, highly visible locations to catch others' attention. In the early 1800s, people began to use a system called a semaphore chain, in which men opened and closed shutters, flashing signals from tower to tower. Everything changed in the early 1830s when American artist and professor Samuel Morse, along with two other inventors, introduced a single-circuit telegraph. When the machine's operator pushed the key down, pulses of electricity traveled across a wire to a receiver at the other end. All the operator needed was a key, a battery, a wire, a receiver... and something to transmit. So, in 1838, Samuel Morse solved that by creating his famous code—a series of beats alternating with periods of inactivity.

At HMCS Saint-Hyacinthe, the women listened to Morse code until it was as familiar to them as the regular alphabet. They also watched it being signalled on a tiny light, and if the lights weren't enough, they used semaphore with flags. They got so good at Morse code that they sometimes chatted to each other across the mess hall by signaling with their fingers. Imagine a cafeteria filled with silent conversation!

In the novel, Dot and Alice were assigned to HMCS Coverdale after graduating from training. Coverdale was a signals intelligence post across the river from Moncton, New Brunswick, and it was staffed entirely by women. As Dot learned, real intelligence work required every Wren to sign the Official Secrets Act. Why? One simple reason is the example of Operation Fortitude. Tens of thousands of Germans were purposefully misled into believing Normandy would *not* be the site for D-Day. If even one person had leaked the truth, might D-Day have been a disaster? Would the war have continued to rage?

I ran across only twenty-two cases of prosecution stemming from the Official Secrets Act in Canada, mostly to do with the Gouzenko Affair, which involved the defection of a cipher clerk from the Soviet Union to Ottawa in 1945 and his allegations about a Soviet spy ring in Canada. In contrast, I could not find even one record of a Wren spilling secrets. Proof of the women's loyalty often emerged well past the forty-year mark, when astounded sons and daughters accidentally discovered their mothers' role in the war as they dug through dusty boxes in attics or basements. Every one of the forty-five thousand women kept those secrets to themselves. Considering the confidential nature of their work, imagine the strength of character that must have taken!

Some secrets, I think, would have been harder to keep than others. On April 30, 1945, at Coverdale, Canadian Wren Elsie (nee Houlding) Michaels intercepted a particularly important message. In it, German admiral Karl Dönitz informed his forces of Hitler's death, making Wren Michaels the first Allied person in the world to learn the news. It was not until May 1994 that she finally asked a longtime fellow Wren friend to help her keep the astonishingly important message safe. It is now kept at the Canadian War Museum, in Ottawa, Ontario.

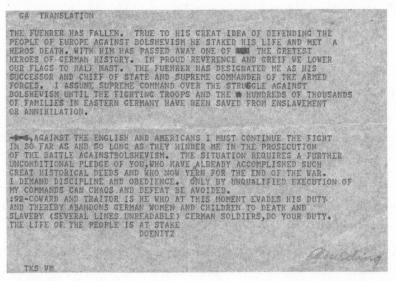

English translation of German admiral Dönitz's message to German forces on the death of Adolf Hitler intercepted by Wren Elsie Michaels.
Adolf Hitler's Death, CWM 19950051-001 reprinted with permission of the Canadian War Museum

Listening Stations were not limited to HMCS Coverdale. These stations were set up all across Canada, from Baccaro—the southernmost point of Nova Scotia—to Ucluelet and Alliford Bay in British Columbia, as well as around the world. Every station operated its own LORAN machine (long-range navigation), a specialized navigation system that operated without the benefit of either voice or radio contact. As an example of how it worked, two stations in Nova Scotia (Baccaro and Deming Island) triangulated with a station in Nantucket, Massachusetts, and this allowed Allied ships and planes to navigate by chart to any predetermined destination while maintaining radio silence. Many warships were equipped with LORAN machines, but the weather in France was so bad on D-Day that all navigational information came from the women at those Listening Stations worldwide.

Wrens intercept German radio transmissions at HMCS Coverdale,
one of Bletchey Parks outstations.
Reprinted with permission of the George Metcalf Archival Collection/Canadian War Musuem

While the listeners specialized in intercepting messages, there is an obvious connection to codebreaking, which I couldn't resist. Most of the messages flying through the airwaves during World War II were done in Morse code, and they were usually encrypted. It took sharp minds and brilliant figuring to decrypt them. We know of Bletchley Park from wonderful books such as Kate Quinn's *The Rose Code* and movies such as *The Imitation Game.* I was excited to let Dot (the-Dormouse-No-More) head to Camp X and live the cloak-and-dagger experience she had always craved.

Codebreakers were much more than brainiacs with a penchant for crossword puzzles. They were passionate, brilliant, and innovative. By decrypting the work of the listeners, they (and the listeners) have been credited with shortening the war by at least two years. Yet, despite their staggering contribution, the Wrens were not recognized with medals until 2009. On the back of those medals was engraved: WE ALSO SERVED. As momentous as that was, some of the surviving Wrens never claimed their medals. In a CBC interview, Wren Mary Owen said, "It took me so long to get that medal, because I didn't think I was worth it."

Tens of thousands of women around the world aided in the war effort, and many did not join military organizations. In Canada, a perfect example of that was the Canadian Car and Foundry in Fort William (now Thunder Bay), Ontario. Under the brilliant leadership of Vancouver's Elsie MacGill, CanCar became home to the Canadian version of "Rosie the Riveter." Canada's National Film Board made a short, delightful documentary about our "Rosies of the North" (link below), in which some of the women returned to the factory sixty years later. I love the first sentence of the film's description: "They raised children, baked cakes . . . and built world-class fighter planes."

Vancouver's Elsie MacGill (1905–1980), aka the Queen of the Hurricanes, was the first woman to be admitted to the University of Toronto's engineering programme. After graduation, she worked with an automobile company in Pontiac, Michigan, as a mechanical engineer, focusing on stress analysis in automobiles. She began studying aeronautics and soon graduated from the University of Michigan as the world's first female aeronautical engineer. Then, twenty-four-year-old Elsie was diagnosed with polio.

Despite her paralysis, Elsie MacGill refused to be slowed by the disease. She wrote articles about avionics and drafted aircraft designs during her recovery time at home. In 1938 she accepted the job of chief aeronautical engineer at the Canadian Car and Foundry, where she managed forty-five hundred workers (half of them women) in the construction of 1,451 Hawker Hurricanes for the RAF. Along the way, Miss MacGill added a few of her own extras to the airplanes, including skis and deicing controls. Due to her disability, she was not able to fly, but she insisted on taking test rides.

But many others flew. Learning about the Air Transport Auxiliary was such a thrill for me. I'd never thought about that aspect of the war before. The military required replacement airplanes, as well as soldiers, officers, mail, and medicine, and those would have to be picked up and delivered to where they were needed most, including factories, airfields, maintenance units, and front-line squadrons across Britain and beyond. That meant the RAF needed pilots, flying instructors, ground school instructors, ground engineers, crash rescue teams, drivers, nurses, doctors, administration staff, and more. From that came the Air Transport Auxiliary, of which pilots made up about one third.

In its early days, the Air Transport Auxiliary was exclusively male. The nickname Ancient and Tattered Airmen came from the fact that most were retired World War I pilots. Some, like pilot Stewart Keith-Jopp, flew despite being short one eye and one arm. On January 1, 1940, the first eight female pilots were admitted to the ATA, despite a great deal of criticism and pushback. Opposing voices claimed the women were "taking jobs men could have," and that these "glamour girls of war" "couldn't handle the kinds of planes they'd be required to fly."

Air Transport Auxiliary pilots flew "anything to anywhere," and always within sight of the ground, since they had no maps or radios. When they flew in a group rather than solo, it was called "flying in a gaggle." The trick was to stay in line by watching the wing tip of the plane beside them. They made it sound easy! But it was not all picturesque and peaceful. Anyone flying during wartime was at risk. If strong winds, thick mists, search lights, and antiaircraft guns (ack-acks) weren't enough, there were balloon barrages, tethered to the earth by thick, lethal cables that were practically impossible to see until the pilot was upon them. ATA pilots also flew without weapons; if the airplane was already armed, the pilots were not given ammunition.

ATA pilots were civilians (not military), and each could fly up to ninety-nine different airplanes (most flew thirty different airplanes on average). They worked twelve days on and two days off, and they could be assigned up to five or six flights in a day. Pilots discovered which planes they were flying, and to where, only when they picked up their chits that morning. A typical question from one pilot to another was "What are you dicing with next?" Those words came from a World War I propaganda poem called "Dicing with Death under Leaden Skies" that many of the women felt was a direct reference to what they were doing. "Flying by the seat of their pants" would have worked, too!

The Spitfire (or "Spit," as the ladies liked to call her) was a favourite of most of the ATA girls. In Mary Ellis's book *A Spitfire Girl*, she quoted Squadron Leader Freddie Lister, who claimed, "The Spitfire was a lady in every definition of the word. And of all the WWII aeroplanes she remains the only lady, every line of her—the beautiful ellipse of the wings, the unmatched grace of the tail-unit, the unmistakable sit—as she banked in a steep turn—displaying that feline waist . . . She was sensitive to the touch, and if you treated her right she would take care of you. And if you didn't treat her right—she gave it back to you in full measure."

The Air Transport Auxiliary was made up of 1,320 international pilots. Regardless of their critics' myopic vision, 166 female pilots joined through the war, eventually making up 10 per cent of the ATA's pilots. Members, both male and female, came from more than twenty-five nations, including Canada, Australia, New Zealand, Poland, Holland, Chile, China, Russia, India, and South Africa—even a royal prince from Thailand.

Forty-seven ATA pilots were Canadian. Six of those were women, including Vancouver's Helen Harrison, Quebec's Elspeth Russell, and Toronto's Violet Milstead and Marion Orr. Helen Harrison was a commercial pilot with over twenty-six hundred flying hours; she was an instructor (she taught reserve for the South African Air Force) and a seaplane pilot. She was experienced at flying both civil and military aircraft in three countries, but she was rejected by the RCAF "because I wore a skirt. I was furious. Instead, they took men with 150 hours." Helen became the ATA's first Canadian female pilot. Some of the women, like Canadian pilot Violet Milstead, had to master certain unique challenges. Since she stood just over five feet tall in her boots, she sat on a rolled-up parachute in order to see over the cockpit!

NUMBER 15 FERRY POOL . A.T.A. HAMBLE

JANUARY 1944.

Air Transport Auxiliary pilots at Hamble Airfield, January 1944.
DB Walker-7866 reprinted with permission of the Air Transport Auxiliary Museum and Archive, Maidenhead Heritage Centre

In all, 174 ATA pilots were killed in action. Four of those were Canadian.

With the listeners, CanCar, and the ATA already on my radar, I was eager to get writing. Then I learned about Canada's Spy School. There was no way I could leave that out of the book!

Camp X was Canada's top-secret, paramilitary training school, the only one of its kind in North America. Prime Minister Winston Churchill and others in Britain's SOE (Special Operations Executive) recognized early on that covert communication and solid intelligence were the way they'd win the war, so Churchill directed the SOE to build something that would "set Europe ablaze." That something became Camp X. There, they taught sabotage and subversion behind enemy lines; they recruited and trained resistance fighters; and they found safe routes to help downed Allied pilots or escaped POWs get home. The camp's vast 275 acres were near Whitby, Ontario, fifty kilometres from the United States, across a field from Lake Ontario. In addition to its classrooms and gymnasium, firing range and explosives field, Camp X came with a field of highly sensitive rhombic antennae—and a parachute jump tower. From the base of a ninety-foot ladder, the trainee climbed to a shaky four-foot-by-four-foot platform that offered no railings for either balance or safety. Staying upright would have been a challenge in itself, since they were jostled by strong winds sweeping up from Lake Ontario. From the platform, the trainee grabbed a rope and swung down onto bales of hay provided by a local farmer. Once they hit the hay, their feet dragged until the momentum stopped, then they'd finally let go of the rope. According to the world's expert on Camp X, Lynn-Philip Hodgson, students did this every day, over and over, until they were (a) no longer afraid of heights and (b) able to land safely and not break any bones.

That was just one of the fun and insightful emails I received from Mr. Hodgson over the duration of my research. His contribution to this book was invaluable. It was with great sadness that I learned he passed away on October 11, 2023.

Lynn-Philip Hodgson was also one of the writers for CBC's excellent miniseries *X Company*, which I highly recommend. On the website for the show is a story about a man named Gustave Biéler, an extraordinary, real-life agent from Camp X. Gustave's reputation went well beyond my idea of Gus, but I did enjoy thinking of him this way: "November 18th, 1942: The SOE deploys Gustave Biéler, a former

Montrealer, into France. Despite injuring himself during his parachute landing [he fractured his spine], he goes on to organize countless missions to sabotage German supplies and logistics and is considered one of the SOE's best agents. Biéler wreaks so much havoc that the Gestapo is forced to create a special team to track him down and capture him. Eventually, Biéler will be charged with the monumental task of helping to pave the way for the D-Day Invasion." Biéler was arrested by the Gestapo in Saint-Quentin, France, in 1944. He was transferred to Gestapo head-quarters and tortured, but he never broke. He was ultimately sent to Flossenbürg concentration camp and executed with an honour guard on September 5, 1944.

More than five hundred agents and instructors participated in Camp X's programme, having faced up to fifty-two different courses during their train-ing. They learned "unconventional warfare," including disguises, surveillance evasion, explosives and weapons training (in which only live ammunition was ever used), coding and ciphers, underwater demolition, the interrogation of prisoners, and much more. The most physical exercises, including self-defense, were extremely rigorous. Of the many men and women who trained at Camp X, probably the best known was author Ian Fleming, who went on to share some of what he'd learned in his James Bond novels. Other noteworthy attendees were screenplay writer Paul Dehn, and children's author Roald Dahl.

After the war, the chief of the SOE declared, "Per capita, the secret war was bloodier than the Somme. The only difference was that the cries were muffled and, in many instances, the corpses were never found." Nor were most of the records, since the people in charge of Camp X celebrated the end of the war with a huge bon-fire. After that, the only source of information available was from actual interviews. Those were practically impossible to access, since every person there was still held to that oath of secrecy for the next four decades. Very little Camp X information is on public record even after *seventy* years. Imagine the stories those files could tell!

And then, as Dot would say with a fond sigh, there was Hydra, Camp X's one of a kind, fifteen megahertz shortwave transmitter/receiver responsible for sending and receiving Allied radio (including telegraph) signals around the world. Hydra was the most powerful telecommunications relay station of its kind, "handmade" after a few Canadian amateur radio enthusiasts sold the camp their apparatuses. Hydra was connected to a huge array of rhombic antennae in the field to the south of Camp X's main building, and because of its reach and the topography of the land, it could reach Britain, other Commonwealth countries, and the United States, while keeping both coding and decoding information relatively safe from the prying ears of German radio listeners. Communications officers like Dot were in direct communication with Bletchley Park. In fact, on May 8, 1945, Bletchley Park notified Camp X directly that the war had ended. Seventy years later, they held a reenactment of that moment in Morse code (link in Sources).

One other unexpected but fascinating section of the book came to me rather late—in fact, I discovered this treasure as I was completing my edits. I had already decided Gus would be taken as a POW after that fateful night in France, but I had to think about after the war, when he came home. I began to search for dates of when the Canadian POWs might have arrived in Halifax, and this article in the *National Post* popped up, completely out of the blue: "The Untold Story of How Canadian POWs Helped Liberate the Women of Ravensbrück Concentration Camp."

This was perfect for Gus. Heartbroken by the task of driving three hundred beaten, emaciated women from Ravensbrück to safety, he was stunned into near silence. But Dot knew what he needed: a true listener. No one listened better than she did.

Time lines and facts are tricky sometimes, and while I aim to stick to the truth, fictionalizing a few dates and details can help me out of the occasional rough patch. For example, Dot's interception of U-409 before the Battle of Sicily was fictitious, though U-409 was not. It happened to be the only U-boat skulking around the Mediterranean around that time, which was why I used it. U-409 was actually sunk on July 12, 1943, in the Mediterranean Sea northeast of Algiers by depth charges from the British destroyer HMS *Inconstant*.

Lucky Dash, sailing on the *Queen Mary* and meeting Bing Crosby! The *Queen Mary* was actually sailing to and from Australia at that point and would not return to Halifax until April, when it was assigned to the Atlantic. Who knows where Mr. Crosby was, but that charming blue-eyed crooner did entertain the troops whenever he could.

World War II mobilized thousands of Canadian women for the first time. When the men went to fight, over 1,200,000 women went to work full-time, in addition to raising families and "keeping the home fires burning." They worked in almost every possible job, from factory workers and munitionettes to butchers and typists. They drove buses and streetcars, they ran farms—they even worked in the logging industry, where they were called "lumberjills." Canadian women who had once resigned themselves to having very few choices in life took a courageous step forward and became top-secret listeners and codebreakers, or heroic pilots. As far as I know, Wrens were never sent to work in private industries, like when Dash went to GECO, then Eisens, then CanCar, so I used a little creative license to get Dash into the right places.

I love what I do. I love that I get to learn about history and experience a taste of what our predecessors' lives were like. Where do I get my stories? History is full of them, just waiting to be discovered.

What am I working on next? Ah well, that's a different question. For now, I'm going to keep that secret to myself.

Sources

The following publications and videos are just a few of the many that provided factual information about the story's time and place and the people involved.

BOOKS

Bashow, David L. *All the Fine Young Eagles: In the Cockpit with Canada's Second World War Fighter Pilots.* Toronto, ON: Stoddart Publishing Co. Limited, 1996.

Ellis, Mary. *A Spitfire Girl: One of the World's Greatest Female ATA Ferry Pilots Tells Her Story.* South Yorkshire, England: Pen & Sword Books Ltd., 2016.

Gossage, Carolyn. *Greatcoats and Glamour Boots: Canadian Women at War (1939–1945).* Toronto, ON: Dundurn Press, 2001.

Hodgson, Lynn-Philip. *Inside-Camp X: The Top Secret World War II "Secret Agent Training School."* Port Perry, ON: Blake Book Distribution, 2000.

Hyde, H. Montgomery. *The Quiet Canadian: The Secret Service Story of Sir William Stephenson.* Great Britain: Constable and Company, 1962.

McKay, Sinclair. *The Secret Listeners: The Men and Women Posted Across the World to Intercept the German Codes for Bletchley Park.* London, England: Aurum Press, 2012.

Wheeler, Jo. *The Hurricane Girls: The Inspirational True Story of the Women Who Dared to Fly.* London, England: Penguin Random House UK, 2018.

Whittell, Giles. *Spitfire Women of World War II: The Courageous Heroines Who Flew Through World War II.* Great Britain: Harper Press, 2007.

ARTICLES

Florence, Elinor. *D-Day: Decoys and Dummies*. https://www.elinorflorence.com
    /blog/d-day-decoys/.

Peterson, Anna. "The 'Always Terrified Airwomen' of the Air Transport
    Auxiliary: Defining Femininity Among the Women Who Flew Military
    Aircraft in Second World War Britain" (undergraduate thesis, University
    of New Hampshire, 2007).

Robertson, Dorothy "Robbie." "I Go (Not) Down to the Sea in Ships:
    Recollections of a Canadian Wren" (unpublished memoir, 2005). *Courtesy
    of Jerry Proc.* Available at https://navalandmilitarymuseum.org/wp-content
    /uploads/2019/06/CFB-Esquimalt-Museum-I-Go-Not-Down-to-the-Sea
    -in-Ships.pdf.

VIDEOS

ATA Museum and Archive: https://atamuseum.org

Baxtor, Jason. CTV News. https://atlantic.ctvnews.ca/we-called-ourselves-
    the-spies-wren-veteran-says-of-service-at-hmcs-coverdale-1.4680148.

Bob Wilson's World War I story, based very loosely on: https://lermuseum.org
    /second-world-war-1939-45/1942/leonard-j-birchall-the-saviour-of-ceylon
    -4-apr-1942.

"Canada's female ww2 pilots: ATA women trained to be able to handle any-
    thing" Global News. https://www.youtube.com/watch?v=0pzI9y1AmFA.

Canadian Army Film Unit: https://canadianfilmandphotounit.ca/2014/02
    /24/the-canadian-army-newsreel-on-the-home-screens/.

Canadian Car and Foundry: https://www.thunderbay.ca/en/city-hall/canadian
    -car-and-foundry-.aspx.

Canadian Women Flyers: http://canadian99s.com/women-in-aviation-history/.

Cousin Fred's story, based very loosely on: https://lermuseum.org/second-
    world-war-1939-45/1942/canadian-pilots-in-malta-june-oct-1942/.

Gagnon, Michelle. CBC, *"We Were Sworn to Secrecy': Canadian Women Share
    Stories of Their Efforts to Help Win WWII"*: https://www.cbc.ca/news
    /canada/d-day-code-breakers-women-1.5159789.

German Codebreaking of World War II: https://www.feldgrau.com/WW2 -German-Code-Breaking/.

Gillogly, Jim. NovaOnline, *Crack the Ciphers*: https://www.pbs.org/wgbh /nova/decoding/faceoff.html#cipher1.

Hathaway, Sheri. *The Western Producer*: https://www.producer.com/farmliving /canadians-living-with-rationing-in-wartime/.

Inside Camp X: Trained to Forget, CBC: https://youtu.be/UZt4rvv7Zgs.

Learn Morse Code: https://morse.withgoogle.com/learn/.

Legion Magazine's *Canadian Fly Girls*: https://youtu.be/2f0zz1eF9G8.

McMurtry, Alice. BlogTO: https://www.blogto.com/city/2020/10/geco-muni tions-plant-scarborough-ontario/.

Reenactment (seventy years later) of Bletchley Park transmitting to Camp X that the war was over: https://www.youtube.com/watch?v=08kJhPkRUs g&list=LL&index=11.

Rosies of the North: https://www.nfb.ca/film/rosies_of_the_north/.

"Spy School Secrets: The True Story Behind Camp X." *Canada's History*: https://www.canadashistory.ca/explore/military-war/spy-school-secrets.

"The Secret Life at Camp X," *Legion Magazine*: https://legionmagazine.com /en/the-secret-life-at-camp-x/.

"This Is the Spy School Equivalent of a Fire Drill, and It's Insane," The Smith-sonian Channel: https://www.youtube.com/watch?v=1eCto9BQQI 0&t=19s.

X Company, CBC Gem series: https://gem.cbc.ca/media/x-company/s01.

Toronto Railway Museum, 2021. Locomotive No. 6213: https://torontorail waymuseum.com/?p=724.

Warnicka, Richard. *National Post*: https://nationalpost.com/news/liberation -1945/the-untold-story-of-how-canadian-pows-helped-liberate-the-women -of-ravensbruck-concentration-camp.

The
Secret Keeper

GENEVIEVE GRAHAM

A Reading Group Guide

READING GROUP GUIDE

The novel follows two sisters, Dot and Dash Wilson, who in 1942 contribute to the war effort by volunteering with the Women's Royal Naval Service. Had you known about the history of the Wrens before this book?

At the beginning of the novel, Dot refers to herself as a "dormouse." In what ways does Dot break out of her shell, and what factors influence her transformation?

Vibrant and vivacious Dash always rushes headlong into new adventures, but she's stopped short by sexist attitudes from the other mechanics at the garage where she works, then an assault. To what extent does this experience reveal her character?

With which sister do you most identify at the beginning of the novel? Why? With whom do you identify at the end of the novel?

If you were completing your basic training at HMCS Conestoga, which department do you think you would be sorted into, based on your strengths? Do you think you would be happy there? Why/Why not? How about Camp X? Are you surprised by any aspects of the training Dot receives?

Central to the narrative is the experience of women entering the workforce at a time of global crisis, where they are met with male responses ranging from amusement to indifference, from respect to open hostility. Do you think attitudes toward women in male-dominated fields have changed since then?

In the note to the reader, the author states that Dash didn't just want to fly, she *needed* to fly. Had Dash's uncle not supported her interest, her life would have been very different. Can her uncle be considered an early feminist?

When her father falls deathly ill, Dot seeks permission to see him one last time and is denied. If you were in Dot's position, what would you have done? Would you have taken the same risk, or would you have followed the rules? What's more important in a time of war: loyalty to country, or loyalty to family? What do you think Dash would say?

Another character grappling with loyalty is Gus, who, as a six-year-old German immigrant with limited proficiency in English, finds refuge with the Wilson family. How might his Canadian experience have affected his developing identity as a child and later, as a spy?

Why do you think Gus falls for Dot? And what makes Dot conclude that Gus *must* be in love with Dash and not her? Do you think Dot would have acted on her love earlier had she known the truth?

Discuss the theme of secrets in the novel. Whether honourable or shameful, whether personal or political, secrets have a way of creating disharmony. What kind of damage do secrets cause in the lives of the Wilson family?

Dash flew numerous planes in her journey as an ATA girl, but the "Spit-fire" is her favourite. If you had to pick a plane to fly in the World War II era, which one would it be, and why?

Quiet, introspective Dot is a great listener, but so is Dash, and her memory of an early lesson about listening saves her life. Discuss how the novel shows that listening carefully can be transformative.

Dot and Dash fall in love with men who are in similar fields, who understand their work, their commitment to it, and the need for secrecy. However, others might not have been so lucky. Do you think women working as Wrens who took oaths of secrecy would have had difficulty finding love and acceptance after their service? Why is secrecy so isolating?

The author mentions in her note to the reader that authors like Ian Fleming and Roald Dahl were part of Camp X. Did that change your perspective about these authors and their works? Do you know of any other authors who served in World War II?

After leaving Camp X against orders, Dot goes on to break more official rules when Dash goes missing over Nazi-occupied France. Do you think her actions are justified? How is Dot's bravery different than Dash's?

Why is it so important that Gus tell Dot the horrors he witnessed liberating the women's labour camp? Do you think the divulging of this experience is crucial to his healing?

Consider the title, *The Secret Keeper*. In a novel full of "secret keepers," who is your favourite? Why?

ENHANCE YOUR BOOK CLUB

Want to learn about the ATA girls? Check out the ATA Museum & Archive website: https://atamuseum.org/. Also hear from Canadian ATA pilot, Jaye "Pete" Edwards, in this interview: https://globalnews.ca/video/5357087/canadas-female-ww2-pilots-ata-women-trained-to-be-able-to-handle-anything.

Read about the real Canadian women who swore oaths of secrecy to work at HMCS Coverdale in this CBC article: https://www.cbc.ca/news/canada/d-day-code-breakers-women-1.5159789.

If the scenes set in Camp X whet your appetite for more, check out the TV series *X Company*, a Canadian-Hungarian spy thriller series following the lives of five Camp X recruits in World War II. Watch on CBC: https://www.cbc.ca/xcompany/episodes/season1.

Acknowledgments

All novels contain secrets, but not all of them are based on secrets. Fortunately for me, as well as for the Wilson sisters and many others, the forty years set out in the Official Secrets Act is over, so it's possible now to learn many things that had been concealed. And yet, due to the fierce determination of those secret keepers and the passing of time, a lot of those stories are still buried. Some are waiting to be found. Some are gone forever.

Research is such an interesting journey. Sometimes it can be dry, but most of the time it's fascinating. I am neither a historian nor a trained researcher, so despite the fact that this is my eighth novel based on Canadian history, it's all new to me. Over the years, I have written to some of the most generous and knowledgeable experts asking for help. I introduce myself out of the blue then send a gentle bombardment of questions their way, fingers crossed. I have found that it is a rare thing to be denied answers from these experts. All are passionate about their specialties, and they want the world to understand what they are about. What might seem like a trivial point to others makes so much difference to how I understand the history and my characters, and I am so grateful for their insights and patience.

When I began to write this story, we were all still in lockdown, so I was unable to visit the WRCNS Room at the Naval Museum of Halifax. Then my family and I moved to Alberta, and I have not found any kind of exhibit about the Wrens here, so I relied on the few contacts I had made online. I am indebted to JoAnn Cunningham (retired chief petty officer first class) of the Nova Scotia Wren Association for introducing me to I Memory Project, and in particular the story of Wren Dory Smelts Hocking and the information about the two LORAN stations in Nova Scotia.

My husband thinks it's pretty funny that my favourite soundtrack these days is anything based on the rumbles of Rolls-Royce Merlin engines in Spitfires and Hurricanes. I can't help it. Every time I dig into a different part of our history, my heart awakens to new experiences, and this time it was the growl of those fighters! Special thanks to volunteer Barry Halliwell at the Hangar Museum in Calgary, who gave me a personalized tour of their "Jenny" and helped me understand the differences between the Spitfire and the Hurricane, among other things.

I want to thank Linda Duffield, volunteer researcher at the Kenley Revival Project, which "preserves and protects the heritage of the most intact fighter airfield from World War II," the Kenley Airfield. Linda offered insight into the Air Transport Auxiliary then referred me to the Maidenhead Heritage Centre, of which the ATA Museum and Archive is an integral part. I find it kind of funny that I am terribly afraid of heights, but now that I have spent so much time researching and watching warplanes, I am on the hunt for a Spitfire to fly me somewhere. Anywhere at all. The Maidenhead Heritage Centre in England actually offers Spitfire simulation flights, which is very tempting.

My thanks to Maidenhead Heritage Centre's volunteer researchers John Webster and Peter Rogers for all their assistance in helping me fill in so many blanks when it came to the ATA. Both John and UK Airfield Guide Dick Flute wanted to be sure I mentioned the important fact that while the ATA-girls receive well-earned attention, they made up only about 10 per cent of the whole organization. John was also the one to educate me on the "temporary" airfields located in occupied territories. These basic facilities with steel plank–surfaced runways were given code numbered identification—for example, B-21 (Sainte Honorine) was an actual airfield in occupied France. Interestingly, one of the last surviving ATA pilots, Jaye Edwards (a British-born woman known as "Pete Petersen" when she was in the ATA), flew Spitfires into forward bases in France in support of D-Day operations. Ms. Edwards lived in Canada for many years ˙d died at the age of 103.

ˉˋˋny thanks to the Canadian War Museum for granting permission ˉe the remarkable photos of Wrens intercepting German radio transmissions at HMCS Coverdale, as well as the intercepted communication of Hitler's death. Codebreakers, warplane pilots . . . and now covert agents! Quite a few readers told me in advance of publication that they'd heard of Camp X, but until this book, it was a well-kept secret from me. What an amazing part of Canadian history!

The world's expert on Camp X was the brilliant Lynn-Philip Hodgson, who recently passed away. He was the author of *Inside Camp X*, but he was so much more than that. A passionate teacher, Lynn spoke about Camp X to countless people, including over one hundred thousand public and high school students, and almost every Lions, Kiwanis, Probus, and Rotary Club in southern Ontario. He was the only Canadian invited to the sixtieth anniversary of the Office of Strategic Services (CIA), and in 2013 he was awarded the Queen's Diamond Jubilee Medal for dedicating thirty-five years to preserving Canada's history and heritage. He was the Canadian Association editor of *Eye Spy Magazine*, and the list goes on. So you can imagine how nervous I was to approach him to ask my questions! To my relief, Lynn was incredibly helpful, patiently giving me answers to everything I asked and offering a great deal more insight. Then he told me that his wife, Marlene, enjoyed my books, so I sent her an early draft of *The Secret Keeper* to see what she thought. I breathed much easier after he told me she had "thoroughly enjoyed it."

I hope you feel the same way about this novel and all my Canadian history novels. I started writing these stories because, as a Canadian, I was astounded by everything I'd never learned. Now that I am educating myself, I love creating stories based on our history. It's fun and rewarding for me, but realizing so many readers feel the same way about my books is the most amazing gift. Your support and encouragement mean the world to me, so thank you, thank you, thank you!

To all the dedicated, hardworking librarians and booksellers from shore to shore who champion my books, introducing them to new readers as you do, I am truly grateful for your endorsement.

The Secret Keeper would not be the story it is without the invaluable guidance of my very busy, insightful editing team at Simon & Schuster Canada: Sarah St. Pierre (editorial director), Adrienne Kerr (senior editor), and Nita Pronovost (VP and editor in chief). Big thanks to the superwomen who keep my head on straight, Mackenzie Croft (associate marketer), and Natasha

Tsakiris (publicist), and to the rest of the amazing Simon & Schuster team: Shara Alexa (director of sales, national accounts), Adria Iwasutiak (VP, director of publicity and Canadian sales), Felicia Quon (VP, marketing and communications), Lorraine Kelly (manager, library and special sales), Jessica Boudreau (designer), and, last but never least, Kevin Hanson (president and publisher). A big thank-you to the U.S. sales team, especially Lexi Mangano and Stephanie Calman. Thank you all for everything you do for my books!

As always, my sincere gratitude to my literary agent, Jacques de Spoelberch, for all he has done for me over the past dozen years.

Saving the best for last as always: thank you to my husband, Dwayne, who is my rock and my partner in everything I do. When I lose myself in self-doubt, he shows me I'm on the right path, then he leads me through until I can see it on my own. When I am researching and writing, I forget about everything else, but he doesn't. I couldn't do any of this without him. Thanks, Dwayne, for all you do for me—including that glass of wine at the end of the day that tells me it's time to close up shop for the night. What would I do without you?